The Iron Bound

Book Five of the Iron Soul Series

J.M. Briggs

Contents

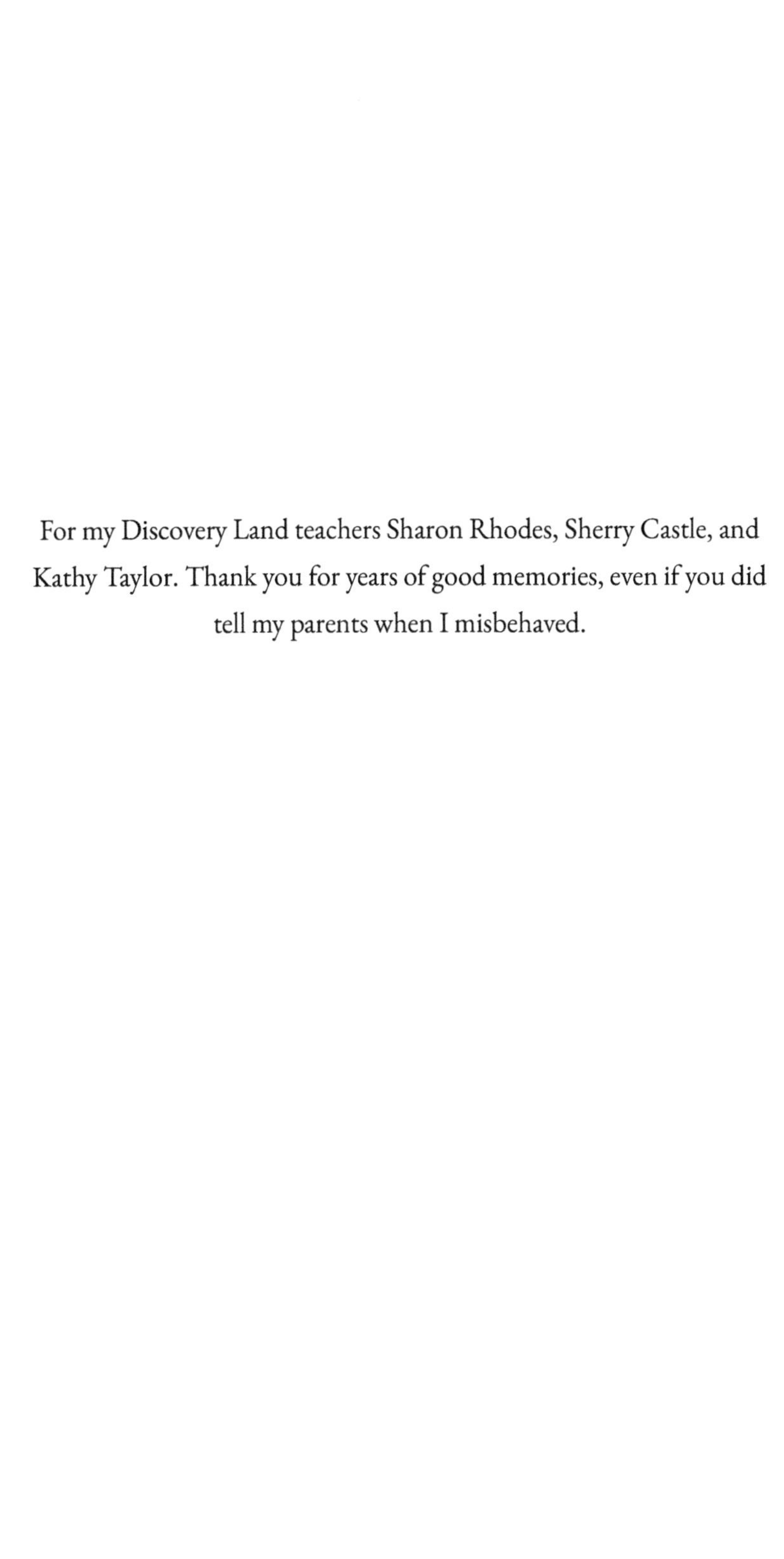

For my Discovery Land teachers Sharon Rhodes, Sherry Castle, and Kathy Taylor. Thank you for years of good memories, even if you did tell my parents when I misbehaved.

1

Cost of Magic

Magic was all she could think about as the windshield wipers came to a stop and she set the parking brake. Alex had managed to keep her mind off of such things for most of the drive thanks to the nasty winter weather and loud music, but now she was back in Ravenslake. Exhaling, Alex eased her fingers off of the steering wheel and turned off the car. The snow was thankfully beginning to ease and a campus snowplow was already at work in the parking lots.

She was back in Ravenslake: back in a town plagued by supernatural events and the site of most of her adventures. Alex just sat silently in the car and listened to the soft thrum of the heater and watched snow begin to collect on her windshield. There'd be magic lessons again, probably even more now that Arthur's true nature was revealed. There were too many things to worry about. Not only did they have to worry about the Sídhe breaking through the one Iron Gate they had built, but also descendants of Fae creatures attacking them plus Arthur himself. Magic had come with far too many strings attached. Shaking her head, Alex told herself to stop being so damn maudlin and get moving.

Alex fumbled in the car for a moment to pull on her heavy coat before climbing out. She grabbed her backpack and duffle bag from the back seat and headed straight for the sidewalk. There were other students in the parking lot unpacking their vehicles and the snow was trodden down on the outer edge of the parking lot towards the sidewalk. As she walked towards the dorms, she could see the university arboretum which looked dark and lifeless alongside the lake. The South Santiam River to her left was silent with a layer of ice across the top.

Gallagher Hall stood amidst the snowdrifts as an impressive looking four-story brick building and in the dim lighting of the cloudy day looked more than just a few years old. The pale bricks looked dark and dirty while the green metal accents were almost hidden thanks to the roof being covered with snow. She was about to set her things down to dig out her access card when the front door was pushed open by someone buried in a heavy winter coat, hat, and scarf rushing out. Catching the door with her foot, Alex hopped forward as the person hurried past her before slipping inside herself.

The front room was blissfully warm and a small group of older students was gathered in the main kitchen laughing while the smell of cookies wafted over to her. A couple more students she didn't know were lounging on a small collection of sofas by the front door. Alex ignored them and headed for the elevator, going straight up to the fourth floor. The elevator dinged and she stepped out into a rather plain hallway with muffled voices echoing around her.

Setting her bag down in front of the door marked 415, Alex pulled her wallet out and found her keycard. The door beeped as she entered her code and it scanned the key just before it unlocked with a soft click. She pushed the door open and nudged her duffle bag into the room with one foot.

"Oh, hi, Alex," a tired voice greeted.

Alex shrugged off her backpack and was in the process of taking off her coat to hang on the coat rack when she caught sight of an older woman walking into the entry room. Her roommate Nicki was shifting nervously and toying with one of her long red braided pigtails. Alex instantly recognized the older woman as Nicki's grandmother.

Samantha Russell had changed a bit since the last time Alex saw her. The local artist had dyed her hair again so it was now short and brown with hints of purple and blue scattered throughout. She was wearing a long blue smock sort of thing with a white scarf and some of her own ceramic jewelry over pinstripe slacks. The eccentric and friendly look was ruined a bit by the way the woman was staring at her. It was a mix between fascination, pity, and anger. Swallowing, Alex forced a small smile and resisted the urge to reassure the woman that being the Iron Soul didn't mean that she chose who was a mage.

"Alex," Samantha greeted in a rather tight voice. "Welcome back." She forced a small smile that was very uncomfortable. "How was your holiday?"

"Uh, going home was good." Alex glanced towards Nicki, suddenly unsure if her roommate had told her grandmother about magic. "It was good to see everyone."

"Did you explain to them..." Samantha trailed off and shook her head as Nicki flinched behind her. "About..."

"Yeah," Alex answered before the woman had to say the word 'magic'. "I did: it wasn't easy, but we managed to get through it and still have a decent visit."

"And your family isn't worried?" Samantha asked in a sharper voice. "They actually let you return?!"

"Well, legally I am an adult." Alex refused to look to Nicki for help even as she wanted to run. "And well, this is what we are, and if we don't fight back then other people suffer. Eventually, we will too, in another way."

It sounded weak to her ears: it had the dozen or so times she'd tried to go over it with her own parents. What excitement they'd had about her having magical powers had dimmed with the truth, and Alex had wondered more than a few times if sharing all of it had been the right choice. Nicki coughed lightly and shifted in between them. She hugged her grandmother while Alex tried not to shift under the weight of the woman's gaze. Samantha Russell then looked back at her granddaughter and cupped her face gently. Her eyes were suddenly teary and Alex made a point of looking at the wall decorations. The door closed behind her a moment later and a loud sigh escaped Nicki.

"Sorry about that," Nicki said. "She's... well, she's not taking it so well. She was really excited about the magic; absolutely lost it when I made an ice sculpture for her, but it wasn't good when I told her the rest of it."

"The rest of it," Alex repeated with a snort. "You mean the fact that there are other universes and they sometimes invade our world? Or maybe that mages exist to serve as white blood cells of our world against invaders? Or did you mean that there are Old Ones from other universes that are waking up and some of them are completely insane thanks to being in our world too long? Or that your roommate's ex-boyfriend who we all thought was the reincarnation of King Arthur was really a traitor who almost killed me? Or that you spent a week in Wales finding a magical cup to heal your best friend who nearly died to save said roommate?"

"Long drive I take it?" Nicki raised an eyebrow at Alex.

"Yeah." Alex groaned, slumping onto the blue couch. "Long week and long drive. The roads were shit."

"You never did say much about your parents' reaction," Nicki said. "Was it bad?"

"Same as you, mostly. Not the magic thing; they thought that was neat." Alex almost smiled. "It was the other stuff… the whole magic is a result of our world being invaded thing and my… ex-boyfriend is actually an enemy of our world."

"He hasn't called again, right?"

"No; I haven't heard anything from Arthur in the last week and a half," Alex assured her. Then she groaned and rubbed her neck. "God, it's only been a week and a half; how is that possible?"

"Sorry. So, they didn't take it well?"

"My parents weren't exactly thrilled. It took a rather long philosophical discussion about responsibility and the knowledge that I was failing my purpose to reassure them at all. Not sure it really worked, to be honest." Shaking her head, Alex snorted a little. "I almost gave my mom Merlin's phone number so he could deal with her."

"Why didn't you?"

"You know that Merlin and Morgana are a bit… obsessive about the Iron Soul," Alex scolded lightly. Nicki's lips turned up into a smile. "I wasn't quite ready to deal with that can of worms. My parents were having a hard enough time with the reincarnation thing."

"How much did you tell them?"

"I tried to keep it simple," Alex replied. She toyed with a strand of her long blonde hair. "Every day there were a few more questions and dazed looks. Honestly, in a lot of ways, I'm glad to be back. Walking on eggshells and worrying about what is going to happen next isn't a great way to spend a holiday."

"Yeah… as you saw my gran is more than a bit worried."

"When did you tell her?"

"Two days ago."

"Why wait so long?"

"It's not an easy thing to explain," Nicki said. "You know that your family wasn't exactly jumping for joy according to you."

"I know, must be hard just being across town."

"Yeah, I sort of envy you, with your family being in Spokane," Nicki admitted. "At least they've got some distance to help them process everything."

"Except that now I'm worried if they are going to be safe," Alex said softly. "You can at least keep an eye on and protect your grandmother. Me, I'm just hoping that Arthur doesn't try to go after them."

The words hung painfully in the air. and Alex tried to think if she could do anything more to protect the house. Her parents had been silent as she hung iron horseshoes over the doors and windows, and she was already plotting ways to add a layer of iron inside the doorways themselves. But that only protected the house; she couldn't secure the hospital where her mother worked or her father's office with iron. Then there were her brothers-

"Stop worrying about it," Nicki ordered. She gave Alex a sympathetic look. "We just have to keep doing what we can and stay in contact with our families. Maybe Merlin and Morgana will have some ideas for protecting your family."

"What, like magic rings to make them invisible to anything from outside our world?" Alex asked, only to pause in consideration.

The expression on her face must have been amusing because Nicki chuckled and shook her head fondly. "Maybe; we'll see what you can do. I'm still not too clear on the limits of making magical items myself," Nicki observed with a tiny smile. "I bet I'd be awesome at making magic items."

"You'd use your games and RPG books for ideas." A soft chuckle escaped Alex at the thought.

"Your point?" Nicki grinned and tossed her hair over her shoulder dramatically. "We have the benefit of hundreds of years of human imagination in literature, art, and yes games to give us ideas. Think of it as a way that the rest of humanity is helping us fight!" Her pale skin flushed to match her red hair as her blue eyes widened in excitement.

"Yes well, if you figure out how to make a dancing sword be sure to let me know." Winking one of her gray eyes Alex offered Nicki a smile. "I look forward to watching you torment Merlin and Morgana in the process though."

A knock on the door made both of them pause, and Alex glanced towards it curiously before moving over to it. Opening the door, Alex was braced for an RA, neighbor or even Morgana or Merlin, but was pleased when she found the boys waiting in the hallway. Happiness rushed up through Alex's chest at the sight of the smiling Aiden. His dark brown hair was a bit of a mess, but his brown eyes were all but sparkling. He was beaming at her and before she could say a word, he stepped forward into their dorm room and swept her up in a hug. Her feet bumped the wall as he walked her into the living room area laughing.

"Aiden!" Alex laughed, clutching at his shoulder. "Put me down before you drop me!"

"Ah, my hero returns!" Aiden announced. He walked further into the room while Nicki laughed behind them. "Welcome back, Alex!"

"Aiden Bosco, put me down!" Alex demanded. Clinging to his arm as she began to slip, she could smell the lingering scent of books from his family's bookstore on his shirt. It was unexpectedly comforting. "Aiden!"

Thankfully, he did as she said and set her back on the ground even though he was still laughing. The door closed and Alex took a few breaths to stop giggling. She pushed a strand of hair out of her face and stepped back to take Aiden in. There was almost nothing to indicate that he'd been on death's doorstep only a week and a half ago. Gone was the pale complexion that lying in a coma had given him, and in its place, his healthy half-Italian glow was back. For a moment Alex couldn't even breathe and felt tears prickling at her eyes. Aiden's smile softened, and a soft half-laugh and half-sob escaped Alex. Stepping forward, she wrapped her arms around Aiden and held him tightly, squeezing her eyes as his arms came up around her.

"I'm sorry," she choked out. "I'm so sorry, Aiden, if I hadn't-"

"Hey, we all thought that Arthur was on our side," Aiden said gently. "I'm just glad that I was able to save you." He chuckled a little and eased his grip on her. "You scared me pretty badly, Alex."

She nodded weakly, unable to imagine how it must have been for Aiden. Bran's vision had sent him rushing to the other side of Ravens Lake looking for Arthur and her as the Old One Chernobog emerged from the water. He'd been fighting off a horde of Chernobog's shadowy monsters to reach them, only to see Arthur stabbing her with a sword.

"I left town too quickly to properly thank you for knocking Cathanáil out of Arthur's hands." Alex offered him a weak smile. "It's easier knowing that at least he doesn't have the Sword."

"Yeah, but we don't have it either." Aiden's smile faltered. "That's less good."

"We'll find it," another male voice assured them both. Alex blushed in embarrassment as she turned to find Bran calmly watching them while she'd all but forgotten he was there. "We found the Iron Chalice to save you after all," Bran reminded Aiden.

Then Bran smiled gently at her, looking relieved at seeing her, and Alex grinned in response. She shifted away from Aiden and stepped forward quickly to hug Bran. He still smelled a bit of his mother's bakery and Alex exhaled in relief into his shoulder. Legs trembling a little, she stepped back and tried to smile. At least the loyal mages were all back together again. But then she noticed that while the metal leg brace, he'd worn for the last year and a half that she'd known him was gone, he was still using a cane. Bran followed her gaze to the cane and chuckled before he leaned it up against the wall.

"It's for appearances," Bran explained. "The story is that I underwent a new surgery during break and am doing special physical therapy. I'll keep the cane through this semester to help sell that."

"Which sadly means that we'll lose our nice big room next year." Aiden sighed as he sank down onto the couch. "Pity; I like that room."

"Honestly next year we should probably rent a house or something," Nicki said. "That way if the Sídhe come looking for us there aren't other people around."

"And there goes the happy mood." Aiden pouted, shaking his head at Nicki.

"Just make yourself at home," Nicki retorted.

"Thank you, Nicki," Aiden said, giving her a wide smile.

Nicki chuckled and shook her head, gesturing for Bran to take a seat. He sat down next to Aiden as Nicki plopped back into the armchair, leaving the black ottoman filled with Nicki's crafting stuff for Alex to sit on.

"So, Bran, uh, how did your mother take it?" Alex asked.

"Well... she got a rather... edited version shall we say," Bran admitted sheepishly. "I told her about being a mage, but I just couldn't bring myself to tell her about the Sídhe or Arthur."

"Bran! The whole point of telling them was so that-"

"I know," Bran cut in. "In case we were killed or injured so that they'd at least have the truth, but, Alex, I just couldn't." He sighed; his smile was gone and he looked exhausted. His fingers went around his neck and pulled a long chain out from beneath his shirt revealing a set of dog tags. "We lost my dad to a war. I don't think my mother could cope with the knowledge that I'm part of one too. I'm sorry, but she's not ready for that."

"So, what... she just thinks that you have magical powers?" Nicki asked carefully.

"I tried to explain it more like tides; that magic comes and goes over the centuries. I explained a little bit about Merlin and Morgana and let her make some inferences there. I just did my best to leave out anything about threats. She knows that magic healed my leg and cried in relief." He paused and looked at the others. "Uh, how about you?"

"Honestly... I pretty much did the same thing," Aiden admitted, looking uneasy. "I told them a bit about Arthur who wants to use his powers for evil but decided against telling them about the potential army that could invade. They know that a magical artifact, that you three went to retrieve, healed me."

"Do they know uh..." Alex trailed off for a moment before gathering her courage. "That you were hurt saving me?"

"No," Aiden replied. "I didn't want to risk them being angry at you. I was the one who chose to save you. We haven't got time to break in another Iron Soul." Aiden grimaced at his own words. "Uh, that didn't sound good. Sorry, Alex. You aren't replaceable."

"Except I sort of am." Shifting uneasily, Alex crossed her arms over her chest. "When I die, be it now or of old age, I'll just be reborn. I'm still trying to wrap my brain around that, given that we actually handled the remains of my first life less than a month ago."

"But it wouldn't be you." Nicki's stern expression and tone didn't leave much room for argument.

"Speaking of reincarnations," Bran interrupted before things could get any stranger. "Has anyone spoken with Lance or Jenny since they left for break?"

"I got a text from Jenny that she got back to California safely," Alex said. "But nothing since then."

"I still can't believe that they went with you guys to find the Holy Grail." Shaking his head, Aiden sighed loudly. "I can't believe that I missed the Quest for the Holy Grail! That is going to haunt me for the rest of my life! All the references, the jokes, and you actually saw a dragon! Jenny and Lance got to see the dragon and do a special magical funeral at Stonehenge and I was stuck in a coma! And I didn't even get a t-shirt!"

Alex glanced towards Nicki, who looked rather bored with the outburst. Clearly, she'd heard it before. Bran mildly patted Aiden's shoulder in false sympathy. Pressing her lips together, Alex felt a laugh trying to escape her. Nicki caught her eye and the redhead began to crack up. Bran's soft chuckle began to fill the room even as Aiden made a noise of protest. The laugh escaped Alex and she shook her head at the utter insanity of her friends and fellow mages. Aiden got put into a coma from using too much magic to save her life, and it was the adventure he'd missed that he was worried about. Maybe they'd get through the semester at least in one piece.

2

Dinner with Mages

It was hard not to run. Hell, it was hard not to fidget as she waited by the entrance of Michaels Cafeteria for the others. Jenny shifted her feet and licked her lips, wondering not for the first time if this was even a good idea. Reaching up one hand, she pushed a long black hair out of her face before tugging at the hem of her dark blue tunic shirt. Jenny pulled out her cellphone to check for any messages, but all there was one text from her father, Carlo Sanchez, that she responded to quickly. Nothing from the mages.

The main doors swung open and a blast of cold air hit her face as a group of students came walking in. They were chatting happily and headed into the student cafeteria after only a moment, leaving Jenny alone again. She checked her phone again and sighed softly at the lack of messages from her friends. Well... after the last semester maybe it was time to acknowledge that she didn't have that many friends. Nibbling at her lip, Jenny wondered if maybe that wasn't entirely true.

Everything was more than a little unsettled right now. She'd only come to Ravenslake for college because Arthur had wanted to. Granted she'd really liked the school and town when they'd checked it out, but she would never have looked twice at it if Arthur hadn't pushed. Jenny leaned against the cold wall and kicked the floor, trying not to look depressed and pathetic. The doors opened again and a blast of cold air hit her in the face, making Jenny close her eyes tightly.

"Jenny," a warm and very familiar voice called.

She opened her eyes in a flash. Lance towered over her, dwarfing her with his tall athletic build and broad shoulders, but smiling so sweetly at her that Jenny had to fight back a blush. She hadn't anticipated how good it would feel to see him again. His smile was hesitant, but his brown eyes were gleaming with genuine pleasure to see her.

"Hi, Lance." She gave him a small smile of her own. "How was your break?"

"Normal, which was really something after... well, Wales and England." Lance shrugged a little, glancing around and rubbing his hands together nervously.

Jenny nodded her understanding. After going to another country with a group of people who could use magic in order to find a magical cup that could heal a person in a coma, and then having to find the remains of your husband from a previous life, and taking part in some sort of magical funeral, all the while being under attack by crazy fairy tale rejects, almost anything would be normal. Just the passing thought of the funeral sent a chill down Jenny's spine. It had been so weird, but there was also a strange, lingering sense of relief that she hadn't been brave enough to look at too closely just yet.

"How about you?" Lance asked, pulling her out of the strange thoughts. "Everything go alright with your father?"

"Well Morgana fulfilled her promise and paid me back the cost of the plane tickets and everything else, but Dad is still a bit confused as to why I went in the first place." Jenny forced a little laugh and shrugged. "It was hard to explain… in the end, I just told him that it wasn't my story to tell."

"He accepted that?"

"Strangely enough yeah; he didn't like it by any means, but Daddy is a lawyer. He does understand that sometimes you just can't talk about something."

"Weird, I was lucky on the family front. I didn't have to try to come up with any explanations," Lance said. He shifted a little and rubbed the back of his neck. "Uh… you haven't heard from Arthur, have you?"

"No." Jenny's whole body tensed at just hearing his name. She felt sick just thinking about him. "And I doubt I will. I was just a means to an end; a way to help convince everyone that he was really the reincarnation."

"Good," Lance sighed in relief. "Hopefully he won't pay too much attention to you now."

Part of Jenny felt a little offended by the insinuation that she couldn't take care of herself even as another part of her agreed with Lance. Arthur was apparently a mage and the reincarnation of Mordred, but he was allied with the Queen of the Sídhe, which didn't make much sense to Jenny. She'd thought that magical powers came from protecting the Earth, but then again, she wasn't a mage. The last part of her couldn't help but turn a bit floaty at the expression of Lance's concern.

"I hope he leaves you alone too," Jenny told him gently, meeting his big brown eyes with her own and giving him a smile. She was going to say something more and Lance licked his lips and swallowed, telling her that he wanted to say something as well.

The door opening sent another blast of cold air swirling through the entryway, and Jenny grimaced at the temperature drop. Lance shifted in front of her and his body heat suddenly seemed to surround her. Fighting back her embarrassment, Jenny peeked around Lance's arm towards the door. A small squeak escaped her as Alex and the others rushed inside and began to shake the snow off of their coats.

"Jenny!" Alex's wide smile was so happy and welcoming that Jenny instantly relaxed.

"Hi, Alex!" Jenny stepped out from behind Lance and returned the smile. She was tempted to hug Alex but held back that impulse. "Welcome back."

"Thanks." Alex pulled her hood back and shook out her long blonde hair. "How are you guys?" Her eyes darted between Jenny and Lance, almost glowing with curiosity and eagerness.

There was a sudden urge to say something about Lance and herself but Jenny held back. She still needed to better understand what was happening. Their relationship had caused a lot of heartache over the lifetimes, and wow that was a strange thing to have to think about. Jenny shifted around Lance and turned her attention to the others. Nicki looked relaxed and content standing next to Aiden and was giving Jenny what was the probably the warmest look she'd ever received from the redhead. Bran was standing neutrally with a cane in his hands that made her frown in confusion, but he gave her a quick wink and smile. Aiden, on the other hand, was looking between her and Lance before he shifted his attention to look at Alex's face. The blonde merely raised an eyebrow at him which made Aiden chuckle.

"Hello, Jenny," Aiden greeted with a wide smile. "Hey, Lance!"

He stepped forward and slapped Lance on the shoulder and then to her surprise he kissed her cheek quickly. As she stared at him in shock, Aiden shifted back and grinned at them impossibly wider. He gestured towards the doors to the cafeteria.

"Shall we?" He asked, with a glance around at everyone. "I'm not sure about you but I'm hungry."

"Even if they only have lousy Italian?" Nicki asked. She smirked and walked forward to link her arm through Aiden's.

"Oh god, no more Italian," Aiden groaned. He pulled open the door with a shudder.

"Aiden! Did I really just hear that?" Nicki gasped, giving him a shocked and curious look.

"I was in a coma: Dad's been cooking Italian nonstop since I woke up to 'help me recover', so yeah, no more Italian please," Aiden explained. He was pouting a little and Jenny had to hold back a giggle.

"Alright you two," Alex chided. She stepped up behind them and pushed them forward. "Pause the comedy routine so we can eat."

Entering Michaels Cafeteria suddenly seemed to reset her world in a way that not even her dorm room had. She followed the others and took a tray from Alex with a smile. Her former roommate gave her a small nod and as the others moved past them, they lingered for a moment. Suddenly Jenny was back at school, and it was strangely easy to imagine that at any moment Arthur was going to come strolling in to join them.

"It's still a bit weird," Alex said with a helpless shrug. Jenny wondered if Alex had read her mind. "But I still mean what I said about wanting my friend to stay."

"I remember," Jenny breathed with a softening smile. She glanced down at her feet feeling a bit silly. "Sorry about the weirdness."

"It was a little easier while we were on a grand, urgent adventure to save Aiden." Alex nodded towards the others. "Real life... little harder."

"Well for what it's worth, I'm still not sure what the reincarnation of Guinevere-"

"Gwenyvar," Alex corrected. Grimacing, Alex froze and started to turn red. "Sorry."

"Okay; I'm not sure what my role will be here. I don't have magical powers, but I'd like to help."

"Well, if nothing else you give me someone sane to talk to," Alex offered, still blushing a little at her earlier interruption. "Because let's face it, Nicki is not totally sane."

Jenny looked at the girl in question to find her flirting with the dark-haired girl working at the hot food counter. Nicki was leaning on the counter with a wide smile and fluttering her blue eyes. Holding back a snort, Jenny glanced towards Alex and found the other girl chuckling.

"She's not... completely insane," Jenny offered with an uncontrollable smile. "She's very spirited."

"No, she's insane," Aiden said. He joined them, grabbed a plate for the salad bar and grinned. "But we like her that way."

Shaking her head, Alex nodded towards the salad bar and gave Jenny a smile. She nodded in return and stepped away from Alex to start getting her own meal as more students began to pour into the cafeteria. Jenny focused on making herself a large salad and got a piece of grilled chicken from the hot food counter. Meeting up with Lance at the drinks counter, Jenny poured herself an iced tea and fell into step with the others.

"What's with the cane?" Jenny asked Bran in a low voice as he moved alongside her. "Is your leg- I mean-"

"It's just a cover," he assured her quickly. "I'm fine."

It was strange to be so close to the group back at school. She'd certainly been close to Alex during last year when they'd been roommates, but Jenny had never spent much time with the others. From their time in Wales, she knew a little bit about all of them, but wouldn't consider them friends and yet now she was sitting at the large table in the back corner of the dining area with them. A round table, her mind unhelpfully added.

Lance sat down to her left and then to her relief Alex sat down at her right.

Her eyes were drawn instantly to Alex and she took in the blond young woman carefully. She looked a little tired, but happy at the same time as her gaze flickered over to Aiden as he sat down. Jenny felt a wave of fondness for Alex wash over her before remembering the awkward truth that in another life, several in fact, that woman had been male and her husband. Jenny shook her head; this was a real head trip, but she really needed to get past it. Besides, wasn't it still better than Arthur really being the reincarnation of King Arthur- uh Arto? She'd have to get used to the real history she was dealing with now rather than just the far-removed mythology.

Alex being the real Iron Soul and Arthur being a traitor deceiving them all meant that she hadn't actually betrayed someone who was good. Sure, she'd cheated with Lance on her boyfriend, but given that he was lying the whole time, surely that wasn't such a horrible thing. She almost snorted; now rather than being former husband and wife she and Alex had a potentially much more distressing connection: the women that Arthur had used and betrayed.

"So..." Alex's fork was poised over a bowl of some sort of pasta on her tray. "Where should we start? I'm sure that the Professors will be contacting us tomorrow for information on what is going on and getting back to training."

"Well, some good news on my front," Aiden offered as he sliced his burger in half. "I used an ice spell against Chernobog's shadows."

"You did?" Nicki reached over to smack his arm, grinning widely. "You didn't tell me that."

"I wanted to tell the group," Aiden defended quickly. "But that really shows that it's time for us to pull out the RPG books again and start trying new things again."

"RPG books?" Jenny asked weakly. Biting her lower lip, she struggled not to burst out laughing. "Are you serious?"

"Yes, actually." Bran chuckled fondly. "Our magic is based on our will and an ability to visualize, so movies, tv, literature, and yeah RPG books are a good source of ideas."

"I hate to bring it up," Lance said carefully. "But have you learned anything new about all those creatures that attacked us?"

"No," Bran admitted. His smile vanished and he shook his head. "Merlin and Morgana said that they were going to start working on it, but they haven't told us anything yet."

"To be fair though, Alex just got back," Nicki added hopefully. "So maybe they'll have something for us soon."

"But this queen?" Jenny looked between the four mages, wishing one of them would say something helpful. "What do you know about her? I mean, if she's really Arthur's mother then where are they? How is she communicating with the Sídhe?"

"Actually, that's the thing," Bran said. "The Queen isn't actually the current ruler of the Sídhe world. She was... well, killed in theory, but was actually trapped in our world somehow three thousand years ago."

"Okay...." Jenny was actually afraid of asking for more details on that madness. "So why do those things obey her if she isn't the Queen?"

"That's one of the big questions," Alex admitted. "Most of them don't really have a reason to want to hurt us. The creatures living in our world were all born here at this point, so they certainly aren't loyal to her."

"We think there is something more going on," Nicki added quickly. "Some sort of controlling magic that she's using on them. We just don't know what."

"So, what's the next step?" Lance frowned, his eyes glancing between the mages with the same sort of confused and uneasy look that Jenny knew must be on her own face.

"Research, probably." Aiden sighed, stabbing at his own salad. "Lots of research."

"The problem is," Nicki said. "I'm not sure if there are any myths or legends that relate to this at all." She grumbled a bit at her own words. "This may be something completely new."

Jenny was silent as the four mages all exchanged a worried look. Alex pushed her pasta around in the bowl and Jenny looked over at Lance, who seemed just as unsure as she did. Clearing her throat, Jenny forced a little smile.

"I'm sure that Merlin and Morgana will have some place to start. So how about we pretend that you're all regular college students for the rest of the night." Straightening up, Jenny smiled and did her best to look cheerful. "What classes are you guys starting tomorrow?"

She caught a small smile on Alex's face in the corner of her eye before Bran drew her attention with a nod of approval. Aiden's eyes crinkled slightly as he smiled at her before he promptly turned his attention to Nicki. Slowly the chatter turned from the fate of the world to more normal young-twenty topics. Sighing softly, Jenny took a sip of her iced tea and shared one more pleased look with Lance.

3

A Man Named Thor

1 15 C.E. Sør-Trøndelag, Norway

A cold wind was rising off of the fjord carrying the scent of salt and the promise of something that he couldn't put his finger on. The carved mountains of gray rock rose around the narrow inlet and almost completely hid the sea. In front of him, a small freshwater stream bubbled down the slope towards the fjord where it would join the ocean. Rich green vegetation covered the rounded edges of the mountains: thick grasses, small spruce trees, and blankets of moss made everything seem alive and fresh, and yet there was something keeping him from feeling at ease.

He lingered and watched the waves in the distance with a detached interest and tried to understand his sudden introspective mood. Behind him, the village was busy with the chores of day-to-day life; something that he should be getting back to. Turning around, he took in the village with sharp brown eyes and pushed a wild strand of hair out of his face. He took a moment to tuck the strand back into his braid before he started trudging back to the village with the full bucket of water in his left hand.

Numerous houses were arranged in a rough u-shape slightly up the hill on a bare well-trodden patch of land. Each one was long and rectangular, made of woven sticks covered with mud and reinforced here and there with small stones. Their steep roofs were covered with thick layers of moss and turf with a large hole visible in each where smoke was escaping. Beyond the collection of houses were several fields where he could see many of the men out laboring despite the advancing hours. Judging from the height of the grain it looked to be a decent year. Smiling slightly, he caught sight of his brother walking towards their own house with an exhausted slump to his shoulders. Further beyond the small fields were the thick spruce tree forests full of deer and wild pigs.

He shifted in his path and moved towards the same house as his brother, but instead of going inside he went to the smaller structure next to it. The building had only three walls with the fourth side open to the air, though some hides and woven mats hung from the roof to provide some extra protection. A sturdy stone-built furnace filled the far interior wall. Tools sat waiting for him on a small bench along with two half-finished axe heads awaiting some work. There was a stack of wood and an already full bucket of water on hand.

Setting down the second bucket of water, he quickly busied himself with putting away the set of hammers and small chisel tools out of reach of the elements. Wrapping himself in a thick animal skin, he checked once more that the furnace was cold before placing the wrapped tools in the corner. He glanced out to see his brother heading back towards the fields with a woven bag as he covered the axe heads. Turning to the pair of buckets, he dipped his hand briefly into the cool water and rubbed his hands together to clean off the thin layer of dirt that the day's chores had created. Glancing around one more time, he nodded to himself and strode to the doorway of the adjacent house.

Long benches lined the sides of the house, providing enough room between them for a person to lie down, with furs and woven blankets piled into bundles. The house carried a chill thanks to the animals being outside in the pasture for the day, but that wasn't stopping his father from conducting his usual grooming. The man's razor and comb were waiting beside the small bowl of water next to him as he perched on the edge of the bench. Thor pulled off his outer tunic and tossed it onto the bench.

"Thor," the large man called as he caught sight of him. "You need to clean up," his father scolded lightly. His brown eyes swept over Thor with a hint of distaste.

"Yes, Father," he grumbled. He knew it was true; his red hair was becoming more apparent as the last lye treatment to bleach his hair was growing out. "I'll see to it soon."

Walking over to his father, Thor quickly unbraided his hair and accepted the offered comb. He was combing out the long reddish strands of his hair and his small beard when his brother entered the house. A bit shorter than Thor, but equally well muscled and carrying a heavy woven sack. He all but tossed it down with a small groan by the grinding wheel and shifted over to join them.

"Father," he greeted with a respectful nod. He glanced towards his brother. "Thor," he said with much less warmth.

"Arvid," Thor greeted. "How was the dirt today?"

His remark earned him a sharp look from his brother, dark brown eyes flashing with irritation. Thor could see streaks of dirt on his brother's neck and there was some mud caked in his brother's bleached hair.

"More productive than playing with your toys," Arvid said with a smirk.

"Enough," their father cut in. "You are finished for the day, Thor?"

"I am," Thor answered with a nod.

"Then I suggest, Arvid, that you finish your tasks."

His brother nodded to their father and gave Thor one more look. Holding back the urge to say something more, Thor inwardly grumbled to himself. Arvid couldn't marry soon enough. Then his brother would move out into another home. Of course, then he'd have a sister-in-law to deal with and soon after that nephews and nieces. Thor groaned softly: maybe looking forward to his brother's upcoming marriage wasn't such a good thing after all.

"You're arrogant, son," his father said. There was judgment and perhaps a hint of amusement in his eyes. "Be respectful to your brother. You busy yourself with the forge but he grows the food for this family."

"Father-"

"Erlendr taught you smithing because you showed talent," his father reminded him sternly. "Not so that you could insult Arvid."

"Yes, Father." Thor held back a sigh of annoyance. "You're right."

His father gave him a look that clearly said Thor's quick agreement didn't mean much to him, and Thor inwardly sighed. He didn't really mind Arvid so much, but his brother was just so aggravating. Thor shifted so his back was to his father and brought his right hand in front of him. Flexing his fingers, Thor breathed out slowly and pulled on the smoldering flame he could feel in his gut. Small sparks of a bright blue color, almost white, appeared around his fingers and he smiled to himself. The sparks shimmered and moved faster, shooting together to form a tiny orb in the center of his hand. It glowed a little brighter and Thor wished that he could allow it to light up the whole house. But it wasn't time yet; this gift wasn't something he could fully harness.

Thor watched as his father and Arvid stepped out of the roundhouse to start bringing in the animals. Shifting quickly, he climbed off of the bench and moved to the large stone-lined fire pit located directly under the hole in their roof. His father had already prepared the fire with thick sticks and small cuts of logs stacked around smoldering tree bark. Holding out his hand, Thor focused on the small pulsing ball of magic and glared at one of the small dry pieces of wood.

The magic jolted out of his hand, arcing through the air like a tiny bolt of lightning before striking the wood. It smoked and the spark of magic caused the wood to burst into low flickering flames that quickly began to spread. Smiling to himself, Thor flexed his fingers and considered summoning more of the power and showing his father exactly what he could do, but he dismissed the thought as quickly as it had come. There was no way to be sure what kind of reaction they'd have, and the more control he had of this power the better.

Thor busied himself with starting the evening meal. It was a simple thick stew that began to fill up the house with its smell quickly as his father returned. Tossing a blanket over his shoulders, Thor inwardly grumbled about the icy temperature that seemed to be setting in for the night. There was a flap of the animal skin in the doorway and Arvid came in with several of the goats trotting along behind him. Crinkling his nose at the smell, Thor adjusted the blanket around his shoulders.

"What's wrong, Thor?" Arvid asked with a smirk. He was holding back his own shivers. "Can't handle the cold?"

Giving his brother a dark sideways look, he was going to reply when their father gave him a warning glance. He stayed silent and almost smiled when their father turned his attention towards Arvid and gave his brother an equally disappointed look. At least it was nice to know that his father knew it wasn't just him causing trouble. Thankfully they were young men who had just done a long and hard day of work, and their thoughts and remaining energy were quickly turned towards the meal. That and the indoor chores that still needed doing kept them busy for a time.

There was a strange rumble from outside of the house that disturbed the peace sometime later as the stew began to bubble softly in the iron cauldron. Frowning, Thor raised his head and listened as another rumble echoed down into the village. It wasn't the familiar sound of a spring thunderstorm: it sounded more like a rockslide. Before his father could say anything, Thor was on his feet and headed out the door.

Outside the sky was quickly darkening with the last rays of the sun vanishing into the sea. A moment later Arvid stepped out of the house with a blazing torch. His lips twitched and Thor nodded to his brother. Looking around, he noticed quickly that they weren't the only ones investigating the noise. It was too dark to see the mountains, but Thor turned to look up towards the dark towering shapes. To his surprise, he could see flickers of light on the mountains above. Not fires or torches, but brighter and made of soft white light.

Around him, the other villages began to notice and point towards the mountain. The deep rumbling sound came down into the fjord valley once again and more lights appeared. Thor took a step towards the mountain even as an icy feeling washed over his body. All of the hairs on his neck stood on end and he could feel all the hairs on his arms and legs beneath his clothes doing the same. His stomach rolled and his fingers twitched on some strange instinct.

Above their heads, storm clouds began to rumble and the world seemed impossibly darker. Breathing in sharply, Thor looked around the village and took in the other residents who were looking around in confusion. He turned his eyes up towards the sky and smelled the sudden rush of lightning in the air. This storm had not been here before: it had been a clear night not long ago. There was a strange scent on the breeze, rotten and thick that was unfamiliar and horribly out of place. In the distance, a strange gargled scream echoed down into the village from the hills.

"What is that?" one of the children asked. He moved closer to his mother as everyone looked around.

A rumbling sound came down off the hill followed by another strange scream, even louder than the last and so high pitched it sent a shiver rolling down Thor's spine. Above their head on the mountains, the lights were spreading out and sparkling over the ridges. He was so distracted by the visible points of light on the hillside that Thor almost missed the flash of light in the trees just beyond the village. Touching Arvid's shoulder, he gestured into the forest. Then the lights all vanished; there wasn't a single ray in the forest or on the mountain. Everything suddenly seemed much darker and another wave of nausea spread over Thor. The villagers all lingered close together with soft whispers filling the night air, but Thor kept searching the darkness where he'd seen the light go out.

Something was moving just beyond the torchlight and Thor took a tentative step forward. In the corner of his eye, he saw two more villagers do the same to extend the light. Then something stumbled into the glow of the torches and Thor froze. The creature was human shaped with pale, almost clear skin that shimmered in in the low light. Long white hair was bound up around horns growing out of its forehead that curved back over its head. Long pointed ears poked out of the remaining hair hanging loosely around its face. Golden decorations covered the horns and golden ornaments were worked into the hair, making the being appear majestic for a moment. But then it moved forward and he heard a collective gasp through the villagers.

Wild black eyes like empty sockets swept over them, and as the being moved closer to the light of the torches Thor could see strange dark lines visible on its lower face. A golden gloved hand reached menacingly towards them and it took another shaky step forward. Suddenly a horn blared beyond the light of the torches, ringing through the fjord and sending a shudder through Thor. Someone began to speak, only for the words to be lost in a shriek of fear.

It was like throwing water on a blazing fire only to have steam explode into your face. The world around him burst into a haze of confusion. Three more of the creatures poured out of the shadows; all of them had black veins stretching over their face and dark eyes. Their faces twisted with rage and pain like a rabid animal and Thor felt his heart jump in his chest. Screams echoed around the village as people began to run.

The creatures crashed into the village, one of them moving right past him with eyes locked on one of the young girls who was staring at them in horror. Violent anger raged through Thor and he grabbed a torch from Arvid. He brought the torch down hard against the creature's neck, hearing a soft crack in both the neck and the wood. Twisting the torch around, he set fire to the creature's hair and heard it release a high-pitched scream.

Another turned towards Thor as the first shrieked and fell to the ground, clawing at its face as the smell of burning hair filled the air. He didn't dare look at the injured one and took a tentative step back as empty eyes fixed on him. It opened its mouth and a long hissing sound came out as the creature moved its lips. For a moment it paused, a strange look of surprise on its face before it moved towards him.

"Die," fell from its lips in a thin and strained voice. "Die!"

A hand with long fingers covered in a golden gauntlet reached for him and Thor stumbled back. Vaguely he heard Arvid shout something, but another one of the creatures came rushing out of the darkness with a high-pitched shriek and lunged towards him. Thor twisted and started to run as his stomach dropped painfully. He needed a weapon: a real weapon, not the cracking torch in his hand. He lost sight of Arvid as the two creatures rushed after him. His feet shifted and he moved towards his house even as his mind spun trying to think of a plan. Something hit him hard in the back and he fell forward. Rolling over, he slashed the burning torch through the air in front of him.

They pulled back and Thor scrambled to his feet. His body suddenly felt heavy and awkward, ill-suited to the quickness that he wanted from it. Holding the torch in front of him, Thor looked around at the village, but more of the creatures were running through it. There were several bodies collapsed on the ground and one of the creatures was dragging a small boy behind it through the dirt. Several villagers had armed themselves with swords and were fighting back, but he seemed to be alone next to his house.

One of the creatures lunged at him, pulling Thor sharply back to the danger he was in. He moved backward and nearly fell into his forge through the animal skin coverings. Dropping the torch, Thor jumped away from the creature and reached blindly into his workspace. He could hear the thing right behind him. In the light of the torch, he fumbled for a weapon. His fingers tried to unwrap the animal skins holding the axe heads, but the creature clawed at his back. Thor heard his tunic rip and grabbed frantically for anything he could reach. His hand closed around the handle of one of his hammers.

There was a hiss of metal as a sword was drawn and Thor swung his hammer around his body with all of his strength. His heartbeat pounded in his ears and he felt the spark in his lower chest flutter to life. Blindly he pulled on it, calling it forth to do something. Thor felt and heard his hammer collide with the creature's head. There was a crunch, but the thing kept clawing at him and a strange snarl ripped out of its throat. Grimacing at the sound, Thor swung the hammer again and pulled on his power frantically. It bloomed in his chest far faster than ever before and flooded through his arms. The hammer flashed for a moment with a brilliant bright blue color just before striking the creature.

The golden sword hit the ground and to Thor's shock began to decay right before his eyes into a pile of dirt. His eyes returned to the creature which was reeling back from him and collided with its fellow. Skins were torn from the structure as they both fell back amidst the pained screams of the first. In his hand, the hammer's glow was beginning to fade and Thor felt his legs trembling more than he'd ever want to admit.

Leaping forward, he brought his hammer down as hard as he could on the golden armor that protected the creature's chest. Under the force of his strike and in a flash of the bright blue power the armor began to dissolve as well. He didn't wait and struck again, now on the unarmored flesh. Thor heard a crack and a scream from the creature just before it began to turn into dark black ash and fall to the ground.

The second creature lashed at him with its golden gauntlets. Thor felt one of the long sharp edges catch his face and slice into his skin. Adrenaline flared inside him and he brought his hammer down on the creature's face. There was no armor to dissolve as he heard the cracking of bone beneath his hands. It too turned to ash. His knees buckled and Thor collapsed against the workbench. On instinct, his fingers closed around the hammer and he chuckled weakly to himself. A hammer wasn't an ideal weapon; he favored a sword himself, but it seemed that in a pinch it could do more than shape metal and build things.

Forcing himself to move forward, Thor stepped out and scanned the village. He could see none of the creatures and villagers were rushing around in a haze of panic and worry. Arvid spotted him with a look of relief crossing his face. His brother jogged over to him, grabbing his arm just as Thor's legs decided to give out and the small flame in his gut dimmed.

4

Mage Meeting

The house of Professor Morgana Cornwall was a little outside of Ravenslake proper, with a shield of trees keeping it out of sight. It was a Victorian-style home, though of modern construction with light gray paint and white trim. Alex found it a bit nondescript as it lacked the iron decorations around Professor Yates' house, but she couldn't deny the sense of safety that she felt here as she climbed out of her little blue car. Nicki was right behind her in climbing out; Aiden and Bran were still unfolding themselves from the back.

"And here we go," Aiden muttered. "What a way to spend our last day of freedom before classes resume."

"Oh, stop whining," Nicki chided without any real bite.

It was silly to be nervous. It was just Merlin and Morgana... The last time she'd seen them had been weird. The strange connection she'd always had with Morgana had finally solidified into a warm sort of affection, and Merlin... well that one was still a little odd. She'd given him the Iron Chalice to look after, but the jury was still out on how that relationship was going to go now that he knew she was the real reincarnation of his dear student Arto.

"Easy, Alex." Bran came up next to her and smiled reassuringly.

The heavy wooden door with etched glass was opened before they even reached the porch and Alex looked up to find Morgana waiting in the doorway. A look of intense relief flashed over the woman's face, but she quickly stepped back from the door to let them in. The small entryway was a bit crowded as the four of them stepped inside and began to shrug out of their coats. Morgana was standing near the doorway to the living room with Merlin beside her.

To say that the two professors didn't look their age was a tremendous understatement: both of them were roughly three thousand years old and yet neither looked beyond their fifties. Morgana's long hair remained a rich dark brown, and her rather regal face had only a few small worry lines around her green eyes. She was dressed in jeans and a dark green sweater; nothing like what one would think an ancient sorceress straight out of legend to look like.

Merlin looked older than Morgana, with soft white hair that contained a hint of auburn and a neatly trimmed gray beard. Dressed as he was in black slacks with a blue button-down shirt, he didn't look like a wizard, but it was at least a little closer. His brown eyes were looking at her intensely, searching for any sign of injury or distress. Holding back a sigh, Alex managed a small reassuring smile and nodded in greeting. In the back of her mind, she wondered if Merlin had followed her back to Spokane over Christmas Break. She hadn't seen him, but for a mage of his age and experience that wouldn't have been much of a challenge.

Alex moved around Merlin, catching sight of his silver triskele pin just to the right of his heart. It matched the necklace that Morgana wore and Alex found herself wondering if she should see about getting something similar. After all, the triskele was the closest thing to a symbol that the magic of the Iron Realm had. Pushing the thought away, Alex walked into Morgana's living room as soon as her coat was hung up and was hit by the smell of cookies.

Morgana was right on her heels and Alex turned to look at the professor. Alex was a little taller than Morgana: a point of amusement to the other woman. For a moment Alex was a little unsure until Morgana smiled and brought her arms up a little awkwardly. Returning the slightly uncomfortable smile, Alex stepped forward and hugged Morgana. As the older mage's arm came up to grip her shoulders Alex relaxed.

"This is still a bit weird," Alex confessed.

Morgana chuckled warmly at the statement. "Well, this may surprise you, but I'm not a hugger," Morgana said. She released Alex's shoulders and stepped back. "It has not been my habit to hug the Iron Soul in the various lifetimes."

"Oh really?" Alex asked teasingly.

"Indeed." Morgana began to move towards the kitchen, allowing the others to follow them into the living room. "Sometimes you've been utterly obnoxious."

Holding back a laugh, Alex let herself smile and sank into one of the vintage red chairs. It was odd, but Morgana's dismissive references to her other lives actually made her feel a bit better. Bran gave her a soft smile as he glanced pointedly towards Morgana. Smiling in return, Alex lowered her face so her smile wasn't too obvious as everyone took their seats. Aiden and Nicki sat on the long sofa together and Bran was in an armchair as Merlin followed Morgana into the kitchen.

They returned a few moments later with a pot filled with hot cocoa and a plate of chocolate chip cookies. Several mugs were floating in the air with a faint green shimmer around them next to Merlin, and he beamed at the look of surprise on Alex's face. She wasn't sure that she'd ever seen Merlin use magic for something so trivial. Morgana shook her head and set the plate of cookies down on the large coffee table. Judging from the smell still lingering in the house Alex guessed that they were fresh.

With graceful moves, Morgana plucked the mugs out of the air and took the pot from Merlin. She poured everyone a mug and passed around some cookies. It was almost like a pleasant winter afternoon. Merlin and Morgana sat down next to each other on the loveseat. For a moment no one said anything as Alex waited for Merlin or Morgana to start the conversation.

"This is weird," Aiden said, voicing what everyone was thinking. "First time we've been back together since..." He trailed off, stilling for a moment before swallowing thickly. Nicki shifted a little closer to him but didn't reach out to touch him. Still, her presence seemed to calm Aiden and he sighed dramatically. "I still can't believe I missed the Quest for the Holy Grail."

"Your presence was missed," Bran assured him. "There are many times where I'm sure we missed the perfect chance to make Monty Python references."

A real laugh escaped Aiden and he shook his head at his friend. Smiling softly, Alex breathed a little easier as the lingering tension began to fade from the room. It wasn't completely gone, but a lot had changed recently.

"So?" Alex asked drawing everyone's attention to her. "Where should we start?"

"Ah yes, that is the question," Merlin said. "Well, firstly the Iron Chalice has been secured in an iron box that I made over the break. It's in my workshop surrounded by even more iron."

"That won't stop Arthur." Aiden's hands clenched into fists. "He worked with iron before, so he doesn't have the Sídhe weakness to it."

"And the creatures they have control of don't seem to be as vulnerable to iron," Nicki added.

"Indeed, the box is a temporary solution. We need the Iron Chalice protected, but accessible in case of an emergency," Merlin agreed with a weary nod. "I'm considering putting a vault into the floor of the shop. Coated in iron or something of the sort."

"Of course, we don't know if Arthur would be able to use the Chalice," Nicki said. "He may not care about it."

"Never leave an enemy with an advantage," Aiden said. "Us being able to heal each other without exhausting our own magic is a critical thing. I wouldn't want my enemies to have something like that."

"I also have a few spells in place to alert me if someone enters the workshop." Merlin gave Aiden an approving nod. "But I do indeed plan to improve the security around the Chalice."

"Pity we can't just bring Emrys to Ravenslake." Nicki sighed even as a smile tugged at her lips. "He'd be one hell of a guard dog."

"I'm still having difficulty believing that a Dragon entered our world in Wales and Morgana and I didn't know about it." Merlin chuckled softly even as he slouched slightly, suddenly looking very old.

"We were rather distracted at the time trying to protect Cathanáil." Morgana too had an uneasy and guilty look on her face.

"Have you had any progress in locating Cathanáil?" Bran asked. "Alex and I were able to combine our magic enough to find the Chalice, maybe we can do the same for the Sword."

Merlin and Morgana exchanged a quick glance, and for a moment Alex marveled at the silent communication the two were capable of. It amused her more than she would have imagined and a small part of her felt a flush of satisfaction at them getting along. She finally took a bite of the cookie and let the fresh warm flavor flood through her mouth.

"Wow!" Alex's eyes widened. "These are fantastic!"

A chuckle escaped Morgana and a little more of the tension faded. Alex couldn't help but blush a little as everyone looked at her. Smiling at Morgana, Alex made a sheepish shrug before taking another bite of the cookie. She watched Aiden take a bite of his own and his eyes widened.

"At three thousand years old I should hope that I can manage chocolate chip cookies." Morgana gave her an affectionate look. "But back to Bran's point: I suppose that it is possible you two could scry for Cathanáil."

"It would certainly be marvelous if we could retrieve the Sword," Merlin said.

"I'm sensing a but there." Nicki frowned and looked between the two teachers. "What is it?"

"But Bran was already having visions of the Iron Chalice when they scryed for it." Morgana folded her hands in her lap. "He was already connected to it thanks to, uh…" she paused and Bran snorted softly.

"My former head being next to it," he supplied bluntly.

"Yes, that," Morgana agreed, earning a laugh from Aiden. "I suppose you could try, though I don't think it would work. However, we need to be careful when you try."

"You're concerned about it?" Nicki tilted her head curiously. "Why?"

"Scrying is searching through everything, Nicki," Morgana reminded her gently. "It's sending your magic spinning out into the world in an attempt to connect with something. If you have only limited experience with the thing you're looking for, it is difficult. Bran has talent, but it would be too easy to use too much magic and hurt himself."

"But you want to train me more before we try," Bran said. "I suppose that's fair."

"Cathanáil is a very powerful object that I've been unable to find. Its magic shrouds it, but Alex's connection might be able to get through that as the Sword does belong to her," Morgana explained. "You and I will work on focusing your magic better into scrying since in this attempt you won't have the benefit of Bran the Blessed's head to help you. Once you're ready we will try."

"And I'll work with Alex in the forge and in meditations so she can hopefully help you find the Sword," Merlin added with a smile. "It will be our project for the semester."

"Alright, well, there's that issue." Aiden reached for another cookie. "But what about those Sídhe creatures, the descendants? Do we know anything about how Arthur and the Queen are controlling them?"

It was like air being let out of a balloon as they watched Morgana and Merlin wilt. Morgana leaned forward, resting her arms on her knees while toying with her hands and Merlin slumped back against the sofa. Holding back a sigh, Alex tried to keep her fingers still as she looked at the others. Judging from their body language they had heard the silent answer.

"I suppose that I can't think of any stories like this," Alex offered softly. "That's a bit funny," she added with a muted giggle. "Everything else has had a story."

"But not originally." Merlin sat up a little straighter and looked more animated. "Those stories came from our original struggles; this is no different. We know that Queen Scáthbás survived somehow, trapped within the magic of the Iron Gates, and she somehow created another half- Sídhe in Arthur. We don't know where they are: the Pendred home has been abandoned, and we don't know how they are compelling the descendants of those that fled into our world."

"She must have at least some sort of magic to have created Arthur in the first place," Bran said. He toyed with a loose thread of the armchair until Morgana fixed him with a look.

"Certainly she has magic, but the scale is the problem," Merlin explained. Pressing his fingertips together in front of his face, Merlin hummed thoughtfully. "I believe she has something helping her achieve it: a magical item of some kind. Perhaps she brought something through three thousand years ago."

"No; we would have found it," Morgana said.

"Perhaps it was caught in stasis with her when you killed her on the Iron Gate," Merlin replied. There was a sharpness in his tone that made Morgana glare at him.

"Okay, so we don't know yet." Alex was very uncomfortable with the looks of irritation on the older mages' faces. "But we'll figure it out."

"Alex is right, you guys, and past Iron Souls have worked your way through a lot," Aiden said. "We'll be on guard for more attacks, keep training, and see what more we can do."

"Yeah, I mean we were talking about making more Iron Gates." Nicki forced a small smile. "Wouldn't that help keep the Sídhe out of the area?"

"Indeed, Nicole, there are things we can do to increase the safety of Ravenslake," Merlin replied. "Including a blood protection spell like the one you encountered at the Tor."

"But if we protect the city too much, doesn't that increase the likelihood of the Sídhe focusing on other places without mages?" Bran pointed out uneasily.

"It does," Morgana admitted. "Making more Iron Gates in the area is our best chance, as that will help protect the world as a whole from invaders, but it won't fix our problem with the Sídhe creatures."

"Is there anything we can do in the meantime?" Alex gripped the mug of cocoa tighter, but it had gotten cold during the conversation.

"Train: we need to focus our efforts on helping Alex control her powers and expand what the three of you are able to do," Merlin said firmly. "If we can retrieve Cathanáil that will give us a powerful weapon in our arsenal."

"And once Bran has more control over scrying, the two of us together might be able to locate the source of the Queen's magical control," Morgana added though she sounded less confident than Merlin.

"Great." Nicki's shoulders dropped and she frowned. "Stalemate."

"For the time being." Morgana set down her mug and raised her chin. "But we have the Iron Chalice, Bran has been healed, and we know the truth about Alex. Arthur and the Queen may have tricked us, but we aren't defeated or stuck by any stretch of the imagination."

"I do have one more question for Alex," Merlin added quickly, earning a sharp glance from Morgana. It had a hint of warning in it that surprised Alex, but Merlin ignored it. "What are you planning to do about Lance and Jenny?"

"What?" Alex blinked at him in surprise. "Uh, nothing. They helped us and I don't think that they're any sort of threat to us." She paused and licked her lips before swallowing. "I don't even know if Jenny will be back next year. With everything that happened she was planning on transferring after she finished her sophomore year and Lance... honestly, he seems pretty focused on trying to get Jenny to give him a second chance."

"You aren't planning to distance yourself from them?" Merlin frowned and irritation flared up in Alex's chest.

"No, I'm not. They went with us to Wales. Jenny and Lance being a bit more removed from this magic stuff meant they noticed things we didn't. They never ran during the trouble and they apologized to Arto's remains during his funeral. Whatever shadow was hanging over them I think is gone."

"But still-"

"Merlin," Morgana cut in. "Leave it be. It is Alex's decision." That earned a look of surprise from both Alex and Merlin. Morgana sighed softly and shook her head. "I never liked Gwenyvar, that is true, but part of it was that she and Arto got married during the puppy love stage. They cared about each other, but he was gone so much and Gwenyvar..." She sighed and waved a hand dismissively. "The relationship that enabled the old tragedy isn't relevant now." Morgana glanced back at Alex with a slightly teasing smile. "Unless our dear Alex begins to have bisexual tendencies."

"I think we're safe." Alex fought back a blush and the urge to kick Morgana. "Though after Arthur I don't think I'll be dating for a while."

"Oh great, we're all single now," Aiden muttered.

"What about Sarah?" Bran asked. He looked over at Aiden in surprise as Nicki flinched.

"We broke up, three days ago. She, uh, met someone."

"Sorry, Aiden." Bran grimaced in sympathy.

"It's fine; she didn't cheat on me at least. She just wanted to be honest and she didn't stab me, so for this group, I'm doing great." He gave Alex an apologetic look for that one and she gave him a small nod in return.

"So, we're stuck living vicariously through the Jenny and Lance romance." Nicki groaned, leaning dejectedly against Aiden's shoulder. "Now that is just sad."

"And on this turn of the conversation let us call it a day," Morgana said. She looked both amused and uneasy at the sudden shift in topic.

"Indeed," Merlin said. "Everyone is up to speed on the situation. I'm sorry that we didn't have better news for you today."

"We will keep looking of course." Morgana stood and picked up Alex's cold mug. "An answer will present itself in time."

"That's it?" Aiden asked with surprise. Glancing down at the half-eaten cookie in his hand, he blinked in confusion. "No training, no pop quizzes on Celtic mythology?"

"You resume classes tomorrow." Amusement took over Morgana's features. "With the... events of your break and the challenge you faced in telling your parents about magic, I suspect that you have not gotten things in order for your classes."

"Seems a bit silly to worry about," Bran said softly.

"Perhaps but bear in mind that this war may go on for years or it may be done in months," Merlin told them in a softer voice. "You need to be prepared for life after magic because once the Sídhe are defeated and our world closed off once again, magic will begin to fade once more."

Nodding slowly, Alex drummed her fingers on the armrest. Her mind was spinning a little at those final words. She'd lived almost two decades without magic, but if they ever had a victory complete enough that it went away, what would it be like? Shaking her head, Alex stood up as Aiden and Nicki marched past her towards the door.

Feeling a twinge of pity for him, Alex considered bringing up Sarah but dismissed the thought. She was pretty sure he'd mentioned it here so it was done and out of the way without a long conversation ensuing. Bran recovered his cane from beside the chair and tossed it in the air, catching it quickly with a small smile before heading for the door. He glanced her way, but Alex found herself lingering for a moment.

"Alex, are you alright?" Morgana asked. Stepping towards her, Morgana touched her arm lightly.

"Just a lot in my head," Alex answered.

"I am sorry if I upset you." Merlin shifted over next to Morgana. "You do of course have every right to decide on what roles Lance and Jenny play in your life."

"I get it, Merlin," Alex assured him. She really didn't want to do this now. "But I watched how much everything affected Jenny. I know she's sorry about it even now, knowing that Arthur was just using her and Lance as a way to convince us all he was the Iron Soul."

She shrugged and glanced towards the doorway where the others were lingering and listening. Nicki grinned as she spotted them and waved one mitten-clad hand towards her before she began pushing the boys out the door. Chuckling, Alex turned her attention back to Morgana as the door shut.

"Beyond that, I don't know." She opened her arms in a wide helpless gesture. "Everything's been happening really fast. I guess we just have to find the new status quo before any real decisions can be made."

"Wise words." Merlin nodded in resignation. "Please do be careful. Neither Morgana nor I wish to see anything happen to you."

"I know," Alex forced out weakly. There was a strange weight on her shoulders at the warm look in Merlin's eyes. "But I've got to live my life too."

Merlin sighed but nodded in understanding. "How did your conversation go with your parents?" he asked tentatively.

"I told them; I showed them magic and explained things, but honestly I think they're in shock," Alex confessed. "We ignored it a lot during Christmas stuff, but every so often they'd ask a question or I'd catch them looking at me funny. I'm kinda surprised they haven't called asking me if it was a bad dream or joke."

"We could speak with them, if you wish," Morgana said with a glance towards Merlin. "In the past, we have explained things to the Iron Soul's family."

"Yeah, but that was back in the days of superstition." Alex tried to smile but failed. "I'll keep that in mind, but they did put up some iron horseshoes, and if it's okay with you, Merlin, I'd like to use the forge to make them some daggers."

"Of course, Alex," Merlin said. "I'll have another key made so you can come by whenever you need."

"Thanks, but I'm pretty sure that Aiden's got figuring out an unlocking spell on the agenda."

"Knowing that group it will be triggered by the word Alohomora." Morgana rubbed the skin between her eyes though Alex caught a smile around her hand.

"Well, they'd never forget it." Alex barely contained her smile. "But yeah, we've got a date with the books again to start working on more forms of magic."

"Well, we can't complain that you aren't creative and working hard," Merlin said smoothly. He grinned at Morgana, who just shook her head.

"Is it creativity if they're taking ideas from books and television?" Morgana countered with a sharp raise of her eyebrow.

"I think its genre savvy then." Alex zipped up her coat with a real smile. "This may not be a book or TV show, but no reason not to seek guidance from them."

She gave the two older mages a friendly wave as she stepped out the doorway onto the porch. The others were already in the car and waiting for her so Alex didn't linger any longer. Classes started tomorrow and there was still normal stuff to deal with. Like getting textbooks... yeah, magic had more than complicated her college life. Her free time was all but gone and her now ex-boyfriend had deceived them all and tried to kill her, but at least she hadn't flunked out yet.

5

Nightmares

The snow was icy on her back. She was so thirsty. Alex could feel her own warm blood seeping between her fingers. Beneath her hands, her stomach was a mess of sliced flesh, torn fabric, and sticky blood. The cold was unbearable, but worse was Arthur looming over her with that horrible mocking grin. His blue eyes were bright with satisfaction, without even a hint of regret or doubt. In his hand was a gleaming sword with a golden hilt covered in blood. Her blood. With his blond hair, square jaw, and broad shoulders, he might have looked every inch the hero if she hadn't known the truth. Unable to bear it, Alex slammed her eyes shut and pressed her hand tighter against the wound.

Then the cold began to fade away as warmth rolled over her like she'd stepped into the sunlight. She didn't feel blood on her hands anymore and opened her eyes. Around her was a strange haze, but she sighed in relief. She wasn't on the shore anymore. It had just been a nightmare. Now that it was over, she recognized the floating sense of a coming dream.

Alex slowly became aware that she was walking down a long and twisting corridor. There were no lights from what she could see, but everything around her was illuminated with some sort of soft glow.

The wall was hazy to her, and she struggled to take in the details of what seemed to be an ordinary wooden wall. Every few feet there were doorways that were unmarked, but each door was a little different. One had a wider dark wood frame around it while the next one had a larger doorknob. She suddenly stopped next to one of the doors and reached out to touch the roughly textured, dark silver doorknob. It was icy to her touch and she paused for a moment in hesitation before turning it. A strange wave of magic rushed over her and Alex slammed her eyes shut.

The smell of the ocean was the first thing she was truly aware of as Alex opened her eyes and looked around. The rush of salt water with a strange hint of something musty and almost rotten hit her extra hard as she took in her surroundings with mild surprise. She giggled nervously to herself as the haze of the strange corridor faded away and she wondered what was going to happen now. Alex blinked as the dream became clearer, and looked around in interest. In a strange variation, she was on the deck of an old-fashioned sailing vessel.

Looking up, Alex let the salty wind catch her hair and gazed at the tall double masts with billowing cloth sails. It was right out of a movie and she couldn't help but grin. There were small flags perched high at the top of the masts above the tiny crow's nest. Shielding her eyes, Alex scanned the ship for anything else interesting and caught sight of a couple of sailors up along the mast. She could hear the crashing of the waves against the wood of the ship and feel the swaying of the vessel, but suddenly realized that her body was moving easily with it. A grin split her face as Alex turned to look at the large boat steering wheel behind her. She couldn't remember what it was called though it teased at her memory.

There was a sailor dressed in loose clothing with a bandana on his head. He looked bored and was slouched against the wheel until he caught her eyes on him. Then he straightened up and stared past her towards the horizon with a nervous twitch beside his eye. Turning away from him, she directed her eyes back across the main lower deck and took in the details. One of the sailors was cleaning the deck near a large grate that led to the hold. Another was checking a series of ropes secured along the mast that Alex was sure had some sort of technical name, though she didn't know it. Frowning slightly, she marveled at the detail of the ship. She'd seen old ships like this in movies, but everywhere she looked the details were crisp and clear. Far more than she thought her hazy memory of movies would permit.

The wind faded a bit, going from the strong constant blast to a softer ruffle against the sails. Alex brushed back her hair and breathed in again. She gagged and coughed, stumbling backward against a wooden railing. The stench of piss and rot hung across the deck like a fog without the wind to carry it away. A few of the sailors paused and grumbled, moving to the sides of the ship, but they didn't seem alarmed by the smell wafting up. Alex stared at them in shock as the smell filled her nose and made her eyes begin to water.

Something rippled up her arms like a cold mist pulling at her hairs. Her stomach turned and she could taste bile seeping into her mouth. Shivering, Alex stared at the cargo hold opening as more of the foul smell poured out. From below she could hear soft, pained, and frightened voices. The stink of rot and bodily fluids caused a rush of fear that made her stumble back as her throat closed.

The creeping feeling of a dream turning into a nightmare hit Alex square in the chest, making her body tense. Suddenly she felt pinned in place. The voices below grew a little stronger for a moment before one of the sailors shouted vicious words down into the hold, making them fall silent. They were human then; able to understand an order for silence.

A strange metallic sound of soft clinks echoed up onto the deck, like a chain moving. The voices softened to the point of fading away.

But the smell lingered even as the wind picked up again. Alex stared at the hold grating, her ears searching against her will for a sound. She was suddenly aware of the heat that even the wind offered only a little comfort from. The groans were becoming louder, and a horrible suspicion was beginning to push at the back of Alex's head. But it made no sense; why would she be dreaming of a prison ship?

"Captain!" one of the sailors with rotting teeth called over to her.

Her eyes snapped open, and Alex peered across her room at the back of her desk chair. There was only the hint of blue light from her laptop's power strip in the dark room. Licking her lips, Alex inhaled slowly to calm her frantic heart. She sat up cautiously and looked around her room. It had been just a dream, but then again it had been something so very real and ominous. Alex had a sense of dread, but the reason why was slipping away.

Before she could talk herself out of it, Alex swung her legs out of bed and stood up. She swayed for a moment as her feet protested her sudden rise. There was no desire to stay in bed: the thought of returning to that dream made her ill. Alex scrambled for her desk lamp. With a soft click, her room gained some light and Alex blinked her eyes even as her hands fumbled for a notepad in the top drawer of her desk. She collapsed into her desk chair and started writing down the dream.

There wasn't much: an old large sailing ship, a terrible smell, people in the hold and a sense of absolute dread. Alex shoved it to the side and rubbed her temple. What was she hoping to gain from this? It was probably just a dream. Alex shook her head but made a few more notes about the details of the ship before they slipped away. Pushing the notebook away, Alex slumped back in her chair and drummed her fingers on the edge of her desk.

She felt wide awake now but didn't dare look at the clock on her phone or turn the computer on. Alex was pretty sure that she'd be disappointed if she did so. Instead, she pushed her chair back and stood up, grabbing the paperback copy of *Beowulf* for her British Literature class. She pulled on her robe over the pajama bottoms and tank top she wore before slipping out of her room. She paused in front of Nicki's bedroom door and listened for a moment, but her roommate was silent. Sighing softly, Alex wasn't sure if she was disappointed or not.

Alex moved out to the living room and groped around in the darkness for a moment before she found the light switch, nearly stubbing her bare toes on Nicki's hat rack by the door. The layout was great if you were coming into the dark room from the hall, but less so when coming out of a bedroom at night. Alex sat down in the armchair and pulled her legs up with her. She tugged the spare blanket over her lap and snuggled down with the book in her lap. For a moment she just sat quietly and listened. Everything was still with only a faint sound of the wind outside the window.

Rubbing her eyes, Alex opened up *Beowulf* and easily found the place she'd left off at. They'd only just gotten started with the old epic poem. For a moment she smiled as she considered the irony of Merlin teaching *Beowulf* as one of the oldest examples of British literature when he was in fact much older than it.

"He should write a book of old legends and stories," Alex said out loud. It was a silly attempt to dispel the lingering nervousness she was feeling, but it helped a bit. "He could pass it off as a gritty reimagining of the oldest stories."

Alex wondered for a moment if Merlin or Morgana had ever been tempted to make records of their lives. Had either of them ever kept any kind of journal? Ever attempted to draw a long-deceased loved one? Her fingers tugged nervously at the pages of the book and Alex shook her head. It was never pleasant speculating on the three-thousand-year lifespans of the two older mages. There had been plenty of hints over the years that the stories would not be pleasant.

She turned her attention to the next passage of the poem, but she couldn't focus on the words. Instead, a nagging little voice in her head suggested that Beowulf might be based on a real person: a real hero that lived long ago. Closing her eyes, Alex breathed out slowly and sternly reminded herself that assuming that because Arthur was based on the real ancient hero Arto that other heroes were real would be a mistake. She'd already been informed rather bluntly that her Welsh life who had made the Iron Chalice had become a god in Celtic mythology and that Thor had in fact been one of her past lives.

"If I was Beowulf too, I'm going to kill Merlin," Alex grumbled. The first stirrings of a headache tingled at the base of her skull.

She opened her eyes and started skimming through the words again, trying to take them in. Still, the sense that she was forgetting something remained and distracted her, like a bad itch when trying to fall asleep. Without meaning to, she began to tap her foot against the armrest of the chair and drummed her fingers on the cover of the book while flipping between pages.

"Alex?" a sleepy voice called softly from the hallway.

Nicki stumbled into the living room, though her eyes were wide and alert as she took Alex in and scanned the room. A moment later Nicki relaxed slightly and leaned sleepily against the wall. Her long red hair was in two braids, and combined with her overly large fuzzy blue pajamas she looked far more like a preteen than a powerful mage who could kill you with ice shards or drown you. Nicki was trying to look nonchalant, but it didn't fool Alex, who lowered her face slightly at being caught. Neither of them said anything for a moment until Nicki huffed in impatience.

"I'd ask if you're okay, but you're up at two in the morning and reading *Beowulf*," Nicki observed dryly. "I have a hard time believing that it was so riveting as to demand that."

"I had a dream," Alex answered honestly. She closed the book and set it on the small table between the armchair and couch. "It felt a lot like the tunnel dream. Sort of a floaty feeling, but lots of details and really clear." She shook her head and sighed, letting her head fall back against the couch. "I have the horrible feeling that I'm forgetting something important."

"Did you write it down?" Nicki pushed off the wall and walked over to sit on the edge of the couch by Alex.

"Yeah, I did; I'll type it up and send it to Merlin, Morgana, and Bran tomorrow, just in case any of them had the same dream." She paused and licked her dry lips. "It's odd but I think... I think I may have been on a prison ship."

"A prison ship?" Nicki repeated with a hint of surprise and interest. "Any particular reason?"

"Just... I don't know. It popped into my head during the dream. It was an old-fashioned ship, like the ones in pirate movies. 17th or 18th century or something like that, but there was this smell coming from the hold."

"Maybe fish."

"I doubt I'd dream about an old-fashioned fishing boat," Alex scoffed. "No, this was an ocean crossing ship; two masts and big sails... I heard voices from below, I think. There were people down there and..." Alex furrowed her brow trying to remember the details. "One of the sailors yelled at them to be quiet and they did."

"Maybe." Nicki reached over and put her hand over Alex's, giving it a soft squeeze. "Look, you won't solve it tonight. It may have just been a dream. An ordinary instance of your brain trying to tell you a story while you sleep."

"I don't think-"

"And even if it wasn't," Nicki interrupted, "You had the dreams of the tunnels numerous times, so if it is important then you'll probably have the dream again."

"I hope not." Alex dropped her eyes from Nicki's, not able to face that intense stare. "That place gave me a weird feeling. It was pretty at first and a nice change, but I don't know." She pushed a tangle of blonde hair back behind her ear. "It was like a shadow settled over me or something. It made me feel sick."

"We'll figure it out," Nicki promised. "I mean come on, we found the Holy Grail, remember? Grail Hunters have been trying to find it for centuries and we found it in like two weeks."

"We had a lot of help." Alex couldn't help but smile at the pride in Nicki's voice. "It also helps if you know you are looking for an ancient Celtic artifact rather than a Middle Eastern goblet."

"Details," Nicki dismissed. However, she looked pleased with herself for managing to get a smile. "Look, Alex, try to relax. It really might have just been a normal dream. A lot has happened lately and I'm sure our subconsciouses are trying to keep up." She paused and softened her tone. "Besides... it was better than the nightmares, right?"

"Yeah," Alex agreed. She licked her lips as her mouth suddenly felt super dry. "It was."

"Okay then." Nicki stood up and held out her hand to Alex. "Can you try to get some more sleep?"

"I... yeah, I probably should." Alex sighed in defeat, taking the offered hand and unfolding her legs.

Nicki tugged her up and then proceeded to half lead/half push her back to her bedroom. The other mage lingered by the door as Alex crawled back into bed. As nice as the mattress and pillows felt, Alex couldn't help but tense up a little bit as she caught Nicki glancing towards the open notebook.

"Goodnight," Alex said, pulling Nicki's attention back to her.

"Good morning you mean." Giving her a warm smile, Nicki reached for the light switch. "Get some sleep, Alex. I'll see you later."

Then the light was off and the door closed. Alex watched the light from the living room slipping in under her door for a moment before that too vanished. Nicki's door closed and she was left alone in the dark with only her thoughts for company. Restful sleep felt very far away.

6

The Strangers

15 C.E. Sør-Trøndelag, Norway

The wind off the fjord was the same as before. The smell of the village was the same. The people were the same as always, at least in appearance, but there was a shadow over his village; something he couldn't see and didn't know how to fight. Something intangible had changed in his home, and Thor hated it. Helplessness and confusion didn't sit well with him. Even now as he went about his normal tasks, he couldn't escape the feeling. It seemed to fill the village itself and spill into the fields and fjord.

Thor shifted back and shook his head as a heavy sigh escaped him. Turning around, he grabbed the bound bundle of thin logs and began moving back towards the village with quick steps. A wooden wall now encircled roughly half of the village where there had been none before. Men at work on the wall and in the fields were carrying swords and axes that he'd been busy making for the last moon cycle. As he walked back towards the village his own sword hung at his side and lightly hit his thigh with each step. It was a comforting weight, but one he found himself resenting.

Pushing those thoughts from his mind, Thor walked through the unfinished section of wall and towards his own longhouse. A flash of blue in the corner of his eyes made him pause and he turned to the right curiously. There was a pair of unfamiliar figures moving up the path towards the village, both of them in cloaks that billowed in the wind. Around him, the others paused in their work and looked up at the strangers.

Erlendr and Thor's father began to move to meet them, both seeming at ease, but Thor could see the tension in his father's shoulders. He couldn't remember such a small party traveling to the village, and certainly none in times like this. His own eyes returned to the strangers and his body tensed, ready to jump to the defense.

"Welcome strangers," his father greeted. His tone was pleasant but demanded attention. "I am Jor."

"Greetings," the first of the figures answered. He nodded and reached up slowly to pull back their hood. "Thank you for the welcome."

The man had gray curls with the barest hint of red like Thor's own natural hair and sharp brown eyes. He regarded the village with a curious and sorrowful look. For a moment his eyes followed one of the young boys as he crossed the village with an armful of wood. Thor tensed up slightly as he watched the stranger move further into the village with his long gray cloak sweeping around him. Others around him were on guard as well, but the stranger didn't seem concerned.

His companion was a woman with a stately bearing and long dark hair bound up in a long plait over her head. Intense green eyes were sweeping across the village and a small tight frown marred her otherwise attractive features. A pin with three connected curving arms was fixed on the long blue cloak she wore. Like the man, she didn't seem at all worried about the fearful and distrusting looks that the armed men were giving them. Instead, she almost seemed amused or bored with them.

Nothing about them was too strange; they wore ordinary clothing, yet there was a sense of power and... something else. He wasn't the only one picking up on it. Thor could see several others in the village looking unsettled by the strangers. He wondered just what it was; it didn't feel bad or wrong. It just... hung in the air around them, like a veil of mist that separated them from the rest of the world. Shaking his head, Thor became aware that he was staring, and lowered his eyes before he drew attention to himself. In his chest, there was a strange itch to approach and find out what was happening, but his aching muscles stilled the impulse for the day at least.

Thor kept eyeing the strangers as they spoke with his father and Erlendr as he moved towards his workshop. He pulled back the animal furs protecting the workshop and grimaced at the darkness creeping in around him. The sun was beginning to set so he swung the bundle of wood off his shoulder and began stacking it beside the forge. Thor noted the harsh heat that had burned throughout the day was almost completely gone. Smoke lingered on the walls of the workshop and his clothes, but the day was well and truly done.

As he stacked the wood, Thor did a mental inventory of the supply and the amount he had used each day. Thus far the season was proving colder than normal, making it harder to keep the forge hot enough. His supply would get him through the next day, but at some point, he was going to need to bring some of the village children along if everyone continued their current demand for iron weapons and tools. He was done stacking the wood and was covering his workbench when he heard someone moving up behind him.

"You are the local blacksmith?" the woman asked. She looked him over as Thor stood up and turned to face them.

"I am one of them," Thor answered calmly. He turned to study her, but she had already looked away from him. "You've already met Erlendr who is the other."

She nodded, still not looking at him. Without another word to him, the woman examined the pile of iron axe heads and the two rough swords on the bench. A flare of irritation blasted through Thor and he frowned at her. Drawing himself up to his full height Thor glared at her back and grit his teeth. Thankfully the man stepped forward and offered him a slightly softer smile.

"Please forgive my companion; we've been traveling alone for some time," he said in a warm voice that sounded a little forced. "I am Merlin and she is Morgana."

"Thor," he offered politely. He turned his full attention to the man and met the unfamiliar brown eyes.

His workshop melted away as the scent of a thick forest enshrouded him and he eyed the unfamiliar trees. Soft morning dew settled on his face as sunlight filtered through the canopy above. He could hear the rustling of the leaves and birds all around him. The air tasted differently and he could feel something brushing over his skin. Panic clawed at his chest; he gasped for air and then thankfully the world fell away once more.

"Easy, lad," Merlin said in a much warmer voice. A surprisingly strong grip guided him down onto the bench. "Sit down."

"Well." Morgana chuckled, sounding amused as Thor lowered his head and blinked his eyes. "The smith, that is interesting. A pleasant surprise."

"That confirms the situation." Merlin patted Thor's shoulder almost fondly. "New mages are being born. As strange as Erlendr's descriptions of the creatures may have been, we may be once more facing our old war."

"But it can't be the Sídhe," Morgana insisted. There was a strange, sharp note in her voice that made Thor's shoulders tighten. "They can't enter the world."

"We're some distance from Arto's Iron Gates, perhaps far enough."

"Ridiculous, you felt the magic the same as I did."

"What-" Thor gasped out, his fingers digging into the wood bench. "What was that? Who are you?" he demanded as his strength began to return. He forced himself to look up only to find Morgana's green eyes focusing on his face. His stomach knotted and he felt his own power surging uncontrollably in his chest.

He was suddenly on a tall, unfamiliar hill with a strong wind rolling across his shoulders and ruffling his hair. A water soaked plain with numerous small islands filled the land before him with the glistening sea beyond. He breathed in the thick and familiar smell of the sea as a strange sound threatened to draw his attention.

"At least that is out of the way," Morgana said.

Thor swayed on the bench, the world still spinning a bit. The flutter of power in his chest was stronger than he'd felt before, but it was wild and slipped away from him like a mountain brook. Swallowing back the fear and confusion, Thor took a deep breath and straightened up. The old man, Merlin, was looking at him with a hint of amusement and Thor grabbed onto the surge of anger spinning through him. Standing up, Thor drew himself to his full height and frowned at the man who now stood a few inches below him. Merlin regarded him calmly, seemingly unconcerned with Thor's aggression.

Suddenly the blast of a horn echoed down through the valley making Thor tense. He noted that Merlin and Morgana both straightened up and their expressions turned cold, but he strode past them. Outside of his workshop, the sun had begun to set and a chill had settled into the air as the last rays of the sun vanished. The other men were gathering together with torches and their weapons drawn in the center of the village. Two of the women were running forward and laying wood in the large new fire pit next to them. One of them pulled out softly smoldering coals and tossed them onto the piles of dried moss.

It caught in an instant, and as the flames began to lick at the large pieces of wood Thor turned and looked up towards the mountain. Another blare of the horn brought the other men out of their homes with their weapons at the ready as a few small points of light began to appear on the mountain. In the corner of his eye, he spotted the strangers Merlin and Morgana leaving his workshop. On the tip of his tongue were the words accusing them of being in league with the strange things about to descend, but he couldn't force them out.

Frightened silence took over. The women and children fled towards the side of the village protected by the new walls. Thor shifted towards the unfinished openings with the other men. His fingers were tight around his sword, and he flexed them carefully as soreness began to invade. He was aware of Merlin and Morgana moving to join them, and a few of the men giving Morgana looks of surprise, but none of them said anything. Arvid caught his eyes with a hint of worry and curiosity.

Then the sounds of something moving out in the fields drew their attention. Everyone was still as more of the lights appeared out of the trees and drew closer. A strange relief that the creatures weren't carrying torches and lighting the fields on fire washed through Thor. They arrived at the edge of the walls together like a violent wave against the rocks of the fjord. Their glowing stones fell from their gold-covered clawed hands as they grappled for their weapons. One of them screamed in pained rage as its black eyes reflected the glow of the fire.

"By the ancestors!" Merlin shouted behind him. His voice was thick with shock. "What the- what has happened to them?"

"Ha!" Morgana laughed with a hint of triumph. "Finally, you suffer for your crimes!"

Thor struggled to catch his breath. Too much was happening. More creatures rushed Merlin and his expression hardened. Green sparks flared brilliantly around the man, casting strange shadows on his face that made his eyes glow and his nose seem long and sharp. Thor froze in place as he watched the stream of green light spin around the man as it followed the movements of his hand. Then Merlin pushed his hand forward and the sparks surged through the air, forming a dozen bolts of green light. They blasted into the group of creatures, shattering through their golden armor and sparking screams as three of them began to dissolve into dust.

A strange glow to his right made Thor turn. Morgana was surrounded by rings of silver light that were illuminating half of the village. The rings lazily spun around her as she glared at the oncoming horde of creatures. They snarled, made pained, broken noises, and then charged. Thor saw Morgana flick her wrist towards the creatures. The rings around her suddenly lashed forward through the air and crashed into the creatures with brilliant flashes of light. Three of them went down with screams of pain and began to decay before his eyes into mounds of dust.

His eyes were wide with shock. For a moment Thor couldn't move. There hadn't been time to consider the strange visions in the forge, but that power and glow were like his own. Villagers were drawing back from Merlin and Morgana as the pair continued to strike down more and more of the creatures. They were swarming around the pair like flies around a rotting animal in the woods. Magic flashed brilliantly around them and Morgana shouted something as a dark look crossed her face. A whip of silver light collided with two of the creatures. They vanished, crumbling to dust. Morgana turned sharply towards yet another one as Thor and the others just stood there in muted shock.

Then somehow, as quickly as the tide of creatures had risen and crashed into their village, the last of them was being struck down by a green orb thrown from Merlin's hand. His throat tightened as Thor took a step towards the strangers. Questions were burning on the tip of his tongue, but he couldn't seem to make his mouth work.

"Who are you strangers?" his father asked. His voice was weaker than Thor had ever heard before. A moment later his father was next to him and gesturing at the piles of dust. "What were those things?"

Merlin and Morgana ignored his father completely as they turned towards each other. Thor couldn't help himself and took another step towards them as the others were drawing back. Small sounds of life were returning to the village behind him and he knew the others would start whispering soon enough, but he was straining his ears to hear the strangers.

"They looked different, but it was certainly the Sídhe," Merlin observed in a low voice. He completely ignored the villagers who were all eying them with a mix of awe and fear.

"But half-crazed," Morgana said with a thoughtful frown. "And did you notice that when destroyed it was more like dirt rather than gold?"

"Perhaps something has gone wrong in Sídhean."

"As much as I would love that to be true, I think it is more likely something to do with Arto's Iron Gates."

"That would fit," Merlin agreed. Then he looked up towards the mountain. "But just what is it?" In the distance there were still a few flickers of light on the mountain, but rather than moving towards the village one by one they vanished into the valleys and over the hills. "And how does it change things?" Merlin added with a dark look in the firelight.

7

Reincarnates

One thing that Jenny hated about living in the Northwest was the icy chill that settled into her bones during winter. She'd grown up in San Francisco and the way that fog could cling to a person was no stranger to her, but Ravenslake always seemed worse. A soft mist enshrouded the campus, making the world hazy and the winter evening seem all the colder. Her footfalls on the cold, but thankfully clear sidewalk echoed around her despite the voices of other students who were still coming and going.

Her messenger bag thumped softly against her hip with each step and Jenny absentmindedly adjusted it as she looked up towards the library. The four-story old brick building with its metal and glass expansion was an eyesore to her, but her architecture major roommate loved it. She supposed that the library was the building on campus that represented the awkward collision of classic brick and slightly gothic buildings of the original land grant college with the new modern buildings that had been constructed as it grew. Still, she preferred the more classic look.

Walking inside, Jenny paused and let the warm air melt her frigid body. There were only two people at the front counter, both of them sitting behind desks and looking very bored. Jenny quickly made her way upstairs. She glanced into the nearest study room and froze in surprise. Bran was seated at the table in one of the small study rooms. His cane was propped up against the table and he was leaning back in the chair with a book in hand. His green eyes were dark with concentration and his expression was one of intense thought. Jenny lingered in front of the window as she debated with herself if she wanted to go inside.

Taking a deep breath, she knocked lightly on the closed wooden door and waved hesitantly when Bran looked up through the window. He smiled and shifted the book he was reading to one hand gesturing her inside. As she opened the door, Jenny felt her stomach flip in her gut but reminded herself that she'd spent time with Bran in Wales while the others were busy with other things. Not a lot of time, but it was something.

"Homework already?" Bran asked.

"Uh, yeah," Jenny answered quietly. She set her backpack in the chair and began having second thoughts about sharing the room with Bran. "A paper that I wanted to go ahead and get started on. The dorms were too loud right now."

Bran raised an eyebrow at her but nodded. Jenny slumped her shoulders slightly in defeat and shrugged. "My current roommate, a girl named Erica, was making out with some guy in our living room when I came in. Felt like a strategic retreat was in order and I wasn't brave enough to go past them into my room."

"Sorry to hear that; it's too early in the semester for that shit," Bran said sympathetically. "You'd think having separate bedrooms would keep that from happening."

"Her room is a disaster zone," Jenny said. A soft smile tugged at her lips. "She doesn't spend much time there."

"I doubt he'd really care about that." Bran chuckled and shook his head. "So other than an inconsiderate roommate, how are you doing?" Bran asked her. His voice had gone soft and his expression was gentle, as if he was talking to a spooked animal.

"Fine," Jenny answered quickly. Holding back a flash of irritation, she reminded herself that Bran was just being nice and that she hadn't exactly been easy to approach until recently. "We saw each other on Saturday, Bran."

"I know." Bran shrugged and looked down at his books. "Alright then."

Ignoring him for a few minutes, Jenny pulled out her tablet and logged into the campus library Wi-Fi. She distracted herself for a few minutes by checking her emails for coursework and logged into the website for her News Editing and Production class. They were required to do 'discussions' outside of the classroom, so Jenny quickly did a couple of responses to questions from Professor Harper and replied to one of her classmate's posts. It took the whole of fifteen minutes.

Pulling out her phone, Jenny checked her messages and quickly responded to a text from one of her high school friends before looking over to see what Bran was working on. There was a stack of dusty books in front of him and Jenny read their spines quickly. They were all books on Celtic mythology and Bran seemed very interested in the large green tome in his hands. He must have felt her gaze or seen her move because he suddenly looked up from the book.

"How are classes going for you?" Bran asked. He reached for his bottle of water and took a drink.

"Uh fine." Jenny felt a touch embarrassed at getting caught staring. "Nothing too interesting yet."

"Give it time," Bran replied. "My classes are pretty much the opposite. I've already sat through several intense lectures."

"You guys have one of Mer- Professor Yates' classes together, right?" Jenny tucked a long strand of dark hair behind her ear. "You mentioned it the other night."

"The Bible as Literature," Bran agreed with a nod. "I wasn't originally going to take it, but given how important mythology is to the war we're in, it seems wise to familiarize ourselves with as much information as possible." He grinned at her. "Besides it's nice to have one class with the others. This is probably the last one: I'm not sure if Merlin will be able to keep convincing the university to let him teach weird mythology classes for the sake of teaching us."

"He has magical powers; can't he just convince them that way?"

"I suppose so," Bran said thoughtfully. He lowered the book and put his elbows on the table. "I know he's used magic to change people's memories in the past, though I'm not sure how he does it. We still have to focus on visualizing an effect to get our magic to work."

"Maybe it's just part of his greater experience."

"Probably, but I wonder what made him decide to try messing with people's heads for the first time." Bran shivered a bit and picked up his pen with a thoughtful look. "I mean Merlin's usually pretty serious about being the good guy." He flipped the pen around in his fingers. "Course, that might just be me projecting since he's Merlin and I grew up with Merlin in the stories."

"Hard to believe." Jenny gave an uneasy laugh, her mouth suddenly very dry. "It all still seems so insane."

"Even after seeing a real dragon?" Bran seemed to relax and gave her a teasing smile.

"Especially after that," Jenny said. Lowering her chin into her palm, she rested her elbow on the table and toyed with her phone. "Everything over there was weird."

They lapsed into silence, but Bran didn't bother picking up his book again. Instead, he watched her out of the corner of his eye as he studied the pen in his hands. Jenny noted that the cap was a little chewed on and almost smiled.

"Uh... you're a reincarnation too, right?" Jenny finally asked. Swallowing, she gathered her courage. "That's what all of that was about? That's how you found the Chalice?"

"Yeah; I'm apparently the reincarnation of a man named Bran." He licked his lips a little, staring at something beyond her shoulder for a moment. "I was a friend of... Gofiben I think was the name of that Iron Soul." Bran shook his head and his eyes seemed a touch more focused. "But yeah, that's what helped me find the Iron Chalice. That skull had been mine and a fragment of my soul, or an imprint of my spirit, was still with it."

"You don't seem to be bothered by it." There was a long moment of silence as Bran just looked at her. "Why?"

"It's something I'm adjusting to still," Bran said. He closed the book and set it to the side. "Are you still having difficulty with it?"

"Let's see, I was the most famous adulteress in all of literature." Jenny gave him a 'duh' look. "Not to mention it doesn't quite fit into the worldview I grew up with."

"I'm guessing by that you mean your religion."

"I'm Catholic; reincarnation is definitely not a part of my theology."

"You're Catholic?" Bran asked. His lips twisted into a small smirk that he tried to fight down. "Hispanic and Catholic, there's a stereotype," he said, clearly trying not to laugh.

"It's part of our culture. Though my dad isn't very religious." Jenny gave him a stern scowl and Bran had the good grace to look sorry. "But Mom loved our religion… I guess it's a way of staying close to her."

"I'm sorry," Bran apologized. "I didn't realize she was deceased."

"It's fine." Jenny resisted the urge to tug at her clothes as her earlier nervousness returned. "I guess Alex never told you."

"No; in the moments when we allow ourselves to talk about something other than magic, we tend to avoid sadder topics," Bran said. "For what it's worth, I lost my dad a few years back."

"Cancer?"

"No. I'm guessing that was your mom?" Bran asked. Jenny nodded in response and Bran once again gave her an apologetic look. "No, my dad was deployed to Afghanistan. He died there."

"I'm sorry," she said before thinking about the words. Was she supposed to say thank you or something like that?

"Anyway, back to the topic at hand before we went off on a tangent." Bran waved his hand dismissively before picking up his pen and toying with it again. "I suppose on some level I'm adjusting to the reincarnation thing a bit easier because I come from a Buddhist background, though my family was never serious about it. Reincarnation is a principal that I've been aware of for much of my life."

"Did you believe in it though?"

"Not really," Bran admitted. "I liked the idea though, even if I didn't really believe. Plus, my branch of Buddhism is a Mahayana tradition that seeks enlightenment for the benefit of all sentient beings. It's pleasant to hope that we don't just vanish at the end of this life and that we can transcend to help others. That was just always an idea that I liked. Heaven and Hell never made much sense to me, but I could buy the idea of our energy shifting or our memories becoming some sort of imprint on another level of reality."

"So, you listen to the Dalai Lama then?"

"No." Bran folded his hands in front of him and shook his head. "My grandfather was a Korean Buddhist, which is a bit different from the Tibetan tradition. 'Course Korean Buddhism influenced the Far Eastern schools of Buddhism, but saying the Dalai Lama is the head of our religion would be like saying the Pope is in charge of Methodists." She must have made a face because Bran laughed, but it got the point across. He shifted in his seat, leaning his elbows forward onto the table. "But like I said I never really believed. It was a nice system of traditions that my family enjoyed honoring a bit. Personally, I don't worry too much, but one thing that I like about Korean Buddhism is that it tried to address inconsistencies within the tradition. I respect that."

"And now?"

"I'm grateful that there was part of me which had this idea planted when I young," Bran said. "I think it's made things easier. I like to think that I was reborn in order to help Alex find the Iron Chalice. My previous self and I... I'm still not sure exactly what happened in Wales, but we were able to connect and help Alex. That's a powerful thing." He paused and gave her a searching look. "You don't have that to help you though."

"No," Jenny said. "Reincarnation... it just doesn't fit with what I grew up believing."

"I suppose not." Bran nodded with a distant thoughtful look. "Christianity is based on a belief of Heaven and Hell-"

"There's more to it than that!" Jenny interrupted.

"Jewish tradition does not include Hell; that was a Christian invention, and the threat of damnation remains a big part of the religion," Bran continued as if he hadn't heard her. "There really isn't room for reincarnation in the traditional interpretation of the religion. Yet, I do know Christians who believe in reincarnation."

"Huh?"

"One of my high school buddies once suggested to me that reincarnation is the real form of Purgatory. People who did enough good to escape Hell, but not enough to enter Heaven." Bran shrugged. "It was a compromise that he found helped him balance the two things that he believed in. It might not match up with Church teachings, but it helped him reconcile things in his own head."

"You're not supposed to do that though."

"It's the twenty-first century, Jenny." Bran laughed with a pointed look. "Don't worry, Alex won't let anyone burn you as a heretic. She's rather fond of you."

"Bran," she said in a warning voice.

"Yeah okay, I'm being a little shit. I think Aiden is rubbing off on me." Bran smiled for a moment before turning serious. "Look, Jenny, I don't think what happened in your past lives makes you a bad person. Hell, I don't think it made you a bad person then; it just made you a person. We can't always control the outcomes of our actions, and I know that you two weren't trying to hurt the Iron Soul in those lives. That does count for something in my book. As for the religious questions, well I encourage you to try and make peace with it. Maybe you accept that the world is greater than people thousands of years ago could understand while they recorded their religious texts, maybe you adjust things a little in your own head, or maybe you reject those religious texts in favor of something else, or maybe you give it up altogether. That's your decision. I don't think there's a right answer here beyond what is right for you."

Hanging her head, Jenny hoped she didn't look too disappointed. There was a flicker of anger in her chest, but she'd been the one who'd started the conversation. She hadn't really thought Bran would have an answer, but she'd been hoping for something more than that. Her religion had been something familiar and comforting since her mother passed, and even when she hadn't been able to get herself to go to church, it had still been there.

"I don't have an answer for you," Bran continued in a softer voice. "Buddhism might help me with the issue of reincarnation, but it doesn't address where the Iron Soul came from or other worlds or what happens next." He exhaled slowly, flipping the pen again. "All of our traditions and beliefs are built on the old stories that helped us understand and explain something, but right now we're part of writing one of those stories. We're part of the new King Arthur story; we're part of the story of the death of a Slavic God. I'm focusing my energy on trying to help write the best story I can."

"You're kind of a dork, aren't you?" Jenny smiled before she could stop herself.

"A bit, yeah." Bran nodded his head and chuckled.

Then his phone beeped from its spot next to his book. He scooped it up and with a few quick movements of his thumb, the relaxed smile vanished from his face. Jenny felt her whole body stiffen as her back straightened.

"Bran?"

"There's been an attack." Bran stood up, forcing his chair back until it hit the wall. He grabbed his coat and pulled it on before reaching for his things only to hesitate.

"I'll take care of your stuff and drop it off," Jenny promised. She gave him a smile and a weak thumbs up. "Go and save the world."

"Thanks." Giving her a nod, Bran grabbed his cane with an irritated look and pulled open the door.

"Be careful," Jenny added softly as he strode out of the study room and vanished around a shelf of books. "Look after Alex."

8

Slice of Life

This was life now. Wake up, go to class, hang out with her friends, and get attacked by Sídhe relatives hell-bent on killing them all. It was a bad television show with the writers trying to figure out what new challenge to torment them all with. Alex grit her teeth and let her magic flow down her arms as a short creature with choppy silver hair rushed her.

The trees of the University of Ravenslake Arboretum provided them with just enough cover that Alex didn't feel too worried about releasing a blast of magic. It was difficult to focus on how she wanted the magic to act when one of the small creatures dressed in a raggedy patchwork set of clothes with long vicious looking talons lunged at her. Dodging out of the way, Alex pulled on her magic and willed the dark silver sparks to zing through the air. They struck the creature on the side as it began to dodge away.

The smell of burnt hair and seared skin filled her nose. Alex began to gag as her magic began to eat away at the creature. Shaking her head, Alex took a few steps back as her feet tried to slip in the blend of mud and snow beneath her. Sweat was trickling down her back and it pooled at the base of her spine as Alex's eyes swept over the area. Aiden and Nicki were both with her, gathered near the shore of Ravens Lake with a large moon hanging over the water and humanoid creatures moving around them.

She could see five of them in the moonlight, all dressed in old cast-off human clothing with hoods pulled up over their heads. Two of them were as tall as Nicki with strands of silvery hair visible as they rushed along in the mud. The three others were smaller and might have fooled someone into thinking they were children if not for the vicious long talons at the end of their fingers.

The creature she'd just injured lashed out at her once again, its long talons slashing at her face. Jerking back, Alex sliced the dagger across the creature's face. With a roar of pain, it stumbled back from her, its violet-tinted eyes glaring at her. The long cut in its translucent skin shimmered as the iron ate away at the edges of its flesh. A cry from behind Alex made her spin on her heel. Another creature was rushing her from behind.

She heard the injured one begin to yell something and pulled more magic forth. Forming a small orb in her hand, Alex tossed it back at the injured being, earning a scream as it began to dissolve. Her distraction had given the creature charging her one moment too many and it leapt through the air towards her. Yellow magic spun around the jumping creature and stopped it midair. Alex used the reprieve to release a burst of magic at another of the creatures trying to flank Nicki down the hill.

Her magic formed into a long bolt of energy and sailed through the air like a spear. It struck the creature in the chest, throwing it back against a tree as it howled in pain. It clawed at the spear of magic as the spear began to dissolve and seep into its body. Alex glanced back to Nicki and found her friend sending a mass of ice shards flashing through the air to shred one of the creatures.

"Alex, to your right!" Aiden's voice snapped from up the hill.

Spinning to the side, Alex gasped as her boots slid to the left and pulled her whole body with it. A bolt of red magic shot past her and she felt the tingle of the energy against her cheek. Her eyes widened as she saw another creature being blasted back. The first one attacking her was still suspended in the air in a field of yellow. The magic around it flickered for a moment, but Alex regained her balance.

Opening her palm, Alex pulled on the warm pulse of energy surging through her veins. Dark silver sparks exploded out of her fingers and spun around her hand awaiting her command. She brought her hand forward with a sharp movement and the silver magic formed a smooth arc in the air. It sailed forward like the blade of a guillotine and sliced into the suspended creature. With a gargled shriek the creature dissolved into wisps. The sound rolled over Alex making her shiver, but she pushed the discomfort it caused aside.

A sharp high-pitched cry of anger and sorrow pulled her attention back to the one Bran had blasted back. It was crawling through the snow with mud caked on its loose hoody. Long talons raked through the frosty dead leaves as it glared at her with violet eyes. Alex paused at the look on the creature's face. Pained, frustrated, and resigned.

"Destroy," it growled. Grabbing at a tree, it climbed to its feet. "Kill Mages. Obey." Another low sob-like sound was ripped out of its throat. "The chain commands."

Staring at the creature, Alex felt an icy sense of familiarity at the words that she didn't understand. Meaning danced just outside of her reach in a haze that Alex couldn't force herself through. Someone shouted her name as the creature threw itself forward with a desperate roar. The sound snapped her out of the strange daze she'd fallen into and Alex threw herself to the side. She caught the legs of the creature with her left leg, tripping it as she grabbed at the rough bark of a tree. A rush of air escaped her lungs at the impact against the trunk, but she was able to stay on her feet.

Turning around, Alex tightened her grip on her dagger and lashed out at the creature again. The tip of the iron blade sliced through the ratty clothing and sank into the cool flesh beneath. Bile filled Alex's mouth as the haze of instinct fell away. Silver blood seeped out of the wound and wide violet eyes met her own gray ones. Panic flashed in Alex's chest and she shoved her magic through the iron blade. It grew hot in her hands and dark silver magic shimmered over the creature's body. Then it dissolved, its head thrown back in a silent scream. Alex stumbled back as the body crumbled, almost releasing her dagger.

Panting, Alex stopped moving but was still braced for an attack. Nothing happened, and she released a slow breath as she looked around. The university arboretum was quiet with the bare trees closing them in by the lakeside, the water lapping gently at the shore. Up the hill, there was the bright glow of the streetlights and dorm rooms and the faint sounds of traffic. The others were braced and waiting for more of the creatures to appear, but none did, and Alex felt her body beginning to relax, though the tight knot at the base of her spine remained.

Taking a deeper breath, Alex carefully shrugged out of her coat and sighed in relief as the cool night air hit her skin. One good thing about magic and these attacks was that it seemed to provide a good cardio workout. Alex closed her eyes for a moment and fought to slow down her breathing. Inside her chest, she could feel a warm, pulsing swirl of energy, and she gently tried to calm it. She fell back on the first meditation techniques that Merlin and Morgana had taught them and felt the energy slowly easing.

She opened her eyes as her breathing evened out and rolled her shoulders carefully. The sleeve of her coat was dragging in some snow and Alex pulled it up into her arms. Turning around, she noted Nicki and Aiden climbing up the slope of the hill. At the sound of someone moving nearby, Alex turned and smiled as she caught sight of Bran stepping off the jogging path towards her.

"Everyone alright?" Nicki asked. She pushed back the trimmed hood her coat and wiped a gloved hand over her shining forehead.

"I'm good!" Aiden trudged back up the hill towards them. There was mud caked on the right side of his wet jeans. He looked irritated, but unharmed. "That was fun."

"I'm alright," Bran assured Nicki with a nod. "Was that all of them?"

"That was the group we caught sight of." Alex looked around carefully. It took her only a moment to spot the messenger bag she'd shrugged off and stashed by one of the larger bare trees. "I'm not sure if there are any more." She trudged through the mud to retrieve her bag.

"Anyone have any thoughts on how to tell?" Aiden asked looking between them. "Some new trick I missed?"

"You were only in a coma for two weeks," Bran said with a raised eyebrow. "We weren't exactly experimenting with new spells." Bran paused and looked out over the lake. "I suppose that these creatures have been programmed as it were to attack us, so since we aren't actively being attacked then we're probably good."

"Oh joy; that'll be great if we're attacked in front of civilians," Aiden grumbled with a deepening frown. "At least we're probably safe during the day."

Alex caught his eyes moving over towards the lake and averted her gaze from the water. They were on the campus side, but it was disconcerting to remember that she'd been fatally stabbed just across the way. And in the middle of the lake... Cyrridven, the mythical Lady of the Lake, had died helping her fight Chernobog. That had been only about a month ago. Somehow time seemed to have become twisted around.

"Alex!" Nicki called, making her jump a little.

At some point, the redhead had moved over next to her and reclaimed her own bag. Nicki was giving her a soft, knowing look, and Alex forced herself to smile and shrug. She dug around in her bag for a moment to find the leather sheath for her dagger and carefully slipped the blade back into place. Her eyes lingered on it for a moment before she put it back into the side pocket. She adjusted the strap on her stiff shoulder and let a soft sigh escape her. A quick glance around reassured Alex that somehow, they were still alone. No one had come to investigate the light show, and she wondered if maybe they were repelling people with their magic. In theory, it was possible, and their magic did what they wanted, but could it be done subconsciously?

"Why were you out here anyway?" Bran asked, interrupting Alex's thoughts. He bent down to retrieve his cane and lazily leaned on it. "Did I forget something?"

"I was at the bookstore," Aiden explained. "Mom wanted to go and check on Grandpa after a nurse at the home called. I rushed over here like you did."

"We were on our way home from a coffee run," Nicki said. "One of them was stalking us from the shadows; maybe waiting until we were alone. Or wanting to get into our dorm with us." She shook her head and sighed loudly. "I hope this isn't going to become a regular after dark thing."

"Yeah, that would mess with everything. We all just need to stay aware of our surroundings," Aiden agreed with a grimace. "Are we still on for fencing club tomorrow?"

Everyone was looking at Alex and she tried not to squirm. "Yeah, we can't just hide in our dorms. Besides some of these things can go out at least in partial daylight, based on what we saw in Wales."

"Then they could attack during class," Aiden groaned, rubbing at his eyes. "Shit, we really need to step up our game."

"We'll train this weekend," Nicki half suggested, half ordered. "See if we can't figure out the Magic Missile spell. So far, I'm not having much luck with the whole hit without fail."

"They're faster than us since we have to focus our magic," Bran said. "We'll get there. Sadly, I don't think I can get away with fencing club yet with my cane."

"Next semester then," Alex gave him a soft smile. "After you can spend the summer in 'physical therapy', it would make sense for you to join in." She paused for a moment and gave him a nervous shrug. "In the meantime, I'm sure that Aiden will show you a few things."

"You got it!" Aiden slapped Bran lightly on the back and earned a dark look. "You'll be up to speed in no time."

"It won't take long," Nicki agreed. Then she turned to Alex and gave her a smile. "And you need more practice anyway. For when we find Cathanáil."

"Trust me, from what I managed to see when she killed Chernobog she's got the basics down," Aiden said.

"I was using it as a conductor," Alex reminded him. She shivered a little at the memory, her heart jumping. "It was hardly a duel for the ages." She gestured towards the path. "Come on, let's not make it easy for anything else that may be lurking."

Alex's phone chirped as a text message arrived, the sound echoing in the silent little forest around them. Pulling it out quickly, Alex checked the message quickly before looking back at the others.

"It's Jenny," Alex said. "She wants to know if we're okay."

"Yeah, she was at the library with me," Bran said. "She actually has my stuff."

"That's a bit weird." Aiden sent a curious look towards Alex. "Her checking on us now. It wasn't like that last semester."

"Our time in Wales changed things a bit." Using her cold aching fingers, Alex typed in a quick text reply to assure Jenny they were all fine. "Though yeah, it is a bit weird to be texting her after a fight." Alex shivered as she put her phone into her bag. "Not bad or anything, just... weird."

"Ah yes," Nicki muttered thoughtfully. "What is the role of the muggle in the story?"

"New rule: we will not refer to Lance and Jenny as muggles," Alex told them all sternly. "They're our friends and we've got to keep the references in check."

"Ah, Alex," Aiden sighed dramatically. "So protective of the ex-wife."

She almost stumbled in shock at the phrase, but Nicki caught her arm and Alex's brain replayed the words. It was so... stupid and so Aiden that she couldn't help but laugh. Something warm and cleansing bubbled up through her chest and Alex giggled uncontrollably. Thankfully the others joined in with her despite it really not being that funny.

"Okay." Alex gasped, trying to both catch her breath and give Aiden a stern look. "I acknowledge that there had to be an ex-wife joke somewhere, but you've now used up your quota."

"My quota? One joke; you are kidding right?" Aiden whined.

Alex struggled not to laugh at his face. Shaking her head, she nodded towards the path and started walking towards the dorms. Over her shoulder, she called back, "Nope, not kidding. You've made your Jenny is my ex-wife joke."

"You guys left your senses of humor in Wales." Aiden pouted and kept walking along behind Alex. "However did you manage without me?"

"It was a difficult time," Bran admitted with a smile. He shared a fond look with Alex and shook his head. "Fraught with unsaid jokes and references."

"Yeah, it was," Alex agreed. A soft laugh escaped her. "But you've still used up your one ex-wife joke." Shaking her head, she gestured towards the dorms visible through the bare branches. "Come on, mages, time to call it a night."

9

The Mysterious Pair

1 15 C.E. Sør-Trøndelag, Norway

Thor did not like feeling nervous. He loathed it, in fact; always had. The only time he could remember ever admitting to being nervous or frightened in the past was right before his very first lesson with Erlendr. Back then he'd actually been ill that morning. Thankfully Arvid had kept it a secret from Father.

A smile tugged at Thor's lips at the random spark of memory. He'd thanked Arvid, but his brother had started holding it over his head about a week later once his lessons with Erlendr seemed secure. A nostalgic feeling swept through him and Thor lowered his head, fighting back a nervous smile. This wasn't the time, and so he took a breath and straightened his shoulders. Glancing back across the village Thor became very aware that everyone was avoiding the small hut that the two strangers were staying in.

Whatever reservations the villagers might have had about the strangers who battled with magic weren't gone, but those fears hadn't stopped the two strangers from being offered shelter in one of the older houses that was awaiting repair. Without animals and with the holes in the walls it would be chilly, but no one lived in it at the moment. Thor moved towards it with soft footfalls and the knot in his stomach tight. He didn't dare look back at the others as they returned to their homes, and couldn't quite bring himself to look straight at the hut either.

The well-trod dirt of the village was firm beneath his feet, and the stars overhead twinkled softly. He could see by the low light of the half-moon and the few torches that were still burning. Glancing towards the opening in the wall Thor took note of those on guard and silently wished them a quiet remainder of the night. Then a faint glow of firelight was spread across the ground and Thor had to focus his attention on his destination.

There were streams of orange firelight slipping through the cracks in the side of the house and Thor sped up his pace. For a moment he debated simply barging in or calling to the strangers. Yet as he came closer and heard the low muffled voices, he felt only raw, nervous curiosity. Silently he reminded himself that the village knew nothing of these strangers. He knew their names, if those were their names, but nothing more than that. Except that in his first moment of eye contact.... Thor shook his head and pushed the thoughts away. He'd made up his mind and wasn't going to change course now and run home like a frightened child.

Creeping forward, Thor felt foolish as the nervousness churned once more in his stomach. He peered through the thin opening between the cracking boards. Thor could see the two cloaked figures pacing around their fire. Their posture was alert and strangely at ease with the chaos that had filled the village only a short time ago. Sucking in a breath, Thor tried to stay still and quiet as he turned his head so his ear was closer to them. He could feel his heart thundering in his chest and the small flame of power lashing about as if reaching to escape. The nerves were stronger than ever and he clenched his fists stubbornly.

"At least we found the boy easily." There was an amused note to Merlin's voice that gave Thor the sense that he'd come late in the conversation.

"Let's not make any assumptions," Morgana cautioned. "It seems a little too obvious for him to be a smith once more."

"Why?" Merlin chuckled, sounding far too at ease for the events of the night. "Given his destiny, his origin, and his powers, surely it makes sense that he would be drawn towards working with iron."

Thor held back a gasp of surprise and a flare of satisfaction. They were talking about him. Strange creatures had attacked his village and they'd only just arrived from some distance away, judging from how they talked, yet they were talking about him. He shifted even closer, his knee dropping into the dirt and pressing against the wooden wall.

"Thor!" Merlin's face nearly glowed in the firelight as he turned towards the wall. "Why don't you come inside and speak with us."

Gasping softly, Thor almost fell back onto the ground. His knees protested as he rose up from the squatting position and Thor stumbled towards the door. Merlin had been kind enough to leave the animal skin in place so Thor was able to take a moment to gather his wits. Taking a deep breath, Thor felt keenly aware that this was his best chance to walk away. All he knew about these two strangers were that they had powers like his.

But that was enough, he pulled back the animal skin and moved into the small hut with strong strides. Merlin greeted him with a nod and a small smile while Morgana merely crossed her arms across her chest and smiled tightly at him. For a moment they observed each other. There was something about them. Something that seemed too large for the small space and made him feel small. He was a large and strong man and loathed the very idea, but it was there.

"You have magic," Thor said to them both only to realize that he sounded a bit dim. "Do you know what those creatures are?"

"They are familiar to us," Merlin said. "And yet they are very alien to us."

"Ignore him." Morgana raised an eyebrow at the man's words. "He is too impressed with himself when he speaks in riddles. Those creatures are Sídhe, or at least they were. Something has happened to them that made them become feral. None of them seemed as strong as they should have been."

A cold shiver ran down Thor's back. Those things weren't as strong as these two knew them to be? That did not inspire any confidence in him. If these things could be stronger and attacked before the wall was ready, they'd be trouble. Three men had died in the attack prior to this one, and two little girls had been ripped to shreds. Even a wall might be worthless then.

Decision made, Thor brought up his hand and breathed out slowly. The spark in his chest flared to life and his tense body was flooded with a reassuring hum of power. He felt taller and stronger as he called it through his arm. Turning his hand, Thor opened his palm and let the bright blue sparks gather above his skin. Tiny arcs of lightning flashed over his flesh, sending pleasant tingles through his hand and up his arm. He raised his eyes to look at Merlin who was grinning brightly at him.

"Well, that is a surprise." A look of real interest appeared on Morgana's face. She eyed him thoughtfully. "The boy has already sorted out a few things for himself."

"Indeed: not subconsciously using magic, but real control," Merlin added with a smile that looked ready to split his face. Then his expression softened and he shifted back to give Thor more room. "I assure you that we mean you and your village no harm."

Thor said nothing, keeping what he hoped was a calm and stern expression on his face in an attempt to mask the rush of confusion and questions bubbling up in his chest. His efforts were clearly in vain as both Merlin and Morgana gave him looks that were an uncomfortable blend of pity, amusement, and in Merlin's case a hint of affection.

"Your power is a gift of our world," Merlin said. He spread his hand out as if gesturing to the whole of the world around them. "You were born with a very special gift: the ability to summon forth the power of our world and use it to defend humanity."

"We call ourselves Mages." Morgana sat down on the wooden ledge of the house and brushed some dirt from her long dark cloak. "Our kind are born when threats to the world manifest and the magic in our world builds."

"I know it is a lot to take in." Merlin stepped over and reached up to grip his shoulder, giving it a light, friendly squeeze. "Morgana and I have been traveling here for some time."

"A very long time," Morgana corrected. "There is no easy way to cross any longer."

"Yes, Morgana," Merlin sighed with an odd smile. "We were guided here by magic, as I'm afraid your homeland is the new battlefield."

"I see." Thor was aware of how silent he had been. For a moment he struggled just to find something to say. "So that is why I have the power," he said more to himself. His mind whirled, trying to assimilate everything, but it was too much at once. "I'm supposed to use it to stop these creatures."

"We'll help you, of course," Merlin promised him with a growing smile. The older man seemed to be having trouble standing still. "We'll train you and stay here to help keep your village safe. That's why we came here."

"Of course, we also need to get to the bottom of what is happening to the Sídhe," Morgana added with a strange, nasty smile. "Though I enjoy seeing them like this, we need to make sure that it doesn't signal an even greater danger."

"Is it just the three of us?" Thor asked. Merlin moved easily enough and he had seen how capable the pair was, but still. "That isn't much of a defending force."

"Maybe, maybe not." Morgana shrugged graceful, tossing her hair over a shoulder. "It's hard to say. We'll have to be on the lookout for other mages that might have been born in the area. If there are others then they're sure to be nearby. We're honestly not sure what determines the number of mages."

"But..." Thor trailed off uncertainly. "You said you came a long way, why would others be nearby?"

Morgana smiled in approval of his question, looking at him with a hint of respect. Thor didn't look away from her as he watched something spark in her green eyes. A shiver went down his spine as he suddenly felt very small once again and remembered just how this woman had cut down the creatures earlier.

"Good." Morgana nodded in approval. "Mages are usually born in the area where the threat is growing. Merlin and I are a bit older than we look. We were born during a previous period of strife."

Given how the pair glanced at each other Thor was certain that something Morgana said had a touch of untruth, but he was unsure of which part. He was debating bringing it up when Morgana distracted him with further explanation.

"You'll find that you have a knack for your magic to take a certain form. This isn't the only way you can use it, but it is the most natural way. Even once we train you in how to use your magic and do more with it, you will find that it is easiest to fall back on that first form."

"Lightning," Thor informed her with a small smirk as her eyes widened. He flexed his fingers thoughtfully and looked down at them as he called on the power once more. Tiny arcs of lightning surged between his fingertips, but there was no pain. "It always seems to look like lightning."

"Well, you are making this easy," Merlin chuckled as he patted Thor's shoulder again. "You seem to have a good grasp of who you are, and that is very important."

"For better or for worse," Morgana added giving Merlin a chiding look. "Still, it does give us a good starting point, and with those things coming through nearby it means you aren't helpless."

"We will start training you right away," Merlin continued with a thoughtful nod. "And see about discovering the tunnel that the Sídhe are using. It might give us some clues as to what is happening. Hopefully, it isn't too close to the village."

The mention of the village pulled Thor out of the stunned, excited fervor that he'd fallen into. Learning to use his mysterious power sounded wonderful, but the realization that everyone was about to find out brought a blend of excitement and alarm forth in him.

"What are you going to tell them?" Thor was unable to think of anything that the pair could possibly say to explain this. "I mean-"

"Don't worry about it," Merlin said. "You'll find that once people are confronted with a magical danger, they are rather happy to accept help from someone with magic."

"If those persons look human at least," Morgana added darkly. She unclasped her cloak and gently folded it up. "But he is right, Thor; that's enough for tonight. You need to get some sleep, and so do we. Merlin and I finished a very long journey today."

"But-"

"We'll see you in the morning and take steps to get started," Merlin assured him. "It will be a bit complicated of course. It always is, but at least we can remain in your village for a time."

Nodding, Thor felt dozens more questions burning at the tip of his tongue, but he took a step back toward the door. Morgana was already setting up her bed for the night with an unimpressed expression on her face. Merlin moved with him to the doorway and squeezed his shoulder one more time. Thor was uncertain as to the odd affection the older man seemed keen to show him but said a quick goodnight to them both.

Leaving the hut, Thor was hit with the cool night air and realized with a start that the hut had been strangely warm for being bereft of livestock. He paused for only a moment before his feet began to take him towards his own home. Pride was mixed with fear in his chest and he couldn't help but smile. He could feel the magic in his gut growing brighter as he thought over everything Merlin and Morgana had said. Strange as it should have seemed, he could feel the truth of it all in his bones.

He'd always known that his power was for something important. Thor breathed a little easier and barely held back a wild grin. His heart was racing and his stomach was twisting in a way that he didn't fully understand. He pulled back the animal skin that protected his family longhouse and crept inside with a glance towards the slumbering figures of his father and brother. Thor shook his head at them and moved to his own pile of blankets and furs. How they could sleep after a night such as this he'd never know.

10

Back to the Forge

S trangely, the heat of the forge served as a comfort to her frayed nerves. Amongst the iron creations of Merlin and Morgana and the numerous items in his tool collection, Alex felt calm. Swinging down the glowing hammer, Alex felt the impact of the tool against the piece of iron through her whole body. Her arm protested only a little and Alex noted with a slight sense of pride that this was getting easier. She could feel the soft hum of her magic traveling through her fingertips and into the handle of the hammer, and she could see the dark silver glow surrounding it in the corner of her eye.

Alex brought the hammer down and watched the red-hot metal shift at the impact of the blow. Small sparks were released around the anvil and Alex watched for a moment as the metal began to darken its shade of red. She grabbed the iron with the tongs and slid it back into the furnace. The charcoal crackled and heat rolled off to hit her face, but Alex felt herself breathing easier.

Catching something moving in the corner of her eye, Alex tightened her grip on the hammer and glanced back. It was only Merlin shifting around near one of the worktables and rearranging a few of his previous projects. Alex relaxed her shoulders and nearly laughed at herself. Being jumpy in a building full of iron was pretty silly, and her eyes moved over the heavy pad that covered the floor safe.

"Am I in your way?" Alex asked Merlin as he shifted into view on her right.

"Not at all," Merlin assured her with a warm smile. "Forgive me, I just hesitate to stray too far when you are in the forge." He moved what looked like a fireplace tool set up onto a shelf.

"You were a good teacher." Alex adjusted the heavy gloves on her hands and rolled her shoulders. "I do know what I'm doing; at least for simple projects."

"It isn't about that," Merlin said. "I suppose I have some lingering concerns about your powers reacting to the iron. Your capabilities are still largely unknown to us."

Resisting the urge to look at Merlin, Alex merely nodded and turned her attention back to the dagger. Using the tongs, she extracted the heated metal from the furnace and quickly positioned it back on the anvil. Alex held it in place with the tongs in her left hand and brought the hammer in her right hand to the ready. She tried to block out the sounds of Merlin moving around her, but she was keenly aware of his eyes on her. Hammering the metal once again, Alex focused on creating the sharper, narrower edge of the dagger. She pushed a little more magic into the hammer and felt the hum all up her arm before she cracked the hammer down once more.

Alex let herself get lost in the clanging of the metal. Every hammer fall sent a jolt through her body as her magic jumped from her into the hammer, and then into the dagger. Panting softly, Alex swallowed several times and licked her lips as the heat began to feel heavier against her skin. She stopped and breathed out slowly as her lungs clenched in her chest. Her arm was beginning to ache more than she liked, despite the stretching she'd been careful to do.

"I'm not in shape for this."

Groaning, Alex set the hammer to the side and carefully rolled her right shoulder. Then she massaged the upper muscles of her arm. It helped a little bit, but Alex could tell that it wasn't going to improve so easily. With a soft sigh of defeat, she eyed the cooling metal. The dagger was mostly done and wouldn't need much more refinement. It wasn't as pretty as one of Merlin's, but she could see the soft flicker of her dark silver magic settling into the metal like flecks of glitter. The comparison threatened to make her giggle. She eased her grip on the tongs and moved the dagger off the anvil.

"I'm finished for today," Alex called to Merlin, certain that he was still hovering within the workshop.

"Excellent," Merlin replied from beyond the second furnace. "Your endurance is getting better, Alex." With a cheerful smile, he strode over to her. "You worked for over two straight hours."

"Really?" Alex laughed in pleasure. "Okay; I'm a little impressed with myself then."

Alex paused and swept her eyes over the area to make sure that everything was in place. Seeing no problems, she shifted to the right and turned the fuel level down. The hot coals and bits of wood shifted as the gas suddenly vanished. There was something about the sound of the shifting coals that sent a pleasant shiver down Alex's spine. She wrote it up as a quirk and shifted away from the furnace.

She pulled off the heavy leather apron and breathed out in relief as the heavy heat against her chest eased. Alex hung the apron up on the nearby rack and looked back to Merlin. He had already shifted towards the forge and was eying the dagger with interest. Then he began to tidy up the tools and rolled the wooden work platform away from the anvil.

"Thanks." Alex brushed another bit of hair out of her face.

"Of course, Alex," Merlin replied with a quick glance up at her. "So how are you finding classes this semester?" Merlin moved around her and began to tidy up one of the worktables.

"Fine. No real surprises, but they are more interesting now that I'm past the general education course. But I do sort of miss having classes with the others."

"Understandable, but the diversity of your educations can be a boon."

"Literature is going to help protect the Earth?" Alex raised an eyebrow as a small smile tugged at her lips. "I know you're an English professor, Merlin, but really."

"Your knowledge of mythology has served you well thus far." Merlin gave her a knowing look and an indulgent smile. "And you have a talent for stepping back and looking at a situation critically; a talent that eluded many of your predecessors."

"Rule one is to be careful of clichés," Alex replied with a casual shrug. "Besides, Nicki and Aiden are the more genre-savvy ones."

"I was under the impression that they were working on your education on that front?"

"They are." Alex shook her head fondly. "But it's slow going."

She tugged off the gloves and tossed them next to the anvil before tucking a strand of blonde hair behind her ear. The messy bun on the top of her head was beginning to fall apart with the hair being weighed down by beads of sweat. Alex looked over at the dagger again and took in the slight shimmer over the surface of the metal.

"I see you're making a new dagger, have you lost the one I made you?" Merlin asked.

"I'm making daggers for Jenny and Lance. That one is for Jenny since I know that Lance will want her to have the first one." Alex looked down at the mostly finished blade. It needed some sharpening and a handle, but she was pretty happy with its progress. "They aren't mages, but if these things get smart and spy on us for any length of time then they're sure to notice Lance and Jenny spending time with us."

"Ah, then Lance and Jenny are doing well within the group," Merlin observed, trying to sound calm and nonchalant, but Alex could almost feel the genuine curiosity and lingering worry.

"Worse; Jenny told me that the boys are having a video game night," Alex laughed a bit forcefully as she turned fully towards Merlin. "They are getting along surprisingly well. At least something is falling into place."

"It looks like you've been successful in putting some magic into it." Merlin brushed a finger over the cooling metal and nodded. "Nicely done."

A soft glow appeared under his finger as if something in the metal was reaching out towards him. Merlin smiled fondly down at the dagger with a strange look that Alex wasn't sure about. She could almost see the wheels turning in Merlin's head, and she wasn't sure that she liked it.

"So, how many of the Iron Souls have been good at smithing?" Alex hoped her question sounded casual.

"A few have been," Merlin answered with a thoughtful expression. "But not as many as you might think... though Morgana and I haven't known all of the Iron Souls. There were plenty of times when magic was at a low level and we didn't need to seek them out."

"Oh..." Alex breathed uncertainly. "I guess that makes sense, though with how protective you and Morgana are it does surprise me a little bit."

"We can be a bit overbearing I suppose, but I must confess that I feel a bit lost when it comes to you, Alex." Staring at her, Merlin slowly shook his head. "I loathe the idea that it's because you're female in this life."

"Half of the species is female, Merlin." Alex didn't look at him. "It was overdue."

"That sounded just like Morgana," Merlin teased with a loud laugh. Alex froze as she realized that he was right. "But perhaps that is the best way to consider it."

"I can't believe I sounded like Morgana," Alex grumbled. She wasn't sure what to make of that. Shaking her head, Alex turned to straighten the already organized hammers. "Sounding like my mother is bad enough."

"I went through the same thing," Merlin chuckled warmly. "We all do, Alex." There was another long pause and the feeling in the workshop changed to something thicker and more serious. Alex braced herself for the questions she knew were coming. "Have you spoken to your parents recently?"

"Yeah, every week or so. Uh, they don't talk about what I told them. I think they're still waiting for me to admit it was just a joke or something."

"Alex-"

"It's fine," Alex said quickly as her throat felt tighter. "It's a lot to dump on their plate, but they've left the iron protections in place." She paused and looked back over at the dagger. "Maybe when they've had some more time, I'll make them some daggers too."

"I'm sorry that times are so different now." Merlin's voice softened further, like he was talking to a spooked animal. "I'm sure things will improve soon."

"Maybe, but until we know more about what is going on I'm not holding my breath." Alex turned to face Merlin, crossing her arms over her chest. "We still don't know where Arthur and the Queen are, what they even are or how they are controlling the Sídhe creatures." Alex shuddered slightly at the mention of the creatures. "It's almost February and we still know nothing. Imbolc is right around the corner and we just don't know what is coming."

"Alex?" Merlin took a step towards her. "Is there something else going on?"

"I'm not sure." She sighed in defeat with her shoulders slumping forward before she looked squarely at Merlin. "Do you ever have the sense that you've forgotten something important? Like it just slipped through your fingers?"

"I assume you aren't talking about forgetting to pay a bill or not finishing grades on time."

"No, it's silly." Alex tried to laugh, leaning back against the edge of the worktable. "I've got something at the back of my mind and it just won't slide into place. It's like I've forgotten something really important and it's starting to get to me."

"Have you had the dream again? The one with the ship?"

"Yeah, but I'm not sure it means anything," Alex admitted as she wiped her sweaty forehead on the sleeve of her shirt. "I've had it a couple of times, nothing really changes, but maybe it's just because I'm fixating on it."

"Yet your instinct is that the dream is important," Merlin pointed out with a thoughtful nod. "Add that to your sense that you've forgotten something and I'm inclined to say that it is indeed important. You've had prophetic dreams before."

"This wasn't prophetic," Alex huffed, holding back a shudder. "It couldn't have been. The ship was too old and- well, it isn't the future."

"The only thing I can suggest is that you meditate and try to take control as much as possible in the dream. Explore the environment, and you may find what you're looking for." Merlin offered her a warm smile and reached over to squeeze her shoulder as he leaned against the table alongside her. "Trust your instincts."

"I know." Alex rubbed at her hairline in an attempt to stave off the building headache. "But my instincts failed horribly when it came to Arthur."

"Morgana and I made mistakes too," Merlin reminded her gently. "It wasn't just you. We're older and more experienced. We shouldn't have been so easy to fool."

"Except I'm the one that dated him," Alex growled. Her chest ached with the familiar rush of anger and frustration that came with discussing or thinking about Arthur. "I'm the one that handed him Cathanáil. I'm the one that slept with him!"

"Oh." Merlin coughed at the end of her statement.

Alex almost laughed at the old mage as he blushed. Three thousand years old and yet he had the most normal discomfort points imaginable. Her sudden amusement eased the tight feeling in her chest, and she sighed.

"Yeah, I slept with him," she admitted. "We were dating and I'd had a thing for him since we first met."

"Alex, you don't owe me an explanation." Merlin's discomfort faded and he looked at her in concern. He paused for a moment and seemed to be gathering his thoughts. "Uh... are you doing alright with all of... that?"

"Jenny and I have appointments at the clinic to get checked over if that's what you mean," Alex replied in confusion, uncertain what Merlin was asking. "Just in case. It was Nicki's idea and she's going along for moral support."

"Do you think he'd use... uh, a sexual disease?" Merlin asked awkwardly. "That's an odd attack strategy."

"No, I don't really think that," Alex assured him with a forced little smile that quickly dropped away. "But my gut instinct has been shit when it comes to Arthur, so better safe than sorry right."

"Indeed." Merlin coughed again. "Uh, what I meant to ask was, are you doing alright otherwise?"

"Well, the positive thing about the stupid ship dream is that I haven't got time for nightmares about my ex-boyfriend stabbing me." She sighed and let her hands fall down to her sides. "But one day at a time, right?"

"Yes," Merlin agreed after a moment. "Believe it or not, one day at a time can get you through a lot."

"Even three thousand years?"

"Especially three thousand years," Merlin assured her. "We'll sort this out Alex. Morgana and I have solved a lot of strange mysteries concerning invaders and strange magic over the years. With the help of the four- uh, six of you, I'm sure that we will find the information we need."

"And until then?" Alex pressed with a frown. "It feels like we are just treading water, Merlin."

"You keep smithing for one, keep practicing ways to use your magic creatively and let Aiden try to figure out how to replicate every spell in those books he's so fond of."

"Laugh if you want." Alex chuckled as a smile tugged at her lips. "But if Aiden does manage even half of those spells, you and Morgana are going to be left in the dust."

"That would be a very pleasant surprise. I know that Morgana would love to see the Sídhe's face when confronted by that."

Smiling, Alex nodded and pushed herself back onto her feet. The furnace had finished burning down and the warmth of the workshop was beginning to seep away. Through the window, she could see the sky beginning to turn into a wash of reds and pinks as the day ended. Merlin caught her eye and gave her a soft smile before nodding towards the door. Alex nodded in return and moved to the doorway where she retrieved her coat and messenger bag. She stopped only for one moment to look back at the unfinished dagger before her eyes dropped to the not-so-secret hiding place of the safe.

They might have lost Cathanáil, but they still had the Chalice, and maybe in time she'd be a good enough smith to make her own powerful object. Maybe it would even be something to help with the madness that seemed to have taken hold of the creatures from the Sídhe worlds. With that in mind, Alex stepped outside into the cold evening air with a quicker pace than she'd arrived with. One day at a time, she reminded herself. One day at a time and one step at a time.

11

That's Okay

"That's it!" Nicki slammed one of the heavy library books shut with a soft growl. "I give up! I can't find any mythological objects or examples of something like this in Celtic mythology! I've been through all the books they have and nothing stands out from any of the Cycles."

Jenny looked over at the redhead whose face was slightly flushed in aggravation, her freckles standing out a bit more than usual. Dropping her eyes down to the open book in front of her, Jenny had to admit that she was in the same boat. The words from the book on Slavic tales were swimming in front of her eyes, and so far, the notepad that she had for notes was empty.

"Okay maybe we're not going to have any luck today," Alex said with a hint of painfully false cheer. "That's okay, everyone." Alex sighed softly and rubbed her eyes. "Anyway, my eyes are starting to get tired."

"Mine too," Bran admitted from his spot at Alex's left opposite Nicki. "It may be time to call it a day." Jenny watched him rub his eyes with his left hand as his right hand dropped to his side. For a moment his fingers lingered over where she remembered his brace used to be and he smiled a little. "We're all tired," he added. "Even if we found the right story, we might not even recognize it."

"Good point." Alex smiled gratefully. "That's enough for tonight but thank you all for looking."

"We're not going to find anything, Alex." Nicki shook her head. "I'm afraid this situation just hasn't happened before." Nicki groaned and folded her arms on the table in front of her, dropping her head down into her arms.

"Now what?" Aiden asked. "We're hitting a dead end with research. There isn't anything that fits in Celtic mythology."

"Well, I'm not through Slavic mythology yet." Jenny watched the reactions of the mages nervously.

"I'm not sure we're going to find the answer in a book," Alex said. Leaning her chin on her hand, Alex closed the book she'd been reading. "As much as I hate to admit that, Nicki is probably right that this just hasn't happened before. There isn't anything similar enough to make me think we're on the right track. This weekend we should probably keep training our magic, see what else we can come up with."

"Well, I'm curious about if enchantment is possible for other mages," Nicki said. "More than just putting a little bit of magic into an item. Actually, making it do something special like Alex can."

"You ready to give it a try?" Aiden turned in his chair to look over at her curiously. "Already?"

"We know that at least some magic can be put into iron by mages other than the Iron Soul, thanks to Merlin putting some magic into our daggers to keep them from breaking or rusting."

"True," Aiden agreed, "But that's pretty different than what you have in mind."

"I'm starting small," Nicki protested. "And sure, the enchantments probably won't hold for the centuries that they do in iron, but I want to try."

"Can you imagine if she can pull it off?" Bran asked kindly. "With Nicki's imagination, it could be amazing."

"Hard to believe Merlin and Morgana haven't tried something like that." Lance frowned a little as his eyes moved between the mages. "Might be a reason."

"They've done some things," Nicki countered. "But they're a bit set in their ways."

"I suppose after three thousand years that's natural," Jenny said.

"Yeah." Alex smiled even as she slumped back into her chair. "So, we'll close up the books for the weekend and focus on training; maybe it'll help us come up with something clever."

Jenny wondered if she should offer to keep looking through the weekend. She didn't have any magic to train, but she wanted to help. In the corner of her eye, she caught a slightly guilty look on Lance's face and wondered if he was thinking the same thing. Her heart jumped uncomfortably when Lance caught her gaze and turned his head just enough to glance at her. For a moment Jenny stared dumbly at him before realizing what she was doing. Looking away from Lance, a tiny sound escaped her as she found Alex smiling softly at her.

The beep of a phone saved Jenny from the comment that was no doubt about to escape Alex, and Aiden fished out his phone just as Alex's phone chirped with a text message. Jenny shifted back to give Alex room to retrieve her phone from the bag slung over the back of her chair.

"Sídhe spotted near Morgana's," Aiden announced as he read the text just as Alex pulled out her phone. "Enough that Morgana alerted us."

"I'm getting sick of this!" Alex pushed back her chair and swung her coat on in one fast movement. "They aren't even all that strong!"

"No, they aren't." Bran stood up and pulled on his own leather coat and retrieved his cane. His own phone beeped with the arrival of the message and he just shook his head. "They attack, we fight, and kill them, rinse repeat."

"We really need to find something," Nicki said. She glanced at her own phone while wrapping a long green scarf around her neck over her coat and sighed.

"Sorry to bail on you two," Alex apologized. Giving both Lance and her warm looks, Alex made a move towards the door. "Uh, this shouldn't be a problem, but just in case-"

"I'll see Jenny home," Lance said. That earned him a wide smile from Alex before she reached down and gave Jenny a quick one-armed hug.

"See you for breakfast," Alex said.

Then the mages were out the door. Staying in her seat, Jenny watched them vanish beyond the rows of books as they all moved quickly and efficiently. She wondered if they even realized what they looked like. All of them were striding purposely with their heads held high, and even from her vantage point behind them, Jenny could easily imagine that they looked more than a little heroic. Which was a feat in itself when dressed in jeans and sweatshirts.

"They'll look after each other," Lance promised. "Try not to worry."

"I know." Jenny debated looking at Lance now that they were alone. "It may be becoming normal and even boring to them, but knowing there are creatures that want to kill them still sends shivers up my spine."

"Yeah." Lance chuckled softly and Jenny finally looked over at him. He was looking down at the book in his large hands with a sad expression.

"It's all still pretty crazy." He paused and closed the book, sliding it onto the table as he sighed. "Worse is being on the sidelines."

"Yeah." Fighting the Sídhe wasn't something that she wanted to do, but knowing that there was a species trying to take over her world... "It's a mess, isn't it?"

"Actually, they seem to have it disturbingly under control," Lance said with a frown. "That's half of what worries me."

"How so?"

"Arthur," Lance muttered with a sympathetic glance her way. Jenny tried not to flinch at the sound of her ex-boyfriend's name as her stomach churned painfully. "He knows all about them, and yet even Merlin and Morgana are at a loss for how he and the Queen even exist still."

"You think they're holding back?"

"I think these little attacks are meant as a distraction." Lance's jaw tightened. "Why aren't they trying to kill Alex themselves before she can make more gates?"

"They're probably looking for the Sword," Jenny suggested. "So, they can open the other gates and let the real Sídhe through."

She shuddered at the idea. The night that Arthur had caught Lance and her and they'd run after him right into the midst of a Sídhe hunt remained her most terrifying memory. And that was including the strange almost possession she'd experienced during Arto's funeral at Stonehenge. Giving herself a small shake, she focused her attention on Lance.

"How can they find it though? Bran and Alex are training so that they can find it using Alex's connection to it, but how the hell would Arthur find it?"

"Oh... I don't know." Licking her suddenly dry lips, Jenny struggled to gather her thoughts. "I didn't know about the training thing. I guess given that they found the Chalice it makes sense."

"Bran and Aiden told me."

"It's nice you've made friends with them." Giving him a shaky smile, Jenny viciously stamped down the jealous feeling clawing at her chest.

Lance gave her a soft smile and met her eyes with a curious expression. "Alex considers you her friend, and I think Nicki is trying."

"I know; it's still a bit... odd with Alex."

"The reincarnation thing, or Arthur?"

"Both," Jenny admitted. "It's just weird all around. Finding out that you were married to your female friend in a couple of different lives and betrayed them in each is a bit much. Plus being used by the same villain isn't the best thing to have in common either."

"Just be careful and never put it that way around Aiden," Lance cautioned her. "He'd have too much fun with that."

A laugh escaped Jenny and she slapped a hand over her mouth, trying to keep herself from making too much noise. Her brain supplied too many comments that sounded like the fire mage and she couldn't help but giggle. Lance grinned warmly at her and Jenny felt her heart do another flip in her chest, which while only slightly alarming did stop the giggles. There was a moment of comfortable silence and Jenny held back a grin.

"We should probably call it a night too," Lance suggested. "I doubt we're going to find anything tonight."

"It's a shame." Nodding her agreement, Jenny began to gather up all the books. "I was hoping that us being a bit removed might help us see something."

"Well, don't count us done yet," Lance said. "Maybe you and I should have a brainstorming session. Just see what we can shake loose."

"I don't know... I'd hate for it to be picked apart by Merlin and Morgana," Jenny said in a soft voice.

"We'll give it to Alex then; she can mark off anything they've already covered." Lance pulled on his coat and picked up a stack of books. "Just a thought."

They took the stacks of books over to one of the rolling shelving carts that were parked nearby and placed them on an empty shelf. One of the library staff who was shelving other books gave them a slightly dirty look but said nothing as they retreated. Jenny felt a little surge of gratitude to her father who was able to pay for her tuition and give her an allowance: work study didn't sound very fun.

She stayed silent as they pulled on their coats, and Lance calmly waited as she tidied up her long hair and buttoned up the long coat. He held the door for her and Jenny held back a small smile. Around them, the library was quiet with a few students sitting at the special desks with locking cabinets that were rented out to graduate students. The squeaking of a cart made her look over her shoulder at the student employee as they reached the stairs.

It was a strangely warm late January with only a few patches of snow left scattered around them. The heels of her boots clicked softly against the concrete as they moved up the sidewalk towards the dormitories in the northwest side of campus. Beside her was the calm and steady pace of Lance's footsteps as he moved slowly so she could keep up with his longer stride. Around them, the lamps provided a warm glow, but Jenny's eyes kept sweeping around carefully for any sign of a Sídhe Hound or another threat. Her fingers shifted towards her purse where the new dagger from Alex was carefully tucked away. There were a few other students moving across campus: a girl with her blonde hair in pigtails and a stack of books, a group of boys with skateboards by one of the staircases and a couple who were moving away from them and giggling.

"Can you imagine fighting monsters becoming ordinary?" Lance suddenly asked her conversationally.

"No, but then again I suppose it was bound to happen," Jenny replied uneasily. "Does seem a bit strange or insane."

"That's putting it mildly." Lance chuckled, but Jenny caught his eyes shifting out towards the shadows between the buildings where there were no lights. "Did Alex give you a dagger too?"

"Yeah, yesterday, just in case. I'm not sure how much damage I can do with it, but Alex says the iron would be enough to make any Sídhe creatures hesitate. You?"

"Yeah, this morning she swung by my dorm room. I actually went to get a strap for it," he said in a low voice. "It's on the back of his jeans beneath my shirt."

"That makes sense." Jenny glanced at Lance's back, but thanks to his loose Ravenslake sweatshirt there wasn't even a bulge. "I should probably get something to carry it for times I don't have my purse."

"There are a lot of different options, but I'm not sure how many options the local sports shop would have for a woman," Lance said thoughtfully. "But Nicki could probably help you make something. Might be a good thing to put that into her head: I think Alex still carries hers in a bag."

"Alex has magic."

"And yet they all still have daggers," Lance said. "Which as their friend I appreciate."

"Fair point."

Lapsing into silence again, Jenny breathed out slowly and watched the faint hint of her breath dance in the air. It reminded her a bit of the San Francisco fog and her heart tightened in a wave of homesickness. Up ahead she could see the dorms, and the sounds of students and music washed over them, growing louder with each step.

Then they were at the front door of Rhodes Hall with other students maneuvering around them to get inside. Above their heads, the warm lights of the building illuminated the sidewalk and made it easy for Jenny to see how nervous Lance was when he turned to her. Licking her lips, Jenny took a deep breath and folded her hands in front of her and waited.

"Jenny, uh, look I've been trying to be the good guy and give you space." Lance adjusted the strap of his bag nervously but kept his brown eyes locked with hers. "But I'm wondering if you'd be willing now to give it a try. A real honest try between us."

Blinking her eyes up at him Jenny tried to gather her suddenly scattered thoughts. She'd known that this was coming of course and she'd admit that she encouraged it a little bit. And yet she'd still somehow been hit with something right in the chest.

"Okay," she heard herself blurt out. Blood rushed to her cheeks and she desperately hoped that the darkness and her olive skin would keep her from visibly blushing as she dropped her eyes. "I mean, yeah I think that would be okay."

"Really?" She looked up at Lance and was drawn into his hopeful brown eyes that suddenly made her think of a puppy. "Uh, if you aren't really ready yet-"

"No!" Jenny rallied against the uncomfortable churning of emotions in her stomach. "I think it's time, Lance, and I do... I do care about you a lot and you've been... well, wonderful."

"Oh! Wow, okay, I wasn't expecting you to say yes," he admitted with a sheepish grin. "What would you like to do?"

"How about lunch tomorrow?" A giddy flush began pushing up through her chest. "Just the two of us. We'll go from there." Before she could become too nervous, Jenny leaned up and kissed Lance right at the corner of his mouth. The tiny brush of their lips made the happy feeling triple in strength and as she stepped back, she knew she was beaming like an idiot. "See you tomorrow, Lance."

"See you tomorrow, Jenny," he replied with a stunned grin.

Moving towards the door, Jenny fumbled for her key card and had to make a point not to look back at Lance. The insane thrum of desire to stay near him that she'd felt when they first met was humming through her, but alongside it, intertwined with it was a softer feeling that made her feel dizzy. She swiped her card and pushed the door open before she turned back to Lance.

"Text when you get home," she told him softly. "Just in case."

"I will," Lance promised. Nodding, he shifted in place like he was torn between moving towards her and leaving. "Good night."

"Good night."

Dashing into the dormitory, Jenny let the door close behind her with a heavy thud. She threw her hands over her mouth to muffle the squeal that burst forth. Rocking on her feet for a moment, Jenny tugged the collar of her coat up to hide her face as if it would keep the world from observing her being a fool. Once she had recovered herself, Jenny ran to the stairs and quickly ascended to her floor by taking them two at a time. She got a few looks but ignored them all as she let herself into her shared suite.

The living room was dark, but the hallway light was on. Jenny went straight into her room, turned on the light and breathed out slowly. Her room seemed empty even though she could hear her roommate Clara giggling in her own bedroom just through the wall. Breathing out, Jenny dropped her purse onto her bed and looked over at her stuffed bear Zoe who was waiting on her pillows. Lance had asked her out and she'd said yes. It hit her hard, like a punch to the chest, and Jenny felt her knees shake threateningly. Pressing her lips together tightly, Jenny fought back a smile but gave up as she collapsed onto the bed.

She had fished out her phone before she even processed the movement. Rolling onto her stomach, Jenny pulled Zoe over to her chest and caught the bear in a one-armed hug. As she began to text Alex, it occurred to her that Alex was probably still out fighting monsters. Even in a car, it would have taken them a bit to get to Morgana's place and that was after they got to whoever's car was closest. Jenny distracted herself for a few moments by checking her texts, including one from her father that she'd reply to in the morning. Then she gave up on that and sent Alex a text to call as soon as she could no matter the time. Tugging off her boots, Jenny kissed Zoe on the head and giggled.

"Weird, isn't it?" she said. "Husband in former lives and yet she's the one I want to tell the most." Dropping the phone onto the comforter, Jenny leaned her chin on her hand. "I.... I guess that's okay."

Smiling to herself, Jenny looked over at her desk and wondered what assignment she could do to keep herself busy until Alex could call.

12

Impatience

15 C.E. Sør-Trøndelag, Norway

Impatience gnawed at him as he could feel magic racing through his blood just below the skin. Thor struggled to keep his breathing slow and steady; tried to focus on the soft sounds of Morgana across the room and the rhythm of village life he could hear through the walls. It didn't help, and Thor tightened his hands into fists.

"Don't force it," Morgana chided.

From his seat on the wooden bench of the hut, Thor was able to open his eyes and look over at the other mage. She wasn't even looking at him and was instead focused on the loom she was sitting in front of. The large wooden frame was leaning against the side of the hut, and thick rough threads hung from the top and were weighted by tied rocks at the bottom. Morgana's fingers deftly slid the new thread through the weighted strands to create the weave of the new cloth calmly.

"You're trying too hard," Morgana continued, completely unbothered by his staring. "You were able to call forth magic before we got here, Thor. Focus the same way you did then: don't worry about the next steps just yet. Just let it come."

"When can I learn to do more?"

"Your breathing and ability to call forth your power are coming along nicely, but doing more is up to you, Thor."

"But I want to learn more than that," Thor protested. "I can make my magic come forth already, Morgana. I want to do something with it!"

"If the other Iron Souls had been as impatient as you-" Morgana muttered before cutting herself off. "Thor, you can't just be better today because you want to be. Surely it took time for you to learn how to use the forge."

"I was the best student Erlendr has ever had!"

"And how many students has he had?" Morgana chuckled, looking over at him with a smirk. "You will learn, Thor, provided you focus. As for what you will be able to do, that depends on your own mind. How creative can you be? I know you can create swords, pots, and axes for the village, but magic requires more than just the ability to create. It requires true creativity. Your magic will do what you envision it doing; it will follow your instructions and if you work hard, you will be amazed."

Holding back a scowl, Thor let the words wash over him and inwardly grumbled at the riddles these two were so fond of using. Their statements were poetic and pretty, but they didn't really tell him anything solid. He needed something that he could grab onto. Instead of risking another lecture Thor fell silent and looked into the low flames of the fire in the hearth.

"What brought you here anyway?" Thor asked after the silence became too much. "You mentioned your journey only in passing."

"When our magic began to grow stronger, I used a special magic called scrying to help me locate the source. It took some time and multiple attempts, but gradually I was able to discover that we needed to head east. Once we arrived on your shores, things became easier. All we had to do was follow reports of elves." Morgana's fingers easily adjusted the threads on the loom. "Almost the moment we arrived we heard rumors of strange creatures. Merlin and I assumed they were the reason for the growing strength of magic in the world and came to investigate. We never imagined that we'd find magically altered Sídhe." Morgana paused and rolled her shoulders with a soft sigh before she chuckled. "I admit that I am curious as to where the name elves comes from."

"There are old stories of fair and wise creatures," Thor offered. He shifted on the bench to be more comfortable and watched Morgana work, noting that the woman furrowed her brow slightly at his comment. He wondered what she was thinking, but not enough to ask. "So, are you and Merlin married?" He looked thoughtfully around the small hu t.

In the mere week that the pair had been in his village, the holes had been patched, though Thor had rarely seen Merlin bring supplies to the hut. The once empty space had a few luxuries scattered amongst the necessary tools of life. Morgana had gotten or built a loom in the last two days and was making quick work on a long piece of blue cloth. The pair certainly seemed comfortable living together and complimented each other in their own way.

"No." Morgana laughed, suddenly sounding younger. "We're not, but due to our shared nature and responsibility as mages it is simpler to remain together." She paused and pulled her fingers back from the loom. "Do many in the village think we are?"

"You don't interact with anyone except for me," Thor reminded her carefully, uncertain of the woman's temper.

"It's easier to keep to ourselves," Morgana said with a wistful hint to her voice. "Though I am a widow since you're so interested."

"Really?" Thor grimaced at how surprised he sounded. "Uh, I'm sorry that he's deceased. Sorry for your loss," Thor amended with slumping shoulders.

"Thank you, it has been some time." Chuckling softly, Morgana tugged on a stubborn bit of thread. "How about yourself? Merlin and I haven't discussed your future plans with you. Are you engaged to anyone?"

"No!" Thor laughed, shaking his head. "I'm not sure marriage is for me."

"Not an unusual declaration for someone your age, but how does your father feel about that?"

"Irritated; even Arvid is moving towards marriage with Embla, which thrills Father to no end."

"She a nice girl then?"

"Embla is an only surviving child so Arvid will move in with them," Thor explained with a shrug. "It expands the family's property which is good I suppose."

"Ah, politics," Morgana said. "I suppose that even here it is an active force of life." She paused for a moment and glanced his way. "My marriage was partially based on expanding my family's position of power. My stepfather introduced me to important men or the sons of important men whose connection with us would give us more control over the bronze trade."

Thor was a bit confused but said nothing. Morgana was smiling wistfully as she used the heddle to tighten the weave. For a moment he closed his eyes once more and tried to breathe slowly like Merlin had instructed, but his mind was too active. Realizing that he was picking at the blanket with his right hand, Thor folded his hands on his lap and gave a sigh of surrender.

"How long will you stay?"

"As long as we need to," Morgana replied simply. "You must be trained, and the threat of these… tainted Sídhe must be dealt with. That may be months or years. Either way, I suppose Merlin is right and we need to make peace with the village."

"Keep helping to kill those creatures and they'll warm up to you," Thor promised. Looking around the hut, Thor gave it an approving smile. "All you need is some animals and you'll be properly part of the village."

"I will not have animals in the house!" Morgana shuddered and looked at him distastefully. "That cannot be healthy, Thor."

"You'll change your mind in winter if you are still here." Holding back a smile, Thor nodded towards the doorway. "I don't think you understand how cold it can be when the wind brings in the ocean fog and chill."

"We will manage: Merlin and I have dealt with worse in our lives," she said. Then she paused in her work and gently stretched her fingers. She looked towards the doorway and then at him. "It is late, Thor, and you've fallen into a mood." He frowned at her observation. "Go home and get some rest. I overheard you get some requests today. Focus on your work tomorrow. Merlin and I need to have some discussions about our next steps."

It was a dismissal and Morgana turned her attention back to her work. Gritting his teeth, Thor kept himself from huffing and quickly left the small hut. Shaking his hands, Thor let his body shudder in pent up frustration before he looked around. The sky was darkening rapidly and already numerous stars were appearing over their heads. At the wall, warriors armed with the iron weapons he'd been busy making were patrolling with serious expressions illuminated on their faces by torches.

A soft sigh escaped him and Thor shook his head. He'd worry about all of this tomorrow. Moving away from Morgana and Merlin's hut, he headed towards his own home even as his eyes shifted up to scan the dark mountains around them. There was no sign of the strange lights, but a chill rolled up his spine like an icy caress. He allowed himself a small shudder while silently reassuring himself that everything was fine.

"Thor," his brother called. Looking around, he found Arvid waiting in the shadow of his forge hut with a pensive expression. "We need to talk."

"What is it, Arvid?" Thor walked over to join his brother.

"Thor, what are you doing with the strangers?"

"Did Father send you to ask me that?" Thor smirked, enjoying the discomfort in his brother's posture.

"No, he didn't," Arvid replied tersely. "Fact of the matter is that Father is rather content to let you spend time with them if it keeps them in the village. Those things are still out there so I suppose I understand, but-"

"Then don't worry about it." Shaking his head dismissively, he started to walk away.

A strong hand caught his arm and held him fast. Thor looked at his brother and found a pair of angry brown eyes looking straight into his own. "Look, Thor, this isn't the time. I know we live for showing each other up, but you are my brother. I don't want you getting hurt because you're around them too much. We know nothing about them."

"They're here to help," Thor heard himself reply softly. He swallowed thickly at the rush of emotions growing in his chest that he couldn't get a grip on. "They're teaching me magic," he admitted in a lower voice. Merlin and Morgana hadn't told him that he had to keep it a secret. "I was able to use it before they arrived, and they are here to help me control it."

A hurt expression took over his brother's face and Thor felt a stab of guilt. He hadn't meant to say that at all. Pressing his lips together, Thor swallowed and tried to moisten his suddenly dry mouth. Arvid's brown eyes were sad even as the hurt expression was schooled into a neutral and stony expression.

"I didn't know how to explain it," Thor said weakly. "I wasn't sure what would happen... having powers was exciting, but..." Thor gestured around the village with a soft huff. "What would happen?"

"Are you admitting to being scared?" Arvid's mouth curved into a slight smile. "The great Thor was worried about what us mere mortals would think?"

"Now you're being obnoxious!" The weight on his chest eased and he sucked in a breath that he hadn't realized he'd missed. "Well, now you know."

There was no apology. He wasn't going to do that, but his brother nodded in calm understanding. For a moment Thor thought that Arvid might say something else. He felt something stirring his chest and considered that maybe he had something more to say. But a shout of alarm from the wall of the village made them both turn sharply.

Men were shouting and rushing towards the gateway with their weapons at the ready. Thor didn't even think as he leapt into his workshop and grabbed the nearest axe. It hadn't been sharpened as much as he would have liked, but he felt a hum beneath his fingertips as he gripped it. The traces of the magic he'd begun to let flow into the metal reached for him and Thor smirked. His confidence faltered as a thunderous crack blasted through the village. Rushing out to join his brother, Thor found the strange Sídhe creatures pouring in through a new narrow hole in the wall. Horrible hissed words escaped them and hung in the air like a low threat whispered in the shadows.

Moving towards them, Thor scanned the small horde curiously. They were a mess with their long hair matted with leaves and dirt. Some of them were missing the golden armor and only a few had weapons at the ready with others clawing at the air with long talon-like nails. One of these leapt towards him with a snarl.

"Poison!" he hissed at him. "Poisoned!"

Startled by its words, Thor hesitated for a moment, but only for a brief one. Swinging the axe, Thor felt a moment of resistance as the axe blade collided with the side of the creature. Without any armor to slow it down, the dull edge sank into flesh and silver blood tinged with dark brown spurted out when he pulled his axe back. The creature screamed and clawed frantically at its arm, struggling to stand as its legs collapsed beneath it.

"Stink of magic," a gravelly voice to his right growled.

Turning sharply, Thor's eyes widened as he found another Síd waiting for him. Thor could see the creature's translucent skin stained with lines of black just beneath the surface that were crawling up its features. Wild, violet eyes were glaring at him and flickering strangely as if their very shade was changing right before him. This one still had its armor and the golden decorations on its horns were longer than the others with fraying braids wrapped around the bases.

Thor felt his stomach turn over as his own pulse echoed in his ears, but he didn't run. A slimy feeling slipped up his arms and the flare of power in his gut fluttered like a cold hand was snuffing it out. His feet felt fastened to the ground as if a hammer blow had fused them to the earth, but he could move his hands.

"Thor!" Merlin shouted from across the village.

Snarling at him, the Síd stretched its hand towards him and Thor gasped as a soft glow began to appear around its hand. However, the glow flickered and a pained expression crossed the creature's face. It was enough to allow Thor to shake his head and stumble back a few steps. Sucking in a deep breath of cool air, Thor risked closing his eyes for a moment and grabbed at the flame in his gut. It flared back to life like a starved fire given fuel.

Magic burst out of his hand and arched through the air in a blast of lightning that struck the creature and the ground. Thor could feel his arm hairs standing on end beneath his tunic and smell the hum of the lightning in the air. For an instant, he could barely see as the bright flash blinded him, but his senses felt stretched outward beyond his body. There was a faint rumble in his bones, but no sound of thunder which confused him. He pushed the thought aside and focused on the creature which was still alive and roaring in pain.

In the corner of his eye silver magic flashed through the air in a smooth arc. Green magic rolled past him and he heard shouting from the warriors. Pushing it all away, Thor called on the magic again and felt a tightening in his chest. It stung as it rushed up his arms leaving a burning trail behind it, but burst out of his fingertips on command. A blast of bright blue energy struck the Síd which shouted again. Then as the energy rushed over it, the Síd began to dissolve into a pile of dirt and ash at Thor's feet.

Panting softly, Thor looked around the village as every muscle in his body tensed at the ready. His nerves were all but burning and the night air felt like ice against the flushed skin of his face. Part of the wall had been broken down with brute force and lay in scattered pieces, but there was no sign of more of the creatures coming through. His muscles felt raw and stretched, but even with the pain in his veins, he could feel the soft hum of his magic.

He grimaced slightly as he wondered if the pain he'd felt was part of the reason Merlin and Morgana were trying to pace him. It was an unpleasant idea, but he breathed out slowly and felt the pain ease a little. Looking towards his house, Thor sighed in relief as he caught sight of his brother and father near their home. Arvid was panting slightly but looked uninjured and his father didn't appear to have been in the fight at all. For good measure he kicked at the pile of dust and ashes, grinding it into the ground with his foot before searching for Merlin and Morgana.

Finding them near the wall was easy enough, but Thor was stunned by what he saw. Merlin and Morgana were standing over one of the creatures with contemplative looks of interest. Its long hair was splayed around its head and the tips of its golden covered horns were pressed into the dirt. He waited a heartbeat for one of the mages to do something, but then Merlin calmly unbuckled his belt and handed the pouch on it to Morgana. She nodded and stepped back without a word. Silver magic filled the palm of her hand and she held it over the Sídhe but did not release it as Merlin knelt down and rolled the creature on its side.

Thor could hear the collective gasp of surprise and alarm as Merlin bound the creature's hands behind it. Violet eyes began to flutter open and it struggled against Merlin only for the mage to stand up and roughly pull it to its feet. The Síd swayed and its legs threatened to give out, but Merlin forced it to keep moving. Without a word to him or anyone else, the pair of mages escorted the Sídhe creature out of the village through the opening in the wall.

13

The Adamses in Ravenslake

Grabbing her packed duffle bag, Alex looked around her dorm room one more time. It wasn't out of fear that she'd forgotten something, but a lingering worry that while they weren't in the dorm room the Fae would come here anyway. An iron triskele sat on the ledge of the locked window and would hopefully keep things out. Her laptop had been stashed beneath a layer of socks in a drawer and there was really nothing else that she felt a need to worry about. Without her there during the night the Fae really had no reason to sack her dorm, and yet Alex had a bad feeling tugging at her gut.

"Alex!" Nicki called from the living room. "You ready?"

"Yeah." Shaking her head at herself, Alex turned off the light. "You've got iron on your windowsill, right?"

"Of course, they're going after mages and we won't be here," Nicki said. They walked to the front door and pulled on their coats. "It'll be fine."

"I know, it's just..." Alex trailed off and shook her head. "I've just got a bad feeling is all."

Nicki's lips twitched, but whatever reference or joke she'd been thinking of making didn't come, and instead her roommate nodded kindly.

"It's probably just the date; Imbolc is one of the seasonal dates and the Sídhe are stronger." Nicki gave her a smile and nudged her shoulder. "Happy anniversary though. It's been a year since they captured you and you escaped with all those kids." Nicki's smile softened. "It's probably just bad memories."

"Maybe," Alex conceded with a repressed shudder. It wasn't enough and Nicki gave her a soft, worried look. "I'm fine," she said quickly.

"I doubt that," Nicki said. "I hear you toss and turn sometimes you know."

"It's been a rough year, but I'm still alive."

"And we're going to keep you that way." Nicki reached over and squeezed Alex's shoulder. "Come on, let's go. The boys will beat us despite making a snack run at this rate."

"They are aware that we'll probably be dealing with the Fae tonight, right?"

"Yeah, but that just means we'll need lots of caffeine to stay awake," Nicki said with a lazy shrug. "Besides, the seasonal days may lower the defenses of the earth, but as these creatures are already in our world, tonight may be nothing special."

Nicki did have a point: the seasonal days were days when the transition of the Iron Realm's seasons affected its natural defenses. They still had their magic, but it was easier for creatures from other worlds to break into their realm. With the new Iron Gates in place, Alex couldn't really be sure that there would be any trouble tonight. It was all just a precaution.

"Hey, Nicki?" Freezing in the doorway, Alex shuddered as a horrible thought occurred to her. "You don't suppose that Arthur sabotaged the Gate, do you?" The idea hadn't crossed her mind before now and she looked fearfully towards Nicki.

The redhead looked worried for only a moment before she exhaled slowly and put a hand on Alex's shoulder. "No, I think we're safe. From what Arthur has gloated about, he and his... mother were interested in controlling the Sídhe's access to Earth in exchange for their allegiance. Since their plan was to get Cathanáil there was no reason, and in fact, it would have been dangerous for him to try and sabotage the gate then with Merlin and Morgana watching so closely."

"That makes sense." Alex nodded slowly, allowing Nicki to tug her out of the dorm suite and turn the lights off behind them.

"Try not to worry so much." Nicki chuckled and nudged her shoulder. "It'll give you wrinkles."

"That would be the least of my problems," Alex grumbled, though she calmly followed Nicki downstairs.

"Besides, you've got Aiden, Bran, and I helping you out this time around!" Nicki laughed as they walked past another student staring at his phone. "Not to mention Lance and Jenny. We'll work through all of it."

"Your optimism is irritating. I think I like you better cynical."

"I'm only cynical about a few things, thank you very much," Nicki huffed with a toss of her red hair. "Usually, I'm a lovely ball of sunshine."

Stepping in front of Nicki, Alex gripped the front door and gave a strong tug to pull it open. She froze in place with the door against her foot as she found herself face to face with a very familiar and surprised woman.

"Mom?"

Sure enough, the woman in front of her was her mother, with her long graying blonde hair up in a bun and bags under her eyes that made her look even older. Inwardly Alex grimaced as it sank in why her mother would be here.

"Elizabeth did you find-" her father's voice called from around the corner moments before he came into sight. He stopped and looked at Alex with wide eyes. She couldn't help but notice that his hair had gone a little whiter since she came back. "Hello, Alex."

"Mom, Dad." Nervously licking her lips, Alex took in their serious expressions. "I'm guessing you're here to talk?"

"You're not calling home much," her mom said. "We know that you're dealing with a lot and maybe we weren't very..." She trailed off and grimaced slightly. "Supportive? Understanding? I'm sorry, sweetheart, but we still don't know how to process this."

"I get that," Alex said. "But this is a bad night to visit."

"Oh." Her dad moved over to stand next to her mother and his eyes dropped to the duffle bag in her hand. "Are you going somewhere?" He looked around Alex at Nicki who was loaded up with her backpack.

"It's Imbolc." Glancing nervously towards the sun, Alex tried to keep her voice even. They had several hours until sunset, but she could feel her stomach turning. "It's a night that... uh, problems are likely." Forcing a laugh, Alex tucked a strand of hair behind her ear. "We're doing a sleepover at Morgana's so that we're all together." She paused and considered her parents, whose faces had paled slightly. "So, what brings you two here tonight? It's not exactly a fast drive, and it's a weekday."

"We just... you didn't call this weekend and we were talking with your brothers," her dad floundered and shook his head. "We just needed to see you."

"You literally picked the worst afternoon possible!" Nicki laughed in a poor attempt to ease the tension. Then she coughed and stepped up next to Alex. "Maybe we should take them to see Morgana and Merlin," she suggested in a softer voice. "Let them explain a bit more."

"Uh yeah," Alex said weakly. "That's probably a good idea, Mom. Morgana and Merlin are the experts. They can probably explain better than I did."

"Alex," her dad began to say before shaking his head. "Sorry to surprise you like this, sweetheart." He stepped forward and wrapped her up in a hug that Alex melted into with a soft sigh. "Good to see you," he murmured with a kiss to her forehead.

"Good to see you too, Dad." Alex's throat tightened and she really didn't want to move. "But really, the professors would probably be the best people for you to talk to now."

"Alex is right." Nicki gave her parents a warm reassuring smile. "It isn't too far away."

"Alright," her mom agreed hesitantly. "We'll follow you then."

Alex was keenly aware of her parents watching her as they headed down the sidewalk towards the parking lot. She could see her parent's car in the short-term parking spot and her own a few cars down in the first row. Resisting the urge to look over her shoulder at her parents, Alex let out a soft sigh which earned her a sympathetic look from Nicki.

"Just bad memories, huh?" Alex asked. Nicki snorted in response.

Despite her reservations, Alex and Nicki calmly climbed into her car after stowing their bags in the back seat. As Alex pulled out of her spot, she found her mom's dark blue car waiting for them by the exit of the parking lot. Nicki wisely stayed quiet as Alex tightened her grip on the steering wheel and told herself to stay calm before pulling out of the parking lot and into traffic. The trip across the river and into the tree covered hills outside of the main area of Ravenslake was usually very short, but this time it seemed to drag on and on. The sight of Morgana's house and Aiden's small truck was both welcome and unpleasant at the same time.

"Easy, Alex," Nicki said. "Merlin and Morgana can help answer some of their questions."

"They didn't really ask much when I told them." Alex's grip on the steering wheel tightened as the car rumbled over the gravel of the driveway. "It just sort of... I don't know; it wasn't ignored exactly, but..."

"It's a lot to take in, even with a practical demonstration," Nicki reassured her. "And it's not your fault. This is just going to be a process."

Their car came to a stop and Nicki grabbed both of their bags like nothing was wrong. Looking over her shoulder, Alex focused on her father's face as he brought their car to a stop behind Aiden's truck. Her mother was out of the car first, but the sound of the front door opening made Alex look sharply towards the house. Morgana was in the doorway and her face showed surprise only for a moment before she looked towards Alex. Swallowing thickly and licking her dry lips, Alex rushed up the stairs to Morgana with Nicki on her heels.

"I'm sorry," Alex whispered to Morgana as she reached the waiting professor. "They just showed up."

"Worst possible day." Morgana sighed, but she smiled calmly if not warmly at Alex's parents as they approached. "I suppose Merlin and I should have expected that sooner or later your worry and curiosity would compel you to Ravenslake. Please come in; we'll try to answer any questions that you might have."

"Relax, Alex," Nicki said softly. "You aren't being led to your execution."

"This way," Morgana called to her parents, leading them inside.

Morgana paused in the entryway to allow her guests to shrug off their coats. As soon as she had done so Nicki vanished towards the guest bedroom with their bags, leaving Alex alone with her folks and Morgana. If the older mage was distressed by the turn of events, she showed no sign of it and gestured them into the living room. Aiden and Bran were already seated in armchairs with cups of tea in front of them on the coffee table. There were a full tea service, a plate of cookies, and a platter of small sandwiches waiting for them along with a seated Merlin, who merely raised an eyebrow. Nicki returned a moment later through the kitchen and leaned against the doorway to watch the proceedings.

"Since we have guests, I suggest we set up watches," Merlin said calmly. "Bran, Aiden, if you wouldn't mind keeping look out on the porch in opposite directions, and Nicki please keep an eye on the back."

Her three fellow mages exchanged slightly irritated but also understanding looks. Aiden snagged another cookie from the plate and headed off towards the front door with Bran behind him. This time Bran didn't even bother taking his cane with him and Alex saw her mother eyeing his leg with interest. As they both moved out of view and Nicki went out through the kitchen, her mom shook her head and focused her attention on the two professors seated across from them.

For a moment no one spoke as Alex slumped into a seat and tried not to fidget. Her parents looked frazzled but determined. They glanced her way a couple of times as they gathered their thoughts but were focused on the two mages in front of them. Finally, her father removed his glasses and cleaned them off before putting them back on and looking intently at Morgana.

"Are you really Morgana le Fey?" Her dad was staring at Morgana in an awkward blend of disbelief and wonder. "And you're Merlin?"

"I am the basis of the mythological figure that you're familiar with," Morgana replied. Settling back in the armchair, she took a sip of her tea and studied Alex's parents. "I'm afraid that with the changing and reinterpreting of the myths in which I appear, much of what you have heard is wildly inaccurate."

"My story is a bit more accurate," Merlin said. "Of course, Nimue wasn't real and many of the elements are wildly wrong, but at least I survived without my character being completely transformed."

Alex glanced at her parents and grimaced. They didn't look very comfortable or reassured. It was almost funny to consider that Morgana was bad at this. Three thousand years old and explanations and reassurances were a problem. Though with her parents looking like they might be sick or have nervous breakdowns, Alex didn't find it very funny. Then her mother took a slow breath and sipped her tea before she set the teacup on the table and straightened up.

"I assume that you aren't going to inform us that this was all a joke?" Her mom looked between Merlin and Morgana.

"No, we are not," Merlin replied kindly. "I am sorry, Doctor Adams."

"Elizabeth," she corrected automatically. "Under the circumstances, formality seems a bit pointless unless you prefer Professor Yates."

"Merlin is fine unless you think you might struggle with calling me Professor Yates in public."

"Honestly I'm not sure we'd ever have reason to see you socially," Alex's dad pointed out, shaking his head. "I'm afraid that while we asked Alex some questions when she told us about magic, it hadn't truly sunk in yet. It isn't normal to learn that your daughter has magical powers and is one of the people responsible for protecting the world."

"No, I suppose not," Merlin agreed with a nod. "Forgive us if we have difficulty understanding your position; Morgana and I are from a very different time."

"We've heard," her mom replied giving Merlin a curious look. "It's all a bit too fantastic to be real."

"So you've indicated; perhaps if you had specific questions the answers might help you understand the reality you find yourself in," Morgana said.

"What is the long-term plan here?" her dad asked, drawing himself up and stubbornly meeting Morgana's gaze. "Are you going to take the fight to them? It sounds as if these... Sídhe outnumber you greatly."

"They do," Merlin agreed. "And we do not enter their tunnels. They have the upper hand there. As for the long-term plan, it is our goal to gradually rebuild the layers of protection around Earth that can keep out the Sídhe."

"And how long will that take?" Her dad was eyeing them suspiciously, causing Alex to grimace.

"I can understand your fears." Merlin's words got him doubtful looks. "I raised the first Iron Soul Arto after it became too dangerous for him to remain with his family. Arto was very dear to my heart and knowing that his powers and purpose put him in harm's way was never easy," he confessed with softening features. "My duty to the Iron Realm means that I have come to know and care for many of Alex's other incarnations, and it is never easy to have to send them into battle. It is why Morgana and I work so hard to identify the Iron Souls and train them. Without understanding their powers, they could harm themselves or be defenseless."

There was a moment of silence and her parents squeezed each other's hands. Her mother recovered first and looked straight at Morgana. "Alex told us that this can be dangerous; that it is a real war. She told us the truth in case she never came home."

"That is true," Morgana confirmed with a nod. "I'm not sure I agree with Alex's decision to tell you, but she is right that someday she may suffer an injury that there would be no easy excuse for. There is even a chance that she might be killed, but please understand that many of the Iron Souls have also lived to old age." Morgana met Elizabeth's eyes and leaned forward in her chair. "Please don't allow yourself to make assumptions about Alex's future. There is a reason why Merlin and I very much wish for all of the mages to continue their educations. This is part of their life, an important part to be sure, but it is not the final purpose of it."

"Exactly," Merlin agreed. "While Alex is a student in my department and I am in fact her advisor, I admit that I am very curious to see how these experiences will guide Bran in his potential future research in the field of physics."

"The point is that Alex is the current Iron Soul. She was not the first, that is true, but each one is important and we will strive to help her and protect her," Morgana said. "And keep in mind that while magic certainly has a price and responsibility; Alex has not only Merlin and I but the other young mages as well. They care about each other and look after each other. Magic has given her good friends."

"I suppose so." Her mom still sounded uneasy with a doubtful expression on her face. "I suppose it is something we can't change, but I still wonder why my daughter. Is it genetic?" Her mom frowned and looked seriously at Morgana. "I mean if you were the sister of one of the Iron Souls and had magic, then does that mean that Alex's brothers could potentially have magic?"

"We'd be aware by now if they did," Morgana replied. "I'm afraid that genetics is a very modern field of science and Merlin and I have not sought to break down that aspect of who is a mage. Magic can be passed on in families, but to be frank, those cases are only in families where they are following formulas to borrow magic."

"That's possible?" her dad asked in surprise. "Alex didn't mention anything like that."

"Alex is a mage," Morgana answered tightly. "She has been gifted power by the Iron Realm itself; she doesn't need to siphon it off."

"Morgana doesn't care much for those who use magic like that," Merlin added with a soft chuckle that did nothing to reassure her parents. "Otherwise, I'm afraid there really doesn't seem to be a magical gene. Incarnations of the Iron Soul have had children and none of them were ever mages, though some did embrace siphoning magic for small scale uses."

"Children," her mom repeated before shaking her head. "I suppose I should have expected that, but it's strange to think about, Alex having children in another life."

"There is no reason why an incarnation of the Iron Soul can't live a peaceful and long life," Merlin told them with a smile. "And in truth, Morgana and I haven't met every Iron Soul incarnation, as we tend to leave them alone when magic stays at low levels."

"So, is there always some magic in the world?" Rubbing at his glasses, her dad seemed torn between dread and curiosity.

"Usually not enough to do much with," Morgana said.

"Because of the creatures in our world?" her mom clarified.

"Exactly!" Merlin grinned like her parents were clever students. "Nowadays there are enough creatures living on Earth with non-native origins that there is always a bit of magic, just in case, I suppose."

"But there's more when there is a threat like now," her dad pressed. "And when this is all sorted out it will go back to normal?"

"It takes time for magic levels to drop," Morgana explained, "But yes, within a few years Alex and the others will only be able to use a few simple spells."

Her parents exchanged a look that Alex couldn't quite read, but it didn't seem too much like relief or disappointment. "And Arthur? Is he a mage?" her mom asked, turning the conversation away from talk of the future.

"No." Morgana's lips twisted with a thoughtful frown. "We're honestly not sure what he is. If he were just a mage then he would have struggled to use magic due to his loyalty to the Sídhe Queen."

"We are at a loss," Merlin admitted with slumping shoulders. "Arthur caused a Connection with Alex, which may be due to them having been cousins in his prior life, but that explanation can't be confirmed."

"And we aren't even sure how the Queen was able to force the reincarnation like that," Morgana added. "Merlin and I in the past have been able to…" She paused and looked uncomfortable. "In one life it became necessary for us to force a reincarnation quickly. He was for the time an old man and very ill. We were able to use our magic to catch the soul and well, shove it, I suppose, into a nearby pregnant woman. It was very difficult and we weren't certain it would even work."

"Wait," Alex cut in with wide eyes. "You hadn't told me about that." Merlin and Morgana exchanged guilty looks and Alex bit her tongue slightly to keep herself from saying something.

Her parents were looking uncomfortable enough as it was and anger began appearing on her mother's face. "You mean that you could just cause Alex to be reborn again?!"

"It is not ideal!" Merlin grimaced and looked a bit guilty. "But if she were to be badly injured then it would allow us to make sure that the Iron Soul would be reborn quickly."

"We've never found a pattern to the Iron Soul's rebirths," Morgana explained. "It isn't like the concept of the Buddha's reincarnation where they are reborn immediately or within a year of death. Years can go by, and while the Iron Soul does always seem to appear when they are needed, Merlin and I hesitate to leave things to chance."

"We have the Iron Chalice now," Alex reminded her parents. It was difficult to ignore their uncomfortable faces and her own discomfort with the idea of Merlin and Morgana doing that to her. "So, it's unlikely I'll ever get hurt that badly."

"Indeed; the Iron Chalice is a powerful asset," Merlin agreed. "And the young ones usually stay in pairs."

"In fact, we're talking about renting a house together next year," Alex said. "That way we can protect each other and not potentially bring the Sídhe to the dorm rooms."

"I hate to interrupt!" Rushing into the room, Bran gestured towards the front of the house. "But Fae creatures are coming up the drive."

"How many?" Morgana asked.

"Enough that Aiden and I shouldn't take them alone," Bran answered with a pointed look at Alex. "You coming?"

"I- yes," Alex managed as she stood up.

"I'll join Nicki out back just in case," Morgana said. Standing up, she nodded to Alex's parents. "Please excuse us."

Leaving the room, Alex grimaced as she heard Merlin quickly assure her parents that they would all be alright. There was a flicker of regret in her gut. She didn't doubt that her parents needed to know the truth. She wasn't questioning that someday if Arthur got his way and killed her, they deserved to know she was trying to save the world. Instead, she just regretted that this was necessary in the first place. No parent should have to fear the death of their child and she'd put that on them. At least she hadn't explained to them what happened last Imbolc. Tightening her fists, Alex breathed out slowly and let the magic churning in her gut flare to life. For once she was a little happy to have the Sídhe or at least their cousins attacking.

14

Realities of a Mage Life

Joining Bran and Aiden on the porch as she pulled on her coat, Alex looked out into the densely forested slopes of the hillside just beyond the edge of Morgana's property. There were still a few rays of the sun shining past the horizon, but the tall trees and rolling hills cast long shadows that shaded the creatures marching towards them. Alex's eyes widened as she took in the small legion of over twenty different Fae creatures: an odd mix of the humanoid ones that she recognized as Sídhe descendants, Redcaps, and a couple less familiar ones.

The first of the Fae creatures stopped and looked at Alex with a blank expression. Its eyes were bluer than any Sídhe related creature Alex had ever seen, and in the loose sweatshirt and jeans with the knit hat covering most of its pale hair she might have mistaken it for a human. For a moment no one moved and Alex exhaled with her breath wafting up through the cold air. Then a Redcap snarled and the horde began to rush them.

Yellow sparks burst forth in a rapid stream and formed a spinning ring above the creatures. In the blink of her eye, the sparks exploded into a shower of small fireballs that began to rain down on the Fae creatures, making them scream and the snow hiss as it turned to steam. Looking towards the boys, Alex blinked in surprise as she realized that it had been Bran who cast the fire spell and not Aiden. There was a smirk on his face and next to him Aiden laughed out loud. Around the Fae, the cloud of steam lingered even after the fire dissipated.

"Nice!" Aiden shouted. Red sparks of magic spun around his hands. They transformed into flames and settled into large glowing orbs of fire in Aiden's palms. "But this is how it's done!" Gritting his teeth, he pushed his hands towards the assembled creatures.

Fire flashed forward through the air like a flamethrower and sent the creatures scattering even as a few of them vanished in puffs of smoke and dust with aborted cries. Noting in relief that they didn't seem any stronger than usual, Alex shifted over near the stairs and brought her hands in front of her. She let the magic flow down her arm to her fingers and mentally conjured a bolt of lightning. Energy flashed between her fingertips and Alex allowed her eyes to fall shut for a moment as she struggled to imagine her latest idea for an attack.

Opening her eyes, Alex shoved one hand forward and sent the lightning leaping off of her fingertips and arching through the air. The bolt struck the first of the Redcaps, making the creature snarl loudly as it lashed at the air viciously. Then the bolt jumped, striking the next small pixie-like target. Alex grimaced as the attack began to dissipate into the air, but didn't have time to reflect on her failure to achieve a longer effect as the first of the Sídhe creatures reached the porch and Alex moved down the steps to engage it. More than half of the attackers had been destroyed in their initial spells, but as the creature exposed long talon-like nails to the cold night air, Alex had no time to consider the speed which they'd dispatched the first forces.

She dodged the first swipe of its claws and began letting her magic gather into an orb against her palm. Bringing up her hand, Alex released the built-up charge of magic by pushing it forward. This time she skipped the mental command for a lightning bolt and watched as the orb shot ahead, lengthening into a bolt only a split second before striking the Síd. It was blasted back off the porch as the energy burned a hole in its sweatshirt and exposed steaming skin below. A snarl pulled Alex's attention to her right as a Redcap leapt off one of the porch railings towards her. A swirl of yellow magic threw it back past the railings and into the snow beyond as Bran came rushing down the stairs of the porch to join her. Fire swirled over their heads and illuminated the snow as Aiden provided support from his position on the porch.

Another one, a pixie this time, came running at her with needle-like teeth exposed. Bringing her hand forward, Alex gripped her right wrist to aim before releasing a bolt of lightning. This time it was strong enough or the creature was weak enough that even the simple attack caused it to dissolve into the familiar ashy dust. She glanced towards Bran as his magic formed a bolt of yellow magic that sailed into another of the creatures and destroyed it. A pair of creatures further back were struck by a fireball that exploded and caused another rush of steam from the snow.

The creature that she'd blasted back earlier was stumbling to its feet and shaking its head as if dazed. Alex paused her movement even as her magic flowed into her open palm and began to hum gently against her skin. It staggered towards her, silvery blood leaking from its mouth and a strange tilt to its head that made the porch light cast odd shadows across its face. Then it rushed for her.

"I'm sorry," the creature stammered out from between clenched teeth. With a cry, it slashed through the air at her. "I- can't- we are bound."

A column of fire dropped from the sky and swallowed the Fae creature up. There was a brief dull scream of pain before the body vanished amongst the flames. Staring into the fire, Alex felt her chest tighten as if a cold hand was squeezing her heart. The strange words of the prior Fae creature echoed in her head and Alex was once again hit with the dizzying feeling that she was forgetting something important.

"Alex!" Aiden called over. "You, okay?"

"Yeah." Swallowing the knot that was trying to form in her throat, Alex nodded. "I'm fine. Nice spell."

"It's a new one." Aiden grinned and rubbed his hands together eagerly. "I like it: nice and precise on what I want to damage."

Looking around slowly, Alex squinted her eyes at the tree line trying to make out if there were any more creatures lurking about. The relief she felt at the end of the battle was dulled by the looming sense of dread and guilt that she couldn't quite shake off. Rubbing her hands against her arms, Alex glanced at the boys who were moving back towards the porch and locked eyes with Bran for a moment. He offered her an understanding nod and Alex felt a tiny bit better. She paused at the base of the stairs and looked around at the trodden snow and marveled once more at how quickly all the evidence of the creatures vanished. Aiden's fireballs had burned away the clothing. There were a few slowly fading traces of silvery blood and lines of ash in the snow. Well, where there was still snow after the fire throwing show.

Straightening her shoulders, Alex strode up the stairs to the porch and didn't look back at the others. Her heart was still pounding and her mouth was dry as the strange words the creature had said echoed in her head. Alex couldn't help but feel an inkling of doubt creeping up her spine. It was easy to see that the Queen was controlling them and there wasn't much choice, but still... there was a bitter taste in her mouth that she couldn't deny.

Alex shrugged out of her coat once she was inside and looked up to find her parents waiting anxiously in the doorway with wide eyes. She glanced towards the window and noted with a sinking heart that the drapes were open. Morgana caught her eye and cleared her throat behind her parents. Nicki was next to her with a sad little smile.

"You two alright?" Alex asked even though she could clearly see them.

"Only a few attacked us," Morgana replied dismissively. She strode across the room and gently took Alex's arm as she examined Alex for injuries.

"One of them talked to me again," Alex whispered. "It said they were bound."

"We already knew that." Morgana sighed, brushing a finger over Alex's cheek before she cleared her throat and looked over at her parents. "As you can see, the mages are becoming very practiced at dispatching threats."

"But those things... those were fairies?" her dad asked in shock. Her mom was frowning and gripping her dad's arm. "Real fairies?"

"Of sorts; there are variations of them, of course, but they all share a weakness to iron. At least they used to before they began to adapt to our world."

"Adapt to our world?" her mom repeated carefully with a calculating look towards Morgana. "Are they or are they not invaders?"

"It's complicated." Morgana rubbed the furrow between her eyes. "You aren't completely off the mark with your question, I'm afraid. While they are not creatures native to our world... they are born here and live here. In essence, they are both: they are native and yet their species are from different universes. They are an invasive species. They are part of the reason why there is always at least a low level of magic."

"Then what's their history?" Her mom's arms crossed defensively across her chest as Alex's father wrapped an arm around her waist.

"Some are descendants of the warrior Sídhe who were trapped on this side of the Iron Gates three thousand years ago. The humanoid ones are the descendants of true Sídhe while the others are descendants of creatures from the same branch of the Tree of Reality of the Sídhe who were enslaved by them."

"We had something of an alliance with them once," Merlin said. The statement earned him surprised looks from all of the young mages. "It was during the proto-Viking period," he told them dismissively. "When the Sídhe were trying to break through the Iron Gates were... altered."

"That is not the biggest issue we have right now," Morgana said. "I understand that fighting them while knowing they don't have full control is... difficult."

Alex swallowed and avoided the eyes of her mother and father. Morgana had just hit on an uncomfortable reality that she personally had been avoiding. Nicki caught her eyes and gave her a sad smile, which reassured her that the others were aware of it too. But she didn't think that they were trying to talk with her fellow mages. That seemed to be confined to her.

"I understand," Morgana continued gently. "But until we understand how the Queen and Arthur are doing this, we have no other options. We don't know what would happen if we tried to contain them. Without knowing how the Queen is doing this, we have no way of knowing what else she might do through them. And should we try to hide from them I'm afraid that Arthur may just have them attack Ravenslake or your families."

"You think that's a possibility?" Her dad looked between Merlin and Morgana. "Alex had us put up horseshoes, and after seeing those things we'll be keeping the iron poker in the bedroom."

"I'm afraid that the iron protections Alex put up in the house for you might not be enough," Merlin cautioned gently as if trying to soothe a frightened stray animal. "Unfortunately, Morgana and I have concluded that Arthur is most likely a half Sídhe being. We aren't certain how the Queen was able to create him, though her control of the Sídhe descendants in this world may indicate that she used one or more of them as a source for Sídhe flesh. His half-human nature means he can bypass iron completely."

"What if I used a spell like the one at the Tor near my house?" Alex asked. A shiver went down her spine as she remembered how her blood had reactivated Arto's ancient spell. "Wouldn't that keep him away?"

"Maybe," Morgana agreed carefully. "His loyalty to the Sídhe would allow the spell to impact him, but speaking from experience the effect is lessened after the initial casting." Alex wanted to ask about Morgana's experience but based on how the woman's face tightened she decided against it while her parents looked nervous.

"You think he'd come after us?" Then her dad shook his head and snorted. "Of course, he would: this is war to them."

"And Arthur was the mythological basis for Mordred in another life," Merlin added with a dark expression. "The stories about him are largely true, minus the incest of course, and he is a twisted creature."

"He killed his own uncle: stabbed Arto's father in the back." Morgana's eyes flashed and her hands curled into fists. "The reality is that we need to think seriously about how to protect your family from him, Alex."

"And this time we don't have the benefit of warriors that we can station around them." Merlin's statement did nothing to lighten the mood.

"It's not just my parents," Alex observed sadly as she looked over at them. "Aiden and Nicki's families are local, but there's also Bran's mom to be worried about, and Jenny and Lance's families. Hell, Jenny's dad knew Arthur and his mother for years."

"And you didn't explain the danger to your mother, Bran?" Morgana asked with a stern look.

"I didn't think she could handle it yet," Bran admitted, shifting between his feet. "To be honest... I really didn't think about the possibility of Arthur going after her."

"He might not, but we have to consider the possibility," Merlin said. "Aiden, Nicole, perhaps your books could provide us with some ideas. A new spell: something powered by Alex's Iron Soul powers could be of use."

"There are a few things that I could think of," Nicki told him with growing excitement in her voice chasing away the melancholy. "Something like-"

"Later, Nicki," Aiden cut off gently with a nod towards Alex's parents.

"Indeed," Morgana agreed. "For their safety, in case there are more coming I suggest that your parents remain here for the night. Please take your things out of the guest room. I'm afraid you children will have to make do with the living room."

"That isn't necessary-" her mom started to say.

"I'm afraid that it is," Morgana interrupted though her features softened. "Ravenslake is the center of our magical conflict. Right now, this is where the Sídhe could try to break through once more, and this is where Fae creatures are being sent. We will work on the problem of how to protect you further, but when you are in Ravenslake you need to be with mages."

Morgana nodded towards the kitchen and the others slowly trailed out. Merlin hesitated for a moment before catching Alex's eye. He sighed softly and moved towards her, putting his hand on her shoulder for a moment before he followed Morgana out. The living room was suddenly very quiet and she was keenly aware of being alone with her parents who had just seen her fighting back Fae creatures. Judging from the unease on their faces they were very aware of this as well.

"Alex," her mom started to say, only to trail off. She sighed and raised her hand to rub at her eyes for a moment. "I'm sorry, we haven't handled this smoothly."

"Well, I don't think there's a parenting book that covers this." Alex twisted her hands together, chuckling weakly. "I'm not mad. I knew that I dropped a huge bombshell on you and that it would take a while to fully process."

"Ed was so excited." Her dad shook his head, looking much older all of a sudden. "I just couldn't understand it."

"Magic can be wonderful," Alex told them softly. "I mean, it's crazy too, but lately we've been working to replicate the sorts of things that you see in movies or read about. There's something..." she trailed off searching for the right words. "Something remarkable and honestly magical about seeing the world change in front of your eyes. Bran understands the physics more than me, but knowing that I'm bending natural laws is amazing!"

"Even with the risks?" her mom asked.

"I'm not going to pretend that it doesn't get scary: it does and I have nightmares about some of the things that have happened, but..." She brought her hands up in frustration, unable to find the right words. "Look, last year... exactly a year ago, in fact, was when I finally got connected to my magic. It isn't automatic, you know. There was a lot of meditation and frankly, some soul searching. You have to know who you are before you can command magic and at first, I didn't. I guess I still don't completely, but anyway last year I was," she paused and hesitated, knowing that she was going to terrify her parents further. "I was taken by the Sídhe into the tunnels. They captured me." The faces of her parents paled as their eyes widened in delayed panic, forcing Alex to keep going before they could start asking questions or expressing their worries. "I saved a bunch of kids that night." Her eyes watered slightly and Alex took a shaky breath as she tried to get her emotions under control. "They don't remember me, but they're free and with their families, maybe even alive because of me and that feeling... it's worth it. I promise you that: it is worth it to know that I can help people. The rest of the world, well human concerns, sort of fall away."

"Shit," her dad swore after a long moment of silence. "What can we say to that?"

"This is all insane," her mom said sadly. "I mean, if you had told us that you just had magic powers that would have been exciting, but the rest of it..."

"Well, it all still seems too crazy to be real sometimes." Leaning back against the wall, Alex exhaled and felt more of the tension drain out of her. "Sometimes I just try to think of it like a story to get some perspective. What would a good character do here? What would they watch out for? I keep thinking about the different elements of great stories and worrying about what is going to happen. What's my fatal flaw going to be?" She lost herself in thought for a moment but recovered quickly. "But maybe being naïve and wanting to be the love interest of the handsome hero was my fatal flaw," Alex suggested with a small smile. "And that's behind us now."

"It's still hard to believe that Arthur was a traitor." Her dad wrapped an arm around her shoulder, giving her a quick, but comforting hug.

"He was playing everyone, but at least he didn't get the Sword and wasn't able to open all of the Iron Gates," Alex said. "Then we'd have Sídhe in both England and Oregon."

"Alex, honey, I know we can't stop you, but please…" Her mom trailed off and brought her hand to her mouth as tears gathered in her eyes.

"If I was a soldier, I'd be in danger too," Alex said. "Bran's dad was a soldier and he died in the line of duty. Jenny's mom died of cancer. Life isn't safe in general. Being the Iron Soul wouldn't protect me in a car crash unless I saw it coming like Bran did- oh god now I'm rambling like Nicki." Groaning, Alex struggled to collect her thoughts. "I promise that I will be careful. We're trying to navigate this war as smartly as we can. Merlin and Morgana are powerful, but they're a bit stuck in their ideas for spells. Nicki and Aiden aren't. We'll come up with something to protect you and we'll figure out what is happening with the Fae creatures."

"Then what?"

"We'll stop them and build more Iron Gates to keep the Sídhe out for another three thousand years," Alex said. Then she forced a grin. "And then it'll be my future reincarnation's problem."

A strange laugh escaped her mother that made Alex's stomach turn over. Stepping forward, she wrapped an arm around each of her parents as they all fell into an uncertain silence. A moment later their arms were around her and Alex could only bask in the familiar warmth. Resting her head against her dad's shoulder, Alex closed her eyes and just breathed.

15

Question of Survival

1 15 C.E. Sør-Trøndelag, Norway

The pounding of his hammer against the metal provided Thor with a focal point as he drove his frustration into the blows. On the anvil, the sword was beginning to thin to a dangerous level and part of Thor was already acknowledging that he'd likely have to redo it. His right hand glowed brightly with his pale blue magic as he pushed it into his hammer and watched it shimmer across the surface of the sword.

Everyone in the village was giving him distance and had been over the last three days since he'd used magic in public. His father had yet to say much to him, but Arvid was remaining close by as if he feared that someone might attack. The idea seemed insane to Thor: who would attack one of the people that could protect them? Someone they'd known for years and years? Still, part of him was grateful for the affection he knew the gesture represented.

"Is it wise to use your... magic like that?" Arvid asked from the doorway of the workshop, once again checking on him.

"I'm building endurance." Thor brought the hammer down once more. Sparks of magic and molten metal flew around him like a shower, but the sword was quickly cooling. With a defeated sigh, Thor thrust the sword back into the heat. "I need to practice."

"Surely Merlin and Morgana will return," Arvid said. "They took that survivor into the woods. Father believes they are questioning it."

"Maybe," Thor muttered, unable to argue with the theory. "But they might have told me what was going on rather than just leaving."

"They were probably worried you'd insist on going with them," his brother teased. "And you would have, Thor. This way you are here to protect the village and it keeps you safe."

"I'm not a child!"

"Stop trying to pick a fight," Arvid scolded. "Don't we have enough to worry about?"

Biting back a retort, Thor offered his brother a small shrug and turned back to his work. As he drew the sword out of the fire, he heard a loud sigh from behind him but did not turn around. He breathed out slowly, almost hearing Morgana's words in his head and felt his magic flowing back into his sore fingers. He tightened his grip on the hammer and felt the metal shudder in his grip. For a moment he hesitated and looking over at the hammer in mild alarm.

It was one of his larger hammers, good for the earliest steps in shaping metal and thinning it out, with a good weight and a broad head. On a whim, he'd wrapped the handle in leather with small embossing on it to mark it as a favored hammer. Nothing about the hammer looked different except for the soft shimmer of bright blue magic just beneath the surface of the metal, and yet it somehow felt a bit different. There was an odd sensation of standing on a cliff in his gut that made him uneasy. Thor eased the flow of magic through the hammer and shifted it in his grip. Suddenly he could breathe a bit easier and the air did not seem so heavy against his skin.

Shaking off the feeling, Thor turned his attention to the sword and resumed shaping the metal once more, this time being mindful of how much magic he was pushing through the hammer and the thinness he was beating the sword into. He let himself fall into the rhythm of his work and soon enough his breathing was synched with the rise and fall of his hammer. Thor repeated the steps of hammering and firing the metal a few more times without any awareness of the greater world.

"Thor," a familiar female voice called sharply, pulling him back to the real world.

Spinning around and instantly forgetting about his work, Thor turned and sighed in relief at the sight of Morgana standing calmly outside of his workshop. She looked a bit worn down, but otherwise unharmed. He shifted quickly, feeling embarrassed at the sudden surge of relief that he felt at the sight of her.

"Morgana," he breathed as he tried to recover himself. "Where have you been? What happened?"

"We were questioning the captive Síd."

"For three days?" Thor slammed his hammer down on the workbench, which shuddered for a moment. "I've been trying to deal with the questions about my magic on my own. Everyone is scared of me and then you both vanished-"

"I apologize, Thor." Morgana looked a bit embarrassed. "I truly am sorry. The timing was bad, but Merlin and I did need to get some answers as to what is happening. We didn't wish to put you in harm's way given how little training you have had."

"And did you?" Thor asked, not wanting to dwell on the insinuation that he was weak.

"Some, but not nearly enough," Morgana admitted. "But please come with me; we need to speak with you."

"What of the Síd- Dark Elf?"

"It still lives," Morgana said. "Merlin hopes that it can tell us more. Whatever happened to it has... altered its intelligence somewhat." She sighed and looked away from him, tightening her fingers in her cloak. "I believe it is time that you joined us."

She didn't even wait to give him time to fully process her statement or put his things away. Thor stumbled around his small workshop securing everything with an uneasy feeling churning in his stomach. As Morgana moved away from the hut to wait for him, a worried looking Arvid appeared in her place.

"Thor? What is it?"

"She wants me to go with her." Thor wrapped up his hammers and picked up a sword. "I'm not sure what's going on, but I'll be back soon." He slipped past his brother before the man could argue with him.

Morgana nodded to him, but her eyes lingered on Arvid over his shoulder for a moment before she turned and led him to the gates of the village. Following Morgana up into the trees, Thor kept his sword clutched tightly in his hand as his eyes scanned the forest. It was dark and the long shadows provided too much cover and opportunity for an attack for him to relax. Morgana was stern and silent in front of him, walking quickly with single-minded determination.

The sound of something moving up in the trees made Thor look up quickly, only to find two ravens perched above them. Both of the birds were on thick branches and watching them carefully. Pausing for a moment, Thor studied the birds with a small frown and a nagging suspicion at the back of his mind. For a moment he considered drawing Morgana's attention to them but decided against it. He had the feeling that Morgana didn't recognize the same gods as he did... if she recognized any gods at all.

Still, he had the distinct feeling they were being followed and heard wings flutter every few minutes overhead. Morgana remained focused on the small game trail they were following, but after a time Thor became aware of how still the forest was. He could hear the bubbling of the various tiny streams that carried the thaw back to the ocean, but beyond the ravens, he didn't detect any other creatures here. Just as this realization was settling uncomfortably in his stomach they came to a small clearing where what looked like a tiny hill was created.

It took Thor a moment to realize that the small hill was actually some sort of earthen shelter. The strange little shelter was like a cave in the middle of the wood with large chunks of earth having been heaved up together to create the small structure. Around the base bits of plant life were still trying to hold on and grow while higher up the uprooted plants were beginning to wilt. Thor stared at it in alarm, wondering for a moment who had built the thing and how before the answer of Merlin or Morgana hit him.

"The creature is inside." Morgana gestured for him to enter and turned to look around with an uneasy expression. Thor studied her for a moment, noting the tightness of her features and the way her eyes were moving about the forest. She'd noticed more than he'd known. "Come along," she told him after a moment as she turned and swept into the small shelter.

Thor hesitated for a moment, uncertain of the small cave-like structure, but the flapping of wings behind him sent a shiver up his spine. Gritting his teeth, he bent down a few inches and stepped into the small shelter. The first thing he noticed was that it was completely bare. There were no bedrolls, no food, and nothing that indicated how Morgana and Merlin had been looking out for themselves.

A low snarl pulled his attention to why he was here, and he swallowed thickly as his eyes settled on it. A column of earth rose up from the middle of the small space to the roof. The Síd was bound to the earth by a long length of chain that gave it only enough slack to slump forward. Merlin was standing to the right of the door with a dark expression as he calmly observed the creature. Lingering in the doorway, Thor noted the way the creature was keeping its eyes downcast, and its skin seemed to have even more of the odd black marks tracing up its face and arms.

"Anything new?" Morgana asked Merlin as she moved further into the shelter towards the Síd.

"Nothing," Merlin sighed. "Everything is the same as when you left."

"I don't understand," Thor spoke up. "What do you mean by that?"

"It keeps changing," Morgana explained darkly. She bent over to get a better look at the Síd's face. "I'm not sure exactly what is happening, but as they enter our world they are being magically altered and it just keeps going." She straightened up and shook her head. "During the other night, they completely snuck up on the village. They aren't using even low lights now; I fear that they might be able to see in the dark."

"We need to be prepared for further changes," Merlin said thoughtfully. "Sadly, I am uncertain of what those changes might be."

Thor glanced towards Merlin, resisting the urge to point out that his statement wasn't helpful. How could you be prepared for the unknown? Instead, he focused his attention on the creature before him. The sound of footfalls outside and a branch snapping made them all jump. Thor spun towards the entrance and looked out the small, rounded doorway. There was a figure at the edge of the glen in the shadows of the trees dressed in a long, worn cloak.

"Who is that?" Thor looked towards Merlin and Morgana. "Friend of yours?"

Merlin moved outside first, looking towards the prisoner one more time and gesturing for Morgana to wait. She paused and narrowed her eyes at the distant figure as it took a careful step into the light before she followed Merlin outside. It took another step towards them and raised its head just enough to reveal a flash of its face to the older mages. Morgana made a sharp move towards their visitor, but Merlin gripped her arm to stop her. Green magic flickered around his free hand and the expression on Merlin's features was unlike any that Thor had yet seen on the friendly man's face. He was eyeing their visitor with a look of intense distrust, but also serious consideration.

There was a silent moment in the small glen, and Thor studied the hooded figure uncertainly. Then it pulled back its hood and his eyes widened in surprise. The being bore a striking resemblance to the sickly creature still bound up in Merlin's chains, with pale translucent skin and violet eyes. Small horns curled out of its forehead, but they were only nubs compared to the longer horns he'd seen on the attackers. Its eyes landed on him for a moment before it took a step to the side so it could see the bound Síd through the doorway. A strange expression appeared on its face that mixed curiosity and revulsion.

"Why are you here Síd?" Merlin questioned in an icy tone.

"I mean you no harm this day, Mages of the Iron Realm," the Síd answered with a slight incline of its head. Thor was uncertain if it was male or female. "We all face a threat from these creatures," it added with a gesture towards the bound creature. "Over the last few weeks many of these... tainted ones have attacked our nearby colony."

"When did you come to these shores?" Morgana asked with a twitch in her jaw.

"Two generations ago. Our ancestors, trapped warriors from Sídhean, came here to establish a new colony," the Síd answered calmly, though

Thor thought he detected a hint of nervousness. "We avoid the humans of the realm and keep to ourselves, though some have come across us in the past."

"That explains the elves," Morgana muttered.

The Síd to nodded in agreement. "Yes; that is the name the people in this region have given us." The Síd paused and glanced between Merlin and Morgana. "I understand that there is bad blood between your people and mine-"

"Bad blood!" Morgana snapped. "Your people invaded this realm. You're only here because your ancestors were sealed on this side of the Iron Gates."

"Yes, my ancestors." The Síd's whole body stiffened. "I nor any of my conclave have ever been beyond the Iron Realm, much less to Sídhean. We were born in the Iron Realm."

"That doesn't make you part of this world," Morgana retorted, but Thor thought her voice had softened a bit.

"What would you have us do?" The Síd met Morgana's green ones with its violet ones squarely. "You may not like us being here," the Síd said. "But we are here, and all of us have a problem in these new tainted Sídhe."

"Do you know anything about them?" Merlin asked, still standing next to the prisoner who was growling softly.

"Yes; we were attacked a month ago, and at first, we feared that some disease had gripped our people, but a count after the first attack revealed that none of us were missing. Messengers to other communities revealed that no plague had infected the others, but they did discover that new tunnels have been constructed."

"Tunnels?" Merlin repeated. "There is more than one?"

"Indeed." There was a flicker of relief in the Síd's eyes at having Morgana and Merlin's curious rather than violent attention. "The one in the mountains near here is the largest, but we have discovered two others in the general area. There are also signs of attempted tunnels, but they were unsuccessful for some reason."

Overhead a pair of ravens cawed and landed on nearby branches. Thor looked up at them uneasily as his stomach churned. Something in the air tasted different, like right before a storm. Shaking his head, he focused on their visitor, who was fighting to stay still under the heavy gazes of Merlin and Morgana.

"We haven't been able to learn much," the Síd continued. "A few of our people braved the tunnels, but there is a clear magical threshold that we dare not cross."

"That would be the power of the Iron Gates," Merlin murmured to Morgana.

"Indeed, when they... push through the threshold, something happens to them. One of ours saw a group being pushed through."

"Pushed through?" Merlin asked.

"Yes, these aren't soldiers any longer." The Síd gestured towards the bound one. "Some are provided with armor, but they seem to be criminals."

"Lovely," Morgana said. "Our world is a dumping ground for criminals once again."

"They transform into these... beasts. We are unsure how intelligent they truly are, but they seem driven to destroy."

"Indeed," a new, deep male voice declared from the trees, making all four of them turn suddenly. "We have observed as much."

There were two cloaked figures standing only a few feet away from them. Thor's throat tightened up in alarm at how they came so close.

Morgana shifted her position and stood directly in front of him and the doorway. Huffing in irritation, Thor pushed out around her and stepped outside of the shelter with his fingers tightly gripping his sword.

Thor eyed the two cloaked figures with a tight frown of confusion. Something about them sent tiny shocks of magic running up his arms, and he could feel goosebumps forming beneath the sleeves of his tunic. It wasn't unpleasant and he peered curiously at the slighter figure which had a long plait of golden hair falling out from beneath its hood.

"Greetings," the larger figure cloaked in gray said, breaking the silence. Then he stepped forward and raised his face towards them letting them see under his broad gray hat.

He was a larger man with long gray hair neatly styled in a series of braids. His left eyelid drooped and Thor gasped softly as the significance of that detail struck him. On instinct, he began to bend his knee only for Morgana to catch his arm tightly and hold him in place.

"We do not bow to those from other realms," she growled. Morgana straightened up and made herself taller. "I can tell what you are." Morgana eyed the pair with a frown. "Old Ones, but we do not know you."

Thor looked at her in mild confusion and did his best to keep his face neutral. He was tempted to speak, but as the man looked at him the words died in his throat. His companion's face was still turned down and hidden.

"I am Odin," the figure said. He gave them a slight smile.

"Ah," Merlin replied with a hint of disapproval. "You're the local 'god' are you not?"

"One of the beings that the locals turn to," Odin agreed carefully, meeting Merlin's gaze evenly. "What they chose to believe is their own affair. Me and mine were born in this world, though my father originated from another."

"And you're aware of the situation with the Sídhe?" Morgana pressed, her eyes shifting between Odin and the Síd.

"Huginn and Muninn have been watching over the area," Odin explained with a smile just before the two ravens that Thor had seen earlier swooped out of the trees to land on either of Odin's shoulders. The smile fell away and Odin breathed out slowly. "It would seem, Mages of the Iron Realm, that we all share a problem."

16

Third Date Unlucky

Central Diner wasn't as simple as coffee or the school food court for a date, but it had the benefit of still being a popular hangout on Friday nights. Jenny had been here often enough that it didn't feel awkward. The checkered black and white floors were slick from tracked in snow and frequent mopping by the staff. Rowdy groups of students had slung their coats and scarves over almost any available surface other than the tables and long main counter. TVs were on around the dining area with various sporting events playing, and groups of students were watching with craned necks.

Jenny toyed with the straw of her iced tea and tried not to feel nervous as she waited for Lance to return to the table. He'd been caught by another member of the football team, and judging from the tight expression on his face the conversation was about Arthur. A soft sigh escaped her right before the other player looked over towards her with a sour look. Jenny did her best to ignore him and not grimace, but she understood how this would look to Arthur's old teammates. He suddenly leaves Ravenslake despite already holding a strong position on the team and his ex-girlfriend is quickly seen dating his friend and teammate Lance. It wasn't hard to put the pieces together, and it was horribly close to the truth.

Determined to ignore him, Jenny pulled out her phone and checked through her text messages. Lately, the texts from her fellow spirit squad members and old high school friends were becoming rarer and rarer. Things had changed; she'd changed somehow in a way she didn't completely understand yet, and she couldn't find it in herself to blame them for drifting away. Over the last year she hadn't been the best company, and in all honesty, she still wasn't.

Yet she had to smile at the latest text from Alex, which was a simple "have fun on the date" with a smiley face. Nicki had sent her a reminder that everyone was getting together for training at Morgana's house in the morning and to let her know if she wanted a ride. There was another text from Bran to schedule when they could work on her latest journalism project that she'd decided to do on Korean American culture in the Northwest. There weren't many other messages and she took a moment to delete some of the older ones.

"Sorry about that." Lance slid back into the booth across from her with a soft smile. "Ryan can be a little hard to escape from sometimes."

"Plus, he didn't like the company you were keeping." Giving him a knowing look, Jenny slipped her phone back into her purse.

"Ignore them," Lance said. Reaching out, he took her hand and gave it a soft squeeze before releasing it. "It doesn't matter, Jenny. They don't know what was going on."

"But they've got a point: we were cheating. I was cheating on Arthur and he was your friend."

"He was also using us as part of a charade." Lance's tone was cautious and a little too affectionate for Jenny's mental state. "He's even admitted to using magic on you. There's nothing to feel guilty about."

"Don't you worry I'll cheat on you?" Jenny asked, avoiding Lance's eyes as she spoke. "I mean, a cheater is always a cheater."

"Honestly, I haven't even been sure if you consider us dating," Lance said with a frown. "But if we are officially dating, then no, I don't worry about you cheating."

Fighting back a blush, Jenny wasn't sure what to say in response to that. For a moment they just sat there in silence with downcast eyes until the waitress brought their food. She picked up a fry and tried to get excited before she gave up and sighed.

"I do consider us dating, Lance." Jenny gave him a nervous smile. "I guess it's time we tried talking about all of this, huh?"

"Yeah, we do just fine when we keep it to classes, music, and even current events, but the elephant in the room is demanding some attention." He paused and took a deep breath. "I get why you feel some guilt and concern, Jenny, I do. What happened on the surface with Arthur was wrong on both our parts; we lied to someone that we cared about and that we thought cared about us, but I just don't see the point in staying angry at ourselves. In the end, I'm just focusing on being grateful that we've got a real chance this time around. Arthur wasn't really the Iron Soul and he was a creep that almost killed Alex and Aiden."

"But-"

"Look, this time around the Iron Soul is Alex, and while I like her and hope we become good friends in the future, it's different with her. Besides, you don't seem to have romantic feelings towards her and she doesn't have any towards you, so we're in the clear there."

"I know." Jenny groaned and shook her head. She struggled to find words for what she wanted to say, but nothing sounded or felt right. "I guess it's just going to be a process. Knowing that even when manipulated I am a cheater... it's just not something I like about myself."

Lance reached over and caught her left hand with his right hand. He said nothing as he used his left hand to awkwardly pour ketchup on his burger and sent it dribbling over the sides. Smiling softly, Jenny held back a giggle but didn't release his hand.

"It's up to you, but maybe it would be best if we helped things along with a story of some kind," Lance said. "Something to explain why Arthur suddenly ditched."

"Like what? Everyone loved him," Jenny muttered tightly. "He was handsome, smart, and charismatic: he even fooled the professors."

"I know, and that still freaks me out," Lance agreed. "But people don't always believe in seemingly perfect people. I bet if we were to say that Arthur was abusive plenty of people would believe it."

"Lance that's not really true," Jenny argued weakly, glancing around to make sure that no one was paying attention to them.

"Yes, it is and he was, though maybe not physically... well, not until he tried to kill Alex, but he manipulated everyone around him. Abuse isn't just about hitting someone. I don't know if it's the result of his mother or the Queen or whatever is going on there, but he's a psychopath: a monster."

"That I slept with," Jenny reminded him. Her stomach turned and her fish tenders looked a lot less appetizing. "As did Alex."

Lance grimaced and glanced down uncomfortably, but he took a deep breath and looked up at her. His brown eyes locked onto hers and Jenny felt a flutter in her chest at the warmth and determination in them. There was anger, but she knew it wasn't directed at her.

"Let's not talk about Arthur," Jenny said. "We can't just focus on that ugly part of our lives." She paused and tossed her hair over her shoulder. "Let's be honest, this is almost our first date; it's the first time we've ever gone off campus together."

"Right. Are you going up with the others tomorrow?"

"I promised Alex that I'd help however I could, even if it means reading through mythology books while they practice magic."

"Aren't you interested in watching?" Lance asked.

"I've seen them fight."

"Yeah, but they can do other stuff too." Lance gave her an excited grin. "I'm looking forward to seeing something other than fireballs, ice shards, and lightning bolts."

"I don't know..." Jenny hesitated, once again toying with her straw. "It's all still so strange. Some days I have a hard time even trying to wrap my head around all of it."

They fell silent and Jenny focused her attention on eating some of her food. It was tasty but somehow muted. Around them, the sounds of other people having fun and rapid conversations seemed to weigh down on her shoulders.

"Still awkward, isn't it?" Lance asked in a defeated tone that made Jenny look up in mild alarm. There was a sad and resigned look on his face that made her feel like someone was squeezing her heart. "It's okay, Jenny."

"Yeah, it is still a little awkward," she admitted softly.

"I feel like I have to ask would you even be here if we weren't..." He gestured between them uneasily. "Reincarnations?"

"It wouldn't be this awkward if we weren't reincarnations." Jenny forced a small smile and prayed that she didn't look scared and panicked. "But I really do want to try to work through the awkwardness," Jenny assured Lance.

His expression eased at the look of determination that must have been on her face. Lance nodded and a small sigh of relief escaped him. "I'll be honest, after Wales and that... funeral, I was a bit overwhelmed," Lance said. "I got some books about reincarnation. Most of it really seems to be junk though, more like the theory and how to connect with your previous lives."

"I talked with Bran a bit about reincarnation." Jenny cast her eyes around to make sure no one was listening. "It helped a little, even if it was weird." She shrugged and smiled. "He's pretty smart about that stuff."

"Well, if you think about it and his powers... I mean, he's got a lot of traditionally psychic sort of powers, so I'd guess that indicates that he's more spiritual than the others."

"I wonder if that is really how it works?" Tapping her fingers against the table, Jenny pursed her lips together in consideration. "Seems a bit cliché."

A warm laugh escaped Lance and she looked back to him, raising an eyebrow. "Cliché? Really, Jenny?" He just grinned at her and shook his head as he picked up the uneaten half of his burger. "We're juggling clichés, story tropes, ancient legends, and new shit that doesn't seem to make any sense. Should we really discount anything?"

"Fair point. Okay, we've gone a little off topic." She took a deep breath and gave her body a small shake. "I'm sorry if I'm seeming a bit... flighty. I do want us to try. I think we can make this work."

The smile he gave her made the awkwardness all worth it, and Jenny had to fight back a blush and a grin of her own. They kept eating their dinners, but the atmosphere of Central Diner didn't seem to be mocking their issues now. After a few bites of her own dinner, Jenny turned the conversation to broader topics, interested in learning more about her boyfriend beyond his previous life as Lancelot or whatever his name had been.

By the time they finished their meals their voices had reached the same loud level of the rest of the college students. Jenny couldn't help but notice a hint of nervousness still shining in Lance's eyes, but she guessed that it was mirrored in her own. Central Diner was becoming more crowded with every passing moment, and when Lance picked up their bill Jenny had to wonder if they'd surpassed capacity. Lance had only taken a few steps away from the table as Jenny checked her phone and grabbed her coat when an angry voice could be heard.

"Seriously, Lance, what is going on with you and her?" she heard someone ask. Her spine instantly straightened in response. Jenny kept herself from looking towards Lance and finding the speaker, but it was difficult. "Have you even heard from Arthur?"

"Look, Pete, trust me on this one: Arthur was a nasty piece of work," Lance's voice cut through the noise of the Diner, which seemed to quiet in response. "In fact, if you hear from him for any reason do yourself a favor and hang up and let me know."

"Lance, what the hell-"

"I'll see you later man," Lance said. "We're finished and have a movie to catch."

Jenny could feel eyes on her as she pulled on her coat and moved towards the door. Lance paid their bill quickly and rushed to join her, dismissing a couple of his teammates with a quick wave. As she began to open the door, Lance put his arm around her shoulders and pushed the door open for her. The cold night air hit them both and Lance let out of long sigh of frustration before shaking his head. Jenny offered him a small smile and they began to head down the street towards Lance's truck.

"One sec." Lance shifted around to her other side. "Let me walk on the street side."

"A gentleman." Smiling up at him, Jenny embraced the little bubble of happiness rising in her chest. "Very nice."

"My dad was always pretty serious about manners." Lance's smile made his own happiness at her reaction obvious. "Hope you don't mind."

"Mind? Why would I mind?"

"Well... some girls don't like it; I guess they think it means I think they're weak," Lance explained in a slight rush, looking a bit uneasy.

Reaching over, Jenny wrapped her arm around his and offered him a warm smile, ignoring the fact that neither of them were looking where they were going. "I don't think that's the case; it's just you trying to be courteous," she assured him. "Now, you try to order me around then we'll have to talk."

"You're the former queen," Lance teased. "I know who will be wearing the pants."

"And don't forget it." Jenny giggled. Then she looked around in mild surprise. "Did we just joke about our own reincarnations?"

"Yes, yes I think we did."

Grinning up at him, Jenny ignored the sidewalk for a moment so she could stretch up and kiss his jaw. Even in her heels, he was just a little too tall for her to easily kiss. The peaceful haze was broken as strange, echoing giggles rolled down the street, and Jenny felt her whole body freeze in recognition. Lance's hand tightened around hers for a moment before he released it and he slipped his hand back under his coat. Swallowing, Jenny glanced around at the other humans who were calmly walking down the street with their friends or chatting on cellphones.

"That sounds like fairies," she whispered. "Do you think they'll attack us out here in the open?"

Other people were stopping and looking around in confusion. One person was pointing to a speaker hooked up on the lamppost as if that was the answer, and Jenny felt herself internally scoff. Her hand shifted into her purse and searched for the smooth cool leather of her dagger's sheath.

"Should we move?" Jenny looked into the nearby alley. The bulb above the back door of the shop was flickering and she could see tiny violet eyes peering out at them. "Will they come into the street?"

"I don't know." Lance sounded just as uneasy as her. Then he took her hand and began to tug her towards his truck. "I think we should move; these things... they seem to attack when they'll be unseen."

"They attacked at Stonehenge." Jenny tightened her grip on both his hand and the handle of her dagger. She wished for a third hand so she could text the mages. "They might here too."

"I think Stonehenge was special." Lance fished out his keys. "Let's not stay to find out."

"But they might attack the other humans!" There was a sinking feeling in the pit of her stomach. "We aren't mages and they seem to be after us."

"Maybe it's Arthur," Lance growled as his eyes darkened. "Trying to get at Alex through us."

"Yeah," Jenny heard herself say. "That would fit him."

"Keep your dagger ready," Lance ordered as he unlocked the passenger side door. "And get inside."

Biting back a retort, Jenny clamored up into the passenger seat and drew her dagger out of her purse. She wrapped her fingers tightly around the handle and rested the dagger on her lap. Somehow the streets were clearing as people moved into the buildings as if compelled by some kind of instinct. In the alleys and spaces between the buildings and along the rooftops the shadows seemed to be shimmering and moving. More tiny violet eyes appeared in the shadows and Jenny's breath caught in her throat.

"Lance!" Knocking on the window frantically, she tried to alert him to the danger. "Lance!"

Thankfully he nodded and began moving around the truck. Jenny kept her gaze sweeping over the collection of eyes, trying to count the pairs. There were at least ten and she could feel her heart pounding hard in her chest. Then the driver's side door opened and Lance climbed in with a huff. He started up the car just as a loud shriek echoed outside. Jenny turned sharply to look out and gasped as something lunged for her window. They roared away from the sidewalk as something struck the side of the truck.

"Okay, bad fairies in Ravenslake!" Lance's hands gripped the steering wheel and he glanced between the window and the road. "Any idea how many?"

"At least ten!" Jenny dug out her phone with shaking hands. "I'm texting the others!"

Something landed in the truck bed making Jenny look over her shoulder. A small, twisted creature with a dingy red cap on its head with long talons snarled at her. As her eyes widened, the creature leapt forward and began to claw at the back cab window.

"Jenny?!"

She grimaced at the terrible sound of the talons against the window. "Keep driving!" Forcing her eyes off the creature, Jenny sent a text to Alex.

The cars around them didn't seem to notice anything, though one person did slow down as another Redcap jumped into the back of the truck and joined the other one in attacking the back window. Jenny saw the campus flashing by in the corner of her eye. She saw the dorms and briefly considered parking and making a run for it, but she dismissed it.

"Head north!" Jenny turned and pointed towards the bridge. "If we can get them to Morgana's then she can help us."

"What about Merlin? I think he's less likely to blast us."

"Not funny," Jenny muttered. "Morgana's house is further out of town."

"Have you been there?"

"No," Jenny admitted. "But it's a Victorian up on one of the side roads."

"That doesn't help much," Lance grumbled, but nonetheless he kept driving as they both ignored the screeching sounds from the Redcaps. Next to Jenny, the glass began to chip and crack.

Her phone chirped and Jenny looked down at the phone. Alex's text was short but included instructions to Morgana's and a promise to be there soon. Despite her dry mouth, Jenny relayed the directions just before a metallic scraping filled the cabin. Lance's jaw tightened, but he just shook his head and turned the wheel sharply. A strange little scream reached Jenny as they spun onto the side road.

The truck accelerated as they raced up into the hills and Jenny looked back at the truck bed. Somehow, they'd gained another two Redcaps who were now trying to swing down onto the sides. The tires, she realized as her heart jumped: they were going for the tires. She looked frantically through the windshield. Up ahead she could see the lights of a house and desperately hoped that it was the right one. The truck jolted and a gasp escaped Jenny. She heard Lance curse under his breath as the truck began to bounce. They jolted again and the bouncing was worse than before. A deep grinding began echoing up through the truck and Jenny didn't dare look at Lance.

It was a Victorian and lights were turning on as they slid on the gravel. The screaming became louder and a Redcap swung over to her side and slammed its body up against the window. Silver light burst out from the porch of the house, blinding Jenny as the truck slammed to a stop. A chorus of screams erupted all around them. Bringing her hands up to cover her ears, Jenny kept a tight grip on her dagger and felt the cool of the blade against her cheek. There was another explosion of light and then everything fell silent. She heard Lance exhale and opened her eyes. Looking up at the house, Jenny's jaw tightened as she found Morgana standing on the front porch, glaring into the darkness.

17

Dark Phone Calls

The rays of the sunrise glinting off of the snow promised a lovely day, but Alex couldn't help but feel tense and frustrated as she turned onto Morgana's road. On the road, she could see tracks where Lance and Jenny must have been driving last night. Alex muttered a curse towards Arthur and his mother under her breath. It didn't help much.

What did help was the sight of Morgana's house and Lance's intact truck parked in front of it. As she pulled her car up next to it, Alex noted that whatever damage that had been inflicted on it had already been fixed. The bodywork was smooth and the paint was shining in the sun like it had just been washed and waxed. A small smile tugged at her lips, but Alex shook herself and reached back to grab the bag in her backseat.

The front door opened as she approached and Morgana stood calmly in the entryway waiting for her. Bounding up the stairs, Alex smiled at the professor who shifted back to let her into the house. She set the bag down for a moment and shrugged out of her coat. Morgana collected it from her and hung it up on one of the hooks without a word. Looking into the living room, Alex breathed out a sigh of relief as she spotted Jenny and Lance seated next to each other on the sofa. They were talking with Merlin and drinking tea with tired but real smiles on their faces. Their clothes were rumpled from their night here, but they were okay.

"They're fine," Morgana's voice assured her. "However, I suspect that they'd like their things."

"Uh, I have some of Jenny's stuff." Alex held up the small bag she was carrying. "Bran said he'd swing by Lance's room."

"Does he have a key?"

"No, but he was pretty confident that he could get the door open."

"Those are keycard locks," Morgana reminded her with a small frown. "Unless he plans to fry the circuits, I doubt he has enough control-"

"Or just use telekinesis to turn the handle from the inside," Alex interrupted. She enjoyed the odd look that crossed Morgana's face and the tiny shadow of a blush on the older mage's cheeks. "Thanks for protecting them last night," Alex added gratefully.

"It was no problem." The corner of Morgana's mouth ticked up in a small smile. "Let's just not make a habit of it."

"Don't like your house being the slumber party center?"

"If we're going that direction then I need to redo a couple of the rooms," Morgana said dryly. "I only have one guest bedroom set up."

"Yeah; given that you've had me here a couple times, my parents, the mages, and now Lance and Jenny it may be time to look at turning the sewing room into another bedroom."

"I suppose so. I haven't had the time since magic returned anyway." Morgana paused and nodded towards the living room. "I take it that Nicki and Aiden will be by soon?"

"They wanted to check around town quickly just to make sure that there weren't more," Alex explained. "They're together."

"Very well." Morgana raised her hand and looked at the small watch on her wrist. "I'm going to check around the house so please stay inside."

Holding back a remark about Morgana's paranoia, Alex instead nodded and walked into the living room. Merlin, Lance, and Jenny all looked at her and Jenny's eyes moved down to the bag. She gave Alex a grateful smile as she set the bag down by the doorway.

"No problems with my roommate?"

"She was fine." Alex sat on the armrest of the sofa next to Jenny. "How are you two doing?"

"Alright," Jenny assured her with a smile. "They never touched us."

"Just tore the hell out of my truck," Lance said. Shaking his head, he couldn't hold back a smile. "But Merlin repaired it all when he got here."

"Glad to help." Merlin nodded pleasantly, but he still looked a bit uneasy. "If you'll excuse me, I need to retrieve something from my car."

The eldest of the mages quickly stood, giving a small smile to Alex, and a nod to Jenny and Lance. Alex watched him head out while trying to convince herself that he wasn't running away. Sadly, her attempt at that only made her chuckle softly.

"He still doesn't like us, does he?" Lance sighed as he slumped back against the couch, moving his arm over to Jenny's shoulder.

"Merlin's still got some previous incarnation issues," Alex admitted. Stretching out, she leaned over the back of the couch. "Despite his bright-eyed and optimistic nature; well, all things considered anyway," Alex amended. "I don't think he knows what to make of you yet. It still sort of throws him off that this time around we're functioning as friends."

"And our behaving exactly as he expected didn't help matters," Lance groaned. "I get it; hate it, but get it."

"Give it time, Lance." Jenny leaned against his chest, resting her head beneath his chin. "We're all still trying to figure it out." She paused and looked towards the bag by the doorway and grinned. "Now if you excuse me, I'm going to take a shower and get into some clean clothes."

Jenny jumped up, forcing Alex and Lance to shift to give her room and scooped up the bag with a spring in her step. She vanished down the hall towards where Alex knew the downstairs bathroom to be, leaving Alex and Lance alone.

"So other than the Redcaps, how was the date?" Alex asked.

It earned her a sideways incredulous look from Lance. He stared at her for a moment as he tried to process if she was really serious. Finally, his lips curved into a smile and he chuckled.

"Actually, it was going pretty well," he said. "And the Redcap attack meant that we spent last night huddling together while Morgana prowled around outside."

"Prowled?"

"Watch her and tell me that she doesn't remind you of a puma."

"You're strange, Lance!" Alex laughed even as she considered the comparison. "But not completely wrong."

Outside a car door slammed, drawing Alex's attention towards the window. Jumping up, she crossed over to it and drew back the curtain. Her whole body relaxed as she spotted Bran out by his car with a bag. Merlin was standing next to him with a much more relaxed smile. Bran nodded at something the older man said before gesturing towards the house. As Bran began strolling over to the house, his cane not in sight, Alex moved away from the window. Opening the front door, Alex smiled in greeting to Bran and stepped to the side to let him into the house.

"Morning, Alex," Bran greeted with a nod, leaning over and giving her a quick one-armed hug. He grinned and headed into the living room with Alex following along behind him. "Special delivery for Mister Taylor."

"Hey, Bran," Lance greeted with a grin, catching the other boy's arm for a moment. "Thanks for getting my stuff."

"No problem." Bran handed over the bag with a shrug. "I still can't believe that you haven't got a roommate and I'm stuck with Aiden."

"He bailed at Christmas," Lance explained. "And don't whine about Aiden. I've been over enough to know that's bullshit."

The ringing of her phone pulled Alex out of the conversation as she battled down a hint of jealousy that was contrasted against relief that they got along so well. Looking down at her phone, Alex barely kept in the short gasp that threatened to escape her. Instead, she tried to look completely calm and normal as she slipped out of the kitchen's back door. The chill outside hit her only for a moment as she brought the phone up to her ear, and her anger overpowered everything else.

"Arthur," she greeted with a growl.

"Alex," the smooth, deep voice of her ex-boyfriend/cousin in an earlier life/would be murderer greeted. "How are things?"

"A bit chilly to be honest." Alex focused her gaze on the empty bird feeder hanging on one of the trees in the backyard. "How about you? What are you up to?"

"Oh, the usual; sending my minions after people you care about. I'll be honest, even I'm a bit surprised how quickly some of them have made it to Ravenslake. Maybe all that magic calls them in like a siren song."

"What do you want, Arthur?"

"Many things, Alex; Cathanáil for one and dominion over the Tree of Reality for two."

"Going the classic villain approach then huh?" Alex mocked. "Seriously, take over the world?"

"Not just the world, all of the worlds, Alex. The Sídhe conquered an entire branch and it was the Iron Realm that stopped their army. I think I can do better."

"Not going to happen, Arthur, and if you're done, I've got things to do. Any chance you could lose my number?"

"Aren't you supposed to be worrying about redeeming me about now?" Arthur asked. In her mind's eye, Alex could imagine him just spinning in a chair with a smirk. "That is how the stories go at this point right? I'm afraid I'll have to defer to your expertise."

"That's not how this story goes, Arthur." Alex couldn't keep her voice even. "I'm not such a fool as to believe that you'll change. You enjoy this too much."

"Harsh, darling," Arthur chided in a mockery of disappointment. "I thought you were supposed to be the good guy."

"I mean it, Arthur: there may be moments where I wonder if you're this way because of how the Queen raised you and there may be moments that I feel something akin to pity for you, but you had a choice. You could have gone to Merlin or Morgana for help, but you didn't. You didn't have to stab me and try to take the Sword, but you did."

"Old habits die hard. I killed you once and just couldn't resist doing it again." His nonchalant answer made Alex's insides crawl. "I blame it all on my reincarnation. Surely you understand that it can be a bit overwhelming."

"You used someone who loved you," Alex reminded him. "As nothing more than a pawn in a chess game to fool Merlin and Morgana. Don't pretend that it was anything other than a choice."

"Ah come on, darling, we both know that Jenny was meant to be with Lance. I led her to him. Honestly, she should be thanking me for that. Well, that and years of great sex."

"You're a pig."

"You didn't deny it though," Arthur countered in the sweet, teasing tone that she'd once found attractive.

Now her stomach just felt ready to turn on her. She gripped at the railing of the back porch. Alex moved the phone away from her mouth so she could take a long, deep breath. She could feel anger clawing at her chest. If she thought her magic could bring Arthur here so she could punch him and maybe slash his eyes out with her dagger she would have used it.

"Arthur, when I think about you all I can see is you smirking at me as you took more of my blood," Alex admitted around grit teeth. "I will never forgive you for what you did. For what you almost did."

"Ah yes, the blood." Arthur chuckled, ignoring her anger. "I'll admit that it hasn't been as useful as I hoped without Cathanáil. Aiden really threw a wrench in the original plans, but I think we've recovered fairly well."

"So, are you going for cliché villainy here?"

"Cliché is such a negative word," Arthur said. "But I think we've done the witty banter enough. We have so much else to discuss."

"I don't know where Cathanáil is," Alex said. Sadly, that was the honest truth. "Stop fishing."

"Actually, that means it is time to start fishing," Arthur countered. "There's a lot of water in the world and it could be anywhere."

"Well, that's more of a problem for you than it is for me. After all, I'm not looking to open the gates."

"True, but that gate won't hold forever, and sooner or later they will break through somewhere else... who knows, maybe Spokane. Imagine the damage they could do there." Arthur paused as Alex absorbed the threat against her parents and younger brother. "Of course, before something like that happens, I suppose I could just have the fairies stop playing hide and seek with the world. Imagine the chaos when bedtime stories suddenly spring to life."

Alex frowned at the words, wondering why Arthur and the Queen hadn't already done just that. Her gut instinct was that whatever they were using to control the other Fae creatures didn't allow for perfect control: at least not like that. Maybe the survival instinct of the Fae against being seen was too strong, or maybe there was some other kind of magic on them.

"So how are you doing this anyway?" Alex asked, deciding to take a chance. "It's a pretty serious spell to send all the Faery creatures after us."

"There are things that even Merlin and Morgana don't know about," Arthur told her smugly. "Honestly, do you think I'm going to start monologuing, Alex?"

"You're the one who keeps calling your ex! Getting a little lonely with only your mother for company, are we?"

"Well, look who's gaining confidence!" Arthur laughed like she'd said a joke. "I remember when you were just the love interest."

Tightening her fingers on the phone, Alex grit her teeth as her stomach churned uncomfortably in a blend of rage, embarrassment, and far more hurt than she ever wanted to admit. She didn't trust herself to speak but hated the silence that was meeting Arthur's last statement. He chuckled on the other end of the phone and Alex wondered once again just what Arthur thought he was getting out of these calls.

"Things change," Alex wished that she had something more impressive to say in response.

"I understand that dear Jenny and Lance were attacked last night. On a date no less; really, Alex, do you feel nothing when you think about them together? Isn't there a tiny spark of rage when you envision them together?"

"No," Alex told him firmly, glad that the truth helped her voice ring stronger. "I don't, Arthur. I'm not a victim of my previous lives."

"Careful, dearest," Arthur replied in a far too confident voice. "You might just learn something that makes you doubt that. Three thousand years is a very, very long time, and there is nothing innately good about humanity."

"Arthur!" a distant voice shrieked, cutting into Alex's confused thoughts and preventing her from speaking. "Who are you talking to?"

The call suddenly ended and Alex looked at her phone in consideration. It had sounded like the Queen didn't know that Arthur was calling her. She nibbled at her lip in thought, wondering if there might be dissent among the ranks. It only distracted her for a moment from Arthur's cryptic words. Chewing at her bottom lip, Alex stared at the phone and considered calling him back, but she couldn't bring herself to do so.

"Alex?" Morgana suddenly appeared around the corner of the house dressed in her dark blue long coat. "What is it?" She strode forward with her feet crunching the snow and her eyes scanning the house.

"Arthur called."

"You shouldn't talk to him," Morgana said in a low urgent voice. "He can't be trusted, Alex. Remember that you don't feel-"

"Don't," Alex snapped. "It isn't that, Morgana... don't worry. I don't love him. Not anymore." She took a deep breath and closed her eyes for a moment. "I don't know... there's just something... I'm not sure what it is. Something that keeps tugging me towards him."

"That isn't reassuring."

"I know it isn't love or attraction or anything like that," Alex assured the professor quickly even as her stomach tied itself into a knot. "But Arthur... there's still so much we don't understand about how he even exists; why he had a Connection with me." She paused and nibbled at her own lip in thought. "Maybe it is related to that."

Morgana just looked at her with those sharp green eyes. Sometimes Alex thought that maybe she understood what was going on behind them, but today she had no idea. Strangely her body seemed to ache just from talking to Arthur and she felt exhausted despite it still being the morning. The expression on Morgana's face softened and she placed her hand on Alex's shoulder with a sad sigh.

"Come back inside," Morgana pleaded, reaching for the doorknob. "We'll make some hotcakes and French toast. Nicki and Aiden should arrive soon and then we'll work on figuring all of this out."

Nodding in agreement, Alex followed Morgana inside and shuddered at the sudden transition from cold to warm. Her phone was still clenched between her fingers as the sense that she was forgetting something nagged at her. Yet the only thing she could think of was the clink of a chain.

18

Alliance Born

1 15 C.E. Sør-Trøndelag, Norway

While Thor was stunned at the appearance of so many legends, Merlin and Morgana hid any surprise they may have been feeling. The ravens on Odin's shoulders released croaking caws, and the forest around them seemed to shudder in response. He looked at the Síd who was standing stiffly to the side with violet eyes darting between the Old Ones and the Mages. Thor felt a twinge of sympathy for the creature but said nothing.

"It would seem that a conversation is in order," Merlin said. "Please give me a moment."

Merlin slowly turned his back on their visitors and Morgana gave all three warning looks while Thor looked towards the older man curiously. Green magic danced around Merlin's hand, and he gracefully moved it through the air, letting the magic build up into a large cloud. He pointed at the small earthen shelter. Beneath Thor's feet, the ground rumbled for a moment before a large slab of earth suddenly ripped itself upwards, followed by another and another.

He shifted further away from the hut, escaping Morgana's watchful eye for the moment and almost backed into Odin's companion. The figure cloaked in gray quickly jumped out of his way with a small laugh that caught his attention. As the earth shifted around the tiny shelter and the earthen wall that had created it fell away, Thor caught a glimpse of the Old One's face.

It was a young woman with regal cheekbones and wide, curious eyes. Thor could feel the power radiating off of her, but it felt comforting, like stepping into a warm house from the cold. As she raised her head to observe the magic at work, Thor was able to see that the long braid of golden hair was just the end of an elaborate braided style woven over the crown of her head. She turned her face towards him and Thor was stunned by her intense green eyes. They were much prettier than Morgana's, and his chest tightened uncomfortably. It took him a moment before he could properly focus on her once more. Her soft looking lips curved into a smile.

"Forgive me," Thor apologized quickly. "I'm Thor."

"Sif." She nodded to him as her smile widened. "A pleasure to meet you, mage of the Iron Realm."

"Are you an Old One as well?" Thor asked softly, not wishing to draw Merlin or Morgana's attention. "I'm not familiar with your name."

"I am Odin's daughter," she explained. "But I am largely unknown to your people, at least for now."

Nodding carefully, Thor was trying to sort out what more he could say when another rumble and a hum from Merlin signaled the completion of the new structure. Sif was eyeing it carefully and Thor turned to take it in. Merlin had expanded the original small structure several feet in all directions, maintaining the circular shape and enlarging the door. From his position by Sif, he could still hear the snarls of the chained dark elf.

"Please." Merlin turned back to Odin and Sif with a carefully neutral expression and gestured towards the door. "Let us speak inside."

Odin nodded to Merlin and said nothing as he moved past the mage, his gray cloak swirling around him. Morgana followed him inside and Merlin looked over to Thor, though his eyes settled on Sif for a moment. Unsure if he should laugh at Merlin's need to impress the Old Ones with his power or sigh at his teacher, Thor nodded and gestured for Sif to go first. She nodded to him and slipped inside with Thor, the Síd, and Merlin following behind.

"Interesting: you managed to capture one." Odin leaned forward to study their prisoner.

"Yes, but we haven't learned much from it," Merlin said. "The Síd came here to inform us of what they have learned. What have your people found?"

"We have conducted our own investigation into the matter," Odin explained calmly as his good eye moved between the three of them. Huginn and Muninn kept their eyes on whichever two Odin was not looking at, which unsettled Thor. "At first these creatures seemed to be part of an invasion force with the traditional golden armor and ornaments, but now conquest no longer seems to be the purpose," Odin added darkly.

"They are making our world a prison," Morgana grumbled with a look towards Odin. "Much like your people it seems."

"So it would seem," Odin agreed without any shred of embarrassment in his voice. "Though given how my father described his home world I had always been grateful that I was born in the Iron Realm and into a form such as this."

"A form?" Thor began to ask before he thought better of it and fell silent.

"In our home world, the world my grandfather came from, there aren't physical bodies like you understand," Sif explained softly. "Our kind is more like... a cloud of energy, of magic. It is bound together by our understanding that it is us. However, such a form wouldn't survive in your world, and we bind our energy into matter." She paused and looked over at him once more and giggled. "You don't really understand, do you?"

It was his first instinct to insist that he did, to scoff at the very idea that she had confused him. Yet Sif's smile was genuine, and he instead found himself bashfully nodding. She laughed a little, making Odin and Merlin look back at them in surprise.

"Where is the tunnel entrance?" Morgana crossed her arms and eyed Odin and the peaceful Síd. "Given the way these creatures are going half feral, we can't just allow this to stand."

"Not far from here," the Síd answered. "I can take you there, but the day is already growing late. By the time we climb up the hills it will be nearing dusk."

"Perhaps it is for the best," Odin said. "We may learn something new if we observe the creatures as they come out."

"Maybe Thor should return-" Morgana started to say.

"No; if you're going to the tunnel then I am as well," Thor cut off quickly. He drew himself up only to get a sharp look of disapproval from Morgana.

"Very well," Merlin said. "I doubt any further conversations would be a benefit until we all see exactly what we are dealing with."

The look on Morgana's face made it clear that she wished to argue, but she stayed quiet. There was a thick silence in the small building as the three different representatives looked at each other. Morgana was glaring at the Síd while Merlin was considering Odin carefully and receiving a very similar look in return. Then next to him Sif cleared her throat and drew their attention.

"Shall we?" Sif gestured towards the doorway. "The daylight will not remain on our side."

Morgana pulled out her knife and grabbed the back of the dark elf's head, using its own pale hair as a grabbing point. Tugging its head back and exposing its throat, Morgana dragged the dagger across the neck and spilled silvery blood out onto the earthen floor. Thor focused on the blood even as the body began to flicker and dissolve into the dirt. There were traces of dark discoloration in the blood, and he found himself wondering how much of the creatures were being transformed. Then the dark elf was gone, and the blood vanished as Morgana calmly slipped her dagger back into its sheath on her belt and gestured towards the door.

Their Síd guide seemed uneasy, but nodded and pulled the hood of their cloak further over their head. As everyone moved outside, their guide pointed towards the nearest mountain before heading towards a light game trail going into the forest. Odin fell into step behind the Síd with Merlin behind him. Huginn and Muninn launched off of Odin's shoulders and the two ravens vanished into the treetops with loud ringing caws. Sif offered him a small smile and followed her father. Thor glanced at Morgana who motioned him to start walking. He sped up and walked alongside Sif with Morgana bringing up the rear. They walked in a heavy silence with only the soft sounds of the forest for company for some time.

"What is your name?" Sif asked the Síd kindly, earning her a grumble from Morgana.

"I am called Frea."

"I'm surprised that you came alone," Sif observed with a small knowing smile.

"It was believed that more than one might alarm the mages," Frea answered calmly.

"Yes; a wise precaution." Sif raised her hem slightly as she stepped over a muddy patch. "Forgive me, Frea, but are you male or female? I fear the features of your race are so fair that I have difficulty distinguishing."

"I am female." Frea stopped and looked around the forest fearfully. "We're getting close."

"How deep is this threshold?" Merlin asked.

Perhaps it was his imagination, but Thor thought that Frea seemed pale. It was a foolish idea, given her almost translucent skin and pale hair, and yet he had the distinct feeling that she was frightened. She caught his gaze and straightened up even taller, fixing her violet eyes ahead of them.

"Not far," Frea answered. "Our spies did not need to travel very long into the tunnel. The barrier seems closely tied to your world. Maybe a half a mile deep."

"Not far indeed," Morgana murmured as she peered into the darkness. "I remember much larger and longer tunnels."

"This is a first attempt at breaking through the power of the Iron Gates," Merlin said gently. "Were you able to observe what occurred at the threshold?"

"It... our spies had difficulty describing it. They said that it appeared like the Sídhe crossing through were poisoned slowly. Magic appeared over their limbs and sank into them."

"I suppose it was the power of the Iron Gates attempting to stop the Sídhe coming through one last time," Merlin said.

The slope of the mountain became steeper and the trees became sparser. Beneath his feet, the ground became rockier and it was more difficult to keep his footing. Thor offered Sif his hand and helped her navigate up the rough trail they were now following. Frea had pulled her hood further over her head as the lack of trees allowed more of the sun to shine down on them. Thor wondered if the sunlight itself hurt her skin or if it was just her eyes though he didn't ask. A quick glance up at the sky also confirmed that the sun was already beginning to descend.

No one said anything about the state of the sky, though Thor caught Merlin looking up with a worried expression. Glancing over his shoulder, Thor found Morgana with a thoughtful and tense look on her face and fought the urge to sigh. To think that his father thought him stubborn. At least he didn't keep heading for the enemy when the sun was nearing sunset. Almost as the thought occurred to him, Frea stopped walking and pointed towards what appeared to be a dead patch of earth piled with rocks ahead of them.

A hand on his shoulder brought him to a stop and he twisted to look over his shoulder at Morgana. She glanced at Sif, but then passed them both to join Merlin near the front of the group. Odin's ravens swooped down and landed on a nearby dead tree that was half twisted from the ground. Cautiously Merlin and Morgana strode around the bend of the mountain with Frea and Odin right behind them. Thor waited with Sif for only a few moments before he followed them into the dying patch of the mountain.

There was a hole torn in the mountainside. Thor could not call it a tunnel or passageway, as the rock had been roughly cut away. Piles of rubble of all sizes were pouring from the opening and the ground all around it was dark and dead. He eyed a nearby tree that was shriveled and twisted away from the opening as if it had died trying to escape. While the sun was hidden behind the clouds and the trees cast long shadows, something about the cavern beyond seemed unnaturally dark. He peered into it, taking a cautious step forward before Morgana caught his arm and gripped it tightly.

Sounds echoed out from the tunnel that made Thor pause. Some of the voices were soft and musical though with a mourning tone to them.

The rest were more like raw growls with the occasional whimper or cry of pain. He risked a glance at the others and found Morgana watching the tunnel with a considering expression. Merlin was eyeing it with disdain and Frea had a look of fear on her features. Then the sounds began to come closer and closer with the musical voices fading away and leaving only the more animalistic cries.

Strange flashes of light deep in the tunnel offered brief flickers of illumination that created long shadows that vanished as quickly as they'd appeared. Without a word being said the assembled group spread out in the dead space around the opening. Morgana remained close to him while Merlin stayed near Odin as both men pushed their long cloaks back and prepared for battle.

Then he caught sight of the first of the Sídhe, or what he should consider Dark Elves, as what came out was very different from Frea. The first Dark Elf stumbled out into the darkening day. It was dressed in an elegant blue tunic, though its hair was a mess with its braids half torn out. Violet eyes focused on them for only a moment before it extended a hand towards them. Backing away, Thor watched in stunned silence as a strange darkening began to spread over its skin as if all at once it was suffering a terrible bruise. It clawed at its own face as a loud scream escaped it.

Lifting his axe in front of his body, Thor dug his toes into the rocky earth beneath him and braced for the attack. More of the creatures were spilling out of the opening, some clawing at their own faces while others cowered in the entrance away from the dying light of the day. Throwing his weight forward, Thor brought the axe through the air and into the chest of the nearest Dark Elf as it tried to claw its own eyes out. An inhuman scream ripped from its body but quickly vanished as its form decayed into dust right before his eyes. Thor's gaze lingered on the empty space for only a moment as more of the creatures began to rush out of the tunnel.

Frea jumped back and drew a long dagger from beneath her cloak as the nearest Dark Elf lashed at her. This one wore light golden armor that didn't quite match and had a real weapon in its hand. Frea slashed forward with the dagger, catching the Dark Elf in the shoulder. It stumbled and Thor left her to finish it off. As another Dark Elf, this one in a mere tunic, rushed out of the tunnel Thor gathered a spark of magic in his left hand. It arced off his fingers and struck the creature as a bolt of lightning, throwing it off its feet.

A strange floral scent reached his nose; confusing him for a moment before he saw a faint trace of light swirling around Sif. Her hood had fallen back and strands of her golden hair had fallen into her face as she narrowed her eyes at one of the creatures. They lunged at her and in a flash of light began to dissolve as Sif stretched out a hand. Odin raised his staff high before he slammed it down against the bare rocks beneath him. Magic shuddered through the air, making the hairs on the back of Thor's neck stand up. More of the frenzying creatures vanished in a wave of light. As another lashed at him, Thor sent another bolt of lightning forth and grinned as it struck his target and then jumped to another.

Beneath his feet, the ground began to rumble. He froze in surprise and took a shaky breath as he looked around in alarm. Morgana was surrounded by ropes of silver magic that were following her arms as she lashed out towards the Dark Elves spilling from the tunnel. Her position was defensive of Merlin, who was cloaked in green magic with his hands reaching towards the top of the mountain. Green magic burst out from the man in a sudden surge of power that knocked the air from Thor's lungs and left him watching in shock.

Above their heads, the mountainside began to collapse. Green magic rained down on the rock and soil like snow; each spark dislodging more and more of the mountain. The roar of the rocks deafened Thor to the world, and his lungs filled with dirt as he struggled to breathe. Everything was shaking as Thor grabbed Sif's arm and pulled her back from the rockslide. He looked back into the tunnel and grimaced as the hole began to crumble into itself and the creatures still within it released horrified cries. Thankfully, his feet kept moving him along the side of the mountain and away from the rolling stones.

The world settled slowly as the dust began to drift away on the soft breeze. His ears rang from the sudden silence until the caw of a raven brought the world back into focus. Taking a deep breath, Thor promptly had to cough as the dirt hit his tongue. He flexed his fingers around the axe and noted with a flush of irritation that his palms were sweating. With another, more cautious breath he looked towards the tunnel, but it was long gone. Part of the mountain had slid down to cover the tunnel, and rocks were still rolling off into the ravine below.

A cough drew his attention to Merlin, who was leaning slightly against Morgana and was covered in a layer of dirt. Frea pulled back her hood long enough to shake off the dust, exposing her long braids of white hair to the last rays of the sun. No one appeared to be injured, and while he was clearly exhausted, there was a look of pride and smugness on Merlin's face.

"Are you alright, Sif?" Thor shifted his attention over to her, looking her over for injuries.

"Yes, Thor, I'm fine," she assured him. Sif looked towards her father who now was speaking with Merlin in a low voice. "At least it seems that we have secured the alliance we sought when we came here. That is something to celebrate."

19

Stillness

Her mother had always said that nothing helped the mind reset like a good hair washing and fresh clothes. After the stress of last night and the awkwardness of sleeping in her clothes Jenny now firmly believed her mother's words. Thankfully Alex was a good friend, and while she might have chosen the wrong shirt for her dark jeans, she had thought to grab her shampoo and conditioner. There was even a wide tooth comb at the bottom of the bag and Jenny used it to carefully untangle her long dark locks as she eyed her reflection in the mirror.

She was looking better than she had for the last few months, Jenny realized with a small jolt of surprise. During the crisis with Arthur, she'd just gotten used to looking tired and there being a shadow of guilt with a hint of self-loathing in her eyes. It wasn't completely gone, but it had faded. Finding out that Arthur had just been using her for years had taken a toll of its own, but every day was a little easier.

Now, somehow, she was part of a group connected to a magic war and yet was in better shape than she had been at the same time last year. Glancing around the bathroom, Jenny didn't see a hairdryer and began to braid her long damp hair over her shoulder. She breathed in the warm humid air and enjoyed a few moments of peaceful calm.

Then with a new spring in her step, Jenny left the bathroom and headed back towards the living room. She took notice of the various paintings along the walls that she hadn't bothered studying the night before. Many of the pieces were landscapes and looked old. One of them was a portrait that took Jenny a moment to recognize as Morgana in an old-fashioned dress with her dark hair largely hidden under a headdress. This painting hung in a small alcove away from the windows with a small lamp illuminating it. If she'd been anyone else's house, she would have figured it and the others were reproductions or prints, but she doubted that was the case here.

"Your turn," Jenny said. She stepped into the living room, but to her surprise, Lance was alone with a stack of books. "Uh?"

"Outside." Lance nodded towards the nearest window. "Getting in some practice while Morgana makes breakfast."

"Ah." Jenny caught a flash of fire shooting past the window and grimaced. "I think I'll stay inside."

"Well, Morgana gave me some research homework," Lance sighed as he held up the book in his hand. "Knock yourself out." He stood up and rolled his shoulders with a soft groan. "And if I'm not out of the shower by breakfast then save me some food."

"I will," she promised.

Lance scooped up a backpack that was waiting at the edge of the couch and gave her a nod before heading down the hall. Jenny shifted uncertainly on her feet for a moment before she looked down at the books. They were old and leather-bound books with a strong smell that took Jenny back to her father's study. There was a mix of different mythologies in the stack and she grabbed the one that Lance had been reading. Something exploded outside and made her jump. She rushed over to the window and pulled back the curtain.

Aiden was laughing with a hand behind his head sheepishly. She couldn't see what he had hit, but Merlin didn't seem too distressed as he leaned against the side of his SUV. Nicki skipped over to Aiden and said something Jenny couldn't hear to him. Bran just shook his head at them and turned his attention back to the swirl of yellow magic gathering in his hands. She looked around but didn't see Alex anywhere.

Pulling a chair over to the window, Jenny sat down so she could look up and see the others. The glare of the sun off the snow bothered her a little, but she ignored it and opened one of Morgana's books on German folklore. In the corner of her eye, she kept seeing flashes of light that varied between yellow, red, and blue. When dark silver suddenly appeared, Jenny looked up from a passage about the Black Forest and spotted Alex standing near Bran. There was a tense expression on her face. The sounds from the kitchen became unnaturally loud in the silence.

Jenny did her best to focus on the book in front of her, but the warmth of the sunlight pouring through the window made her feel lazy. As she idly flipped through the book Jenny was once again struck by how little understanding she had. She and Lance were 'helping' with research, but what they were supposed to be finding was lost on her. Was there some sort of artifact that could control fairies? She was fairly certain that Merlin and Morgana wouldn't have forgotten something like that.

The smells of bacon and sausage were beginning to fill the living room, making Jenny aware of how hungry she was. She could hear the hiss of a griddle as Morgana's movements had become softer once more. Jenny straightened up in the chair and allowed herself one more quick look outside. The others had spread out and she could only see Alex. Her friend was standing very still with her eyes closed and her hands extended in front of her. Flickers of dark silvery magic were jumping between her hands and Jenny couldn't help but watch for a moment. Nothing interesting happened, but the look of tension and worry was still on Alex's face. Realizing that she was staring Jenny lowered her eyes and did her best to ignore both the smells of breakfast and the mages in the yard.

An illustration of some sort of small fairy called a Heinzelmännchen caught her eye, and Jenny was reading the translation of a poem about them helping the people of Cologne at night when the sound of footfalls made her look up. Lance strolled into the living room in fresh jeans and one of his many Ravenslake University t-shirts. Jenny found her eyes lingering on him longer than she meant to, earning her a smug smile from Lance.

"That was fast."

Lance sat in the nearby armchair and she lowered her eyes back to her book. "I'm a guy. Not to mention short hair." He studied her for a moment and frowned. "What's wrong?"

Looking up at him in surprise, Jenny blinked and just stared at him. His smug smile had vanished and he was considering her with a soft frown. She wondered if she was that transparent or if Lance just knew her that well.

"I'm not sure." Jenny looked out the window again. "Just... Alex looks worried about something."

Lance peered out the window at Alex with a neutral expression. Jenny followed his gaze and noted that Alex looked calmer now, almost bored. Her magic was spinning in front of her into different shapes. A blast of fire that collided with the snow a few feet from Alex sent a cloud of steam into the air and made Alex, Lance, and Jenny all jump. Alex spun and shouted for Bran to be more careful.

"Bran?" Lance repeated in surprise. "I thought Aiden was the firebug."

"Alex says that they are trying to learn each other's spells now." Jenny shook her head. "Maybe it's nothing."

"Or maybe it is," Lance offered gently. "She'll talk to you if she needs to. We're the ones a little outside the insanity, remember?"

"I guess." Jenny lowered her eyes back to the book and toyed with the edges of the page. "I just wish we could help more."

Lance said nothing as he opened another book and started reading. A few moments later his free hand caught hers and squeezed gently. It was a bit awkward having their fingers entwined and hanging between the two chairs, but Jenny was grateful when Lance didn't let go. Instead, she just kept flipping through the book and taking notes on a small notepad of the different sorts of fairies that might just be showing up to kill them all.

"Tell the others that breakfast is almost ready," Morgana ordered suddenly. Jenny jumped in her chair and looked up to find Morgana staring at their entwined hands. "Lance, come here and set the table."

They exchanged glances as Morgana spun around and returned to the kitchen before jumping to their feet and releasing each other's hands. Neither of them was sure enough of Morgana to risk her wrath and Jenny headed towards the front door. She noted with a quirk of her eyebrow that the others had left the front door open and only the screen door was keeping the cold air out.

As she shifted around the door, Jenny heard voices and paused before she peeked out. Nicki and Aiden were standing on the front porch, with Nicki leaning against the railing while Aiden stood with closed eyes. Jenny could see his exhales as mist in the cold morning air, but noted that the mage was only wearing a heavy knit sweater. She opened her mouth to tell them to come inside when Aiden brought his glowing red hand up in front of Nicki and she was distracted by the flare of magic in the air.

Aiden opened his hand and the flash of red in his hand shimmered. The sparks shuddered and his brow creased in concentration. In another small flash, the red sparks solidified into a small piece of ice that floated above his palm.

"Check it out," Aiden crowed. "Ice magic, Nicki! That's right, the fire mage has managed to replicate your power!"

"I suppose you expect me to be impressed?" Nicki asked with a raised eyebrow and smug smile.

"Well yeah, you haven't pulled off fire yet."

"Oh please, a redhead using fire magic is so cliché," Nicki said. Then a curious expression crossed her face. "When did you pull this off?"

"Uh, actually the night Arthur attacked Alex. I got surrounded by Chernobog's shadow monsters and did a blizzard to destroy them." He chuckled and shifted his hand, which made the ice crystals grow and begin branching out like a large snowflake. "Haven't used it since. Glad it wasn't a fluke."

"That night-You haven't talked about it before," Nicki said, suddenly sounding uncertain.

"What's there to talk about?"

"Aiden, I'm just worried about you. You've been a bit off lately. I mean you're acting normally, but there's just something-"

"Come on, Nicki, I was healed by the Holy Grail! I'm better than okay."

"That isn't what I mean," Nicki huffed in frustration. "Now isn't the time to be an ass, Aiden. It's not just Arthur and the coma. You're bothered about Sarah-"

"Look Sarah and I… even before graduation we talked about it. Long distance relationships are always tough and she was going somewhere new with new people and…" Aiden trailed off, and Jenny once again had the guilty feeling that she really should try to leave or cough at the very least. "We decided we'd try and we made it work through freshman year, but I mean- this summer she's got an internship so she isn't even coming home."

"Not at all?"

"Well for like two weeks right at the start, but the point is, Nicki, that I'm fine. Really; the breakup with Sarah wasn't great, but I'm okay." There was a strained laugh and then a sigh. "Look, seeing Arthur stab Alex…. It was intense, and the feeling when I gave her all my energy… I'm still processing it all. I promise this is just me trying to take my time and cope with the shit that's our lives now. I'm not having nightmares all the time and I can think about it without having a panic attack, so I'm pretty sure I'm good."

There was a long sigh from Nicki that worried Jenny, but when she peeked around the corner, she saw Nicki nod. Aiden smiled at her and leaned forward to wrap the redhead in a hug.

"Hey, I'm still here," he assured her. "From what I've heard from Bran, you had a hard time in Wales. Have you taken time to cope yourself?"

"I'm fine," Nicki insisted stubbornly. However, a moment later she turned her head and buried her face in Aiden's sweater. "Just glad you're okay."

"Yeah, I'm okay, Nicki." Aiden wrapped his arms around her.

The sounds from the kitchen reminded Jenny why she'd been sent out in the first place. Pulling back from the door, she stamped her feet on the ground and made extra noise as she opened the screen door. Aiden looked over at her and to her surprise, Nicki did not move out of the hug.

While he gave her a knowing look, Jenny did her best not to look guilty and cleared her throat.

"Breakfast is ready."

"Awesome!" Aiden released Nicki and she moved away from him with a bright red face that almost matched her hair. "I'm starving."

"Well, it smells good." Jenny gave him a smile. "And with you all eating it I'm fairly confident that Morgana isn't going to poison Lance and me."

That got a laugh out of Aiden and Nicki fondly shook her head. For a moment Jenny giggled and relished a sudden sense of being part of the joke. She stepped back and let Aiden and Nicki into the entryway as Aiden yelled over his shoulder to Bran that breakfast was ready. Nicki paused in front of her long enough to remove her coat before she headed through the living room with Aiden. The sense of belonging melted away as the two old friends kept chatting and Jenny pushed away the melancholy that tried to take its place.

"Thanks, Jenny." Bran walked into the entry and took off his coat, giving her a warm smile as Merlin brushed past them both.

Jenny shifted around the door, still holding it open and waiting for Alex. Looking at Alex's face, Jenny couldn't help but frown. Her gray eyes seemed extra dark and there was a small furrow between her brows. She stopped walking and looked down at the snow beneath her feet for a moment with an expression that Jenny just couldn't read. Then she shook her head and started walking again, this time striding straight to the porch and up the stairs. As Alex came inside Jenny closed the door and lingered as Alex stamped the snow off of her shoes. Before the other girl headed to the kitchen, Jenny reached out and grabbed her hand. She gave it a quick squeeze and smiled at Alex. Neither said anything, but as Alex nodded to her and gave her a small smile in return so Jenny thought that she probably understood just fine.

Jenny found her feet dragging a little as she followed Alex towards the kitchen and felt sad when Alex released her hand. The others were in the dining room and all setting down platters of food with only Merlin already seated. The room was lit by a fancy old-fashioned chandelier and the sunlight reflecting off the snow through a large window framed by pale blue curtains. There was a fine layer of dust on the side table by the door that indicated the room was rarely used though the table had a fresh white table cloth across it.

As Morgana directed everyone to their seats, Jenny was surprised when Alex pulled her into the seat next to her. Lance took a seat across from her while Morgana quickly sat to Alex's right, giving them a curious glance. Nicki caught her eye and smiled reassuringly from her place across from Alex before picking up the sausage and getting breakfast started.

"So, what's on the agenda for today?" Alex asked in a forced cheerful voice.

"Well, more practice would be a good idea." Merlin scooped up some scrambled eggs and gave the mages a look. "More variation of course-"

"Aren't we beyond that now?" Aiden asked with a disgruntled expression. "I've used fire, ice, and healing magic now. We all know how to pull off effects beyond our normal magic. We've got the basics down! I can replicate Nicki's ice spells and we know how to visualize our magic to make simple things happen. If Arthur and the Queen are going to keep using advanced magic against us then we need to learn more of it ourselves."

"He's right," Bran agreed. "Morgana, you've been working with me on scrying and Alex keeps doing metalworking, but we're at a turning point. Right now, we're just in a holding pattern. If we're really going to find out what is going on and stop it then we need to step up our game."

"You don't understand-" Merlin began to protest, but Alex cut him off.

"Those creatures, they aren't attacking us because they want to," Alex reminded him as the others fell silent. "They are being compelled to. They're the descendants of slaves or soldiers who were trapped here. They were born in this world... the Iron Realm is their home too, even if they aren't children of it. Doesn't that mean anything to you?"

Merlin and Morgana looked at each other, their eyes locking and for a second Jenny could almost feel the silent conversation occurring. She wondered if their magic let them use some form of telepathy or if it was just three thousand years of being together.

"It's complicated," Morgana finally said. "We care to a certain extent, but in the end, Alex... well, I'm afraid that Merlin and I are just a little old to care that much." Morgana stared into her teacup. "It weighs on you. Those creatures are very unfortunate, of course, but we will always value the lives of mages more."

"What about the blood spell?" Alex asked after a quiet moment. "The one that I activated in Glastonbury? Can you teach it to me so that I can at least protect my parents?"

"That spell is very dangerous." Merlin's voice was so serious that Jenny swore the temperature in the room had dropped. "Arto was trained by me for years before he ever used that spell. It is beyond difficult to control, Alex."

"And yet Bran is right," Alex said. "Right now, we're just in a holding pattern. We're letting Arthur and Scáthbás throw innocent creatures at us while they search for Cathanáil and do who knows what else. We aren't protecting the world like this. Sure, we needed some time to heal from Arthur's betrayal and process it all, but not all of us are immortal. I'm the Iron Soul, and I need to learn how to do what I was born for."

Jenny set down her fork while silence reigned around the table and everyone waited with baited breath for Merlin and Morgana's reply. She dropped her hand out of sight just below the table and found Alex's softly shaking hand. Wrapping her fingers around her friend's hand, Jenny kept her face as neutral as possible and focused her eyes on her hotcake.

"Merlin," Morgana said, breaking the silence. "Teach her the spell."

The elder man exhaled slowly, drawing Jenny's gaze, but then he nodded. Alex's hand tightened around hers and Jenny barely kept back a smile. Maybe she wasn't a mage, but as she heard a small sigh of relief from Alex, she felt her own chest swell with pride. The only problem was that Alex didn't seem in a hurry to return her right hand to her. It was more than three minutes later during which she ate her bacon as the only finger food on her plate before Alex released her hand. Still, Jenny could live with that.

20

Blood Spell

Blood trickled down her palm and off the tips of her fingers, the droplets rhythmically hitting the ground. Aiden had melted a patch of snow with a fireball, leaving her with a bare if damp space to work in. Alex turned slowly and kept her arm outstretched so the blood droplets were creating a circle around her. The weight of Merlin's gaze was heavy on her back, but she kept up the slow turn until she was once again facing him.

In the corner of her eye, Alex caught Nicki curling her nose up at the sight of the blood before the redhead vanished back around the house. Alex understood. There was something both beautiful and creepy about watching blood flow, and it was made even weirder by it being your own. Only last year the sight of blood had made her squeamish, but now it didn't seem to matter.

She cautiously pushed her magic into the blood, letting it flow out of her with every drop and supercharge the iron contained within it. The droplets pulsed with a soft glow that only brightened as it splashed on the ground, and Alex struggled to focus on the present as her mind kept jumping back to Glastonbury. She could remember the rush of magic around them when her blood had reactivated the ancient blood ward laid by the first Iron Soul.

Her distraction was a mistake and Alex gasped as she felt the magic begin to slip. In her mind's eye, she saw the flares of magic that had been in Glastonbury and her magic rushed to replicate it. Alex grabbed at her magic and pulled it back fiercely as it began to slip away like water. It resisted her for a moment; the thrum of the earth beneath her feet pulled on her magic and beckoned it to return from whence it came.

Closing her eyes tightly, Alex fought back the wave of panic rising through her chest and eased her own frantic pull on her magic. Instead, she focused on her own heartbeat, willing the magic to gather in her chest. For a moment she feared it had failed but then the magic slowly began to shift. The flare of power in her chest grew and the tug of the earth faded away. Stumbling back, Alex clutched her hand against her chest, completely ignoring the blood she was smearing on the outside of her jacket. The wind whipped around her and sent her hair flying around her face. Relief gathered in her chest like an expanding balloon and she took another long shaky breath.

"Easy," Merlin said. Alex became aware of the older mage holding her shoulders carefully. "That was a good try, Alex. Just breathe now."

"That was-"

"I know," Merlin assured her. "I know. You're alright, Alex; you re-gained control."

She certainly didn't feel that was the case, but Alex inhaled and exhaled slowly. She closed her eyes and focused on the beat of her heart and the thrum of her magic beneath her skin. Without a word to Merlin, Alex tried to send her senses outward beyond her body. As she felt a whisper of magic react to her silent call, Alex opened her eyes and smiled as she spotted soft shimmers of light in the air. For a moment she hesitated, feeling a hint of fear at the notion of trying this without Cathanáil, but the ache in her chest and the burning in her lungs made the decision for her.

She pulled at the magic flickers in the air and almost smiled as they swirled towards her, turning into long threads of energy. Focusing on the flickers, Alex willed her own magic to gather them up. Extending her hand, Alex braced herself as the first little spark of dull light touched her finger. It remained its neutral dull white for a moment before turning a dark silver color. Then it vanished into her skin, melting into her flesh as a jolt of energy shot up her arm. Alex felt the tingling in her arm growing stronger and stronger.

It quickly became too much as the dark silver magic spun into an orb in front of her, and Alex heard a sharp intake of breath from Merlin. She ignored him and pushed the magic away as the rattling in her bones became too much. Her skin felt raw like she'd been holding her hand over a hot surface, and Alex felt more than saw the thread between the orb and her hand break.

The magic lingered in the air before her as Alex caught her breath and fought to stay still. The energy thrumming beneath her skin made her want to run a few miles or jump some hurdles. Her lungs felt a bit raw though, like she'd already been running for at least an hour, aching even more than they did after a soccer game.

"Have to practice that a bit more," Alex choked out as she tried to slow her panting.

"Alex..." Merlin started to say, worry echoing in his voice.

"I think...." She paused to consider how to best explain what she was feeling. "I think that I'm gathering up the leftover magic in the air from the other's spells." Alex licked her lips and risked a glance in Merlin's direction. "It's a bit difficult to control, but I can sort of absorb the power or reuse it, like I did in the tunnels that first time, except not just catching immediate magic in the air."

"Your power is remarkable." Merlin was thoughtfully watching her.

Alex held back a smile as the magic settled into her bones and eased the earlier ache. Merlin already was looking uncertain and Alex didn't think that her bouncing back so quickly would help matters. She turned her attention back to the dark silver orb and watched it curiously as some of the magic slowly dissipated off of it. Part of her wondered just how long the energy would remain like this, just waiting for her to use it, but she dismissed the thought. This wasn't the time.

Instead, she brought a hand back up to the orb and carefully brushed her fingers over it. The magic sparked beneath her fingertips and she could feel it barely connecting with her own internal magic. It was an odd sensation, and she stood there silently trying to take stock of it. She did smile at the realization that she only pulled the magic into her if she wanted to, otherwise, it seemed to just... linger for her to use.

"Hold still," Merlin ordered. He reached out and took her hand. For a moment she thought he was going to heal her hand, but instead, he wrapped a long piece of gauze over the cut. She must have looked surprised because Merlin quickly explained, "We'll heal your wounds at the end of the day. You're doing your little magical absorption trick so much today it has me a bit concerned about using healing magic on you." Merlin tied off the bandage and patted her hand carefully. "Just... don't overdo it, Alex."

"Oh..., right," Alex said. She licked her lips and swallowed, suddenly realizing how dry her mouth felt. A hand on her arm guided her over to the bench on the side of the yard as her feet crunched in the snow. "So, how strong can I make the blood protection?" Alex asked. "I mean, what sort of limitations does it have? It was really impressive in Glastonbury, but you didn't place them all across England."

"For starters, you have just experienced how difficult it is to control the blood spell," Merlin said. "As for the power, it depends on the power the mage is able to pour into their blood," Merlin explained in a thick voice. "Arto became very… skilled at this spell, and didn't have to spill much of his own blood. My mother, on the other hand, slit her own wrist to get enough blood and even then, had to use my magic to make it work."

Freezing, Alex's mind tripped over itself before trying to find some point of reference again. She'd never heard Merlin talk about any family. Morgana had mentioned her brother plenty of times and her long-dead husband, but she couldn't remember Merlin ever speaking of his family. Part of her had almost assumed that he was a creation of the Iron Realm somehow and he's sprung out of the ground.

"It takes almost perfect concentration, Alex. Your magic tries to slip away from you and return to the earth when you cast this spell," Merlin continued, cutting into her confused thoughts. "Just like healing magic, it is very easy to lose control. And as you know, if you use too much magic you can die."

Alex kept her eyes focused on Merlin as she nodded and did not look over at Aiden. "We have the Iron Chalice now." Alex gave him a small, forced smile.

"Indeed, but I wonder what limitations the Iron Chalice might have." Merlin leaned back in his seat. "In truth, we need to test it: we need to learn how long it can go without being charged by your magic. If it needs to be charged by you then it can never be used to save you, only others." Merlin hummed softly and nodded to himself. "That would fit Gofiben's character and power. He was a good lad: a bit simple compared to other incarnations, but compassionate."

"When you say simple...?"

"Oh, he was intelligent enough," Merlin chuckled. "But he was straightforward and calm. Honestly, traits that I've wished the other incarnations had. Then again, I suppose had he lived longer and had I known him better, I might remember him differently."

"Do you have a favorite?" Alex asked. "Other than Arto I mean?"

"A favorite?" Merlin repeated cautiously, giving her a searching look. "I try not to. Each Iron Soul is distinct and many come from different cultures. Arto and I may have been a generation or two apart but we grew up in the same culture and the same area. A comparison isn't really fair."

"That's evading the question," Alex said with a smile. "Come on, Merlin; I'll even tell you outright to remove me from the equation. Was it Thor?"

"Thor? Goodness no. Thor was a good man, but impulsive and arrogant. Didn't know what he was doing or why half the time, if that." Merlin laughed fondly. "Well, if I really had to pick a favorite, and keep in mind of course that this removes you, Arto, others that I raised, and those Iron Souls that I didn't interact with because magic was so low... maybe Lokpal."

"Lokpal?"

"Around 620 B.C.E. in India. He was an intelligent young man and was unafraid to challenge Morgana and I. He is the reason we don't have to worry about the Demons in India much. The Old Ones who make up the Hindu Pantheon keep an eye on them for us in part due to Lokpal's actions. He was a gifted young man." Merlin paused and looked towards Alex with a smile and added, "He didn't quite see it either."

"See what?" Alex asked even as a suspicion of exactly what Merlin was referring to crept up on her.

"How capable he was as the Iron Soul," Merlin said affectionately. "You've recovered brilliantly from a terrible betrayal, Alex. You rallied to save Aiden and you're focusing on expanding the scope of your natural talent."

"I'm not... it still bothers me."

"Of course, it does. You're human; I'd be worried if you just brushed it to the side." Merlin's tone softened. "I have nightmares sometimes of the things I've seen, and not all of it was magical. I know Morgana does as well. That doesn't make you weak."

Swallowing, Alex decided against trying to say something clever or witty. Merlin would see right through it and give her that look. It was odd to imagine that three thousand years ago he'd probably given Arto the exact same look.

"I want to try again," Alex said, earning her a worried look from Merlin. He pointedly looked at her wrapped hand. "I'll be fine. Practice is important, and if I'm going to use the spell in Spokane-"

"Spokane is very large," Merlin cautioned her. "It is almost 60 square miles. And the blood protection spell isn't absolute after its first casting. It weakens the Sídhe, but doesn't always destroy them."

"Are there other protection spells?" Alex met his gaze evenly. "If there are other options, Merlin, then please let's look at those too. But Arthur could easily go after my parents. He killed Arto's father after all and Uther raised him."

"Uthyrn," Merlin corrected. Alex almost rolled her eyes at him. "Well, the blood spell will keep Sídhe creatures from the area, but it won't hide your parents. Arthur will still know they're there."

"We need to try something," Alex insisted, glaring at the man. "I know to you and Morgana my family may not be all that important but-"

"They are important, Alex," Merlin cut in with a sad expression. "We do know that, and while we are prone to worrying about you much more... we do understand how important love and support is to life. Neither of us wishes to see you lose that." He smiled at her; his expression still touched with sorrow. "But I'm sure your parents wouldn't want you risking yourself for them."

"No," Alex agreed a bit begrudgingly. "But I have brothers to worry about too."

Merlin made a face and looked towards Morgana's house with a small grimace. Alex almost laughed at the expression and wondered if Merlin might not be a little frightened of Morgana. Then again, she knew from experience the odd way that the older mages were protective of her.

"I'm fine," Alex said with a little smile. "Just got a bunch of energy and you'll be healing my hand later. If you want, we can even go to your house and use the Iron Chalice."

"Your hand has got to be hurting." Merlin turned his attention back to her.

"It stings," Alex admitted. In truth, it was worse than simply stinging. "I'm getting used to ignoring it."

He gave her a long look that Alex wasn't sure how to translate as he reached for her hand. Alex stayed still and Merlin carefully lifted the bandage and looked down at the cut. Blood was still oozing out of it and Alex watched the thick red liquid with a strange fascination. After Arthur had held her and harvested vials of her blood, she supposed that she should feel repulsed, and yet as she caught the faint hint of iron, she actually felt reassured.

"I'm sorry," Merlin suddenly said pulling her attention back to him.

"Sorry?"

"I am sorry, Alex," Merlin tried again with a slight frown. "I know that you don't think that I see you, but I do. You are far more capable than you think you are."

Swallowing, Alex struggled for the right thing to say. "I'm not sure I'm really cut out to be the Iron Soul," she whispered, lowering her eyes.

"It doesn't work that way," Merlin chuckled. "You were born with that soul, and thus you are the Iron Soul. There isn't any choosing that goes into it. You were born and you are."

"Seems like a rubbish system," Alex muttered. "Not as bad as pulling a sword out of a stone, but bad."

"I'm actually rather fond of that part of the story myself," Merlin said. "It came from how we used to cast bronze swords: we used stone molds."

"Stone molds? Really?" Alex looked up at him in surprise. "That's... neat I suppose. So, when you made a sword, you literally pulled it from a stone."

"Indeed." Merlin chuckled as his shoulders relaxed. "I still remember my first successful sword. I was nervous because the last time I'd tried, charcoal had gotten into the mold and compromised the cooling bronze. I spent many hours polishing and sharpening that blade."

"What happened to it?" Alex asked.

"Oh, eventually it wore down. Not to mention it wasn't very useful against the Sídhe so I began to lean much more towards magical combat. Eventually, it was melted down to recast."

"That makes sense I guess." Alex felt an odd hint of sadness at the thought of the first sword that Merlin remembered so clearly. "Did you teach Arto to work with bronze or just iron?"

"I did teach him bronze working," Merlin said wistfully. "In the early days of him being in my care, we lived a quieter life. We lived in a small village in southern Wales, not too far from modern Glastonbury to be honest, for a few years and I served as a smith. I wanted to lay low and teach him slowly so that I could keep him safe. He was the first Iron Soul and back then I had no notion that he would be reborn."

"You thought he was it?" Alex pressed her lips together as something in her gut twisted uncomfortably. "I suppose that makes sense."

"If you wish to try again then I'll allow it," Merlin told her with a soft sigh, patting her shoulder gently. "Just be cautious, Alex."

Nodding, Alex smiled a little but tensed up as she saw the others come around the house. She received a curious look from Bran as she stood up and walked back out to the empty patch of the yard. She unwound the bandage and shoved it into her pocket before reaching back to the dagger secured on her belt. The sturdy leather band keeping it secure flexed a little as Alex wrestled open the clasp and pulled the dagger free.

Before she could change her mind about trying again, Alex began to slice into the wound on her hand to aggravate it. Then the sounds of something in the forest made her pause and she raised her eyes to look towards the trees. Above their heads, the sun was between a pair of billowing clouds. Nonetheless, she saw violet eyes peering out from the trees and gave a shout to warn the others.

Sídhe descendants rushed out of the trees, their faces half-covered with hoods and several wearing thick sunglasses. The sight gave Alex pause, but blood was already trickling down the lines in her hand and dripping off her fingers. She gasped as her magic suddenly reacted, feeling as though something had reached up and began to pull it straight out of her chest. Around her, the blood on the ground began to flare bright red.

Merlin's hand on her shoulder helped steady her, and she breathed out slowly as she struggled to regain control. As the creatures lingered at the edge of Morgana's yard and the blood magic flowed slowly around them

Alex was too aware of just what Merlin had been warning her about. In the corner of her eyes, she saw columns of red magic flare up from the earth itself and grab the creatures. One turned to dust with an aborted scream and the ache of her magic grew.

She only distantly heard the shouting of the others as they fought back. The air was shimmering and in the corner of her eye strands of magic were appearing. Alex tried to look at them as the threads spun around the Sídhe creatures, but she couldn't hold her magic under control. There were screams, flashes of magic, and a blood red glow all around them.

Everything was hazy and her legs trembled beneath her, but Alex could see shimmering lines ahead of her amongst the dark shapes. They vanished in a burst of vibrant red magic from Aiden's fireball that exploded across her vision as heat washed over her face. Closing her eyes, Alex dismissed the strands and pulled on her magic. She tried to coil it up in her chest and felt her body bending over as she inwardly curled around the spark. The tug of the earth beneath her feet lessened and she could breathe a little easier.

Then everything quieted and there was another set of hands holding her shoulders. For a moment Alex felt like she was floating as the world just drifted away. Her eyes fell shut and her muscles uncoiled. At the last flicker of consciousness, Alex heard the clank of a chain and a soft voice asking what she had wrought.

21

An Old Soul

1 15 C.E. Sør-Trøndelag, Norway

Thor was unsure of what to think as the last of the dust settled and their odd company began trekking back down the mountainside. Merlin and Morgana had created small light orbs that floated at the front and back of the group. He glanced back towards the pile of rubble and the new high scar of the mountain several times before it became too dark to see. Above their heads, the stars were beginning to show themselves and Thor wondered if there were more of the creatures waiting for them in the darkness.

"Are we returning to the village?" Thor asked, as loudly as he dared. "The Dark Elf is dead and the tunnel is closed."

"That won't stop them forever," Morgana said, looking around carefully.

"It might," Frea said. "It may not be worth the effort now that they have lost the tunnel. They are not easy to make, and as they can only go so far... at least according to the old stories." She trailed off and looked between the mages and the Old Ones. "You don't think so?"

"The Sídhe are expansionists," Odin said uneasily. "From my understanding, it is a part of their culture."

"You'd be right." Morgana scowled with anger flashing in her eyes. "They believe that they are meant to rule the whole Tree of Reality."

"I see." Frea adjusted her cloak and pulled up her hood. "I need to return to my people. My absence has been longer than I had planned."

Morgana gave her a sharp look but said nothing, which surprised Thor a little. He was unsure as to what sort of history Morgana had with the Sídhe, but it was clearly a haunting, ugly thing. Frea excused herself with a deep nod to Sif and Odin and a slightly more cautious nod to Morgana and Merlin. He watched the Sid woman hurry back into the forest with a hint of curiosity as to just where her hidden village was. Based on how Morgana was watching her, he was certain she was wondering the same thing. The stories of the Elves were diverse, and Thor was now unsure what was true and what was false.

"I am uncertain of what the Sídhe's next move will be," Odin said. They watched Frea vanish from view and Odin sighed. "Yet preparation for an invasion force may be wise."

"The Sídhe that come through that tunnel are in no way an army." Morgana's lips twisted into a nasty little smile.

"We don't know what happens to them after time passes," Merlin said, seemingly unbothered by her smile. "They may begin to regain their minds or become something even worse or more powerful. They have been exposed directly to the magic of the Iron Gates."

"Surely you and your Iron Soul are prepared for open combat by this point?" Odin made a pointed look his way. "He's clearly a warrior and after so long-"

"Memories and knowledge are not retained," Merlin cut in quickly. He gave Odin a warning look. "And this is a matter for the mages of the Iron Realm, not for outsiders. No matter if they are our allies."

"Cyrridven is trusted by you," Sif said. Her voice was calm and soft, alerting Thor to how much Odin and Merlin had already raised their voices. "We were born in your world and have loyalty to it."

"I do not wish to be ungrateful for your peace towards humans," Merlin assured Sif in a rather forced but polite tone. "But Cyrridven stays in the water to hold off the side effects of living in this world. You and your people do not take such precautions, and thus I am inclined to remember that you could become an enemy."

"A fair point, Merlin," Odin replied evenly. The ravens on his shoulders stiffened and Odin's eyes darkened. "But we are your help in this matter. If the Iron Soul is indeed a new child with each rebirth, then while his power is useful, he is limited."

Thor fought to stay still but caught Sif's eyes as they widened in realization and surprise. Gritting his teeth, Thor nearly demanded an explanation of Merlin and Morgana right there but fought his temper back. It was an effort that his father would have been proud of in other circumstances. There was a tense moment of silence until Odin nodded to him and extended his hand to Sif.

"We will depart so that you may return to the human settlement," Odin said. "May I send Huginn and Muninn to fetch you in the future?"

"Yes," Merlin answered before Morgana could say anything. "That would be wise. I do not believe that this is over."

"And even if the Sídhe are dissuaded, there is still the matter of the creatures already in our- this world. It is difficult to anticipate if they will adjust as we have."

"Indeed." Morgana raised an eyebrow and pursed her lips. "Farewell, Odin. Farewell, Sif."

"Farewell, Mages of the Iron Realm," Odin returned with a respectful nod.

Thor waited for Sif and her father to vanish into the trees before he turned towards Merlin and Morgana. His expression must have betrayed his question because Merlin held up his hand to silence him.

"Not here, Thor," Merlin ordered wearily. "It is dark and we are in a forest that we know our enemies may lurk within."

"He's right." Morgana brightened the orb of light in her hand and nodded towards the path. "Let's return to the village before anything more happens."

Before he could say anything or press on the subject of this Iron Soul, Merlin and Morgana started down the faint game trail towards the village. Thor stomped after them, glaring at their backs for the first few paces before his common sense won out and he quieted. As they came down the hill, he caught glimpses of the low glow of fires in the village and occasional flashes of a torch between the trees.

It took them far too long to reach the village, and thankfully the guard pulled the gate open for them. Thor lingered for a moment and eyed the wooden structure; wondering just how long it would truly hold up to a large group of the Dark Elves. He didn't like the answer his mind came up with and he hurried after Merlin and Morgana.

Following them towards the small hut, Thor glanced around and spotted his brother heading for them. He paused and waved his brother back, but offered his sibling a warm smile to reassure him. Arvid nodded in return to him and looked towards Merlin and Morgana with a question in his eyes. Shaking his head, Thor followed them inside and inwardly smiled, wondering when he'd suddenly become able to communicate with his brother without words. Perhaps it had always been there, a small voice in his head suggested.

The thought almost made him smile, but Thor focused on Merlin's back as he followed them into the hut. His chest was tightening with anticipation: it was almost the same as before a battle, and that realization made his heart speed up. The inside of the hut was chilled from their absence, but Morgana waved her hand towards the pile of dried wood in the fire pit. Silver magic flared and warm flames were suddenly licking at the logs and casting a glow through the small hut. Thor watched the fire catch properly for a moment before straightening up and turning to face Merlin.

"What is the Iron Soul?" Thor asked calmly, facing the question head on with his chin tilted up. "I think it's time that I understood what is happening."

"The Iron Soul is difficult to explain." Merlin sank down onto the bench and tented his fingers with a soft sigh. He looked tired and for a moment Thor was tempted to let them delay the conversation, but only for a moment. "It is a creation of the magic and power of the Iron Realm, this world, itself. Our world is connected to many other worlds, many of them very different from the last. The Iron Soul exists to protect the Iron Realm from beings from other worlds. They have access to the spark of magic that is almost always present now."

"It's the result of so many unnatural creatures living in our world," Morgana said with a dark glance towards the door. "You need to understand, Thor. that while some Old Ones are peaceful and even care to some extent about humans such as Odin does, the fact is that even those born in our world suffer from living in it."

"Add to that the descendants of the Sídhe warriors and the descendants of their escaped slaves, and there is always something in our world that does not belong," Merlin continued. "The Iron Soul was born when these dangers began to grow due to the Sídhe invasions when I was young."

"Born from what?" Thor questioned. "Some sort of deity? Is it alive?"

"Not as far as we know," Merlin replied. He shrugged and didn't look very concerned, much to Thor's shock. "I suspect, due to the things I have seen, that there is some sort of consciousness behind it, but its exact nature eludes us. I would not, however, call it a deity. It has never made itself known to us."

"The Iron Soul is human," Morgana said. "It is born in times in need and does battle with invaders to the Iron Realm."

"And I am this Iron Soul, born once again due to the threat of the Dark Elves?" Thor crossed his arms over his chest and breathed out thoughtfully.

"Indeed," Merlin said.

Thor watched the two older mages for a long moment as he waited for them to say more. They were looking at him expectantly; clearly waiting for something. What, he wasn't sure. Did they expect him to be shocked? He had power and had discovered it even before they came along.

"I see," he replied with a nod. "I suppose that makes sense."

"Is that it?" Morgana asked. "That's all you have to say about it?"

"It isn't really surprising, is it?" Thor shrugged, uncertain as to why Morgana was so aggravated.

"He can't be the reincarnation of Arto!" Morgana spun back to Merlin, her hands shaking with rage. "He can't be, Merlin! We must be wrong!"

"And yet we are not." Merlin ignored the irritated look that Thor knew must be on his own face. "He is not Arto and is, therefore... different."

Frowning, Thor decided he didn't like the turn of the conversation. He narrowed his eyes at Morgana and when she swung back to look at him, glared outright at the female mage. She scoffed, clearly unimpressed with him and Thor tried to think of something clever to say. Nothing came and instead he gave in to his churning irritation.

"You don't have to like me, Morgana," Thor said. "You don't even need to stay if you don't want to!"

"Thor!" Merlin began to cut in, but Thor ignored him.

"I am the Iron Soul; I'm not surprised by it. I've known that I was special for a long time."

"You are so arrogant," Morgana all but growled. "You don't know as much as you think, Thor!"

"Which is why we need to teach him!" Merlin jumped to his feet and gripped Morgana's shoulders. "Calm down, Morgana, you too, Thor. You two need to learn how to work together. Today's journey was just the start of this, I fear."

"Do you really believe that?" Thor asked with a frown, looking away from Morgana to meet Merlin's gaze. "We destroyed the tunnel."

"What we said about the Sídhe's militant nature before was very true," Merlin assured him with a serious nod as he released Morgana and stepped around her. "They now know that the Iron Gates can be battled against. It will take a major defeat, far more than this, to dissuade whatever warlord is currently in charge."

Morgana's shoulders slumped and her fingers tightened into fists, but she said nothing. Questions as to her history danced on the tip of his tongue, but Thor kept himself in check as Merlin gave him a warning look. As the older mage set a hand back on Morgana's shoulder, this time to comfort, Thor began to feel like an intruder.

"It's late," Merlin said. "And I for one brought down part of a mountain today and could use some rest."

Thor nodded quickly, a shiver going up his spine at the reminder of what this man had done just a short time ago. The notion that he might someday achieve that sort of power himself gave him a heady feeling.

"Of course," Thor forced out. "Good night, Merlin, Morgana. Rest well. We'll talk more in the morning."

Merlin nodded to him, relief clear in the man's brown eyes. Thor returned the nod as a lump began to form in his throat. Feeling a little too powerless, Thor turned and left the hut. The cool night air hit him and washed over his exposed skin, sending a shudder through him. Nonetheless, it was welcome and Thor turned his eyes up towards the night sky as he moved away from the hut. Above his head, the stars were bright with only a sliver of the moon illuminating the sky.

Breathing out slowly, Thor shook his shoulders and did his best to dismiss his irritation. There were things that he was clearly unaware of, but he couldn't fixate on that. Still, it made him angry, as did Morgana's reaction to him. Did she expect him to be this Arto? Shaking his head, Thor stomped away from the hut only to catch sight of a figure in a very familiar cloak lingering by the gate. Thor wondered why the gate was still open for only a moment before a flash of golden hair beneath the figure's hood made his feet start moving. As he approached Thor felt his hands becoming a touch sweaty and swallowed thickly as the implications of that settled on his shoulders.

"Sif," he greeted. Glancing towards the guard, he found the man staring at him in alarm. "Welcome to my village."

"Thank you, Thor." Sif gave him a small smile. "I hope you don't mind."

"Of course not," Thor replied quickly. "I'm not interested in sleeping just yet." He looked at the guard who was staring at Sif with a blend of interest and fear. "Shall we speak outside?"

"That might be best."

Giving the guard one more look, Thor stepped outside the gate and smiled at Sif. He was fully aware of how angry Merlin and Morgana would be, but that made him a little pleased.

"You reacted to Odin's announcement earlier," Thor said uneasily. Watching her in the corner of his eye, Thor noted that she looked a touch embarrassed. "You knew about it?"

"I've heard a bit about the Iron Soul," Sif said. "We don't know much about it, but it is said to be a testament to the power of the Iron Realm. My father has theorized that your world's position at the top of the trunk in the Tree of Reality is the reason for it. Your world touches so many different worlds."

"Were you surprised to learn that I was the Iron Soul?" Truthfully, Thor was unsure of what answer he hoped she'd give as he stored the information she'd given him away.

"The Iron Soul," Sif echoed. "That's not surprising really."

"I know." Thor chuckled and gestured back to the village. "They seemed to expect me to have a different reaction."

"Many would be surprised." Sif looked a bit too amused. "But then you are... very confident in your abilities."

"That's you being polite about my arrogance." Smirking, Thor let his amusement bubble up in his chest. It didn't bother him when Sif pointed it out like it did when Morgana did so.

"Well, I can't say that you don't know yourself. From what I understand about the magic of the Iron Realm that is a vital part of it."

"How does your power work then?" Thor asked before he could consider how personal the question might be. "I mean, you aren't a mage."

"I'm not human; I just look like one," Sif said. Thor watched her lick her lips as she looked at a nearby tree in thought. "It's a bit hard to explain really, but I am still a being of energy, Thor.... Just contained in a flesh vessel." He must have grimaced or made some foul expression because Sif flinched a little. "I mean, this is what I look like, this is what I was born as, but it also isn't the whole of it. I hold myself together through intent, through the need to survive in your world." She paused again and considered him with a slight smirk of her own. "In fact, perhaps we aren't so different. At your core as the Iron Soul, you are magical energy held together by the intent of the world."

"Perhaps," Thor answered shortly, uncomfortable with the suggestion.

"Well, my magic is me using some of my natural energy to bend the rules of your universe. The principles of control are the same as you and the Sídhe I suppose, but unlike you and other mages who draw power from the earth I use my own living energy."

"So, you could die by using too much then, correct?"

"Indeed, time is the only thing that recharges my power, but from what I understand a mage can use too much magic and burn away their own body, so we both must be cautious."

The sound of someone by the gate made them both pause in silence for a moment. As the footfalls moved on Sif relaxed and smiled gently at him. "I shouldn't linger, Thor, I was just concerned."

"About what?" Thor asked. "Surely not that Merlin and Morgana would harm me."

"I wasn't sure how you would react to the news." Sif tilted her head so her golden braid slipped out from beneath her hood. "I realize now how foolish that was."

"Perhaps." A smile tugged at his lips despite his best efforts. "But I am grateful for the sentiment, Sif." He paused and looked out into the darkness. "Will you be alright by yourself."

Sif laughed a sweet musical sound that made Thor flush and his stomach twist. She gave him a knowing look before leaning up on her toes and kissing his cheek. "I'll be fine, Thor," she assured him. "I'm sure we'll see each other soon."

Without another word, Sif gracefully moved away from the village gates. Thor watched her until she vanished into the dark trees. Still, in a daze, he reached back and knocked on the gate. As they opened to allow him back into the village, Thor glanced back one more time hoping to catch another glimpse of Sif, but she was gone.

22

The Enslaved

She was having the dream again. Alex hated that it was becoming so frequent that she was fully aware that she was dreaming. And yet despite everything she'd ever heard about lucid dreams, she couldn't wrestle control of this dream from her subconscious. It wasn't enough that last week she'd been knocked unconscious after the Sídhe attack for an unknown reason, it wasn't enough that midterms were only days away, but she had to keep having the same awful dream.

There wasn't anything she could do to change it though. With a sigh of defeat, Alex stepped out onto the bright deck of the gently swaying ship. By now the dream had long since lost whatever beauty the blue sky and ocean brought to it. Still, Alex had to admit that it was better than the reoccurring nightmare of the Sídhe tunnels that had plagued her... was it really just last year? Yet there had been a sense of warning to those dreams, a sense that she was doing something and maybe learning something even when the prophetic nature of the dream eluded her. But with this recurring dream, she had no understanding of why she was having it. Judging from the old-fashioned ship and the period clothing this was at least a couple centuries in the past, so why was she seeing it?

Alex felt her body moving forward against her will. Her stride was long and strong, making her body feel off balance when combined with the sway of the ship on the waves. Yet there was no hesitation in her body, no matter how she might feel. Alex marched to the ship's steering wheel, helm a voice in her head whispered. Her footfalls seemed to echo against the wooden planks of the upper deck and she easily adjusted her body with the rise and fall of the ship. It was almost comforting as she breathed in the scent of salt, but the air was once again tainted with the foul rotting smell. Then she looked down at the deck. The air rushed from her lungs and Alex's eyes widened in horror and shock.

There were rows of dark-skinned and naked men moving around on the deck. All of their eyes were downcast with looks of defeat marring their features. All of them were stained with filth but were obediently jogging in large circles. Sailors were circling them like predators, some with smirks while others looked uneasy. She found her eyes landing on a younger looking sailor who kept lowering his eyes and she felt her mouth twist into a sneer. A rush of irritation coursed through her that Alex couldn't stop and felt ashamed of.

Then her eyes shifted back to the rows of men and she took them in with a critical eye despite her urge to snap her eyes shut. This was new, horrifying and new. She wanted to wake up, but she didn't. Two of the men were missing arms with scarred stubs in their place. They were slim with their ribs beginning to show: fed just enough to keep them from dying. One of the men swayed dangerously and was caught by the others beside him. A voice called for a doctor and a small man came rushing out of the cabins below the helm.

She just watched as the doctor in his neat clothes examined the fainted man. He opened the man's eyes and peered at them before opening his mouth and studying his throat. The others were herded by sharp words by the sailors and pressed back towards the grate leading to the hold. Alex swallowed thickly as they quietly marched below deck. Moments later the low sound of metal chains echoed up onto deck along with the thick stench that had always haunted this dream. A cold hole opened in her gut that threatened to swallow her whole. It was a slave ship.

The ill slave was taken below deck, but she didn't move or try to speak. Alex was still until another group of slaves was brought up onto the deck. One made a dash for the side of the ship only to be grabbed roughly by two of the sailors. They threw him back into the group of slaves who cast down their eyes. Her eyes narrowed on that slave who sank to his knees, a look of utter despair on his face before he was pulled up to begin the exercises. She glanced back towards the fainted slave and doctor, but there seemed to be no change. Alex didn't move and just kept observing the men being put through exercises by the crew who watched them carefully. A deafening roar of anger and despair washed through her and Alex desperately hoped that she'd do something, say something to stop this, but nothing came out.

Suddenly one of the black men lashed out at a crewman and hit him squarely in the jaw. Two of the soon to be slaves tried to grab him, shouting at him in an unfamiliar language. More of the crew rushed forward and grabbed the rebellious man with sharp, brutal movements, slamming him against the side of the ship. Alex inwardly flinched, but her body didn't move an inch. Fear clawed at her for a moment as the men fought, but for the slave rather than the crew.

"The usual, Captain?" a sailor asked. He sounded bored.

"Yes," Alex felt her lips reply, though a much deeper and colder voice rolled out. "Watch the attempted jumper. If he tries anything again remind him that he'll be returning to his homeland as a headless spirit."

"Yes, Captain," the sailor answered. His voice was calm, clearly used to the ugly words. "Anything more, sir?"

"We're almost through the Middle Passage. Double check provisions; tomorrow I want to start fattening the slaves up again. Increase their rations."

"Should make them behave better," the sailor said. "Except for those that throw themselves overboard."

Alex would have been shaking with rage at the remark, she would have been screaming, and she would have been fighting back the urge to be physically ill if she'd had any control over her body. Instead, she just stood there as the slaves were all taken below deck once more. Her eyes lingered on the entrance with a churning sense of dread and the hope that she'd never go down there in this dream. History had never been her subject, but she could remember fragments that she'd learned about the slave trade in American History. Now she felt that she knew too much.

A sharp pain on her face made Alex twitch, her whole body moving just the tiniest bit. At first, she was surprised; it had never reacted to anything from her before, but then she felt the pain again. It was deeper this time, and her skin felt like it was burning. Around her, the ship began to blur and Alex struggled to understand where the pain was coming fr om.

Eyes snapping open, Alex felt like she was falling as the rocking of the ship vanished out from under her. The air was suddenly dry and stale and the world felt hazy around her. She gasped for air just as a sharp pain along her face brought her back to reality. The pain was followed by another and on instinct she snapped her hand out to the right, striking something even as she threw off her comforter and rolled off her bed to the left. Something was running down her face and a dull ache was present near her right eye.

Alex brought her hand up and wiped at the warm sticky fluid dripping down her face, but didn't pay it much mind. Instead, she tried to see what had attacked her as her heart pounded so loudly it echoed in her ears. In the darkness, Alex couldn't see what was in the room. The soft blue light of her laptop charger beneath the desk only cast a faint glow that made the room seem larger and eerier than it truly was.

She backed up and collided with her desk chair. Searching the darkness, Alex fought to still her breathing, but she couldn't hear anything for a long moment. Then she heard a soft rustle of something small moving in the bed, but she couldn't pinpoint the creature. Her fingers began to creep across the desk towards the lamp, but a sudden sound from the bed made her stop moving. It sounded like grumbling and there was a muted flash of light that burned itself into her eyes.

As her vision tried to clear, Alex shook her head and tried to search the room again. There was a flicker of magic in the air, faint, but she was certain it was there. She smirked at the realization that she could find whatever had attacked her. Taking a deep breath, Alex forced her eyes closed against every instinct. She felt her magic flare up through her chest and pushed it outward all around her as a cloud. It brushed over a thin thread of magic and she opened her eyes to find a faint line of dark silver magic shimmering through the air. It led to her bed where something small was moving beneath the covers she'd thrown back. For a moment Alex was frozen in surprise as she examined the thread. It was similar to the line of magic that had connected Chernobog and his shadow monsters. Frighteningly similar.

Reaching out, Alex touched her index finger to the thread. The moment she connected with it a rush of energy flew up her arm and struck her in the chest. Gasping for air, Alex grabbed at the magic and pulled it, trying to drag it away from the creature. A soft cry of alarm and pain from the bed wasn't enough to stop her, and she grit her teeth. She could feel the magic rushing over her fingers, trying to flow towards the creature, but she tightened her grip. Her own magic swirled and spun around her other hand, and to Alex's surprise, the alien magic suddenly rolled back towards her. It blended with her own power without any effort and swam up her arm.

Her mind went blank as the magic filled her chest and gut. She couldn't breathe for a moment as her heart beat against her ribs. From the bed, she vaguely heard a strange groan and then weeping. Her legs buckled and Alex scraped her back on her chair as she collapsed to the ground. The world spun around her and Alex barely held the panic at bay. Yet nothing attacked her, and the world slowly stabilized.

Grabbing her chair, Alex carefully pulled herself up onto her knees and kept listening. The soft tiny sobs were still audible but began to ease as she moved. Whatever was in the room with her was aware of her recovery. She made it to her feet and tried to see the source of the sounds once again, but only saw part of her comforter shift a tiny bit.

"I'm sorry," a small voice called out of the darkness.

Reaching over her desk, Alex flicked the switch of her desk lamp and illuminated part of the room with a soft glow. Her comforter jumped again and then a shape began to move around under it. As her eyes widened, Alex tracked its progress as it moved towards the bottom of the bed. She stopped breathing as it reached the end of the comforter and pushed it back before leaping forward onto the baseboard.

The creature was a small humanoid only a few inches tall with pudgy facial features and tiny, but very pointed and slightly floppy ears. Tiny black eyes peered up at her in surprise as it stayed perched on the top of the footboard. There were shiny tear tracks on its cheeks that it rubbed quickly almost like it was embarrassed. As it didn't seem to be a hurry to move, Alex leaned back and knocked on the shared wall with Nicki. She couldn't seem to find her voice and her heart was still racing from the rush of magic. The small creature shifted nervously as sounds began to come from Nicki's room, and Alex took the chance to get a better look at the thing. It was dressed in what looked like old doll clothes that had been altered to fit it and tiny leather boots.

"Alex?" Nicki called. There was a soft knock on the door. "You okay?"

Forcing her legs to move, Alex shifted around her desk and past the bookshelf to open the door. She pulled it open and gestured for Nicki to stay quiet. The creature had turned to keep watching her and tensed up as Nicki came in the room.

"You're bleeding!" Nicki raised her hand to Alex's cheek, pushing back her hair to inspect the wound. "Almost got your eye!" Nicki flexed her fingers and an orb of blue magic swirled into being.

"Nicki." Alex nodded towards the bed pointedly.

Nicki turned so quickly that her red braid struck Alex's shoulder and her blue eyes widened comically. She fumbled behind Alex's back and the ceiling light came on, temporarily blinding Alex. The small fairy threw up an arm to shield its eyes from the light. For a moment Alex was completely at a loss. Her mind fixated on the strange realization that she was in her pajamas, bleeding, and looking at a Brownie on her bed.

Then the creature lowered its hands and blinked its small eyes at them. It seemed to have adjusted and was shifting nervously, watching, and waiting to see what they would do. Nicki took a step forward with her magic glittering dangerously. Alex waved a hand, signaling her to wait.

"Are you going to attack us?" Alex heard herself ask, not having thought about the words.

"No!" Its voice was surprisingly low and had an odd echoey quality to it. "Don't wish to harm anyone."

"But Faery creatures are under a spell," Nicki protested suspiciously. "You already hurt Alex."

"Spell broken now!" the creature cried. It leapt around joyfully for a second before slumping. "At least spell broken on me." It raised its eyes to Alex and studied her. "Your magic broke spell. Thank you. Sorry for harm."

"That's okay." Holding back a nervous giggle, Alex tried to organize her thoughts. "Uh, who and what are you?" She grimaced at her words. "Sorry if that's rude, but uh, we're a bit confused at the moment."

"I am Timothy." The creature swept into a bow. "I am a Brownie."

"A Brownie," Nicki repeated. The blue orb in her hand dispersed into the air. "Named Timothy?"

Alex almost laughed at Nicki's disbelief. It was an odd name for a Faery, but then again what should they be expecting? Oddly she remembered the old girl scout Brownie rhyme very clearly at that moment. Yet she had to admit that the small creature certainly fit her limited knowledge of fairy types.

"Yes Brownie, helper creature," Timothy said. "Ancestors enchanted to serve as labor to the Sídhe. We have a little magic to help with chores." Timothy looked down and scuffed his foot against the wood of Alex's baseboard. "But it was bound and turned against mages. So sorry."

"It's okay," Alex assured him. Tears were glistening in his tiny eyes again. "That's not your fault." She swallowed, feeling a rush of illness at the reminder that the Faeries they'd destroyed lately had all been under a spell. "You're not going to hurt us now, right?"

"No!" Timothy almost fell off the bed in a sudden burst of movement. "Don't want to hurt anyone."

"Okay, then we aren't going to hurt you," Alex promised. "But maybe you can help us. We don't know much about what is happening or how to stop it."

"Can't stop it," Timothy cried. "Can't break bindings."

"Yet Alex must have," Nicki said. "After all you aren't... bound, are you?"

"No, I'm not," Timothy agreed slowly. He looked up at Alex with wide eyes. "I'm not!"

"Look, we should get dressed, alert the others, and get to Merlin or Morgana's." Alex tried not to shift under the look she was getting from the Brownie.

"Grab some clothes and get dressed in the bathroom," Nicki said. "I'll keep an eye on him."

Alex hesitated. Her head was spinning and she wondered if she was still asleep. Raising a finger up towards the lingering pain on her face, she brushed over slightly warm liquid and pulled her hand back to study it. Red blood covered her fingertips and she could still feel a slight trickle down her face.

"Get your cut cleaned up, I can heal it without much effort," Nicki added in a softer voice. "But we need to get moving."

Nodding, Alex glanced back at Timothy who was still watching her with an expression that was a blend of awe, hope, and guilt. She forced herself to look away from the Brownie and grabbed some clothes from her drawers. Before she left the room, she snagged her phone and as she shut the door of the bathroom, Alex was already texting the others to meet at Merlin's house at once.

She took a deep breath and looked up into the mirror. There was a shallow but long cut running from the edge of her cheekbone down past her eye. A small shudder ran up her body as she realized how lucky she'd been with Timothy. He'd gotten past the defenses and attacked in her sleep and yet she was okay. Shaking her head, Alex wet a washcloth, cleaned up the cut, and put a bandage over it. Grabbing her clothes, she checked her phone one last time to find a reply from Merlin and Morgana agreeing to meet before she changed and tried to brace herself for whatever else was going to happen tonight.

23

The Brownie

Jenny had never really been a morning person by nature: just by necessity. Morning required a cup of coffee, time for a nice hot shower, and plenty of time for hair and makeup, so she'd long been in the habit of waking up at least two hours before she needed to be anywhere. On days that she really wanted to look nice it was best to add an extra half an hour to that. Yet at 2 a.m. today she'd been awoken by a text message that had her throwing on the first shirt she could put her hands on and yesterday's jeans.

Merlin's house seemed as far out of town as Morgana's, and Jenny couldn't help but worry that they were meeting there because of the Iron Chalice. She desperately hoped that no one needed the Chalice, but Alex's text hadn't offered much information. As she pulled up to the one-story light green house that was half hidden by a massive oak tree in the front lawn, Jenny checked for Alex's car and tensed up when she confirmed it wasn't there. She tightened her grip on the steering wheel, wondering why she hadn't checked their dorm room first instead of just rushing here.

A moment later, Aiden's blue truck pulled up behind her, just off the main driveway. His headlights turned off and she watched in the rearview mirror as Aiden and Bran both clamored out of the truck. Up ahead Morgana's red car was parked alongside Merlin's SUV and Lance's truck was coming up the drive behind them. Everyone was here except for Alex and Nicki.

Bran knocked gently on her window, and there was just enough light from her own headlights and Lance's truck that she could see his worried expression. She nodded and turned off her car. Bran stepped back and she climbed out with a soft exhale as the night air hit her face.

"Do we know anything?" Jenny asked as Aiden joined them.

"No." Aiden looked around as if he could make them appear by force of will. "I didn't even check in their dorm. I figured the text meant that they were already on their way here."

"Me too," Jenny admitted uneasily. "I hope it isn't anything too bad."

"Hopefully not," Bran agreed, nodding towards Lance as he came jogging up to them. "But Alex wouldn't disturb us all at this hour unless it was important."

"Good thing we all keep our phones close," Aiden sighed. "'Course, this is why we do."

"You okay?" Lance moved to her side, giving her a soft look.

"Yeah," she assured him with an uneasy smile. "Sorry I didn't wait for you... I just bolted."

"It's okay," Lance assured her. "Come on, guys, let's get inside just in case. It's too dark to be waiting out here."

She'd never been to Merlin's house before, though Alex had given her the address and instructions to run there should anything really bad ever happen. It wasn't as grand and imposing as Morgana's Victorian style home and seemed rather normal in comparison. A pair of winged gargoyles were standing in shrubs by the stairs leading up to the porch, a dusting of snow still present on them.

"Merlin and your family," Bran chuckled. He reached down and dusted some snow off the head of one of the gargoyles.

"Huh?" Lance asked.

"Oh, my parents have some smaller gargoyles at our house too," Aiden explained. "A few years back the local gardening store got them and I think we were the only households to purchase any. It's sort of funny I guess."

Jenny didn't feel amused and was grateful when the front door opened for them. Merlin looked exhausted with his short curls a mess and a steaming cup of coffee in his right hand. He glanced over all of them, and Jenny could tell he was disappointed that Alex wasn't with them.

"Come in," he said quickly. "There's coffee in the living room."

Merlin's home was much smaller than Morgana's, but they seemed to share a fondness for antique furniture. Or maybe when you were immortal with the magical ability to repair things you avoided furniture shopping. His living room had a large fireplace where a small fire was burning opposite a set of stairs leading into a basement. Several dining chairs had been brought in to provide enough seating for everyone around the worn green sofa and pair of dark blue armchairs.

Most importantly, however, was that on the coffee table before the fireplace sat the Iron Chalice. The polished dark metal was shining in the light of the flames and seemed to be glowing with power. Jenny stopped and stared at the magical object from her place by the doorway for a long moment before making herself move forward.

As she sat down on the sofa and shifted so Lance could sit next to her, Jenny looked around the room at some of the photos on the mantle. Many of them were quite old and she didn't recognize anyone in them. There were a few scattered paintings and photos on the wall and a corner shelf that was filled with little knick knacks. Her attention shifted as Bran moved around the sofa and towards the fire. Bran was eying the chalice with a very odd expression as he sank down into one of the armchairs. It was a thoughtful expression, and she wondered just what was going through his head.

"Relax, Fisher King," Aiden said. He chuckled weakly. "It's probably just a precaution."

"Indeed," Morgana said as she came out of the kitchen. "We haven't heard anything to indicate that Alex or Nicki was injured." She looked over all of them with wide, almost fearful eyes. "Did anyone check at their dorm room?"

"No; we figured they'd already be on their way," Aiden admitted as he sat down on one of the dining chairs.

Jenny took the opportunity to study Morgana. Apparently, she hadn't been the only one to just roll out of bed and rush here. The woman's long dark hair was messy and she was wearing an oversized flannel shirt over a simple black tank top and jeans, which was by far the most casual that Jenny had ever seen her. It was a bit worrying in truth. The older woman directed Aiden into the kitchen to get some coffee.

She remained quiet as Aiden got up and Lance stood to join him. Bran was still looking at the Iron Chalice with intense concentration and Jenny felt very alone in the quiet room. Lance returned a few moments later and handed her a warm Ravenslake University mug filled with coffee before he retook his seat. The silence hung in the room with only the crackling of the fire and the soft ticking of the grandfather clock behind her filling the empty air.

Unable to sit still, Jenny stood up and moved over to the front windows. Behind her, she could hear the others talking quietly and a couple of people moving, probably just as nervous as she was. She parted the dark beige curtains and peered out into the dark driveway. Outside thick clouds were hiding the moon and hinting at snow, but otherwise, the world seemed peaceful. Jenny didn't trust it. Then, thankfully, Alex's dark blue sedan came up the gravel drive and parked right in front of the h ouse.

"They're here!" Jenny rushed towards the door.

Morgana somehow beat her there and pulled the door open. As Morgana stepped out onto the narrow porch, Jenny lingered by the doorway and tried to watch to see what would happen. Lance joined her and grabbed her hand, giving it a soft squeeze.

"I'm sure she's fine," Lance said. "She would have said something in her text if she wasn't."

"Still..."

An exhausted looking Alex stumbled into the house a moment later, her hair pulled back into a messy ponytail which only let Jenny get a good look at the bags under her eyes. She had to wonder how much concealer Alex had been using lately before her eyes dropped to a small bag that Alex was carefully holding.

"I'm fine," Alex said. She gave them a forced smile as she moved past them into the living room. Her eyes fell on the Iron Chalice and she seemed to hesitate for a moment. "Bran, hold onto that for me, will you?"

Bran gave her a surprised look, but nodded and leaned forward to pick up the Chalice. Alex licked her lips and looked back towards Nicki who was locking the front door. Without a word, Nicki moved over to the curtains Jenny had opened earlier and pulled them closed.

"Girls, what happened?" Morgana demanded, watching them with confusion. "Were you attacked?"

"Something like that," Alex said. "But it became a bit more complicated."

Alex moved over towards the center of the living room and sank down into the free armchair. The bag was sitting carefully on her lap and Alex glanced down at it with an odd expression that caught everyone's attention. Then the bag shifted on its own. Jenny bit her lip to hold in a squeak of surprise.

"Alex-" Merlin began to ask, but Alex shook her head.

Alex motioned for the others to be quiet and set the small bag down gently on the coffee table. Before anyone could say anything else, she unzipped the bag and a small head popped out from underneath the arm of a rolled-up hoodie. Alex leaned forward, resting her elbows on her knees, watching them with a small smile.

"This is Timothy the Brownie." Alex giggled, with a hint of hysteria creeping in.

Alex extended a hand and the Brownie grabbed onto her extended fingers, letting Alex lift him out of the bag. He released his grip and landed on the wooden table with a soft thump before straightening up and dusting off the tiny coat he wore. Jenny stared at the little creature even as a small part of her noted the resemblance between the real thing and the illustration in the book on German folklore. The Brownie shifted nervously amongst them and looked around uneasily. It wrung its hands together for a moment before toying with a small plastic clasp on its jacket. Jenny couldn't help but notice that the coat looked a bit like one she'd had for a male doll when she was young.

"What happened?" Merlin finally asked. He groaned slightly and rubbed his eyes.

"Well, he... uh attacked me," Alex said. Jenny swore that Morgana's eyes flashed silver at those words. "Just a small cut and Nicki already healed it," she added in a rush. "But when I was trying to find him in my room...

I spread my magic out to try to find him and saw this thread of magic connecting to him."

"The binding of the control spell," the Brownie said. His head was lowered and he scuffed his foot against the top of the table.

"Yeah, and I, well I guess I broke it when I pulled on it because the next moment Timothy was apologizing and offered to talk with us."

"You broke the spell?" Merlin gasped in surprise before a wide smile took over his face. "Remarkable! Did you pull on the magic again?"

"Exactly!" Alex nodded with a relieved expression.

Jenny just stared at the little creature; completely uncaring as to if she was being rude. It was a Brownie, an actual Brownie. She wasn't sure if she should just sit there quietly in shock, laugh, or run out of the house screaming. The Sídhe were one thing: she knew to run from them and get to a mage as fast as she could. Jenny knew from experience to flee from any of the fairy creatures, but now there was one just standing on the coffee table in front of her. And this was a rather cute and nervous looking thing that was twitching like some sort of stray puppy unsure of its welcome.

"Do you know what bound you?" Merlin eyed the small creature intensely.

"Not sure," the Brownie answered in a small voice. "First there were nightmares.... Terrible nightmares of red human blood and this voice..." The small fairy creature shuddered and wrapped its arms around its torso. "I couldn't understand it at first, but it... sank in. It bound us to it. Magic surrounded us and chained us to her will and there was nothing we could do."

"Her will?" Morgana repeated. "Are you aware of who bound you?"

"Yes, the old mad queen Scáthbás," Timothy answered. "It was her voice that called to us!" The Brownie tugged on one of his ears and rocked on his feet. "She didn't tell us much... it was very fuzzy, but it was her." Timothy shook his head and tears gathered in his eyes once more. "There were always stories. Tales of the old worlds that were swallowed by the armies and enslaved. Stories about our ancestors who fled into this world when the Iron Gates were forged to escape her grasp."

"Scáthbás was killed," Morgana said. Then she shook her head. "At least, we thought she was."

"Her magic strong," Timothy said. "Somehow bound all creatures of Tree of Reality branch."

"This magic," Morgana folded her hands. "Can you tell us anything else about it? Did you see a magical object, hear any special words, or see a particular color of magic?"

"I could taste it," the Brownie replied, tugging on the hem of his jacket. "As it took over me, I felt it and could taste it."

"I'm not sure that helps us," Merlin told Morgana. "He has different senses to ours."

"It tasted like her magic." The Brownie pointed one long finger towards Alex only to shrink into himself. "I'm sorry. Maybe I'm wrong. So sorry."

"No, it's alright." Alex gave the Brownie a forced smile. "You've been very helpful."

As soon as the words were out of Alex's mouth, she collapsed back into the armchair. She turned her head and looked in the flames of the fire leaving everyone, including Timothy, staring at her. Someone moved, but Jenny didn't look to see who it was as she tried to sort out what was happening with Alex.

"This is good, right?" Lance asked, breaking the silence. "Doesn't that mean that Alex can break this spell?"

"She almost collapsed again after doing it." Nicki returned with two mugs of coffee and handed one to Alex.

"Yeah." Alex sighed before she took a sip of the coffee. "Thing is that I saw the lines of magic again like I did with Chernobog. That's what happened during that attack at Morgana's house. I'm seeing the magical connection between the fairies and Scáthbás."

"If you can control it then you might be able to at least free those that attack us," Bran suggested carefully.

Alex turned her head and her eyes dropped to the Iron Chalice with an odd look on her face. Under other circumstances, Jenny would have just thought she was staring off into space, but this was something else. Something more. Lance covered her hand and gave it a reassuring squeeze. Breathing out a little, Jenny looked between the Brownie and Alex, and wondered just what changes this new development was going to bring. Based on the look on Alex's face, she was very confident that she wasn't going to like it.

24

Dark Tidings

15 C.E. Sør-Trøndelag, Norway

"I don't like this, Merlin," Morgana said as she ducked under a low hanging branch in the forest. "Being summoned by those damned ravens cawing all night." Her cloak caught on a trunk for a moment before she tugged it off. "We have to be cautious."

"I am aware, Morgana," Merlin replied. "I was aware the first twenty times that you made this argument, but Odin and Frea have been honest with us thus far."

"This is not their world," Morgana countered. Thor sent Merlin a pitying look from his place at the back of their small group as they hiked through the forest. "We cannot trust that they truly wish to protect it," Morgana argued.

"Frea and her community have nothing to go back to," Merlin reminded her calmly, giving Thor the impression that this argument truly was just a repeat. "They would never be welcomed in the Sídhe worlds even if they could safely pass through the barrier of the Iron Gates."

"We don't know for certain that they can't! All it would take is one spy amongst her people traveling into the tunnels and reporting our actions to them in exchange for a lordly position."

"I suppose that is possible," Merlin conceded. "Though after generations of living in the Iron Realm, I highly doubt that the Sídhe would trust them any more than you do."

Morgana bristled at the remark comparing her and the Sídhe. Merlin kept moving up the small path as Morgana glared fiercely at his back. They were both tense, and the faint cawing of crows in the distance alerted Thor that they were getting close to the meeting point.

"There is still the Old Ones to worry about," Morgana reminded Merlin after only a few moments of silence. "The locals think them deities."

"And others back home see Cyrridven as a Goddess," Merlin said. "That does not mean that they mean harm to the Iron Realm. In fact, it would be to their benefit to take an active role in keeping this world safe."

"I just don't trust them, Merlin; we cannot be sure of their motives."

"Do you two always have the same arguments over and over again?" Thor asked. They both turned quickly to stare at him. "Do you two even like each other at all?"

"Thor!" Morgana scolded with a flash of hurt on her face.

"Morgana and I care about and are usually friendly with one another, but we have different perspectives on the world." Merlin laid a hand on Morgana's shoulder. "As such, we do have disagreements on how to proceed."

Thor gave them a doubtful look, though he couldn't help but notice how physically comfortable the pair seemed to be next to each other. Frowning, he remembered how he and the villagers had originally assumed them to be married. Morgana's green eyes were boring into him and Thor felt a flood of discomfort.

"But that makes no sense; you've known each other for so long and yet you keep arguing over this."

"Time has nothing to do with it," Merlin said, apparently picking up that Thor was a little sorry. "We grew up under very different circumstances. What unites us is our dedication to the Iron Realm and to the Iron Soul." Merlin sent a stern look his way, but Thor refused to shrink into himself.

"I believe that we can trust them. Frea has too much to lose to not help end this threat, and my people do see Odin and Sif as gods already," Thor offered quickly as he looked to Morgana. "I don't believe they would risk what they could lose against what there may be to gain."

"As I said it only takes one traitor," Morgana growled. "That is all it takes, Thor; one traitor."

The tone of her words gave Thor pause, and he stopped walking to stare at her back for a moment. Something twisted in his gut at the note of regret, sorrow, and anger that her words had carried. Shaking his head, he started walking once more but stayed silent this time. Morgana muttered something to Merlin in a voice too low for him to hear. He had a feeling she was complaining about him once again. Oddly it didn't inspire the anger that it had before, but Thor pushed the odd thought away. He wasn't interested in analyzing his feelings on the matter just before they met with their allies.

Thor was almost feeling back to normal when they reached their destination and was able to shake off the lingering uncertainty. The clearing was small with towering trees swaying in the wind all around them, but it was in the shadow of the mountain and far enough from the village that Thor didn't need to feel concerned. He clenched and unclenched his fists a few times, wondering if his hair was still neat after the hike. Merlin sent an inquiring look his way and Thor forced himself to relax just before the sounds of someone coming through the trees across the clearing could be heard.

Odin stepped out of the trees a moment later with Sif and another unknown figure, one dressed in light armor and armed with a sword and axe. He towered over Sif and shared her brilliant blonde hair. Merlin shifted and stepped in front of him before Thor had a good chance to get a look at the unknown man. He was quickly distracted from his annoyance at the protective gesture by Frea stepping out of the trees and into the clearing, though she stayed in the shadows of the trees with her face turned down and a hand raised to guard her eyes.

"Put your hood on," Morgana said. "We can see it is you."

Frea did not wait another moment before pulling the hood of her cloak over her head and letting the top of it settle over her face, shielding her eyes from the sun. Her shoulders relaxed and Thor found himself wondering how painful direct sunlight was for the Sídhe descendants. Frea moved around the tree line to come a bit closer to them but stayed to the shadows.

"Thor, Merlin, Morgana," Frea greeted with a small bow. "I trust you are well."

"We have suffered no injuries as of late," Morgana replied dismissively.

"That is good to hear," Frea said, and an awkward silence ensued. "Greetings, Odin. Greetings, Sif." She nodded to the Old Ones respectfully. "I trust you and yours are well?"

"We are. This is one of my sons." Odin gestured to the blond male. "Baldr. He has been tracking the movement of some of the Dark Elves to the north of here."

Thor eyed Baldr critically, taking in the being's height and bright blond hair. His own bleached hair was dark in comparison to the shining locks. Baldr was looking at him with equal curiosity, and Thor smirked in amusement. He'd heard of Baldr in the past, though his name wasn't as well-known as Odin. Thor wasn't completely sure what Baldr was supposed to be the god of. He'd heard healing and light, or maybe it was peace and justice. Hopefully, it was something useful to them.

"It is a pleasure to meet the Mages of the Iron Realm," Baldr greeted with a deep nod. Then he turned his attention to Frea. "And I welcome you, peaceful daughter of the Sídhe."

Frea seemed at a loss for how to respond to Baldr's greeting. Thor couldn't tell if she was flattered by it or if she took offense at her connection to the Sídhe being recognized. Whatever she felt, she pushed it away quickly and turned her violet eyes to Thor for a moment before she looked towards Merlin.

"I am afraid that there is a concentration of these Dark Elves to the north of here, as my father said," Baldr explained. "I have been attempting to track them, but they vanish into the shadows too easily during the night and do not show themselves during the day. We do know their rough area though, where they spend most of their time."

"I fear that I can explain that," Frea said. She shifted in the shadows, clutching at her cloak nervously. "Our scouts have discovered a new settlement being built by the tainted Sídhe to the north, most likely in the same area that you have been noticing them."

"A settlement?" Merlin repeated with widening eyes. "How sophisticated?"

"It is underground in a series of caverns that they have already begun to alter. They are carving out their buildings and expanding the caverns themselves. No houses yet; they seem to be using barrack style quarters. They also have some sort of weapon production, but we are uncertain of what metal they are using or where they are getting it from."

"It couldn't be iron," Morgana muttered uneasily, looking to Merlin. "But how would they secure the materials for bronze?"

"Some of our people have developed a resistance to iron," Frea pointed out carefully. "Exposure to this world has gradually lessened our weakness to it. Perhaps passing through the Iron Gate barrier granted them the same?"

"Let us not jump to conclusions," Odin said. "Frea, do you know what sort of social structure they have in place? Do they seem to be loyal to the Sídhe or are they forming a military of their own?"

"We don't know that yet," Frea admitted. A frustrated sigh that sounded all too human to Thor escaped her. In the corner of his eye, he watched an odd expression flicker over Morgana's face as well. "We've only been able to observe from the outer edges of the settlement thus far, and they are adding new patrols and guards every day. We don't know if they are forming a military force beyond that, and I hesitate to send our scouts too far in. These creatures are developing differences compared to us. I fear it would be impossible for any of mine to pass as one of them. Those lines of magic on their bodies are dispersing across the rest of their flesh and making their skin darker than ours, and the way they move..." Frea shook her head and a small shudder went through her.

"It sounds as though we cannot wait for them to gain more power," Morgana said darkly. "These Dark Elves are not remaining the feral creatures we hoped they would. If they are regaining their minds, then loyal to the Sídhe or not, they are a significant threat."

"Agreed," Frea said. "They haven't sought us out, so they aren't seeking help surviving in this world. My concern isn't just the danger the Dark Elves already here pose. If the Sídhe establish another tunnel like you think they will, then their numbers will just keep growing."

"Yes." Merlin rubbed his beard thoughtfully. "It would benefit them to grab new arrivals immediately and hold them until they adjusted."

"Anything on how long it takes them to adjust?" Odin asked Frea. "Is there a timeline for when they begin to regain more of their minds?"

"I'm not sure of that either." Frea twisted her pale hands together. "To be honest at this point we aren't even sure how much of their minds they are recovering. We just don't know if they are forming a primitive group or if they have truly retained their more advanced knowledge."

"It is distressing that we know so little." Odin shook his head sadly before offering Frea a smile. "But it is a start, and we have a location. I will have Huginn and Muninn keep an eye on the area if you provide me with exact details. We may learn something by observing their patterns of movement outside of the caverns."

"And scrying magic may be of some use," Morgana added thoughtfully. "If nothing else it will help me get a sense of how much magic they have access to."

"There haven't been any signs of magic thus far," Frea said. "And my people usually don't have any magic at all."

"Usually?" Baldr questioned with a tilt of his head.

"Occasionally one of us has some magic, but it degrades our bodies. We aren't certain why it manifests, as the Iron Realm does not grant us power."

"You are not mages of the Iron Realm," Odin said. "It is the same for our kind in this world. But the question of their magic could give us a clue as to what exactly is happening to them. If they do have magic, then there is still a link between them and their home world. If not, then perhaps the transition from their world to ours through the barrier of the Iron Gate cuts off their connection to their home world."

"Speculation at this point," Morgana interrupted. "It is unlikely that they have magic, but we have to be ready for anything. Let's focus on this settlement, not debate the likelihood of these creatures retaining a connection to Sídhean."

"Do we know anything more about this settlement," Thor asked, both out of curiosity and hoping to keep a dispute from breaking out. Sif caught his eye and smiled at him. "An estimate of their numbers, the ratio of warriors to non-warriors?" He paused and shrugged. "What are they eating? Are they hunting animals or doing something else?"

Merlin turned and looked at him with surprise shining in his eyes. Odin was giving him an approving look and that little smile was still on Sif's face. Stilling his body, Thor fought back his smirk and met Merlin's gaze as calmly as he could. A soft chuckle escaped Morgana.

"They seem to be gathering roots for the most part during the nights," Frea said. "There is no sign of them trying to consume any of the animals of your world." She paused and considered him for a moment before adding, "We rarely consume the flesh of creatures of your world, and when we do it requires extra preparation."

"To avoid the iron of the blood," Morgana told him softly. "They dare not consume it."

"Exactly," Frea agreed. "It is a challenge to avoid iron in your world, but if they are like us then they will be able to consume small amounts. As to your other questions, we do not have a good estimate on how many there are. The sentry groups are five each and we know of at least four such groups."

"There are more questions than answers," Odin said. He frowned and glanced up at his ravens. "We don't know enough to take any action against the creatures. Have they attacked the human settlements lately?"

"No," Thor answered. "Since we caused the tunnel to collapse there haven't been any attacks."

"Let us hope it stays that way, though now I wonder if that is because they are focusing on their settlement," Odin announced with a shake of his head. "Shall we meet in three days' time?" Odin asked as he surveyed their odd group. "And report our findings?"

"Huginn and Muninn will be limited in what they can see." Frea looked up at the ravens and shook her head in resignation. "I'll see about volunteers to go deeper into the new settlement. With any luck, they'll be able to find out some real details."

"Be careful," Sif said softly, which surprised Frea and drew a small smile from her.

"Morgana and I will do what we can with our magic," Merlin added. "In three days, we will meet here."

"Then we are agreed," Odin concluded with a smile. "Very well, go in peace, Mages of the Iron Realm and Frea."

Morgana and Merlin did not move as Frea dashed into the cover of the mountainside. Her dark cloak hid her well and she quickly disappeared. The three Old Ones left together at a much slower pace with Odin leading the way. Thor's eyes lingered on Sif until Morgana glanced his way and he had to fight back a flush.

"Maybe we should go and take a look at this settlement," Thor suggested as they began to head back towards the village. "There are so many unknowns, and it isn't right to keep putting Frea and her people in danger."

"We can't put you in danger either," Merlin replied. "It is out of the question, Thor. Too much could go wrong."

"So, what, we just let them keep building up their forces, becoming more organized until they sweep over my people?"

"Patience is valuable, Thor," Morgana reminded him. "They have to be eating something: we can arrange observation points around this settlement and pick them off, study them from safety, and build a plan. With any luck, I will be able to scry into the settlement and learn more about whatever leadership is in place."

"That's it?" Thor all but growled in agitation. "But the three of us are mages, we could go and attack them and destroy them."

"War is not won by fools," Merlin scolded. A dark look suddenly took over the man's face and made his brown eyes appear black. "And it would seem that a war is what we will be dealing with. We do not know enough to risk a full-frontal attack. For all we know, right now they could still be working with the Sídhe, or they may now be their enemies. There may be twenty or there may be two hundred."

"So, we just let them grow stronger?"

"Not exactly." Merlin gripped his shoulder tightly. "We keep an eye on them, destroy the ones who stray away from this settlement, keep the Sídhe from banishing more into this world, and we help you grow stronger."

Thor could have growled in irritation. More of the same it seemed. He balled his hands into fists and desperately wished he was back in his forge where he could hammer something. Merlin met his eyes with a disapproving look but said nothing more as he nodded towards the village and started walking. Morgana fell into step behind him, and Thor huffed as he turned on his heel to follow them.

25

Facing the Dream

Alex struggled to keep calm as her mind raced. She was vaguely aware that Jenny was watching her, and she could also feel the weight of Morgana's worried stare on her back. Shifting in the armchair, Alex licked her lips and tried to figure out just how to start the conversation she was dreading. She thought that she could still taste salt on her lips no matter how much she knew that it really didn't work that way. Bran caught her eyes and frowned. In his hand, the Iron Chalice gleamed in the light of the fire and Alex forced herself to sit up a little straighter.

"I think that my dreams are connected to this somehow," Alex said, giving voice to the disquieting thought that had been lingering in her mind for days. The strength and calmness in her own voice surprised her.

"Your dreams?" Morgana repeated as the room fell silent.

"Yeah, I've been having a reoccurring dream lately. On the surface, it doesn't have anything to do with magic, but I've just got this feeling that it is important."

"What happens in this dream?" Bran gave her a sympathetic look. "Anything in particular?"

"I'm on a ship," Alex explained vaguely. She struggled for a moment to find the right words. Her eyes landed on Lance and she quickly looked away from him. "It's a slave ship. History isn't my thing but based on the clothing and the style of the ship it's probably like 16th or 17th century. It's hard to describe really, but I'm having it all the time. In fact, I was dreaming about it when..." Alex gestured towards Timothy but didn't want to upset the Brownie.

"What happens in these dreams?" Bran asked kindly. "I- I can't imagine that they're pleasant."

"No, they aren't and before you ask, no, I'm not one of the slaves in the dream." Alex lowered her eyes and peered into the fire, watching the flames twist around each other. Shame filled her chest and she braced herself. "I'm the captain."

There was a heavy silence in the room. No one rushed to reassure her and Alex dared not look up at Morgana or Merlin. They'd admitted in the past that they didn't track every Iron Soul. If magic was low and there was no threat then they left them alone. Tightening her fingers around the arms of the chair, Alex swallowed and fought to regain some sense of balance. Hot tears were beginning to gather in her eyes. The horror of the dream was fresh in her mind and she could only imagine what Lance might be thinking.

Someone moved and a moment later a heavy, warm hand rested on her head. Something about the gesture was familiar and sent a rush of warmth through Alex. It untangled the knot in her chest and a soft sob escaped her. Desperately she tried to keep it under control, but a tear slipped out of her eye followed by another and another. Someone said something and there was a rush of noise as people moved.

Then there was an arm around her back as she slumped forward in the armchair. Alex caught a glimpse of Morgana's hand as the woman laid her free hand over Alex's left one. Blinking away the tears, Alex looked up to find Merlin standing in front of her with a soft and sad expression on his face. The weight of his hand on her head remained in place and he calmly met her gaze without a word.

Her whole body tightened. Alex couldn't find any words and the churning storm of emotions in her chest was making it a struggle to even think. Risking a glance around the room, Alex noted with relief that the others had gone, leaving her alone with the two older mages. Morgana rubbed the back of her hand with her thumb gently and said nothing. Closing her eyes, Alex licked her lips again, once more tasting a phantom of salt, or perhaps this time it was from the tears.

They let her sit there in silence: the only noises were the occasional small sounds that escaped her until the crying eased. She thought that she heard something coming from Merlin's kitchen, but she couldn't quite focus on it. The smell of coffee was just hinted at in the air, and she sort of wanted a cup as her emotions finally regained some equilibrium.

The embarrassment was beginning to set in and Alex could feel a deep blush heating up her cheeks. Her fingers somehow tightened even further into the upholstery of the armchair. Alex doubted that this had ever happened to Arto or Thor or Lokpal. Bad enough that Arthur had tricked her and used her and she'd handed him Cathanáil, but now she was probably being haunted by another life. The question of "Why" was one that she was terrified to have answered.

"Easy, Alex." Morgana said. Her voice was almost too soft and gentle. "It's alright."

"Arthur knows about it." Alex rubbed at her eyes, unable to look at Merlin and Morgana just yet. "He outright told me that there were things I didn't know. He hinted that the Iron Soul had evil lives."

"Alex-" Morgana started to say soothingly.

"No: being active in the slave trade is evil," Alex insisted. She shook her head as a fresh wave of tears tried to build. "Trust me... this person was horrible. God, what Lance must think of me!"

"Lance knows you. He only left so you wouldn't worry about his reaction. He was visibly worried about you," Merlin assured her. "Besides, it might not have been another life of yours."

"Yeah right," Alex snorted. "Then how or why would I see it?"

"Why do you think it is important?" Morgana questioned softly, tightening her hold on Alex, and hugging her gently. "Any particular reason or is it just the timing?"

"I- I can't control anything," Alex said. She managed to take a deep breath only to cough around another wave of tears. "Uh, last night was the first time I really saw the slaves. The dreams seem to be getting longer and longer. There is just... this sense that the hold is important."

"The hold?" Merlin repeated thoughtfully. "I'm not sure what you'll learn there."

"I have no clue." Alex laughed bitterly and wiped away the tears. "But my magic or my subconscious wants me to play the dream through." She coughed and shuddered. "And some of the Sídhe creatures have... thinking back on it, some of them seemed to be trying to tell me something. I didn't think much of it the time, but there's a lot of little things that just seem to be building up."

"Okay," Morgana agreed gently. "Okay, it is worth a try." Morgana paused and looked towards the kitchen and then back at Merlin. "Would you like to eat something first?"

"No," Alex answered in a low tone. "After... well, I'm feeling a bit sleepy now, so this is probably a good time to try."

Then there was silence, and Alex knew without looking that Morgana and Merlin were having one of their silent conversations. She closed her eyes and busied herself with taking a series of deep breaths while they debated the matter. Her heartbeat was slowing and Alex was feeling more and more in control with every passing moment. The sense of embarrassment was still there, but she was now able to remind herself that all forms of the Iron Soul were helpless against the shame of an evil incarnation. After all, this man, whoever he had been, was the reincarnation of Arto just as much as she was or Thor or Lokpal. She just had the misfortune of coming after him.

"I'll fetch Bran," Morgana said, breaking the silence and slowly removing her arm from around Alex. "Just wait here."

Alex really wanted to say something clever in response to Morgana's order, but she just couldn't summon the energy. As Morgana moved away, Alex collapsed back into the armchair which pulled her head away from Merlin's hand. He made no move to return it to its prior position but shifted himself so he was next to the chair. His arm came up to rest at the top of the armchair and Alex could feel him standing beside her.

"It is odd," Merlin said.

"What is?" Alex asked, hearing her voice quiver slightly.

"The others have never had memories surface," Merlin reminded her carefully. Alex thought she detected a hint of doubt in his tone. "They have never been aware of their other selves except as historical people or myths."

"Maybe that funeral we did at Stonehenge changed the rules," Alex offered in an uncertain voice. Then she paused in true consideration of the idea. "I wasn't able to use the Iron Chalice until we did that, but Arto wasn't the creator of the Iron Chalice."

"You're suggesting that something lingered in Arto's body?" The surprise in Merlin's voice almost made Alex look up at him. "I... suppose that is possible. There is so much we don't know."

"Yeah, but something definitely happened at Stonehenge," Alex said. Pausing, she thought back to the strange funeral. There had been so much magic and so many strange feelings that it was still hard to really pin it all down. "It's fuzzy, but I sort of remember..."

"What, Alex?" Merlin leaned over so she could see his face. "What do you remember?"

"Faces," Alex answered tentatively. "I didn't mention it because it wasn't really clear, and then we were attacked and came back with the Iron Chalice. I sort of forgot about it, but maybe-"

"You may be right then," Merlin agreed with a soft sigh. "It pains me to think that Morgana and I may have damaged the cycle of the Iron Soul, but you may be right."

"Not your fault," Alex assured him quickly. There was an odd pain in her chest at the very idea that he might blame himself. "Just... when I die make sure that everything is cremated."

"Have you told your parents that?"

"No." Alex grimaced as she heard people walking back towards the living room. "I'm not going to try and have that conversation with them just yet."

Alex was saved from having to continue down that dark train of thought by Morgana returning to the living room with Bran. The others peeked around the corner of the kitchen. To her surprise, there was only soft concern on their faces. She almost wanted to talk to them, to accept hugs, and anything else they offered, but she just couldn't. Alex sniffed and turned her attention towards Bran and Morgana. It was obvious that the pair were both nervous, but Morgana calmly folded her hands in front of her and nodded into the room, encouraging Bran to come closer.

"Bran." Alex stood up from the armchair and tried to act like she hadn't just been crying. "I need your help."

"The dream?" Bran asked. "Morgana says that you think it holds a clue."

"Yeah. We combined our power in Wales; I'm hoping that by doing the same now I might be able to play the dream through to the end and find out what I'm supposed to be seeing."

"Given the setting of the dream, Alex, this isn't going to be pretty," Bran cautioned her. "And we had the Chalice to focus on when we tried this in Wales." He toyed nervously with the Iron Chalice still in his hand.

"I know," Alex said. "But the dreams have had me worried for a while now, and with Timothy being freed by my magic... well, I'm a bit worried about what else I might have done in another life."

There were noises from the other room and Merlin gestured at the others to stay quiet. Alex was grateful, she felt like she was enough of a mess as it was. To her surprise, Bran nodded in understanding, though he sighed a moment later. He raised his free hand and rubbed the back of his neck.

"Okay; I'll try to give you my power and see if you can connect to the dream again," Bran agreed. "But one thing first, Alex."

"What?"

"Keep in mind that if you're right and it was your soul, it still wasn't you." He met her eyes squarely. "Whoever that man was lived and died centuries ago. The things that shaped you in this life are different than those that shaped him."

Swallowing thickly, Alex nodded. "I'll try."

"I suppose that's the best I can hope for," Bran said. Then he turned and held the Iron Chalice out towards Merlin. "Hopefully we won't need this."

"Let's hope not." Merlin gave them a painfully forced smile. "You don't have to-"

"Alex had dreams of the Sídhe tunnels before she was taken," Bran cut in quickly. "And I had dreams of the Chalice and my previous self's skull with it. We don't have dreams on repeat unless they're important."

Alex looked back at Merlin and tried to give him a reassuring smile. It was obvious from his expression that she failed, but he nodded to them and glanced towards Morgana. When she said nothing, Merlin stepped away from the armchair and motioned for them to follow him. Their path thankfully took them away from the kitchen, and the low voices of the others faded away as Merlin took them to the end of the hall.

The guest room was much smaller than the one at Morgana's with pale wallpaper dotted with small blue flowers. It was a bit musty, confirming to Alex that Merlin really wasn't the sort to have guests. Instead, it probably just fulfilled the need to have one in case of emergencies. Alex nearly laughed at herself; apparently, she was doing anything she could to avoid thinking about what they were about to do.

Alex lay back slowly on the bed and tried not to feel awkward about Bran sitting down on the edge beside her. He gave her a small reassuring smile that revealed his own nervousness. Reaching over, he took her hand and laced their fingers together as he exhaled slowly. Alex felt a flutter of magic against her hand and looked down curiously. There was a warm yellow glow around Bran's hand. She closed her eyes and dropped her head back. Resisting the urge to move her feet and tap them against the footboard, Alex couldn't help but wonder if she shouldn't be touching the earth for this. Maybe a sleeping bag outside with one hand touching the ground would work better.

"Try to relax." Bran chuckled softly, not hiding his own worry. "We've done this before, remember?"

"We found the Iron Chalice." Alex rested her other hand on her stomach and tried to make herself comfortable. "Bit different than trying to help my dreams last longer." She laughed and shook her head. "God, that sounds stupid."

"It's worth a try," Bran assured her. "We've both had dreams trying to show us the future before. This makes sense, Alex."

"This isn't the future," Alex said thickly. "Can't be."

"Well, just breathe and try to follow the dream." Bran gave her a reassuring smile and squeezed her hand. "I don't know what else to tell you. I'm right here, and Morgana is right outside the door. Once you're asleep I have no doubt that she'll come in."

"Yeah," Alex agreed. She released a shaky breath. "Merlin explaining to the others?"

"Probably, but don't worry about that," Bran replied. "Try to relax."

Huffing softly, Alex closed her eyes and tried to focus on the feeling of the soft bed beneath her. Unfortunately, she was also very aware of Bran lingering beside her and holding her hand. Her palm was already becoming sweaty and she regretted not using the bathroom first. Pushing the thought away, Alex licked her lips and started one of the meditation exercises that Morgana had taught her.

She just laid there in silence, breathing slowly and imagining a field of wheat blowing in the wind. It was soothing, but it didn't seem to be working. She shifted on the bed, trying to adjust her body into a more comfortable position. In truth, she was a side sleeper, but the idea of being sprawled over a pillow in front of Bran was a touch embarrassing.

Opening her eyes again, Alex looked down at their hands and almost gasped at the strange sight of Bran's yellow magic turning dark gray as it flowed into her fingertips. A shimmering line of magic was growing from her own chest and the other end vanished into Bran's chest. She watched it in fascination for a long moment in both surprise and confusion. Her eyes dropped back to their joined hands and she wondered just what was happening. Was this a representation of their magic connecting them?

"Bran?" she started to ask but as she blinked, Alex lost sight of the thin thread of magic.

"What?"

"Nothing," Alex replied. She licked her lips and tapped her fingers against the comforter. "Let's give this a try."

"Try to focus on something from the dream," Bran suggested softly.

Searching her thoughts, Alex tried to figure out what to focus on. She needed something to direct their magic towards. Closing her eyes again, Alex did her best to remember the feel of the ship. The waves that made it roll slowly beneath her feet and the taste of salt on the air had all but stained her lips.

Her body felt floaty like she'd just become lighter. She couldn't feel the bed beneath her anymore. The sound of her own breathing had become louder and the rhythm of her heart echoed evenly in her ears. Yet the sounds of Bran and the others had faded away. Heavy eyelids separated her from the rest of the world and the warmth of her magic wrapped around her like a thick blanket. Alex would have smiled at the realization that she was falling to sleep, but consciousness eluded her.

She inhaled, but this time a rush of salty sea air with a hint of seaweed hit her tongue. She opened her eyes and looked around as she found herself not on the deck of the ship, but rather a small room. Beneath her, Alex could feel the gentle rocking of the ship as it rolled across the waves. A small port window was open across the room from her and Alex breathed in again, almost jumping in surprise when she felt her body breathe in time with her.

26

Darkness Below

Excitement, nerves, and terror all filled Alex with the urge to jump around frantically until she was exhausted. Instead, she took another breath and again felt the body breathe with her. She tried moving her fingers, but there was only a faint twitch. Still, a rush of excitement rose through her chest. She might not yet be able to control the body, but she at least had a little influence now. The sense of excitement was short lived as she moved without any control towards the desk.

With a burst of desperation, Alex made the body stumble as she tried to take over the speed but was unable to. Grumbling softly in her own mind, Alex had to once again concede that she was mostly along for the ride. As her eyes swept through the small, but comfortable looking captain's cabin Alex reminded herself that she wouldn't be back here if it wasn't important. She'd been haunted by this dream for weeks and now Bran and her combined magic had sent her back. There was something she had to learn here.

Large hands with small scars scattered over the flesh reached out for the bottle of wine. Alex watched the fingers move, noting that the pinkie on the left hand was completely gone with only a stump left. The wine hit her tongue and Alex tried once more to take control as a mirror in the corner of the room caught her attention. At first, nothing happened, but then as the wine glass was drained, she leaned forward.

She only caught a brief flash of the reflection in the mirror, but it was enough to make Alex's heart thunder in her chest. It was a middle-aged face with a cruel sneer seemingly fixed into place. The eyes were dark and unfeeling, the nose was rather broad and long and the jaw was strong and square. It was an unforgiving face that in another life might have been reasonably attractive. A call from on deck broke whatever control she had as they turned and headed for the doorway. Confusion swept over Alex, uncertainty for what was happening and why as she stalked out of the cabin and onto the deck.

One of the crewmen glanced towards her and Alex tried to turn away. Instead, she felt her eyes narrow and watched the man scurry away. A wave of satisfaction flashed in her chest and Alex shoved the feeling down, not wanting any part of it. Something in her chest flared and Alex gasped, feeling the thick lips move in time with her. It took her a moment to recognize the warm glow growing in her chest and once she did, she just stood there in stunned silence.

Her magic was somehow reacting, though it felt a little odd like it was spread too thin or was a few degrees too cold in her chest. Still, it was familiar enough that she tugged at it. Something inside stretched painfully at the attempt. The world went fuzzy around her: the crewmen seemed to slow down and all the sounds and smells became muted. Alex was certain that she was waking up, but then the ship snapped back into place around her.

Confusion took over as Alex could still feel the thrum of her magic pulsing through her. It felt better now, more correct as strange as that thought was. She stretched her fingers out and gasped as she suddenly realized what she was doing. Completely ignoring a nearby crewmember,

Alex raised her hand up to her face and smiled slightly as it did as she wanted. The sight of the unfamiliar hand shocked her for a moment, but Alex pushed it aside. This wasn't the time for another breakdown.

Slowly she became aware that the crew was watching her uncertainly. She wondered how her odd behavior was affecting them. Part of her had been sure that she was just replaying a memory, but now the line between memory and dream was becoming blurred. Giving a sharp look to one of the nearest crewmen, Alex inwardly grimaced as he slouched back and lowered his eyes.

There was an undercurrent on the ship that Alex didn't fully understand. In the back of her mind, she knew that this was a slave ship and that the sort of men who did this work would be made of harder stuff than her, but there was still something. It was like a faint scent on the air that you couldn't place or a name that you just couldn't think of when you needed it. The longer she thought about it the worse the feeling of wrongness became, and Alex forced herself to move forward.

Alex descended the stairs, noting the odd stride of this body and trying not to think about the fact she was suddenly a man too hard. It was a challenge, but as the hatch into the hold came into view and that strange sick feeling intensified, she was quickly distracted. Alex waited to wake up, waited for something to stop her as she marched to the entry, but the dream remained intact. She stopped at the top of the metal grate and looked down uneasily. After all the talk about this being important and necessary and getting Bran's help, there was nothing she wanted less than to go down there.

"Going below, Captain?" Alex nodded in reply, not trusting herself to speak. "They're in the middle of feeding," the voice explained. A smaller crewman stepped into view and pulled the metal grill off to the side.

There was a small wooden staircase leading below, and a faint glow of lanterns that didn't make her feel any better. Nonetheless, she forced one foot in front of the other and carefully descended into the hold. She was hit by a horrible wall of stench that almost knocked her over. It had been present on deck, but the salty wind had apparently done a fine job of clearing it away. Here it was fresh, thick, and threatening to swallow her up.

That was until her eyes finally focused on where she was and what was around her. It was a dark sea of people, all crammed together in tiny rows that left only a tiny sliver of a pathway for the crew to move in. Long wooden structures rather like bunk beds were built into the sides of the ship with more slaves lying crammed into the small extra layer it created. Alex desperately wanted to drop her eyes and thankfully a moment later her eyes did indeed lower away from the people. Below her feet was a filthy deck awash in human waste that threatened to choke her. The heat was unbearable: the hold felt like it was baking them all with each torturous passing second.

Then she realized that it had gone silent in the hold. The sounds of crying and the soft voices that she'd heard above were suddenly gone. Everything had gone still the moment she'd climbed down, and a sense of dread washed through Alex. Her eyes turned up again against her will, her emotions weakening her already limited control. Stepping forward, she moved into the tiny pathway amongst the rows of crowded slaves and looked at a long chain that ran down the center of the ship. Dozens of collars and shackles were attached to it, looping around to keep the slaves in place. The long chain was wound through dozens of heavy metal rungs. Alex focused on it, trying desperately to ignore the smell and the soft moaning of the slaves. It shimmered with black sparks of magic that filled her with dread.

Looking at it caused her head to ache as a rush of something very strange and wrong washed over her. It crept over her skin, leaving goosebumps in its wake. Closing her eyes, Alex willed the sudden headache away and gave herself a moment. Around her, the roll of the ship continued and Alex was struck by a hint of alarm that the pain hadn't woken her up. Opening her eyes, she forced herself to keep examining the hold, but she avoided looking at the long chain though she kept seeing small flashes of light in the corner of her eye.

Crewmen were walking around amongst the slaves in the tiny aisles, completely calm and seemingly unaffected. Alex watched in horrified fascination as one of them shoved a strange fat tube into one of the slave's mouths and squeezed the tube until a thick paste-like substance dribbled out. They were feeding them, Alex realized with a turn of her stomach that made her want to run back on deck. She dropped her eyes. Her knees buckled beneath her and threatened to send her falling into the layer of human waste under her feet.

Alex let the world fall away and instead tried to focus her thoughts on the magic she'd seen in that chain. Something was nagging at her, but it was difficult to overcome the horror clawing at her chest. Tears stung at her eyes, but Alex knew this wasn't the time. She had to focus, had to figure it out, but she just wasn't sure how to even begin. Finally, she raised her eyes and let herself look at one of the slaves. It was a large strong man with a pronounced nose, but his eyes were downcast. All of them were in fact. None of the hundreds of bodies packed into the cargo hold were looking at her. She waited and was hit by the stench of human waste, dried sweat, and rot once more.

"Hey," Alex called, but another voice echoed through the hull. It was deep with an accent to it that sounded a bit English, but she wasn't sure.

Still, none of them looked up at her. "Look at me," Alex tried once again; grimacing at the order came out in the same masculine voice.

They all shifted their heads and looked up at her. Their eyes were glazed and half dead, but worst of all was that the long chain running down the rows was glowing an ugly black color. She could see the shimmer of magic radiating off it and tiny dark threads connecting the chained slaves to it. Alex's stomach turned and she struggled for air as she stumbled back from them. The order not to look at her died on her tongue as they just stared at her and waited for the next command. The wrongness hit her hard in the chest, sending Alex stumbling back. A crewmember called something to her, but she didn't hear and did not reply.

Her eyes dropped back to the chain and she forced herself to look at it. The awful feeling crept up her body again, making her shiver. For a moment she felt it brush against her magic and her own power retreated, but just for a split second before it grabbed onto the oily feeling. Gasping for air, Alex was hit with a wave of vertigo as the magics blended. It was her magic seeping into her and yet it wasn't. Somehow, someway in this low magic environment, in a time period with so little magic that Merlin and Morgana hadn't even bothered to find this incarnation he had used magic.

The chain. It hit her all at once. She'd heard the rattle of a chain before, somehow in the back of her mind. One of the Sídhe descendants had mentioned a chain and yet she only now understood. Somehow this incarnation driven by his lust for control and willingness to buy and sell human beings had created a magical iron artifact.

All the air rushed out of Alex or whoever's lungs. She felt dizzy and found herself suddenly questioning if you could faint in a dream. But this wasn't really a dream, was it? Reaching to the side, Alex gripped one of the support beams of the slave racks. Her eyes met those of a young woman chained by a collar on her neck and the sense of weakness returned tenfold.

"I'm sorry," Alex whispered, but the thick male voice seemed to stumble over the words.

A pain in her gut nearly made her double over as if someone had kicked her. Alex tightened her grip on the support and looked back at the iron chain. Taking a slow step forward, she released her grip on the wood and forced herself to examine the chain. The sight of it felt wrong and she was struck once again by the desire to look away. Fighting against the urge, she knelt, ignoring a question from one of the crewmen and studied the thing carefully.

The first thing she noticed was that the main chain wasn't really all that long, only a few feet and it was this section that contained most of the dark glow. However, the collars and other lengths of chain were connected to this master chain and small ripples of magic were traveling from the main chain and through the iron of the other chains to the poor slaves. Alex wasn't sure if it was a relief to know that this dark Iron Soul artifact was that small or if that worried her.

Hesitantly, Alex reached out for the chain, ignoring the sight of the wrong hands. Her first thought was that the metal was cold unlike the warmth that Cathanáil and the Iron Chalice had carried to her when active. Distantly she wondered if even the magic itself knew that the creation of this had been wrong and twisted. It sparked under her fingertip and there was a startled gasp throughout the hold. The chain tugged on her magic and Alex pulled her hand back sharply even as she felt some of her magic slip into the cold metal.

Standing up, Alex distanced herself from the chain. It was too much being so close to it and she spun back to the stairs leading to the deck.

Two crewmen looked towards her sharply only to lower their eyes a moment later. Alex could only wonder if the power of the chain extended somehow to them as well or if their captain's ability to control the slaves left them with such terror.

"Captain," a sterner and stronger voice called.

She turned to look towards the voice despite herself and met the gaze of a man up near the helm. Alex's feet were moving before she could stop them and she felt the control she'd gained earlier slipping away. Frantically she tried to pull on her magic again, but everything was too unsteady. The chill of the Iron Chain lingered in her chest.

"Jacob." Her body climbed the stairs to join them. She nodded to the crewman at the helm and he quickly stepped back from the wheel. Grasping it in both hands, she turned her gaze away from the man and looked out onto the sea. "What is it?"

"Cuthbert, was it necessary to throw that slave overboard?" Jacob asked. Alex shuddered at the name he gave her. She didn't want to know his name and prayed he wouldn't give her a surname, wouldn't make this person any more real. "You have the slaves cowed."

"Apparently not," her stern voice answered.

A strange faint feeling was seeping over Alex and she half feared that the chain had done something to her after all. Jacob's answer to her comment was lost on her as a wave of vertigo rushed over her. Around her, the ship melted away as an icy feeling settled over Alex as the sky paled and the fog began to surround her.

Everything rippled around her and Alex tried to grasp at the helm, fearing that strange sensation was her magic or her becoming ill. Her fingers passed through the helm and the world around her dissolved, leaving her falling. She didn't wake up in her bed and instead fell through the darkness with panic trying to claw its way up to her heart.

27

Fear Awakens

15 C.E. Sør-Trøndelag, Norway

1 Winter in these lands had never been pleasant, but to Thor, it seemed to be rolling in much faster than usual. Frosts were already destroying parts of the harvest and there was never much to spare. Already some farmers were trying to determine which animals to slaughter, thanks to a frost causing an entire field of hay to be lost. Despite his concerns over the Dark Elves, he'd been forced to turn his attention to helping the village.

Yet, there was a tension building in his shoulders with each passing day. He helped Arvid in the fields and worked at his forge long into the night to keep everyone equipped with tools. When he slept, he should have been exhausted, and yet his mind kept going back to the question of what the Dark Elves were doing. Even though they'd known of the settlement for half a moon cycle, they had yet to take action against it and Thor could not understand.

Drying his hands after washing them in the cold water, Thor moved towards Merlin and Morgana's hut. Around him the other villagers glanced his way, giving him small nods, but largely keeping their distance.

Another boring day working in his forge and trying not to worry too much about what was going to happen next. He hated it.

"Merlin?" Thor called as he reached their hut. "Morgana?"

"Thor?" Merlin answered back, making Thor relax a little. "Oh, come in, come in."

Pulling back the animal pelt, Thor stepped into the hut and noted two packs on the bench near the door. He turned to find Morgana braiding her long hair into a crown around her head, something he'd notice she did when she expected trouble. Thor looked towards Merlin and found the older man fastening his cloak with a stern expression on his face.

"Are you going out again?"

"We're going to have another look at the settlement." Merlin picked up one of the packs and slung it over his shoulder "We've been studying the area; trying to determine where they are gathering food, getting water, and find any signs of them expanding."

"We haven't found much." Morgana glanced his way with frustration glowing in her eyes. "We've decided to head into the tunnels. Frea's spies have gone in a ways, but we want to have a look for ourselves."

"I'm coming with you," Thor said, hoping that his voice sounded more confident than he was.

"That's not necessary," Merlin was quick to say. "We don't want you being injured."

"I need to know what we're up against too." Thor felt nervous at the mention of tunnels and the reminder that the Dark Elves lived underground. He was uncertain as to the source of the feeling and shoved it away as his stomach tightened. "I need to be aware of things too, Merlin. I can't just rely on secondhand information from the two of you."

"Thor, we don't know how this is going to play out yet," Merlin said in that annoying and smooth voice that Merlin used to convince people of his point of view. "For all we know they may settle into peaceful lives like Frea's people."

Thor doubted that. Something in his gut almost made him snort at the idea. In the corner of his eye, he saw a doubtful expression cross Morgana's face and knew she agreed with him. Merlin sighed and looked between the pair of them.

"Now we have to give them a chance," Merlin said sternly. "While the first ones through were warriors sent to take slaves, towards the end they were prisoners. For all we know they were exiled for standing up to the lords, trying to end slavery or something else noble." Morgana did snort now and Merlin looked at her sharply. "We cannot assume that they are evil. Now that they are stabilizing in our world, we need to determine what they are going to be to the Iron Realm before we attempt genocide."

Thor didn't have a response to that. There was a note in Merlin's voice that warned him against even attempting to find a counter argument. Next to him, Morgana merely nodded and said nothing before turning and picking up her pack.

"I'm still coming with you," Thor said. His words broke the thick silence. "I'll be right back."

He didn't give them time to argue and quickly left the hut. As he moved back to his family's house, he was hopeful that they wouldn't simply leave without him. He paused and looked around his home village. It was still so strange to see the houses surrounded by the wall while knowing that the fields beyond were vulnerable.

Thankfully his father and brother were already out in the fields, leaving the house empty. It smelled heavily of the animals who were now huddling inside each night, but Thor ignored the thick scent as he collected a few supplies and his sword. Rushing outside, he ignored the curious looks once more and spotted Morgana and Merlin near the gate. They had waited for him, though Thor could tell as he approached that Morgana still wanted him to stay here. Part of him desperately wanted to prove himself, but he ordered the urge to stay buried.

Outside the walls, the animals were in pasture and Thor could see people busily milking the cows. Others were bundling up the dried hay and taking it into the village so it could feed the animals in the coming winter. Much of the barley had already been processed and only one small field of rye remained to be cut. Over the course of the last few weeks, most of the onions, turnips, and leeks had been harvested from the smaller gardens inside the walls. Still, Thor was uncertain that it would be enough.

They hiked in silence with neither Merlin nor Morgana providing him any additional details. It took longer than he liked to realize why: the forest itself was very still and quiet. While winter was fast approaching and they'd suffered early frosts, there was not yet snow on the ground. Yet the forest seemed empty of birds. There was no scurrying of animals in the underbrush and he could see no recent tracks on the trail. For a moment he felt a flash of guilt as he understood the renewed tension in the village: the hunters hadn't been finding any game and he hadn't noticed.

"We're almost there," Merlin murmured ahead of him. Thor nodded despite Merlin being unable to see him. "Now, Thor, it is vital that you do what Morgana and I say. If you think you have a reason to disobey us then tell us quickly, otherwise do not delay. We do not know how these Sídhe... the Dark Elves will react to us coming so close."

"Understood," Thor forced out around the lump forming in his throat.

He was beginning to feel a bit ill as the unnatural silence surrounded him. The chill in the air was sharper than it should be and the scent of the forest itself was off. Thor shuddered despite himself at the growing sense that he really should have stayed behind. His fingers itched to be back at his forge. Magic flared in his chest in response to his fear, and Thor felt a flash of panic as he willed it away. Sparks danced across his fingertips for a moment and he glanced down to watch the tiny bright blue lightning bolts arc off his fingers and move across his palms. The momentary distraction helped him center himself even as the magic dissipated.

"Almost there." Merlin shifted just enough to look over his shoulder at Thor. "Be ready, just in case."

The older mage didn't seem to notice that Thor's magic had already flared up, and that was fine with the embarrassed Thor. He followed along silently, minding his footing as they shifted onto the rocky terrain of the slope. Looking over his shoulder, Thor could see his village down near the water, but he had the sense already that this settlement was far closer than he wanted it to be.

Leading him further into the trees, they headed down into a ravine that had been carved by ice long ago, and Thor hesitated as the rocky sides of the ravine began to rise above his head. The memory of that small sink hole so long ago nagged at him, and a flash of worry jolted through Thor at his own reaction.

Thankfully they didn't linger in the ravine for long, but Thor was keenly aware of sweat dripping down the back of his neck despite the chill in the air. Up ahead small pockets of snow remained hidden in the shadows of rocks and trees as they moved higher up the mountainside. Then they stopped, and Thor had a moment of disorientation as he looked around.

The so-called entrance was more of a giant crack in the side of the mountain with rock partially folded over it, thanks to another layer of stone that was turned on its side. Thor had only been in a cave once before and hesitated at the entry. Before him loomed the dark stone of the earth that appeared ready to swallow him up, and the pathway quickly vanished in a sharp slope down even deeper. He wasn't prepared for the jolt of alarm that raced through his body at the sight of the cave. The reality of his sudden problem was settling on him, and Thor hated to even give it form through thought. He was afraid; afraid of going into the ground again.

Swallowing thickly, Thor contemplated making some excuse to remain on the surface and beneath the sky. Morgana turned and gave him a questioning look that made him straighten up and march for the cave mouth. However, he couldn't help but take in one last long breath of fresh air. Morgana conjured a small orb of light in her hands. She lifted it just enough to illuminate the small curving tunnel of the cave. There was a faint sound of dripping that was echoing up to them, and it made another shiver go up Thor's spine.

"Thor?" Merlin turned back towards him with a frown. "Are you alright? Have you been here before?"

"No," Thor answered honestly before realizing what he'd said. "I haven't been here before." He swallowed and tried not to fidget. "It's been a long time since I was in a cave... ten years maybe."

"Oh?" Merlin asked with a hint of suspicion in his voice. "Anything special?"

"Not really, it was more of a sink hole. Arvid and I were exploring and not paying attention. My foot got caught and Arvid had to go and get Father to help me." He rubbed his jaw, letting the hairs of his beard scratch his hand. "Bit embarrassing. I was hearing about it for months."

Merlin kept looking at him thoughtfully with eyes that told Thor this was his last chance. He all but snorted at the idea. Was he supposed to just wait for them beneath the opening because he apparently didn't like the idea of going underground? Forcing a confident smile, he nodded down the tunnel and waited for Merlin and Morgana to lead the way. From behind Merlin, Morgana gave him an impatient look and he could imagine what she was thinking. Merlin started his descent with Morgana right behind him. After one last deep breath, Thor followed.

Every step was difficult. The low light in Morgana's hand was barely enough to see even a few feet, but it was enough for him to always be able to see the walls of stone around him. The small entrance quickly opened into larger tunnels with smooth looking walls glistening from faint traces of water dripping down them. Thor kept breathing as slowly as he could and kept his eyes fixed on Morgana's long dark braid in front of him.

"I can hear voices up ahead," Merlin said softly.

Thor nodded, mostly to himself as the other two couldn't see him, and wondered again if being between them wouldn't have been better. Glancing up at the roof of the cavern, Thor eyed the stalactites pouring out of the ceiling with a growing sense of unease. His mind flashed back to the way Merlin had made the hillside above the Sídhe tunnel crumble and he shuddered. Without thinking, Thor murmured a soft prayer to Odin that no harm would come to him in this dark place.

They walked forever. Thor's heart pounded in his chest and he struggled to breathe. All around him the tunnel was becoming tighter, no matter how easily Merlin and Morgana kept slipping through the crevices. From time to time some paintings on the walls or signs of the Dark Elves were able to distract him, but it never lasted long.

Then the tunnels expanded. Rough stone and antler tools were scattered on the ground in piles of rock dust. Roughly woven baskets and awkward clay vessels were filled with larger pieces of rock, leaving Thor torn between worry and gratitude that the Dark Elves were expanding the tunnels. He breathed a little easier until he turned and eyed the pitch blackness behind them. His stomach turned and his knees quivered.

Merlin and Morgana stopped and Thor was suddenly aware of sounds echoing up the tunnel. It took him a moment to recognize them as the sort of noise that filled his village every day, thanks to the echoing effect. They began to move again, but much slower this time. Up ahead, as the sounds grew louder there was a series of tall rocks they could huddle behind.

Peering around the rocks, Thor wasn't able to hold in the small gasp that escaped him. Stretched out before them amongst the rocks were wooden buildings supported against the natural formations of the cave. Dozens of the Dark Elves were moving amongst them, their paths illuminated by the low burning torches. There was a thick haze of smoke in the air and a layer of soot gathering on the rocks, but the creatures didn't seem to care.

"I can't see much," he whispered.

"Neither can I," Merlin said. "I can't get a good count, but I see at least twenty."

"They are using torches," Morgana added softly. "Their night vision must still require some light like the Sídhe." She paused and then in a happier tone said, "But I see no magical lights, so they may not have any magic. That's good to know."

Briefly, Thor wondered if they could simply bring this mountain down on top of the Dark Elves but quickly dismissed the idea. This was no simple rockslide like the tunnel had been. They would need to shake the very foundations of the mountain, and the idea filled him with dread.

"I need more light than this," a deep voice bellowed from one of the structures catching Thor's attention. His magic tickled for a moment, but he ignored it and focused on the new voice. It lacked the musical quality of Frea's voice or the low even tone he'd heard from the Dark Elves. Instead, it was thick and gruff. "If you expect us to keep doing your metalwork then we need better light and a better space."

"What the?" Merlin leaned forward curiously.

A small figure stormed out of one of the buildings with a Dark Elf marching behind him. At first glance, Thor almost mistook him for a human. He was a little under five feet tall with warm sepia skin that had a slight hint of green and sunken dark eyes. Small wrinkles across his face made him look old, but somehow that didn't seem right to Thor. Thick, wild black hair that faded to brown at the tips surrounded his face and flowed into a long beard that was tucked into his belt.

"Dvergr causing trouble," the Dark Elf said from behind the small creature as another Dark Elf moved over to them.

"What is that?" Thor asked Merlin in a low voice. "I've never seen anyone like him. What's a... Dvergr?"

Merlin didn't say anything and Thor crept forward to the edge of the rocks. Both Merlin and Morgana were staring at the small being with looks of utter confusion on their faces.

"Merlin?" Thor tried again a little louder this time. "What is a Dvergr?"

"I have no idea," Merlin said with widening eyes. "I've never seen anything like it before."

And somehow that statement worried and frightened Thor even more than the tons of rock above his head just waiting to crash down around him.

28

The Queen's Spell

Alex was falling through the darkness. She was untethered and yet she could feel the pull of gravity. Around her, there were flashes of scenes like she was falling past dozens of television screens. Most went past too quickly for her to see, but there were dark streets, more old-fashioned ships, and even stages with people lined up on them. There seemed to be no end to them as she just kept falling.

Then her body suddenly seemed to right itself and the fall turned into a slow, floating descent. For a moment Alex thought she was a bit like Alice falling down the rabbit hole. Her feet settled onto something solid, and in a swirl of colors, the world reappeared around her. Blinking in surprise, Alex dumbly took in the space she suddenly found herself in.

She was no longer on the ship or anywhere that she'd seen in the flashes as she fell. Instead, she was in some kind of cellar with old brick walls. Sunlight was streaming down through a small high window, illuminating the space. The room was almost completely empty with a bare concrete floor, a large heavy wooden table, an old wooden cabinet, and a bookshelf that had old leather-bound notebooks stacked on it. There was nothing outwardly odd or magical in the room, and Alex turned slowly in confusion. Through a small doorway, she could see a large clothes washer next to a dryer along with a shelf of cleaning supplies. On the other side of the room was a staircase leading up to a closed door.

Alex was becoming confused as to where she was and why when the door at the top of the stairs opened. Turning her head sharply, she looked up as a woman with a full pregnant belly made her way down the creaking stairs. Alex moved closer to the stairs to observe the woman, but she looked very normal in a blue maternity dress. Once again, Alex was confused as to why she was here. Between the washing machine and the woman's wardrobe, this seemed fairly recent.

She backed up as the woman came down the stairs and prepared to duck into the shadows, but the woman showed no signs of seeing her. As she stepped into the light of a ceiling lamp Alex was able to get a better look at her. The woman was tall with long blonde hair pulled back in a severe bun and dark brown eyes. There was a harshness to her features that Alex couldn't quite understand, and something about her tugged at Alex's memory. Her belly was full and pregnant, but she was looking down at it with an impatient expression.

The woman moved across the room to the large wooden cabinet, which creaked as she opened it. Glancing around, Alex wondered if she was supposed to go upstairs for this vision, but the clanking of a chain caught her attention. Her eyes widened as the woman turned and brought a long, heavy dark metal chain out of the cabinet and dumped it on the table. For a moment Alex could only stare at the chain, trying to convince herself that it couldn't possibly be the chain she'd just seen on the ship.

But then she caught a faint flicker of magic inside the metal as the woman touched it. Just a tiny brush of power, but it was enough to make Alex's knees feel weak. It was the same chain; the central chain that had been linked to all the smaller chains in the ship. Alex eyed the chain with trepidation, but none the less inched towards it. She barely noticed as the woman removed a simple wooden box from the cabinet and placed it on the table next to the chain.

She opened the box and Alex's eyes were drawn towards a small shimmering piece of metal. It was iron that was a little rusted along the edges and looked as if it had been roughly cut from something larger. The woman picked up the piece of iron carefully with a pleased smirk and brushed one finger across the surface carefully. A moment later she set it back in the box and Alex crept closer, still watching the woman for any sign that she was aware of her presence.

Then the woman picked up the chain with a small grunt, letting one end of it fall to the ground with a clatter while she wrapped the other end around her enlarged waist. Reaching over to the box, she picked up the piece of iron with a smirk. Moving it slowly, she watched it as if expecting the dull thing to shine. The smirk stayed firmly in place and she brought it down to the chain, placing it snugly between the chain and her belly.

"This better work," a familiar voice said.

The woman pulled up the rest of the chain from the floor and kept wrapping it around her waist. Alex frowned, trying to remember where she'd heard that voice before. On some strange impulse, Alex tried to grab the chain, but her fingers passed right through it as if she was a ghost. The woman closed her eyes and whispered a series of strange words that teased at Alex's mind. She could feel her magic pulsing as something tried to activate, but it seemed muted and distant. Alex tried pulling on her magic and felt the magic flare, but she couldn't fully manifest the power in her hands.

Magic flashed off the chain and the smell of burning hair flooded Alex's nose. She coughed and looked towards the woman in concern. Her hands were burning against the flashing metal, but she was gritting her teeth and her hands remained firmly in place. Alex took a step towards her, frantically trying to understand what she was doing and why. The chunk of iron against her belly turned white and a gleaming smile took over the woman's face. Her blue eyes widened and Alex gasped softly, alarmed by the dark gleeful glint in the woman's eyes. Magic spun through the chain and Alex's teeth began to ache as the pressure in the room sharply rose. Her hands were shaking as she stepped back, her eyes still locked on the chain. She was torn between an overwhelming desire to reach out and grab the chain or run away.

A wave of pressure hit Alex in the chest, sending her stumbling back. The world around her flickered like a bad recording. Looking back at the woman, Alex could see strands of black magic spilling out of the piece of iron tied to her by the chain and seeping into her stomach. Small sparks of magic rolled across the surface of the chain and the small piece of iron began rusting rapidly in front of Alex. Red dust and flakes fell to the ground, and in mere moments the piece of iron was gone. The pressure in the room eased and the woman placed her hand on her stomach as she allowed the chain to clatter to the floor. She made a nasty smile.

Around Alex, the world dissolved. The basement became fuzzy and she sighed in defeat only for the basement to suddenly sharpen around her. Suddenly the air was different; thick with moisture and soft whimpers bouncing off the wall. Alex swallowed thickly as her heart began to race. Something was wrong, and she spun around to search the room.

Behind her, a slumped figure was huddled in the corner with its head lowered on its knees. Alex stared at the dejected figure dressed in an oversized hoodie. It took her a moment to recognize strands of long white hair spilling out from under the hood. She looked down at its hands and swallowed at the sight of the pale, almost shimmering skin.

Taking a step forward, Alex frowned as she took in the creature with confusion and a flare of sympathy.

The door at the top of the stairs crashed open and Alex spun around. The blonde woman was striding down the stairs with dangerously high black heels clicking against the wood. She was no longer pregnant and was now wearing form-fitting clothing, but Alex's eyes were drawn to the carrier in her right hand. A scowl was present on her face as she looked through Alex at the captive creature.

"Stop whimpering," the woman commanded. She reached the bottom of the stairs and marched past Alex. "Have some dignity. You descend from the greatest race in the whole of the Tree of Reality, even if you are tainted."

The woman set the carrier down next to the table and Alex's eyes widened at the soft gurgling coming from it. Moving over to the woman's side, Alex looked down in shock at the infant that was swaddled in thick blankets. She glanced back at the woman in confusion. Of course, she'd known she was pregnant, but what was going on now? This was all happening so fast in comparison to the weeks of dreams about the ship.

Watching the woman retrieve the chain from the cabinet again, Alex felt her stomach turn over and swallowed a rush of bile. It suddenly occurred to her that she was following the Chain. Not through its entire history, but the important bits. This was important, and magic wanted her to see.

Alex backed away from the woman and the Chain, glancing fearfully at the tiny baby. Its blue eyes were wide as he watched his mother. A tuft of bright blond hair covered his head and a sinking feeling weighed down Alex's limbs.

"No," she whispered, shaking her head. "Not possible. You can't be."

Of course, no one in the room spoke in response to her words. The woman turned towards the Sídhe descendent chained to the wall and Alex followed her gaze. It had raised its head and its violet eyes were dark with fear. The Síd creature tugged at the chains holding it in place and looked up at the woman with completely white features. For a long moment, they just stared at each other, a sneer taking over the woman's features.

A cry from the baby broke the heavy quiet, making Alex jump and flinch. She crossed her arms over her chest and rubbed her arms nervously. The woman huffed, turned on her black heel and looked at the baby. With a roll of her eyes, she knelt and picked the infant up. As the blankets fell away, the baby began to cry louder and louder. With a sneer she set him on the table, protected only by his blanket with nothing to keep him from rolling off.

"Hush, Arthur." She glared down at the infant. "Enough wailing!"

Alex wrapped her arms around herself at the confirmation of the baby's identity. She looked towards the frightened Síd as a horrible suspicion settled in her stomach. It was difficult to look back at the woman, Elaine Pendred, her mind provided, but Alex forced herself to. She was supposed to learn something, and she did not want to go through this again. Somehow Scáthbás had learned of the Iron Chain, found it, and used it.

"What are you going to do with me?" the Síd asked. "What are you?"

"You are going to help me create something very special," Scáthbás answered. "The Iron Realm has Merlin, and Morgana betrayed me, but I can make a new hybrid."

"I- I don't understand." The Síd tugged at its chains.

Rolling her human eyes, Scáthbás turned back to the chained Síd and sneered. Alex shuddered and moved away from the look. "I am Queen

Scáthbás," she informed the Síd. "And you should be honored to serve me with your life."

"You can't be," the Síd whispered in terror, violet eyes wide with horror. "Scáthbás was destroyed: the mages killed her."

"The greatest ruler of Sídhean, and yet now just a mere myth!" Scáthbás kicked the Síd in the side. "A boogeyman to the children of those that served me and failed." She kicked again, this time much harder, and then again and again with a gleeful expression twisting her features. "If your ancestors had done their jobs properly, we would have taken the Iron Realm. It would all be over!"

Silvery blood was trickling from the mouth of the captured Sid by the time Scáthbás finally stopped her assault. She stepped back and cleared her throat as she fixed a few strands of blonde hair. Scáthbás smoothed down her shirt and made a soft sighing noise as she tossed her head. It was disturbing to see the woman swing from enraged to seemingly calm, and Alex just stared at her with a growing sense of dread. She knew what was to happen already and really didn't want to see it.

"Okay," Alex called out. "I'm good, I get it. I don't need to see it."

She closed her eyes for a moment, willing it to be over, but the sounds of Scáthbás moving drew her attention. Torn between a fierce desire to hide in the corner and the fear that she'd be forced to witness this again, Alex opened her eyes to watch Scáthbás. The long heavy Chain rattled as Scáthbás dropped it down onto the table next to the whimpering infant. Rolling her eyes, Scáthbás leaned over the infant and glowered down at him.

"Honestly, Arthur, enough of this," she huffed, but the infant released another sob. "Medraut, I mean it. This is all necessary, and you behaving like a simple human infant is not helpful to the cause. I've already bound your soul into this body. We just need to get the body properly attuned if my plans are going to work. We'll test it on you and then it will be my tu rn."

Scáthbás went to the cabinet and pulled a long, vicious looking knife from inside it. Swallowing thickly, Alex glanced back towards the bound Síd as Scáthbás advanced on it. The Síd released a long and desperate scream that echoed in the basement. Alex turned away and slumped against the wall. The scream of the Síd turned to a gurgle and then was gone. A strange grinding sound filled the room, and even the whimpers of Arthur weren't enough to hide the sound of the Chain being moved once again.

Keeping her eyes closed, Alex focused on the soft crying sounds of baby Arthur rather than the odd fleshy thumps happening across the room. She shook her head and wondered if she could become ill in a dream. Afraid to look, Alex covered her ears and shivered. She waited, listening to the muffled sounds until finally, the basement went still. There was a strange scent lingering in the air that Alex couldn't identify. Taking a deep breath, Alex forced herself to turn around and open her eyes.

There was a pile of carved flesh on the table by baby Arthur, but unlike any that Alex had seen before. It was pale with silvery droplets still running down the smooth surface of the muscles. The Chain was spread over it and Alex felt her stomach turn over as she realized that the power of the Chain was keeping the Sídhe flesh from vanishing. Climbing to her feet, she swallowed back a rush of bile but did not approach the table as Scáthbás set the long knife down on the edge of it.

Scáthbás grabbed the pile of flesh with her bare hands, her long human fingernails cutting into the muscle and skin as she hefted it and the Chain to the center of the table. With silvery blood on her hands, she pulled the blanket away even as Arthur hiccupped softly. The baby's cries intensified as she set his small naked form down into the nest of flesh.

"Your consciousness as Medraut cannot return soon enough," she grumbled to the infant. "Stop crying."

The Chain rattled as Scáthbás shifted it so that Arthur was now wrapped in its links. She pulled it tighter and tighter. Arthur shrieked as his body was forced deeper and deeper into the nest of flesh. Alex's heart clenched and she jumped at the Queen as her instincts demanded she stop this. Her hands passed through the Queen like a ghostly limb and she could only watch as the Chain began to shimmer and glow. Alex reached towards the Chain and gasped softly as her fingers touched it as if it were solid. It shimmered and flashed once again, tearing a scream from Arthur as his tiny body and the flesh began to glow dark silver.

Stumbling back, Alex covered her mouth as Scáthbás grinned in glee. A sloshing sound filled the room followed by a terrible grinding sound that made Alex slam her eyes shut. Arthur's little cries faded away and her eyelids burned with a brilliant flash of light. The sick feeling in her stomach returned as her vision did and she watched the pieces of flesh melt into Arthur's tiny body, making his entire form glow and his blue eyes flash violet. Then thankfully as her limbs started to shake, the world around Alex dissolved and faded to black.

29

Tale of Arthur

The world slowly came back into focus. Thankfully she was no longer in the basement, but Alex knew it was still the Pendred house. She was in a large master bedroom that greatly favored white with gold accents. Scáthbás was sitting calmly at a large white vanity and applying her makeup. She toyed with her blonde hair, shifting it around into different styles while she smiled at her own reflection with bright red lips. It was so normal that Alex was left stunned.

Alex just stood there watching Scáthbás even as her mind pointed out that the former Queen was hardly going to start explaining things to her reflection. Still, Alex watched her for another long moment, wondering how the Queen had managed all this. They had some answers to the mysteries that Arthur posed: he was part Sídhe like Merlin and Morgana, but also had a connection to the Iron Soul thanks to the Iron Chain. She was pretty sure that the piece of iron Scáthbás had used with the Chain while pregnant came from one of the ancient Iron Gates and contained Medraut's soul.

But now Scáthbás herself was a mystery. Was she some sort of ghost or shade who could possess humans because of being sealed in the Iron Gate, or was there more power hiding in her? The body she was in seemed human, or at least it had been, Alex amended as she remembered Scáthbás' comment about testing the Iron Chain on Arthur first. The thought made Alex even more uneasy as another loud wail erupted from the next room.

"For the glory of Sídhean, Arthur, be silent!" Scáthbás snapped just before the phone rang.

"Elaine Pendred." Scáthbás picked up the phone and inspected her long manicured nails. "Oh, it's you." She scowled and was silent for a moment. "Look, Marion, I'm not interested. Yes, Marcus was your brother, but he's dead! I can care for our son on my own." A dark look crossed Scáthbás' face, twisting the attractive features into something ugly. "I wouldn't say things like that if I were you, Marion!" Scáthbás slammed the phone down into the cradle. "Foolish human."

Shifting back, Alex decided that if her connection to the Iron Chain was going to give her access to the old home of her enemies then she'd better make the most of it and take a look around. Besides, there was a sick feeling growing in her chest at the mention of the names Marcus and Marion. She knew that Arthur's father was dead, but he'd never mentioned an aunt. She suddenly had a feeling that Marion had probably met with a terrible death for trying to interfere with Scáthbás' little warrior.

Turning around, Alex strode out the doorway and glanced into the neighboring room where the infant Arthur was whimpering softly by himself. Everything about the nursery seemed normal with a pretty white crib in the center of the room, a matching changing table, and a rocking chair. Yet the room lacked any spark of life. It was just window dressing, and Alex found herself moving towards the crib before she'd even had time to consider it. The infant Arthur was crying softly as the mobile hung lifelessly above him. Staring down at him, Alex couldn't help but notice that he looked just like any other baby, with bright blue eyes and only the slightest bit of hair on his head.

"Why did you turn out like that?" Alex heard herself ask. "Is it Medraut's soul? Her magic? How she raised you?" Of course, the infant had nothing to say; he didn't even know she was there and Alex sighed before looking up at the ceiling. "Why am I even here? I know about the Iron Chain now. I know that the Queen used it to fuse Medraut's soul into the baby her human host was carrying. I know that she then…" Alex trailed off and shuddered at the memory. "Made him half-Sídhe like Merlin and Morgana, but is there more?"

Alex looked at Arthur for only one more moment before she fled to the hallway. It was just too weird. Her fists clenched just thinking about the games Arthur had played with them. Looking around, Alex had to admit she had no idea of what she was looking for until her eyes landed on a heavy looking closed door that stood out in the hallway. Her hand passed through the doorknob and Alex allowed herself a grumble of frustration at her inability to open the door. The next moment, however, she felt like a bit of an idiot and reached out a hand and watched it vanish through the wood. Chuckling nervously, Alex stepped forward through the doorway.

The room was a bit fuzzy; Alex could tell it was an office and a fancy one too with a large dark wood desk, high-backed leather chairs, and built-in shelves heavy with books, but everything seemed to be just a little out of focus. Nonetheless, she looked around quickly, hoping to see something that might be useful. Ideally a blackboard with the steps of the Queen's master plan or a map with little pegs, but of course there wasn't anything like that.

Alex eyed the desk thoughtfully only to remember that while the ability to pass through things was useful on doors it meant that she couldn't actually pick anything up. Sighing in defeat, she looked around the room one more time and her eyes fell on a framed photograph that had been put to the side. A younger Elaine Pendred and a tall young man who looked a lot like Arthur were smiling for the camera with their arms around each other. Judging from the background they were at a restaurant and Elaine was holding her hand at just the right angle to show off an engagement ring. They both looked happy and Alex didn't see even a hint of trickery on Elaine's face.

"Scáthbás destroyed you, didn't she?" Alex felt a wave of guilt and sadness. "Both of you." She swallowed and turned towards the door. "I'm sorry."

Once she'd passed through the door again, Alex tried heading further down the hallway. She stopped in her tracks, feeling a sharp tug in her gut that wasn't familiar. She took a step back and felt the pull ease. Taking a step forward again, Alex felt the pull increase to the slight pang she'd felt a moment before.

"Okay," she sighed. Alex headed back towards the nursery. "Only seeing this because of my connection to the Iron Chain, so I guess I can't stray far from it." She paused and looked into the nursery suspiciously. "Or is it Arthur?"

She felt a flash of magic and straightened up with a sharp gasp. Around her, the world started to blur and this time Alex simply closed her eyes and waited. Magic washed over her, but she remained calm even as her stomach tightened as she wondered what she'd be shown next. Just the edge of her awareness she could feel the cold magic of the Iron Chain pulsing and reaching for her.

Except that she was right back in the same hallway a few moments later as the world shifted back into focus and the tug in her gut eased. Alex rubbed her stomach muscles uneasily as she looked around. She recognized that while she hadn't moved things had certainly changed. There was a series of photographs hanging on the wall that followed Arthur growing older, with the latest one being of a young elementary school boy. Staring at them, Alex was again struck by the reality that Arthur had been a child, a real child.

Swallowing, Alex shook her head and moved towards the stairs as she heard soft sounds below her. Thoughts about Arthur in a sympathetic light wouldn't lead her anywhere good. This wasn't some teen romance where love would redeem him or he'd switch sides. Alex felt stronger remembering that, but couldn't ignore the pang she felt at the notion. This whole thing was messy and she was caught right in the middle of it.

The downstairs of the house provided a bit of distraction. There were large photos of Scáthbás in her human body with Arthur and a few of her alone. Alex sneered at the nearest one of Scáthbás looking a bit too sultry that was hanging near the front door and moved into the living room. Elegant parquet was teamed with fancy old looking tables and sofas that were oddly reminiscent of Morgana's own decorating taste. Alex would never mention the similarity.

A coffee table was pushed to the side and a young blond boy dressed in shorts and a plain white shirt was sitting in the middle of the empty space. He was breathing slowly and deeply with closed eyes. A faint aura of magic surrounded him and Alex stilled as she recognized a young Arthur. Alex cursed loudly, knowing they wouldn't hear her.

With guarded blue eyes, the small boy looked up towards her and Alex gasped in surprise. It took her a moment to hear the person moving behind her and realize that he was really looking at them. Jumping to the side, she tripped through an armchair as she turned to find Scáthbás looming over the boy. She didn't look any older Alex realized curiously, and she wondered if Scáthbás had made her human body half-Sídhe. Were she and Arthur immortal like Merlin and Morgana?

The thought was frightening and Alex was half aware that her mind was jumping all over. There was so much to process, but she forced herself to focus on Arthur. He slammed his eyes closed as Scáthbás came closer and the glow around him brightened. Magic flowed over Arthur's fingertips, but unlike the bright white that Alex had been familiar with his magic was darker and duller.

"Focus!" Scáthbás smacked his head sharply. "White! I said white!"

"I'm trying!"

Scáthbás' human blue eyes flashed and she leaned down to strike the boy across the face. The sound of flesh meeting flesh resonated in the room, and a bright red mark was left on the boy's face as the magic around him dimmed. Reaching out, Scáthbás gripped Arthur's hair and tugged his head back.

"Focus, Arthur! You'll have to do battle with your magic in the future. A small pat on the cheek is nothing!"

The off-white magic flared again and brightened only a little more, but Alex could tell that the boy had lost control. His features tightened up as he fought to keep the magic manifested, but an exhausted gasp escaped him. Around him, the aura began to dim.

"Does it really matter?" Arthur's off-white magic faded and he scowled at his mother. "I mean it's hard for me to control the color it manifests. Can't I just do it normally?"

"Arthur, what color was Arto's magic?" Scáthbás folded her arms across her chest and gave the boy a dark look.

"White," he answered with a soft sigh and a nod. "I understand, Mother." He lowered his gaze and bit his bottom lip, holding back the tears that Alex could see glistening in his blue eyes. The angry red mark across his cheek seemed even brighter now.

"Oh, my dear little boy." Scáthbás dropped her knees next to him and gently rubbed his head, combing her fingers through his hair. "It's important that Morgana and Merlin truly believe you are the Iron Soul."

"I'm sorry." Arthur lowered his head. "There isn't much magic and it feels..."

"You have a great challenge ahead of you, Arthur." Scáthbás wrapped an arm around him, rocking the boy gently. "Your power is... well, it is stolen, to be frank. Stolen from that Sídhe descendant who could not use it and powered by the earth thanks to the trickery of the Iron Chain. You weren't a mage in your former life and I know it is a great change, but you will master it. I know that you will."

"But will it be enough?"

"It will have to be," Scáthbás murmured. "My spies watch those damned Abominations. They are already waiting for their precious Iron Soul to return. Don't worry, my boy, we'll trick them. We've both waited too long to fail now."

"Yes, Mother," Arthur answered with a nod, eyeing the floor. "Do- do you think I'll ever remember everything?"

"I've told you to embrace the dreams," Scáthbás said. "If you let them in then yes, you will remember everything about your life as Medraut. You will understand why this is all so important." Scáthbás leaned over and kissed his forehead. "Never forget, Arthur, that you are my Chosen One. You are my Prince. My Champion and our salvation."

The scene was too much for Alex and she turned and started walking blindly out of the living room. If a person hadn't been listening to Scáthbás they might think that she was a doting mother by how she held Arthur. Of course, she'd struck him only moments before so Alex knew better. Holding back a shudder, Alex felt a rush of bile in her throat at the hint of what Morgana's childhood had been like. There was a rush of sadness and anger that Alex wasn't completely sure was just her own.

Shaking her head, Alex looked around the entryway of the house and peered out the stained-glass windows that surrounded the front door. A man with a dog was walking past and his image was distorted by the glass. Then it distorted even more and Alex straightened up and glanced around at the house. Everything was shifting again. Alex focused on the sensation of her magic, feeling it fluttering over her skin again even as the cold jolt from the Iron Chain made her shiver.

The transition felt rougher this time with the icy pull of the Chain rattling her whole body. Fear flashed through Alex and for the first time since she'd started the series of visions she had to wonder if connecting herself to the Iron Chain had been safe. It was silly to think of an object as evil, but the familiar thrum of her own magic tainted with all that horrible intent made her feel sick. As her knees trembled, the world came back into focus, and Alex found herself back in the same entry hall just as the door opened.

Arthur stepped inside and dropped a backpack on the floor, and Alex swallowed down a rush of emotions at the sight of him. He was a bit younger than she'd known him with a hint of baby fat still on his features, but he already had those familiar broad shoulders. Despite knowing that she was less than a ghost to them, Alex flinched back from him.

He moved right past her, heading into the living room. After a moment of hesitation and a tug in her gut, Alex followed him. The living room was virtually unchanged except for a few upgrades on the electronics. Scáthbás was lounging in an armchair with a book in her hands. Arthur shrugged out of an unfamiliar leather jacket and tossed it over the back of the sofa. Scáthbás raised an eyebrow at him and closed her book with a deliberate thud, setting it to the side.

"Well?" She regally folded her hands in front of her.

"It went fine," Arthur assured her with a hint of distaste on his face. "I'm certain that she's the right one." He met his mother's eyes and smirked. "Jennifer Sanchez. All the signs and scrying point to her."

"It's important that she falls in love with you," Scáthbás said. Her tone was almost urgent.

"Don't worry, Mother." Arthur chuckled, running a hand through his hair. "A little bit of magic and a lot of charm. She was practically panting for me by the time I dropped her off."

"Good," Scáthbás demurred.

She stood up and stepped towards Arthur. Alex blinked as Scáthbás moved very close to him and paused only inches from him. Scáthbás ran a long fingernail down Arthur's jaw with a small smirk tugging at her bright red lips. Arthur returned the smirk and shifted a little closer to her as Alex's eyes widened and she backed up so quickly that she stumbled back through the armchair. Scáthbás' other hand twisted in Arthur's hair and tugged him down, meeting his lips in a bruising kiss.

"Oh God!" Alex closed her eyes and rubbed them as a rush of illness churned in her gut. Her legs threatened to give out. "I've kissed that guy!"

"Just remember, my precious boy, that the little girl is just a pawn," Scáthbás breathed a moment later. Alex dared to open her eyes, but it wasn't safe as Scáthbás was brushing her lips teasingly against Arthur's as her hands traced the muscles of his chest. "Keep her happy and in love, but don't forget your Queen."

"Like I ever could forget you." Arthur grasped Scáthbás' hips and pulled her against him. "She's just a little girl after all."

"That's, my darling." Scáthbás smiled and toyed with Arthur's hair again. "I recall you telling me that you left her panting for you."

"I'm certain of it," Arthur bragged. "By the time everything comes together she'll be completely mine. The Abomination will have no doubt that I'm his precious Iron Soul."

"Such a clever, resourceful boy," Scáthbás cooed. "I should reward you."

"Yes, my Queen," Arthur breathed eagerly. "You should."

They sank down on the couch together, limbs already intertwining and lips joined again. Alex bolted through the wall into the kitchen, ignoring the painful sharp tug in her gut as her magic tried to pull her back towards Arthur. Bile was filling her throat as her mind unhelpfully reminded her that, before the soul and Sídhe flesh fusion, the infant Scáthbás had used had been the biological child of Elaine Pendred.

"Shut up brain!" Alex closed her eyes and shook her head, desperate to rid herself of the sight. It was burned onto her inner eyelids. "Get out get out get out get out! I'm ready to go, come on help me out here magic. Time to wake up or move on!"

Maybe it really was time or maybe her own magic was reacting to her desperation as a long moan filled the room, because a moment later, Alex felt a rush of vertigo. The room around her faded to black and she began to fall.

30

The Dvergr

1 15 C.E. Sør-Trøndelag, Norway

Thor drew his sword slowly, trying to not make a sound as he eyed the Dvergr in front of him. It was all strange enough to distract him from the fact he was underground. He focused on the movement of the Dark Elves within the settlement and the placement of the buildings. Parts of what he could see were messy, but further from them just at the edge of the torchlight, he could see signs of construction and a much straighter and stronger building taking form. They were becoming more organized, and the idea chilled him.

"Careful." Merlin moved to push Thor back.

Everything happened at once: Thor's foot slipped and his knee crashed into the stone, pulling a loud curse from him that drew the attention of the Dark Elves at the same time that the odd creature took a swing at the nearest one. A hammer crashed into the stomach of the Dark Elf sending it staggering back, but then the Dvergr hesitated, looking back towards one of the huts. He began to move towards it, but over a dozen Dark Elves suddenly rushed out of the darkness.

Thor gasped softly as he saw them. Their eyes were glowing slightly in the darkness before they burst into the light. One of them grabbed a torch and extinguished it against the stone floor and another made a move towards another torch. This seemed to make up the Dvergr's mind and it spun around, rushing towards them. A ball of fire spun through the air and exploded against one of the Dark Elves making him stumble back into one of the buildings. It burst into flames, bathing the whole cave in a red glow as the smoke began to thicken.

"Morgana!" Merlin's green magic sailed through the air as dozens of green darts. "Watch it! We need to breathe long enough to get out!"

The Dvergr looked towards their voices, ducking under one of the Dark Elves as it tried to grab him and hurried towards them. Thor licked his lips and pulled on his magic, grateful when it responded despite his locked knees. A bolt of lightning flashed off his fingertips and struck one of the Dark Elves that was closing in on the Dvergr. Then the Dvergr rushed past them, glancing towards Thor with confusion, worry, and curiosity all flickering in its dark eyes.

Bolts of silver and green sailed through the air and struck the first of the Dark Elves rushing them. Both creatures shrieked and collapsed to the ground, convulsing as they began to vanish while their fellows just kept charging. There were more of them now, pouring in all around them like water into a hole.

"Fall back, Morgana!" Merlin shouted while still releasing waves of green magic.

"But-"

"Do you mean to be inside the caverns when this becomes too much and it collapses?" Merlin grabbed Morgana's arm, dragging her back.

The word collapse sent a bolt of terror down Thor's spine and when Merlin looked his way, he was already moving back the way they'd come. Up ahead he could hear the Dvergr moving through the tunnels and frantically followed. His lungs were tight like someone was sitting on his chest, and in the corners of his eyes, he could see the cave walls threatening to close in. As the glow of the fire vanished behind the first curves of the tunnel Thor had to stop himself long enough to create a small orb of light.

Breathing out, Thor was torn between relief at the light and another jolt of terror as the stone walls came into view. A shout behind him spurred Thor into action. He struggled with his footing going up the slope but scrambled his way up. Thankfully the route out was easy without any large branches. He caught sight of the Dvergr up ahead and sped up as fresh air washed over his face. With a final burst of speed, Thor climbed the last slope of the cave and sucked in a deep breath as he all but fell out of the cavern entrance.

The Dvergr rushed out into the sunlight ahead of Thor but shrank back from the sun a moment later as he covered his eyes. Around them, a fierce wind was blowing, making the trees quake and bend. There was a hint of a storm on the wind and Thor thought he could smell energy building in the air: a thunderstorm then. He risked a look up at the sky and smiled gratefully. Indeed, dark clouds were rolling towards them, contrasting with the bright blue sky, and shining sun overhead.

Thor's knees almost gave out on him as he moved away from the tunnel and inhaled the sweet air of the outside. The sky above his head was most welcome, and the trees around him felt comforting rather than confining even as they reached up far above him. His relief must have been clear because the Dvergr looked at him a bit oddly, so Thor tried to calm his expression and straightened up. Turning back towards the entrance he tried not to feel ill at the sight of the small hole in the mountain.

"Keep moving!" Merlin ordered behind him. "We need some room to fight!"

"Fight," Thor repeated dumbly, still feeling out of breath.

Nonetheless, Thor shifted back away from the entrance. Then the wind on his face gave Thor another burst of energy and he tightened his grasp on the sword. Magic sparked in his left hand around the orb he was still clutching. He felt stronger, and he inhaled deeply. The air tasted of lightning and for a moment he thought it was magic sparking in his hand, but a distant rumble reminded him that the storm was coming. Around them, the wind was picking up and Thor ground his feet into the soil as he eyed the cave entrance.

The Dvergr grunted and raised his hammer to fight rather than fleeing. Despite not being sure what the creature was, Thor felt his respect for it rising. Sounds from the tunnel forced him to turn his gaze back to it. His stomach shifted uncomfortably, but the smell of the storm reassured him that he wasn't in the cave. A Dark Elf climbed out of the entrance with flashing, dark purple eyes. In the strong light, Thor could properly see the being, and he drew back in surprise. No longer were they fair creatures like Frea, but the dark lines he observed when they'd first entered the world had spread completely over their skin leaving it a dark, shimmering gray color. Its cheekbones were more prominent and its lips had turned a dark silver color.

Thor raised his hand and allowed the magic orb to flare between his fingers. Light flashed around Morgana's hand and Thor saw it transform into a ball of fire cradled in her palm. Merlin brought his hands forward with green sparks flashing around them as two more Dark Elves climbed out. They lingered in the shadow of the mountain, watching them all carefully.

"Let's just collapse it," Morgana growled to Merlin.

"No!" The Dvergr turned towards them in horror, making Thor hesitate.

"Morgana, we don't know enough yet." Merlin's eyes moved pointedly towards the Dvergr and Morgana made a tiny nod.

As another Dark Elf came out, Morgana unleashed a bolt of magic at the first one. It dodged it for the most part but screamed as the magic tore across its arm. Another one snarled at them and all three moved forward. As they stepped out of the shadow of the mountain and into the sunlight all three froze in place. Blinking, Thor looked at them in confusion as expressions of panic took over their features. Their skin was lightening in the sun and after a moment he realized that their clothing was turning the same gray color. Strange panicked noises escaped the creatures from barely moving lips, but then they were silenced. Their eyes and faces turned a dull gray and all the life vanished from them.

For a long moment, no one moved. Thor was still bracing himself and felt the magic in his hand begin to vibrate faster and faster. Little shocks were traveling up his hand and through his arm. Risking a glance towards Merlin, Thor opened his hand and released the built-up magic in a brilliant bolt of lightning. It hit the first of the Dark Elves, which exploded into a shower of rock and dust, crumbling to the ground.

"What the-" Thor stuttered, taking a step back.

He heard the Dvergr grumble something but didn't look away from the other two stone figures. Blinking his eyes, Thor waited for something else to happen. They were still Dark Elves, but they weren't moving. They were stone, surely this couldn't be real. Yet Merlin moved forward with a thoughtful frown on his face. Morgana's magic flared and she extended both hands, ready to defend them if necessary. But nothing happened even as Merlin stood right beside the figures.

"They're stone." Merlin laughed as he tapped the first of the remaining two figures. The old mage's brown eyes were bright with amusement and astonishment. "Remarkable."

"Oh, marvelous!" Morgana said, stepping forward to study them.

Then with a small smile, she shoved the third statue over and watched it strike the mountainside. Thor grimaced as the statue collided with the stone and a large section of the head crumbled away. There was no blood or brain matter, however, only a pile of stone fragments. The Dvergr rushed past him and before Thor could say or do anything the other two statues were harshly knocked against each other. They both cracked a little and the small Dvergr knocked them together again while Morgana laughed. With a third smacking, the two stone figures began to crumble with bits of them falling into the cave entrance.

"Apparently even once they... adapt to the changes the crossing made, they still have some interesting weaknesses." Merlin reached down and collected a piece of the rubble. He sniffed at the rock and turned it over in his hand thoughtfully. "Do you suppose that they are aware of it?"

"Possibly." Morgana frowned and looked down into the entrance. "We weren't followed by many. Could be just the young and stupid ones that came after us."

"Well, they come out at night," Merlin agreed softly with a nod.

"They can see in the dark," the Dvergr grumbled, crossing his arms. "They only have light so we can work."

"Ah yes, our guest," Merlin breathed as he turned back to the Dvergr. "I apologize for the rudeness, but I am unfamiliar with your... kind."

"And where you come from," Morgana asked sharply. "And how you got to the Iron Realm!"

"I am Brokkr, I am a Dvergr," Brokkr replied with a touch of impatience. Then he sighed and his shoulders drooped as he glanced towards the tunnel. "I am a long way from home. My brother and our friends were traveling when this.... hole opened in front of us. We fell in while looking at it and found ourselves not far from here. Those things captured us and brought us here."

"To what end?"

"We are craftsmen." Brokkr sounded insulted by the question. "This lot needed help and enslaved us to make them weapons and whatever else they need."

"That explains the weapons." Morgana sighed, rubbing her eyes. "We were curious as to how they were managing that."

"Well, they are shoddy work," Brokkr grumbled. "Bad metal and worse forge."

A roll of thunder overhead interrupted the odd conversation and Thor looked up into the sky. The section of the sky that had been clear was quickly shrinking and the smell of lightning was growing stronger. Giving Merlin a look, Thor could tell that the older mage was conflicted. Morgana was eyeing the entrance and Thor wondered just how bloodthirsty she really was because she looked ready to go back down there.

"Thor, would Brokkr's presence in your village be a problem?" Merlin was looking straight at him now with a mixed expression of worry and excitement that made Thor uneasy.

Blinking in surprise, Thor looked back at the small being. In the better light, he could see the elegant detail work on Brokkr's heavy hide vest. There were small tools on his belt and the Dvergr was looking at him with equal curiosity.

"I'm not sure," Thor replied honestly. "None of us have ever seen anything like him." He shrugged weakly. "I suppose we can try. With everything that has been happening I don't think anyone will try to hurt me."

"And what of my fellows?" Brokkr demanded with darkening eyes. "Do you mean to free them?"

"We can't have them making arms for the Dark Elves," Merlin assured Brokkr, but Thor noted that he didn't really answer the question. "What we know about them has changed. We need to meet with our allies and decide our next course of action."

"The fact that the Dark Elves are either capable of opening portals, or that the magic of the Iron Realm has been so badly affected by the Sídhe forcing themselves through the barrier, that it is causing portals is certainly a worrying development," Morgana said.

"Do you know where your world is on the Tree of Reality?" Merlin asked Brokkr, only to get a blank look in response.

"Tree of what?" Brokkr had a doubtful look on his face.

Thor felt a bit better that he wasn't the only being who was lost around Merlin and Morgana. Another roll of thunder made Merlin look up sharply at the clouds with a deep frown.

"We need to return to the village," Merlin said. "I fear that the Dark Elves may attack tonight. They caught us spying, we killed several, and the four that followed us and a prisoner are missing." Merlin hummed thoughtfully. "The problem is that we don't know if they have other entrances in the area so trapping them and killing them off here isn't the solution."

Thor tensed at the words and looked towards Morgana, hoping that she might say something to the contrary. Instead, she nodded in agreement and gestured towards the path leading away from the cavern. Turning towards Merlin, Thor licked his lips and struggled for something to say. He didn't want to go back into the cave, but those creatures couldn't come to his village again. There had to be something that they could do.

Merlin met his gaze and without a word turned back to the cave opening. Green magic flared around his hands and he pushed a cloud of the green sparks towards the mountain. The ground shifted beneath his feet and Thor sucked in a panicked breath until he saw that the mountain was remaining intact. Instead, a mass of earth rose up and covered the entrance as if it was dripping mud only to solidify a moment later.

"That won't hold them back long," Merlin said. He leaned on his staff as he began to sway. "But it will buy us a little time and may change their minds about an attack. And it won't harm the prisoners."

Brokkr nodded his understanding and relaxed slightly while Thor felt even tenser than before. Glancing towards Morgana, he turned on his heel and began walking down the path. There was an urge to stay and guard the entrance battling against the desire to return and protect his home. He glanced back at the now sealed cavern and another shudder ran down his spine, but at least the others were now following him back towards his home.

31

Waking the Mage

The darkness was welcome. Alex sighed in relief as she floated in the sea of magic. She could now feel it pulsing around her, dragging her towards something else. As long as she didn't have to watch her ex-boyfriend, who stabbed her, make out with his mother. The thought sent a shudder through her body as the world began to reform.

Magic swam over her skin and this time she found herself in a dark wooded area, unable to make out anything for several long moments. Around her, Alex could hear thick breathing and the small sounds of giggling. She could smell the evergreens and hear the wind rushing through the branches, and for a moment she was lost. There was a flicker of magic brushing over her skin that she couldn't identify.

"Quiet," a deep and familiar voice ordered.

Alex's eyes finally adjusted and she moved towards the sounds. Her feet were silent as she stumbled down the dark hillside and passed through the fallen branches with a growing sense of dread. Up ahead she could see artificial lights and something was nagging at her, a tugging feeling that was much stronger than before. The sounds of things moving in the underbrush were growing louder and she was closer to the light. As she passed through a low hanging branch, ducking to avoid it before remembering that she didn't need to worry, Alex caught sight of a human ahead.

It was Arthur: much changed since she had last seen him. His blonde hair was longer than before, swept back from his face and damp from the rain. His lips were curled into a sneer as he eyed the assembled Faery creatures. Forcing her gaze away from him, Alex looked at the large group of gathered Faeries with confusion. Overhead, she heard the rumbling of a storm. There were dozens of Fairies, some small and hidden in the shadows and others that were full human sized Sídhe descendants. All of them had dead looking eyes, and Alex's stomach turned in understanding of what had put it there.

Turning back towards Arthur, Alex gasped as lightning flashed overhead and illuminated his face making his blue eyes glow dangerously. They were colder than she remembered; no longer masked beneath a veneer of compassion and concern. But worse was when she looked beyond him and spotted Merlin's house. In front of the well-lit, one-story light green house were familiar cars, and she caught sight of Jenny walking past the window.

For a moment Alex's mind was completely frozen. Arthur was back in Ravenslake. If this was a vision of the present then he was right outside the house with Faeries ready to attack. Faeries bound by the same Iron Chain that had created him. Bile rushed into her mouth and Alex fought back a full body shudder.

The sounds of more creatures moving made Alex turn around. Several dark creatures that walked like dogs were moving towards Arthur. They reminded Alex of Chernobog's Shadows: the shapes were fuzzy and the faces kept blurring as if they were trying to slip out of view. Alex wondered for only a moment if that was the power of the Iron Chain or something else before the full reality of what was happening sank in.

Rushing past Arthur and down the hill, Alex felt a tug in her gut, but it wasn't pulling her back towards Arthur: it was instead leading her into the house. She passed through the door and spared only a glance towards Jenny and Lance who were talking quietly in the living room, completely unaware that enemy forces were gathering outside. The pull of magic was becoming stronger and Alex tried to yell at Merlin who was seated in one of the armchairs, but there was no response.

The pull of the magic was getting stronger and Alex felt it dancing over her skin. She sucked in a sharp breath as she realized that it was pulling her towards her body and ran down the hallway, almost walking through Aiden and Nicki in her haste. Morgana was lingering by the door of the guest room like a sentry and the room was dark except for the light of the bedside lamp.

Her body was lying on the bed, motionless with closed eyes. Bran was leaning on the bed with his back twisted in what looked like a painful position. Alex was stunned for a moment, but only for a moment. Without considering how this magic was working or what she should do, Alex followed the tug right up to the end of the bed. Reaching out towards her own body, Alex felt another jolt of magic as her fingers connected with her hand.

There was a spark and her vision went white. Air rushed into her lungs as if she'd been holding her breath and Alex felt the crush of aching muscles as her magic tingled up and down her limbs. There was a soft hum of Bran's magic against her right hand as Alex fought back the fog that was trying to roll in over her mind.

"Arthur!" Alex's eyes snapped open, leaving her looking at the plain white ceiling of Merlin's guest bedroom.

"What?" Bran's groggy voice asked next to her.

She turned her head to find her friend sitting up in his chair and blinking rapidly as Morgana came rushing into the room.

"Alex!" Morgana smiled in relief. "You're awake! You've been asleep for-"

"Arthur's in Ravenslake!" Alex began to sit up as her heart raced. "He's just up the hill!"

Her stomach ached and her muscles protested the sudden change in position after who knew how long. Bran stood up and pushed back his chair as both his and Morgana's eyes narrowed on her. Swinging her legs off the bed, Alex carefully put her weight on them and started to stand.

"Arthur is in Ravenslake," Alex repeated. "Coming down from the hill; he's just outside the house!" Alex insisted as she stumbled towards the doorway. "There's a bunch of Faeries with him. They're going to attack!"

She stumbled into a wall but kept moving. At the edge of her senses, Alex could feel something beyond the walls of the house. It was like smelling a lingering scent or tasting something in the air; absolutely there, but just beyond her understanding. Someone grabbed her arm, but Alex shook them off as Nicki and Aiden came up to her. Nicki reached for her, but Alex shook her head.

"Arthur is here!" Alex struggled to catch her breath. "He's got Faeries outside, lots of them!"

Seeing worry and confusion take over Nicki's face, Alex pushed past her into the main room. Her legs were feeling stronger as the muscles stretched out and Alex ran to a window. The others were gathering around her and Alex shuddered at the sense of being surrounded.

"Alex." Merlin put a hand on her shoulder. "Calm down and then tell us what is happening."

"There isn't time!" Alex shook her head. "There isn't time to go into all the details, but I connected with the source of the magic controlling all the Faeries. It's connected to Arthur too and showed me how he was created and then showed me that he is outside. They were all gathered up; they haven't spread out yet."

"Okay." Merlin nodded and Alex blinked at him in surprise. She'd really been expecting more of an argument than that. "They haven't started their attack yet, so let's be smart about this. Everyone, get your shoes and coats on."

"Nicki and Aiden should go out the back and try to flank them once they rush the house," Morgana suggested. "Jenny and Lance stay inside the house. Bran should support from the porch and Merlin and I will stay near Alex." Morgana looked her over with barely veiled concern.

"I'm fine," Alex insisted. "Really. I have to fight him."

She couldn't elaborate on that and thankfully no one asked her to. Vaguely aware that her palms were becoming sweaty, it took her a moment to realize that she didn't have her shoes on and Alex was beginning to look around just as Bran held out the pair of tennis shoes.

"You, okay?" Alex asked. She accepted the shoes and used the wall as support as she pulled them on. "I didn't hurt you?"

"A bit tired," Bran admitted lowly. "But I'll make it. You?"

"Yeah," Alex replied automatically before she shook her head. "No, I'm not sure. I've got some serious issues to sort through later."

"The dream?"

"I didn't like what I saw to put it lightly." Alex pulled a hair tie from her jeans pocket and tied her hair back in a messy ponytail. "But this first."

She moved towards the door, softening her steps as if Arthur was right outside. A wave of fear rolled down her spine, but Alex picked up her coat as calmly as she could. In the corner of her eye, Alex saw Merlin pulling several sheathed swords out of a cabinet. He handed one to Lance and then a smaller one to Jenny, speaking with them in a voice too low for her to hear.

Merlin was holding a tall wooden staff that Alex vaguely remembered seeing before with symbols carved into it. Something nagged at her memory, but Alex shoved it away unwilling to be distracted. The sounds of giggling suddenly exploded outside, and Alex knew Arthur was ready for the attack. No one looked surprised or startled, and Nicki and Aiden suddenly rushed towards the back door through Merlin's kitchen.

Calling on her magic, Alex formed a small dark silver orb in her right hand just as Morgana pulled open the front door. She didn't look first. Alex threw the orb forward and it blasted into the chest of a Redcap holding a long, jagged knife. It screamed and began to dissolve. Another creature jumped forward, but a flash of silvery magic from Morgana flung it back. A stream of green magic flooded out the door beside Alex and expanded into a field, pushing Faeries off the porch and further from the house.

Small explosions echoed through the air and Alex's eyes widened as Bran tackled her to the ground. A nearby window shattered and she heard glass falling. Alex could hear splintering wood, metal, and glass cracking in a cacophony of destructive noise. Risking a look up, Alex spotted a silvery bubble of magic around them. Merlin was by the door with a swirling fog of green magic around him and sparks spinning around his staff. His features were dark and angry, sending a shiver down Alex's spine.

Around them, parts of the front door were scattered on the ground in chunks of wood and fallen glass. Alex couldn't see Morgana, but as the clicking sounds of the firearms being reloaded outside echoed into the house, Merlin's eyes almost glowed with rage. There was a moment of stillness and then the small army outside opened fire once more. Green magic flared around them and burst into the darkness beyond the doorway sending light pouring in through the broken windows. Shifting forward, Alex gasped softly as bullets slowed down in the air and were crushed in the field of magic.

"You should know better than that, boy!" Merlin shouted into the darkness. His hand glowed and the symbols on the staff flashed.

"Thought we might get a lucky shot, old Abomination," Arthur's voice taunted from the tree line. "But the old-fashioned way it is!"

Outside the noise changed and Alex heard the sounds of sticks cracking and large beings moving through the vegetation at the edge of the forest. Rising to her knees, Alex spotted Morgana who was pressed against the wall with a hand extended, creating a shield over her and Bran.

"Jenny? Lance?" Alex called frantically; her mouth suddenly very dry.

"Yeah, we're okay!" Jenny replied in a soft voice with a slight tremble to it. There was a pause and Alex heard muffled voices. "Aiden and Nicki too."

"I can't believe he brought firearms," Morgana muttered angrily.

"Like he said a lucky shot is a lucky shot." Bran climbed to his knees and looked at Alex. "Make them come inside or fight outside?"

"We'll have more room outside," Alex said.

Despite the lingering exhaustion and weight on her chest from the visions, the magic roared through her. Alex felt it coiling in her chest and the heat racing down to her hand. That much was reassuring, and she stood up. Morgana nodded to her as she and Merlin shifted closer to the door. Their hands flashed and orbs of bright pulsing magic appeared. Alex barely had time to blink before they were thrown outside. There was a floosh as they collided with something and a wave of pressure came crashing back into the house. Outside Alex heard the car alarms activate before the noise sputtered out. Alex hoped that Arthur had been smart enough to make his magic mute the noise or that Merlin had done so. The police showing up at reports of gunfire was the last thing they needed.

Leaping out the door, Merlin swung his staff at something Alex couldn't see and Morgana lashed out with her magic forming a whip of light. Moving outside, Alex flinched as she saw the damage to the front of Merlin's house. The windows were shattered remnants and large chunks of the walls had been torn open. Parts of the driveway were smoldering and the smell of ozone was thick in the air. Several of the cars were now showing dents and had been knocked into each other. And by the cars were small Faeries clamoring over them and larger ones moving around them.

Merlin stepped in front of her, sending another wave of magic crashing forward. Morgana's whip of light lashed out, striking a Redcap that was climbing up the porch. Rushing down the stairs, Merlin touched the first of the stone gargoyles beside the porch stairs. From her position, Alex couldn't see everything, but a layer of green magic spilled over the stone and seeped into the statue. A moment later it was moving and gave a flap of its wings.

More Faeries were closing in around them on the porch. Throwing her hand forward, Alex felt and saw a blast of lightning jump off her fingers and strike the first of the Sídhe descendants, sending it crashing back into the side of Lance's truck. A flash of yellow in the corner of her eye as another Redcap was launched into the air reassured her of Bran's presence. Another gargoyle flew into the air with an aura of green magic surrounding it and clawed at the nearest Faery.

Magic was pulsing in the air and beneath Alex's feet as she followed Merlin and Morgana down the steps. The pair of older mages kept ducking and twisting as they launched attack after attack. Fairies were being entangled in glowing shrubs as Merlin struck the ground with his staff and small volleys of silver bolts were pouring from the sky into the lines of attackers. There were flashes of red and blue at the side of the yard as Aiden and Nicki pushed their way into the flank.

Moving forward, Alex's head felt foggy as streams of light kept appearing in the corner of her eye. She blasted two more Sídhe creatures and her fingers twitched uselessly for her iron dagger which she'd foolishly left in her bag. Letting her magic build in her hand, Alex slipped between Merlin and Morgana to the front. She saw the small Redcaps in their blood dyed hats giggling and rushing for her alongside the unfamiliar dark indistinct canine shapes. There were small Brownies like Timothy, green-skinned beings that moved clumsily on the land, and dozens of small unfamiliar pixie-like creatures all moving towards her.

Alex pulled hard on her magic and felt the world around her ripple. Magic was spinning around her and a wave of vertigo hit, but Alex pushed it outward. Her dark silver magic exploded around her like an expanding cloud. Terrible shrieks filled her ears and Alex felt something snap over and over again in the air. She couldn't breathe as the stray glittering strands of magic in the air fluttered in the corner of her eyes like cut threads.

Arthur stepped out of the trees and Alex felt a jolt in her chest as their eyes met. She hadn't been prepared for it and the memory of Scáthbás striking him as a boy shoved its way forward despite her best efforts. Thankfully it was followed by the memory of dying in the snow while he collected her blood, and Alex felt her resolve steel.

"Hello, Arthur."

"Hello, Sweetheart." Arthur gave her a boyish grin "Miss me?"

32

Arthur Returns

Her mouth was dry. Alex just stared at Arthur. She was distantly aware of the others fighting the Faeries, but whether they'd been ordered to or Arthur's presence frightened them, the Fae creatures were staying back from the pair of them. Then Arthur moved forward and waved his hand, sending a wave of dark gray magic out through the area. It was close to the color of Alex's own magic, and she felt an uncomfortable twist in her stomach. For a moment she wondered if it was a good or a bad thing that Arthur wasn't forcing the color of his magic to change. As he came closer and the intensity of the sparks grew it was enough to help her move again.

Alex threw her magic forward. Pressure rolled over her, hitting her chest as their magics collided. The sparks of her magic flowed over Arthur's and he grabbed one of the nearby Sídhe descendants, hauling them in front of him. Guilt crashed over Alex as she watched the creature scream and dissolve. The image of the slaves chained in the hold of the ship and their empty eyes flashed in her mind.

Arthur wasn't affected. As the creature vanished in a swirl of dust Alex had to dodge a dark bolt of magic racing at her. She rolled across the pavement of the driveway, her hands scraping against the ground.

Leaping back to her feet, Alex tossed her head to get a strand of blonde hair out of her face and glared at Arthur.

"Can't say I've missed this ridiculous little town." Arthur's hand rested on the hilt of a sword strapped to his hip and leg. The hilt was silver with black wrapped around the guard. Not Cathanáil then.

Arthur's sudden shift from offensive to calm set her on edge. Her shoulders tensed and despite the urge to look around Alex kept her eyes on him. She had to trust the others to watch her back. Behind her, Alex could feel a rush of heat and heard a floosh, probably from a fireball. Arthur's gaze shifted to something behind her, but Alex didn't look away from him.

"I see that Aiden is still alive," Arthur observed. "And Bran is walking quite well for a former cripple." He wasn't surprised: that confirmed a lot to Alex and she remained silent as his eyes returned to her. "Nothing to say, dearest?"

"Where is the Iron Chain?" Alex fought to keep her expression neutral.

Arthur just smirked at her and a wave of nausea rolled through Alex. It wasn't as easy or simple as she'd hoped it would be. The phone calls had been hard enough, but now he was here in the flesh and there was a faint quiver in her body. Alex raised her chin and narrowed her eyes at him.

"Where is the Iron Chain, Arthur?" Alex asked again. "I'm not here to play games with you."

"Well, I suppose I should congratulate you on finally learning about it." Arthur chuckled and shrugged lazily. "Took you long enough. Honestly, what's the point of your immortal keepers if they don't stay up to date on your lives?" Arthur gave her a nasty grin. "After all, even my mother learned of it and found it."

"It does answer a lot of lingering questions." Alex eyed the nearest of the Faery creatures. Redcaps, by the looks of them, who were eyeing her hungrily, but still keeping their distance. "Like why I had a Connection with you and no one else did. It had nothing to do with you being Medraut in another life or any past family member bullshit like that. I was just reacting to my own magic."

"Very good, Alex," Arthur said. He was grinning, but there was a spark of suspicion in his eyes. Alex felt a flash of pleasure at his confusion but wondered how long it would take him to realize that she'd used visions to learn that. "But really, sweetheart, I'm not going to reveal its location or the plan."

"I suppose not."

Suddenly Alex was at a loss of what to do. In the stories and movies, this was the part where they were supposed to fight, but she felt only a sense of weight in her feet. He was staring at her too, even as the sounds of the others fighting echoed around them. Alex knew that the others could be in trouble, but she couldn't help but think of a quote that cautioned against the first move.

Breathing in slowly, Alex focused on the sounds around them. It was all she could do to stay still as every movement on the gravel, every cry of pain, from she hoped the Faeries, and the sound of anyone's voice just made her want to jump. Arthur calmly watched her with narrowed eyes. Behind him, Alex could see more dark shapes moving in the trees, and she wondered just how large a force he'd assembled outside of Ravenslake.

Dark magic flashed around Arthur's hand for only a split second before he shoved it at her. Alex threw her hands up and felt a wave of magic wash up her wrists and palms. Dark silver sparks flew into the air and caught the sudden onslaught. The bolt twisted amongst the sparks of her magic and Alex turned her eyes back to Arthur. He ducked to the side, glaring at her before sending a volley of small bolts flying through the air.

Pulling on Arthur's magic, Alex felt it rush to her outstretched fingers as the small bolts turned to wisps midair and reformed in her own palm. It was a disquieting sensation and she barely held back a shudder. Arthur didn't say anything in response to his attack being stopped, and Alex could feel the magic vibrating against her skin. In the corner of her eye, she saw one of the Faeries leaping towards Morgana and quickly released Arthur's appropriated magic as a bolt.

Arthur didn't say anything; his face remained a calm mask as he merely nodded to himself. Magic spun around his hands, but rather than throwing it towards her, he blasted it out to the right. It arced through the air, spinning past her. There was a loud crash from the house and Alex swung back to look towards it. Part of the porch was beginning to collapse as two of the support beams were broken in two.

Faeries were rushing towards the house as a mob, their voices high-pitched and almost frantic. She could see Aiden and Nicki throwing magic at them. Shards of ice rained down, followed by beams of tightly concentrated fire that fried those at the back. Some fell back and deviated to fight Nicki and Aiden, others vanished when the damage became too much, and still others kept moving towards the open front door.

Two figures came running out of the house, avoiding the collapsed section, and Alex's chest constricted as she saw the look of fear on Jenny's face. A pair of Redcaps were right behind Lance and Jenny, giggling as they lunged for their legs. Moving near the cars, Jenny climbed up on the hood of Morgana's red car and lifted the sword Merlin had given her up. Lance twisted away from the first Redcap, only to swing back around on his heel and bring the iron sword down sharply on its back. It howled and collapsed to the ground, part of its skin beginning to dissolve. A guilty, but determined expression took over Lance's face and he swung the sword down again.

A jolt of alarm rushed up Alex's spine. Spinning back around, Alex found Arthur with his sword drawn and advancing on her. Their eyes met and she cursed herself for ever turning her back on him. She needed to be smarter than that, but her internal scolding was cut off by Arthur casting another spell. The air around her began to spin faster and faster, pulling the oxygen out of her lungs. Fear surged through Alex, but she opened her hands and pulled on the magic. The dark magic sparked in the air, she heard Arthur curse, and the small storm he'd created around her broke apart.

More creatures were moving out of the trees. There were so many different shapes and colors that Alex's eyes were starting to hurt. Some, like the descendants of the Sídhe, looked almost human while others had an obvious otherworldly quality. Some walked like humans, others on all fours, and a couple even seemed to float just above the ground. They were closing in around her and the others. Keeping an eye on Arthur as he began to shout orders to his little army, Alex released a chain of lightning through the air into a group of Faeries. It wasn't powerful enough to destroy them, but three collapsed with muted screams.

In the corner of her eye, Alex saw Merlin move. Flashes of light from Aiden's fireballs were illuminating his face, and the low green glow of his magic made Merlin look more like a vengeful spirit than a man. The symbols on his staff were glowing brightly and he raised it above his head. Alex shivered as she felt and saw shimmers of magic spinning into the top of the staff. Then Merlin crashed it down against the ground. Magic rolled over the yard and the ground trembled. Spikes of earth shot up from the ground. A large hole opened beneath a group of the Faeries and closed up a moment later. The desire to shout at Merlin welled up in Alex's chest before common sense caught up with her. What else were they supposed to do?

Turning sharply, Alex nearly laughed as she caught sight of Timothy on the head of the nearest Sídhe descendent and pulling sharply on its long white hair. It shrieked and tried batting him away. The small Brownie stomped on the head, causing the hood to fall back the rest of the way revealing the Sídhe descendant's pale face. Its eyes were dark and Alex pushed some of her magic outwards, letting it ripple around her.

"Help!" Timothy cried out, his voice barely audible. "They don't mean to! Please!"

As another Faerie turned to dust to the right as a shard of ice lodged in its chest and pierced its heart, Alex nodded. Pushing out more magic, Alex felt it humming in the air around her, dancing across her skin, and filling her lungs. Breathing out, she extended her senses and tried to clear her mind. She connected to the magic and willed it to become her eyes, uncertainty flaring in her chest.

Opening her eyes, unsure of when she'd closed them, Alex found herself surrounded by long glistening lines of magic. They were connected to all of the Faeries, except for the Redcaps, and the lines stretched out into the distance, vanishing from sight. Alex reached for the strands as the world became blurred and shadowy. Everything around her suddenly appeared to be under a filter, but she could clearly see the shimmering strands of magic around the Faerie creatures. As one rushed towards her, Alex reached out and brushed against the strand.

Magic rushed up her arm and hit her chest, making her heart stutter for a painful moment. The thread of magic snapped and she saw a shape drop to the ground with a loud, pained sigh. More power slid into her body. She tugged at another one, calling the power of the Iron Chain back to her and away from the Faery. Again and again, she grabbed at the threads and pulled.

"What are you doing?" Arthur demanded with a frantic note in his voice.

Sídhe descendants and Faeries whose threads had been cut were pulling themselves to their feet. Some were running off into the woods and others were tackling their fellows and holding them down. Emotions were spinning through Alex too fast for her to process so she shoved them aside and just kept pulling on the magic. Long gleaming streams of magic were flowing towards her as more and more of the threads began to snap. It was building up too fast in her chest. A sharp pain was beginning to sink in and spread into her limbs. Biting her bottom lip, Alex pushed the new burst of magic out into her hand.

An orb of glowing magic flashing different colors gathered in Alex's hand. Shifting her hand away from its surface, Alex kept reaching her hands towards the strands of magic glittering in the air. More and more sparks appeared in the air and flew into the expanding orb. The color shifted to Alex's own dark gray and cast a soft glow around the front yard. Arthur stepped back, eying the pulsing orb uncertainly.

Rather than flowing through her, the magic of the broken connections was sweeping straight into the expanding orb of magic. Her hand dropped away from the edge of the magic field and it expanded quickly into a shimmering pillar beside her. It kept growing, pulling in more and more magic without Alex even having to focus on it, still running on her intent to break the connections. With each new burst of magic, Alex could feel a shock in her chest as her magic was stretched out and then snapped back to her.

Yet the sensation was settling into her chest, tightening around her heart. Closing her eyes, Alex exhaled and tried to trace the lines of magic back to the Iron Chain, but they just stretched out of sight and no vision rushed to her. Instead, the threads kept snapping, faster and faster and more at a time as her magic rippled through the air. Unlike the wave of Merlin's power, hers was a whisper and Alex opened her eyes to look around.

Arthur was shouting at the creatures running into the trees, waving his sword through the air like he was throwing a tantrum. Movement to the right caught her attention as Lance went down, clutching at his side as blood began to spill out. With a scream of rage, Jenny lashed out with her sword, the iron flashing in the lights of the house and colliding with the Faery. It began to dissolve into dust and she swung at another. Wild swings kept them back, but they were closing in on her. More and more of the freed creatures were running into the hills, their fear overcoming anything else. Somehow a groan from Lance echoed through the area and all Alex could see was him on the ground, bleeding and more creatures advancing.

The guilt couldn't matter. The Faeries were being controlled and that wasn't their fault, but if the mages all died here then it wouldn't matter. Arthur and Scáthbás would just enslave more and more. Eventually, they'd find Cathanáil, and if Merlin and Morgana died here then they wouldn't even be able to guide her next life. At least that was what she told herself.

Decision made, Alex curled her fingers inwardly and did something completely new. She willed her magic to cut her skin and felt the sharp pain as the flesh of her palm was pulled open by the flash of magic. It was both painful and hot, but the very feel of her own magic in the wound was instantly soothing, like a cool burst of air. Warm blood began to gather in her palm and Alex met Arthur's eyes. They were widening with panic.

Never looking away from him, Alex brought her hand forward and slid it into the mass of magic beside her. Magic rippled over her skin and when she opened her hand to fully expose her bloody palm to the air, the magic pulled at the energy in her blood. It swirled around her, enveloping her in a pillar of magic. It burned and a scream was ripped from her throat as the magic backlashed through her body, setting every nerve ending on fire.

There were faces: so many faces that she thought she'd seen before, but that flew by too quickly for Alex to be certain. Strange landscapes and cities passed before her; some familiar from books while others were completely alien. A familiar gleaming Sword, a rusty Chalice, an odd-looking Hammer, some kind of Trident, that horrible Chain and many others went by too fast for Alex to process. A pounding at the back of her skull made her groan in pain, but she fought through it all.

The blood in her palm shimmered dark silver and glowed in time with her pulse as more magic flowed into the small pool. Blood dripped off her fingers and hit the ground, sending a wave of magic rolling outward like a boulder into the water. At the eye of the storm, the air around her stilled and the world seemed to fall silent for a long moment. Then the air began to vibrate around her and the earth beneath her feet trembled. A roar like a dozen rolls of thunder all at once and unending echoed around Alex making her heart jump.

"Don't kill the freed," Alex whispered frantically, unable to hear her own voice. A wave of fear and guilt spilled over her, but she kept repeating the words. "Don't kill the freed. Let them run."

She had no idea if it would make any difference. It was building and building around her as streams of red flowed across the ground. Alex could hear shouting and screams, but they couldn't overcome the roar still filling her ears. The world exploded into red. Alex could see the shapes of the mages rushing about as glowing red figures while the Fairies and Arthur were cool blue figures in stark contrast. Her vision began to clear and she could see Fairies collapsing to the ground as the small rivers of glowing red blood poured out around her, climbing the hill and illuminating the edge of the forest in front of her.

Arthur dove away from the rush of magic and one of the streams of blood, throwing his hand out to create a mist of dark sparks that spun around like a storm. He rolled back to his feet and took off running down the hill. Towards the lake, Alex realized weakly. She licked her lips and tried to speak, but the hum racing through her body was too much. The pain was gone, leaving her dazed and heady as she stumbled forward. Around them, the red glow was fading into the soil, but she could still feel it there just beneath the surface.

Stumbling forward, Alex's body felt heavy as exhaustion weighed down on her. Around her, the air was still shimmering and she could only see Arthur thanks to the dark mass of his body and the ripples he was creating in the mist of magic that was hanging over the whole area. Still, she ran after him. They were following the road down towards the lake and thankfully there was no traffic. It was difficult to keep up with him and with every second he pulled further and further ahead as his longer legs and lack of exhaustion gave him an advantage. Up ahead Alex could see glistening water in the light of the moon and tried to move faster.

Water surged up at the shore of the lake just as Alex reached the crest of the hill. Alex shouted for Arthur to stop, but he didn't look back at her. Instead, he leapt forward as the water began to spin and swirl like a vertical whirlpool. Throwing her hands forward, Alex tried to pull on the magic as Arthur vanished, but her knees rattled. The world faded away as Alex collapsed forward. Her knees hit the rocky shore of the beach and the pain gave her only a brief rush of adrenaline. The water portal vanished and Alex sighed in defeat. Falling forward, she caught herself on her hands as her arms trembled. Behind her, she could hear Morgana shouting her name and lowered herself slowly to the ground. Inhaling the thick musty scent of the earth, Alex let her eyes slide closed, secure in the knowledge that Morgana would find her.

33

Hammer of Thor

1 15 C.E. Sør-Trøndelag, Norway

It was a clear night as they waited beyond the gates of the village. Thor's eyes moved over the line of tinder and wood set spread in a semicircle in front of them. Torches were waiting for the first sign of the Dark Elves, but Thor was beginning to wonder if they would come at all. Nearby Brokkr was growling lowly and staring into the darkness as the humans all drew away from the strange creature.

Sweeping his eyes up the hillside, Thor did his best to stay calm. The Dark Elves were fierce and their ability to see in the dark had him concerned, but there were three mages present along with the warriors of the village. Surely, this would go well, Thor told himself. A dull, heavy silence hung over them and Thor glanced towards Brokkr who was sniffing the air. The wind shifted suddenly and Thor straightened up.

The wind almost muffled the sounds, but he could hear the faint footfalls of the Dark Elves. Grabbing a nearby torch, Thor watched the forest and listened for another moment to confirm. In the distance, he thought he could see something moving in the fields. The sounds of their approach increased and low voices began to echo on the wind. Tossing down the torch, Thor watched with satisfaction as the line of dried moss and kindling on the ground ignited.

Dark Elves began to swarm out of the darkness only moments later as the fire spread rapidly around the village. Flames roared up before them as the fire spread in a large ring. Dark Elves were shifting back from the flames shielding their eyes, and for a moment Thor felt a rush of confidence. It didn't last long as the Dark Elves began to kick dirt over the flames, dimming them just enough for the front line to leap through the fire.

Swinging his sword at the nearest one, Thor grunted as its armor buckled slightly beneath the force of his blow. The Dark Elf stumbled for a moment before spinning around and striking at him with a long spear. Avoiding the attack, Thor thrust the sword forward. A blast of silver magic caught his attention just before balls of fire and light began to spin around Morgana, striking the Dark Elves that approached her. Pulling on his own magic, Thor tried to focus on dodging the attacks and his desired effect at the same time but found it difficult. Bright blue sparks shot forth from his fingers and swarmed out in a wave of wild heat and sparks. Despite his lack of control, it was enough to force the Dark Elf back.

There were more Dark Elves advancing on him and Thor flexed the fingers of his left hand. He was grateful that his smithing had trained him to use both hands as he summoned an orb of magic in his free hand. Pushing his hand forward, Thor pointed at the nearest Dark Elf and smirked as lightning flashed off his fingertips and struck it in the chest. It dissolved into dust and he turned his attention to the next one. Beyond the wall of flames, more Dark Elves were coming forward even as spikes of earth sprang from the ground in a mist of Merlin's green magic. Energy flashed around Thor as the other mages shifted their attacks to protect him; something which he was more grateful for than he liked. The Dark Elves crowding around him began to fall and Thor destroyed another with a well-timed swing of his sword at the Dark Elf's neck.

A scream erupted from the village and two of the men pushed open the gate. Merlin and Morgana were sending waves of magical attacks raining down on the Dark Elves swarming out of the darkness. There was no sign of retreat from either of them. Turning on his heel, Thor rushed through the gates and followed the screams, gesturing for the others to stay in position. The guards posted inside were already running across the village with their weapons raised.

Dark Elves were pressing their way through a roughly hacked hole in the village wall. Thor could see women and children fleeing from them across the village enclosure and rushed towards the Dark Elves. Thor felt the ground beneath his feet hum as another orb of power formed in his left hand. Throwing it forward, he willed it to destroy the Dark Elves and watched as it transformed into a bolt of lightning that flashed out like a chain of light striking three of the Dark Elves.

Thor rushed for the group, all but forgetting his magic as he swung his sword at the nearest Dark Elf. The weak metallic armor squeaked beneath the force of the blade and the Dark Elf stumbled to the ground. Twisting his sword in his hand, Thor brought it down on the creature's head. There was a satisfying splash of black tinted blood and the thing began to turn to dust. As a mother scooped up her young son and ran towards the far side of the village, Thor took stock of where they were. His own home was only a few feet away and he couldn't see any sign of his father who'd remained as one of the guards inside of the village.

Taking advantage of his temporary distraction a small group of Dark Elves dashed forward, their crude weapons swinging wildly towards him and displacing the air. Stumbling back, Thor swung his sword hard enough to disarm one of them but had to keep moving to avoid the attacks of the other two. In the corner of his eye, Thor could see that the defenders were holding back most of the other Dark Elves by the gate. Other guards had rushed to the hole to defend it. That left the half dozen Dark Elves or so inside the village to him.

One of them hit him from behind, knocking him forward into another Dark Elf. As a club impacted with his stomach, the air was knocked out of Thor and only his armor kept the impact from shattering his bones. Stumbling back, Thor panted and blindly swung his sword around. It collided with one of the creatures, sending it falling to the ground with a shriek of pain. As his vision cleared, Thor was hit again from behind in the shoulder. His sword was wrenched from his hand. Seeing him weaponless, they poured in around him, forming a tight dangerous circle.

Fear tightened his throat as panic began to claw at his chest. Thor released a wave of sparks all around him to force them back with a roar. Waves of bright blue erupted outwards forcing back the Dark Elves. Thor took in a greedy breath and stumbled back, putting distance between himself and the group. Looking around, he couldn't find his sword as the creatures began to rise. Thor turned and rushed up the small incline to his workshop in search of another weapon.

When Thor got to the door of his forge, he turned back to check on the Dark Elves. Their violet eyes were glittering in the low light. He called magic forth into both of his hands. The light of his blue magic only made their eyes glow more brightly, but he launched a pair of orbs at them. Beyond the wall, he could still hear the sounds of battle and the glow of the flames was still illuminating the smoke rising into the air.

Thor released another bolt of lightning, trying to think of what else he could use his magic for. He hadn't tried anything complex yet and didn't dare try to open the earth as Merlin could. He launched another wave of magic and pulled back the hide covering the entry to his forge. One of the Dark Elves rushed forward and thrust a sword towards him. Lunging to the side, Thor's fingers wrapped around the first thing he found. Not an axe or the hilt of a sword, but rather his primary work hammer. Thor smashed it into the head of the nearest Dark Elf, and magic thrummed beneath his fingers. It was faint, but it was there and Thor tugged at the magic before he even thought about what he was doing.

Thor smirked as his hammer pulsed in his hand. He could feel magic stirring within it, though he was not sure from where. It was not draining from him, and yet it felt like his own power. Stepping back outside, he scanned the village and brought the hammer up in front of him. As the Dark Elves rushed at him Thor found he didn't care in the slightest. There was a rush of magic into his chest, making him feel stronger than he'd ever felt. Heady on the sensation, Thor swung the hammer again. It struck one of the Dark Elves in the chest. A flash of magic jumped off the hammer like lightning and made the creature scream in pain as it dissolved.

Swinging the hammer again, Thor hit another Dark Elf as magic jumped from the hammer into his target. They just kept coming and with fast movements, he dodged their attacks and struck them one after another with the hammer. Then the remaining two Dark Elves backed off, stumbling back down the hill and looking back at him with fearful eyes. Thor launched himself after them, reaching out to grab the long whitish hair of the one closest to him. With a slight roar, Thor swung his hammer again, catching the Dark Elf in the shoulder. It fell to the ground and as he moved to strike it once more another bolt of lightning arced off the surface of the hammer. Bright blue magic washed over both creatures, turning them to dust which settled on the dirt below him.

Thor looked around the village but saw no more of the Dark Elves. Running back to the gates, Thor stormed outside the walls and saw that the fires were beginning to die down. The thrum of magic in his chest was growing stronger and stronger leaving Thor aching to release it. The Dark Elves were closing in around the warriors and he could see some of the villagers dead on the ground. Merlin and Morgana were surrounded by magic which was churning like a storm.

His magic jumped as an idea came to him and he felt another lightning bolt rolling across the hammer. Raising the hammer above his head, he called more magic forth and visualized a storm of his own. He would rain lightning down on the Dark Elves, but the magic spun out of his chest and back into the hammer. The metal began to glow as small bolts of lightning flashed off of it, striking out at the nearby Dark Elves. It shook in his hand, but Thor didn't let go and watched the hammer in awe as the magic spread out around him.

Lightning flashed above their heads as dark clouds rolled in from nowhere. The wind howled and Thor could smell lightning and magic on the air. Yet he could feel his own magic churning into the storm and was unafraid. He eyed the Dark Elves who were shifting into an organized battle formation and frowned at the realization. It seemed that the time of wild beasts was indeed now past. Narrowing his eyes, Thor tightened his grip on the hammer and felt the wind speed up.

People were screaming and Dark Elves were snarling as rain began to fall. Thor frowned, not wanting the rain to interfere with his ability to fight. Suddenly the rain around him stopped, creating a dry zone around him. He didn't have time to marvel at the strange event as the first line of Dark Elves rushed forward.

Thor brought his right hand up, pulling on his magic and forgetting about his hammer for a moment. A bolt of lightning blasted down from the sky, striking the hammer. Pure, raw power crackled off the metal and lashed through the air, arcing wildly to strike all of the nearby Dark Elves. There was a blinding flash of light as the world went white and a deafening roar of thunder as everything trembled around them.

His whole body was frozen in place as every muscle shook and the air was forced from his lungs at the rush of magic from his body. Thor's senses abandoned him until the roll of the thunder finally faded. The winds lessened and the pressure in the air eased, though the scent of lightning lingered gloriously in the air. Thor inhaled deeply as a burst of warmth spread through his body. He felt stronger than ever before: felt invincible and completely victorious. Then he opened his eyes.

Ashes were fluttering through the air before settling on the ground. There were small scorch marks scarring the earth, but no Dark Elves. He waited for more to appear out of the darkness, but there was nothing. Slowly, he exhaled and began to smile as the thrum in the hammer lessened to a soft pleasant hum.

"Did you see that?" Thor spun to face Merlin and Morgana. "That was beyond anything I ever imagined I could do!"

He tossed the hammer up in the air a bit and caught it with a widening grin. In the corner of his eye, he could see those who had fallen and yet he just couldn't contain his excitement. Something was still humming through his body making every part of him feel stronger and better than before. His father came stumbling to the gates with wide eyes and his brother rushed to join him. Whatever residual fear Thor might have been carrying vanished, leaving only the heady feeling of victory behind.

Merlin and Morgana were staring at him with surprise etched on their features. It was both amusing and a bit worrying until he followed their gaze to the hammer he was still holding in his hand. A faint pale blue glow was still surrounding the metal and Thor smiled at the pleasant hum having the hammer in his hand caused in his chest. He shifted his grip on the leather wrapped handle, admiring how perfectly it seemed to fit into his hand; better than it had before. Stepping closer to him, Merlin reached out and touched the metal of the hammer carefully.

"When did you do this, Thor?" Merlin's voice was reverent as he looked down at the hammer with wide eyes. "How did you know what to do?"

"What are you talking about?" Thor drummed his fingers against the hammer's wooden handle, noting that it felt a bit different in his hand now. Thoughtfully he ran his fingertip over the handle's leather wrapping, wondering what had changed. "The hammer?"

"Yes, the hammer!" Morgana gasped as her eyes dropped down to it. "What did you do, Thor? When did you manage this?"

"Are you talking about the magic that the hammer possessed?" Thor questioned with a slight frown. "I believe it has built up from me working with it," he informed Merlin as he glanced between the pair of older mages. "I've been pushing magic through it like you told me to in order to improve the iron weapons."

"This is surprising," Merlin remarked thoughtfully with a tilt of his head. "Though I suppose it does make sense."

"Gofiben was a smith and nothing like that ever happened." Morgana seemed torn between being impressed and in a frantic worry.

"Who is Gofiben?" Thor frowned at the clear comparison. "Another Iron Soul?"

"Yes, one of your prior lives," Merlin explained quickly. "Gofiben created the Iron Chalice and did not spend much time smithing to fight a particular enemy."

"Supposedly created a Chalice," Morgana scoffed. "We have only his brother's word for that and the stories he spread."

"This is not the time Morgana," Merlin scolded with a stern frown before looking back to Thor. "I apologize, Thor, we are merely surprised. We were not aware that the Iron Soul could create such a magical item accidentally." Merlin paused and looked at Thor very seriously with a searching look. "You were not trying to enchant the hammer, correct?"

"No, I wasn't," Thor admitted, feeling compelled to be honest by Merlin's hard gaze. "I've just tended to use this hammer lately." He paused and licked his lips before admitting, "It has been easier to push magic through for the weapons I've been making lately."

"Ah yes, that would have been a clue," Merlin informed him as his shoulders relaxed. Then the older mage chuckled. "Well, it is surprising, but I have no doubt that it will be of use."

"What is the significance of the hammer?" Thor looked down at the hammer in question.

He noted that the iron gleamed in the light and that the metal was smoother than it should have been. It had always been his largest hammer, but he could feel a strange heft to it that was less familiar. Magic flowed up his arm from where his fingers brushed the metal head, making him feel powerful again. Thor rather liked the feeling.

"I'm not sure," Merlin said. "Some of your predecessors have created special objects of great power. They are different from the swords and axe heads that you make. While those carry only a few sparks of magic, these objects carry much more magic and have a connection to the Iron Realm itself."

"We believe they can help you call more magic from the Iron Realm without putting your body at risk," Morgana offered. "But our experience with them is very limited."

Frowning at them, Thor tried to calm the odd feeling churning in his gut that warned him they were right. He could feel his magic, a part of himself echoing back at him through the Hammer. It was both comforting and distressing, and he wondered how much of himself he'd given away without even realizing it. Merlin seemed to be aware of his discomfort and said something to Morgana in a low voice. The two elder mages fell back to speak with a group of people including his father and brother.

The caw of a raven made Thor look up towards the roof of the longhouse. There watching him were two ravens that he was certain belonged to Odin. Smirking slightly, he nodded to them and watched them spread their wings and take flight. Next meeting with Frea, Odin, and Sif they would have something interesting to report at least. There were questions of where Brokkr's people had come from, how they'd gotten here, and how to deal with the Dark Elves. Thor exhaled slowly and pushed the questions away. He wouldn't answer them now.

Thor looked down at his Hammer thoughtfully. A Hammer would not have been what he would have chosen to imbue with his power. It would have been a sword or maybe a good axe, but as he watched faint glimmers of magic dance over the surface of the metal Thor had to admit that it wasn't all bad. The only problem was that it was a bit plain with its heavy front and narrowed back side for a grand object. He smiled to himself and hefted the Hammer up. If it was magical and strong then maybe, just maybe he could use his magic to make some embellishments on it. After all, with the issues still troubling his village, he'd need to play the part of an impressive warrior.

34

Outside Looking In

After living together for almost an entire semester in a single room freshman dorm, Jenny had thought that she'd seen Alex at pretty much her worst. She had been very wrong. She'd seen Alex sick with a cold once and seen her utterly exhausted, but never in this state. Morgana had returned to the house with Alex floating in the air unconscious, wrapped in a blanket of silver magic. Alex's hand was still oozing blood, her face was pale with streaks of dirt on it, and her long hair was matted with old dead leaves.

She still wasn't sure what had actually happened. Alex had woken up in a frantic state, all but shouting a warning about Arthur just before they'd been attacked. Professor Yates- Merlin had given Lance and her swords to protect themselves with, and within moments everything had gone crazy. Merlin's front yard had been filled with lights and fiery attacks against all the creatures. She and Lance had stayed in the living room, close together and peering out through the broken windows at the chaos. When the cracking of wood had echoed in the room and the porch had begun to collapse, she'd followed Lance outside. That had put them amongst the creatures and let her take a good look at Arthur.

Her former boyfriend had been staying near Alex; mostly just watching her with a calculating look that had made Jenny's limbs turn to ice. His betrayal still shocked her. There were many days that she woke up in confusion, certain that everything had just been a nightmare, because how could Arthur do such things? That cold look; that expression of utter apathy for the distress he was causing made Jenny believe that maybe that confusion would finally go away. If Lance hadn't been there... Jenny shivered slightly. She wasn't sure how she would've reacted to Arthur. Part of her was grateful that he'd been so focused on Alex that he hadn't even looked her way, and yet another part of her was hurt.

Standing up from the armchair, Jenny glanced down the hallway that led to the guest room where Alex was recovering. Merlin was in an armchair in the living room, soundly asleep while Morgana was sitting in a chair right next to Alex's bed. Nicki was sitting on the sofa next to Aiden with her head drooping every few minutes as she fought back the urge to sleep. Looking out the window, Jenny marveled at how normal the world appeared outside.

Parts of Merlin's lilacs had been damaged, but the creatures as a whole had avoided the back side of the house by the iron workshop and all the wrought iron furniture. The large oak in the front yard showed no signs of damage at all, presumably due to the iron bench around its trunk. There were small craters scattered throughout the front yard. Half of their cars had been at least a little displaced, and she reassured herself that the damage could be fixed.

Jenny wasn't sure how she felt about all of it. They'd talked about the creatures being under Arthur's control, and yet they'd still fought them. Intellectually she knew that there hadn't been a choice: fight or let the Fairies kill all of them, but she was still unsettled by the whole thing. Around them, some of the Fairies had collapsed only to run off. Others had tackled other Fairies to the ground and held them until they seemed to pull free of the control.

No, not pull free, Jenny reminded herself as a headache crept up on her. Alex had freed them somehow. Her friend had been waving her arms around like she was conducting an orchestra in the midst of the battle. That glowing pillar of light by her had just kept growing, and then there had been that.... explosion was the only word Jenny had for it. Some of the Fairies had vanished in flashes of blood red and dark silver, while others had been able to run. Timothy the Brownie had been shouting as he jumped around the streams of red magic flowing across the yard.

Then Arthur had run. Alex had gone after him and everything had gone silent. Some of the collapsed Fairies had gotten up and run away, seemingly unaffected by the magic, and Jenny wasn't sure why. Nibbling at her bottom lip, she tugged at the hem of her shirt and pulled out her phone. There were no text messages. The people she knew best at this point were all here in the house. And what did that say?

Jenny wasn't sure what to do with the stillness that had taken over the house. After Morgana had found Alex, Merlin had used waves of green magic to repair the damage to the house before collapsing in exhaustion so that it was safe to take Alex inside. She and Lance had watched in silence as the beams supporting the porch were knit back together, as splintered wood swarmed up into the air and reformed bits of roof and trim. Jenny had been rather sternly reminded of just what the mages could do. However, they were all now unconscious or nearly so, and she was uncertain of what to do with herself.

Lance had pulled a chair from the dining room over by the window and was peering outside with a closed off expression. The sword Merlin had given him was propped up in its sheath against his leg, his right hand resting on the hilt. There was a ridiculous little flutter in her chest at the sight of Lance standing guard over them, and Jenny turned her flushing face away from him quickly. The sword Merlin had given her was back in its sheath and leaning against the wall of the living room. Waiting, just in case she needed it.

The sound of someone moving in the kitchen surprised her, but Jenny went to investigate. Bran was in the kitchen and Jenny could see him opening cabinets and pulling down plates and glasses. Merlin shifted in his sleep as Bran accidentally knocked two plates against each other. Timothy was walking across the counter, carrying an empty pitcher on his head that had to be several times his weight. Jenny giggled as she wondered if Brownies weren't a bit like ants in that regard.

"Can I help?" she asked softly. Jenny moved further into the kitchen with a slight smile.

"Sure." Bran gave her a welcoming smile before nodding to the fridge. "Merlin has some sandwich makings in there. I figured I'd make up a couple and see if that didn't help people regain some energy."

"It's late though," Jenny pointed out with a look at the clock. "Almost one in the morning. Shouldn't they be sleeping?"

"We don't know what else is coming." Bran glanced out the window with a frown. "Arthur got away again. I can't imagine the Queen would want to risk coming here, but...." He shrugged and shook his head. "I'm not sure what Alex's blood spell actually did."

"Oh." Jenny was unsure if she liked the fact that she wasn't alone in confusion or not. "What was it supposed to do?"

"Well, from what Merlin and Morgana have told us I figured that it would... uh, destroy all the Sídhe and Faery creatures," he admitted with a glance towards Timothy, who lowered his head uncomfortably.

"But Alex said Merlin and Morgana are half-Sídhe." Jenny looked back at Merlin as he was beginning to snore a little.

"Yeah, they are, good point," Bran agreed. "Maybe it only activates against those who mean the people of the Iron Realm harm. It would explain why all the Redcaps were destroyed. Those all seem like miniature psychopaths."

Jenny said nothing. What could she say in response to that? She vaguely remembered reading about Redcaps in one of the numerous books she'd been looking through. According to myth, they were vicious Faeries that soaked their hats in the blood of the humans they killed. They were one of the sorts of Faeries she'd desperately hoped weren't real.

Bran suddenly swayed on his feet, grabbing at the edge of the counter. Taking hold of his elbow, Jenny took on some of his weight and watched his face as it began to clear. His green eyes were cloudy for a moment, but he shook his head and forced a smile.

"Sorry about that," Bran said. "I'm still pretty exhausted myself."

"Well, you were helping Alex with the dreaming thing earlier," Jenny replied nervously.

"Yeah. Still, I thought I was alright from that. I even stayed back in the fight so I didn't get in the way."

"It turned out alright," Jenny offered, unsure of what to say.

"True." Bran pushed back from the counter and rubbed his leg for a moment as he looked down at it with an odd expression.

"It isn't hurting, is it?" Jenny asked.

"No," Bran assured her. "Just a phantom pain. I'm still adjusting to everything being healed."

"Must be nice." Jenny smiled as she turned her attention back to the sandwich she was making, loading the bread with sliced ham and cheese. "Having your leg healed, I mean."

"Suppose so." Bran shrugged, causing Jenny to look at him in surprise. He looked up at her and she could see a shadow in his green eyes. "I mean yeah it's good and I'm happy, but it's also a bit complicated."

"How so?" Jenny questioned, surprised by the answer and his honesty.

"I got used to being disabled. I figured out how to live with it and I made some kind of peace with it," Bran explained in a slightly frustrated voice. "It's hard to explain, but I almost feel like I betrayed something. Maybe I just haven't wrapped my head around it yet." He shrugged and shook his head, returning his focus to the sandwiches. "Then again I suppose I'm the Fisher King, so it had to happen."

"That's something else I don't understand," Jenny said. "How could you be part of that myth? I mean it predates you. By a lot."

"Well, it might be that my past incarnation had visions of me in the future like I had visions of him in the past," Bran said. "Or some other seer did. I mean, a lot of my visions just seem like dreams, so in theory, someone with a bit of magical power could have a vision of us in the future and tell the story to someone. That's potentially where the Welsh myth of a blonde-haired person opening the cave where the Chalice was hidden came from."

"So, you don't know?"

"This is real life, as crazy as it is," Bran reminded her with a humorless chuckle. "I suspect there will be many things that we never really get an answer about. You just have to take what knowledge you do have and move on."

"That would drive me crazy."

"Right there with you." Bran laughed before nodding towards the living room. "Explains a bit about Merlin and Morgana though, doesn't it?"

"I suppose so, in a way." Jenny considered Professor Yates in the armchair. Sometimes she still had trouble looking at him and fully understanding that he was Merlin. Though after watching his magic repair half of his house, that might be easier in the future. "I'm not sure how it hasn't driven them mad."

"I'm not sure that it hasn't."

"Mages are strange," Timothy said, causing Jenny to jump as she'd forgotten that the Brownie was there. Timothy was calmly leaning over the edge of the sink and scrubbing at one of the dirty knives. There was a bit of soapy water in the sink and he looked ready to tumble in.

"I'm not a mage," Jenny replied before she thought the statement though.

Timothy looked at her a bit oddly and she expected him to ask what she was doing there. To be honest she might have felt better if he had, but instead, the Brownie just shrugged and went back to scrubbing the edge of the knife.

The sound of footfalls in the hallway made Jenny perk up. Picking up the plate of finished sandwiches, she looked at Bran, who nodded and moved into the living room. Jenny grinned as she caught sight of Alex stumbling down the hall with Morgana right behind her.

Alex had dark bags beneath her distant eyes. Jenny offered her a small smile and Alex nodded in response before she moved over to the sofa and sank onto it with a grateful sigh. Nicki woke up at the noise and elbowed Aiden lightly to wake him up. Morgana moved over to Merlin and called his name, waking the oldest of the mages. With a hesitant step forward, Jenny set the sandwiches on the coffee table and Bran put down the pot of coffee and the first set of mugs.

No one spoke for a few minutes as she went back to the kitchen to retrieve a few more mugs. Timothy leapt off the counter, landing on the floor by her with a soft thump and instantly trotted out to the living room. Jenny followed him, careful not to step on the Brownie or trip over him. Bran was pouring cups of coffee already as she set down the rest of the mugs.

"Timothy." Alex sighed in relief as the Brownie bounced up onto the coffee table in front of her. "I'm glad you're alright."

"Yes, Iron Soul," Timothy greeted with a grin. "Thank you for freeing so many."

"They're alright then?" Alex licked her lips and rubbed the side of her head. "The freed weren't affected by the spell?" She clarified as she looked over at Morgana.

"Affected, yes," Timothy confirmed, tilting his head and scratching it thoughtfully. "I felt a great weight pressing down on me, but then it flowed off of me."

"I asked the spell not to harm the freed." Alex picked up the mug of coffee, cupping it in her hands. "I didn't want to hurt them."

"Interesting." Merlin shifted in the chair, still looking exhausted with his wrinkles much more prominent than before. "You were able to control the effect of the magic far more than I thought possible."

"Well, Alex was also channeling more magic than I've ever seen one person wield in centuries," Morgana said. There was a proud little smile on her face.

"There was a lot of magic in the air," Alex groaned, rubbing at her temples. "At least I was able to break the connection between the Iron Chain and the Faeries nearby."

"The Iron Chain?" Merlin asked gently. "What did you learn?"

"That I have a previous life who was a slave ship captain." Alex gave Merlin a dark look as she slouched back. "I'm not sure how, but he slowly enchanted one of the chains in the hold to... control people. The eyes of those slaves were so vacant... Thing is, I don't think he even knew about the magic, not really."

No one said anything, and Jenny moved over to sit next to Alex on the sofa, reaching over to take her hand. She caught Lance's eye from where he was still sitting by the window with a dark expression.

"I'm sorry, Alex." Morgana placed her hands on Alex's shoulder, standing protectively behind her. "That's... an unpleasant thing to learn."

"Yeah," Alex whispered. Jenny squeezed her hand. "Anyway, the Iron Chain seems to have the power to bind things together or bind a being to whoever controls it. I'm not sure how the Queen found it or is able to use it, but that's how she put Medraut's soul into Arthur. She had this piece of iron, probably from the Iron Gate they were stuck in and used the chain to bind his... soul, I guess, into her pregnant body."

A small sound of horror escaped almost everyone in the room, but Jenny bit her lip and stayed silent as Alex's grip on her hand tightened. Jenny felt a twinge of pity for Arthur that she hadn't been expecting and wondered just what else Alex had seen in those visions of hers. Alex seemed calm enough, but Jenny didn't believe the act. She remembered all too well the problems with learning that you'd committed a great wrong in another life.

"Her ability to use it may sadly be based on the fact she was caught in the magic of the Iron Gate," Merlin theorized in a dark tone. "She would have been... surrounded in a way by the Iron Soul's magic."

"Wonderful," Morgana growled with a strange tone in her voice. Merlin gave her a sympathetic look and Jenny guessed there was a bit more to it than she knew. "But Arthur also needed Alex's blood, so perhaps her ability to use the Iron Chain is limited. After all, Arthur only handled Cathanáil once Alex's blood was on it."

"The character of the item itself may also have some impact," Merlin added thoughtfully. "Based on Alex's vision we can assume that... well, the life in question didn't value the lives of those in the Iron Realm. Perhaps that makes it easier for them to use the magic." He looked towards Alex with sad eyes.

"Anyway," Alex said. "The Iron Chain is the source of the Queen's control over the Faeries. Maybe she is using my blood to achieve an effect of this scale, after all, she'd had the Iron Chain for years and only just did this. More importantly, what do we do now?"

"I assume you looked at the flow of magic when you were freeing the Faeries?" Merlin looked, with a hint of worry, down at Timothy who, Jenny noted, was gazing up at Alex with a star-struck expression.

"I did, but it stretched far off into the distance. I don't think I could affect it."

"Maybe not," Merlin said. "Was there anything else?"

"Arthur and probably the Queen are half-Sídhe like the pair of you," Alex added. "Uh she used the flesh of a... well she used the Iron Chain to combine Arthur as a baby with... you know. I didn't see her do it to herself, but she remarked that Arthur was a test run for her."

"That fits Scáthbás," Morgana muttered darkly from her place behind Alex.

"Beyond that... uh, bits of Arthur's childhood. The power of the Iron Chain in him is what connected us. When we first met it was my own magic that I was sensing," Alex explained with a slight quiver in her voice. "There were... other things too."

The way Alex said that told Jenny a lot. Unbidden her thoughts turned back to some of the strange things she'd seen and heard around Arthur's home. She remembered the way his mother Elaine had looked at her the first time they met and shuddered. Maybe she was reading too much into it, but the feeling in her gut didn't think so.

"But that isn't the issue." Alex straightened up and raised her chin. To Jenny, she just looked tired and uneasy, but the rest of the room seemed ready to at least pretend. "How can we break the connection between the Iron Chain and the Faeries? Better yet, how can we break the connection between Scáthbás and the Iron Soul's power? They'll run out of my blood eventually, but they might be able to get more."

"A fair point." Merlin looked past Alex to Morgana. Jenny glanced back in time to see Morgana nod in agreement. "Thor's Hammer may be our best option. It was a tool for not only creation but destruction as well." He smiled a little; a look that Jenny was learning meant that he was remembering something from his long past. "And the Hammer did prove capable of breaking unusual magical connections."

"How do we get it?" Aiden asked. He was starting to look excited. "Is this going to be another fetch quest? I'm still irritated that I missed the last one."

"No," Merlin chuckled. "I know where the Hammer is. My TAs can finish midterm testing for me and I'll leave at once." He gave Alex a soft smile and stood up. He put his hand on her head and Alex almost melted at the gesture. "The spring equinox is fast approaching. I'll bring you the Hammer, Alex. We'll help you gather enough magic to break this terrible connection Scáthbás has created."

The mages nodded and Alex sank back into the sofa with an audible sigh of relief. Alex's grip on her hand loosened and Jenny gave her a reassuring smile.

33

What Will Come

Midterm week was always an odd beast at Ravenslake University, well probably any university Alex amended as she looked towards the University Commons from her place on the lawn. The sun was shining overhead and it was truly feeling like spring with only the mildest hint of a chill in the air. Despite it being only Tuesday of midterm week, the population of the campus was already beginning to drop as professors had exams early or students turned in midterm papers before the deadline. Everyone was in a hurry to escape for their week of vacation, yet Alex had no set plans and a sense of dread that she couldn't shake to look forward to.

Professor Yates had already vanished and his TA had apologized for his absence, saying it was a family emergency via an email. Alex wondered if using that as an excuse ever bothered Merlin as he had no family anymore. Though she supposed leaving before midterm to retrieve an ancient magical hammer might not sit well with the administration, even if he did have tenure.

Alex's hands shook slightly as she raised her sandwich to her mouth and took a bite. The flavor was muted and bland, but Alex wasn't sure if that was the sandwich or her. Inhaling slowly, she closed her eyes for a moment only to flinch as the hold of the slave ship flashed before her eyes. Their hopeless vacant eyes meeting her own as the Iron Chain glowed softly, binding them all to Captain Cuthbert Allard.

If she looked him up, would she find anything? Alex wasn't certain. She certainly viewed him as the worst imaginable sort of person; slowly and maybe unknowingly using the gift of his magic to bend those around him to his will. But to history, he was probably just another ship captain, one that may have had lower incidents of mutiny or killing of slaves on his ship. Alex shivered: she couldn't stand the idea that he might have been recorded as a fair captain. Magic may have been at low levels then, but with so many beings from Avalyens like Cyrridven and Chernobog living here there was always some, and his single-mindedness had slowly enchanted a terrible object.

Alex looked down at her tablet, reminding herself that her midterm was only an hour away. It was her last one, but she still needed to be able to write an essay on some question about the Bible. With Professor Yates gone she wouldn't even have the benefit of Merlin grading it, so she needed to focus. She should be reviewing her notes.

The sound of grass crunching behind her made Alex tense up, and she slid her hand into her messenger bag. As her fingers closed around the hilt of her dagger, Alex both realized what she was doing and heard Nicki laugh at something. Looking over her shoulder, she relaxed as Nicki, Aiden, Bran, Lance, and Jenny all walked up. Nicki looked calm and was smiling, while Aiden had a small smile on his face. Lance was stoic as always, but Jenny and Bran were both looking at her in concern.

They all sat down around her and Alex barely held back a sigh, bracing herself for the conversation they would try to start, again. She got it; they were worried and she'd been rather anti-social since leaving Merlin's house. They were her friends and they were worried. She did appreciate that, but couldn't they understand the concept of distance? Unless Morgana had told them to keep an eye on her, which wouldn't surprise her.

"How are your midterms going?" Jenny gently offered her a warm smile. "Anything major?"

"No surprises so far," Alex replied. She raised an eyebrow, looking at the group expectantly. "But that's not why you all came over together."

"So, what will happen now?" Lance questioned as he shifted on the grass, leaning back a bit. Alex almost smiled when she noted Jenny sitting down next to Lance and her body shifting towards his. "Are you all just going to wait for Merlin to come back?"

"Yeah." Nicki shrugged casually, but there was a shadow of uncertainty on her face. "This mage thing has two basic speeds: look out they're trying to kill us and waiting."

"It's a bit more complicated than that." Bran chuckled a little bit. "But I see your point." They were silent for a moment before Bran caught her eye. "Do you want to talk about it?"

"No," Alex answered shortly. Looking down at her sandwich, Alex picked it up and took another large bite.

"Okay," Bran agreed with a nod. "But if you need us, we're here."

They were all quiet again as Alex nodded and chewed her sandwich. She hated that the conversation seemed to be requiring her input. Jenny toyed with some grass and Nicki shared a look with Aiden. Only Bran and Lance seemed truly comfortable with the silence, but Alex couldn't take it.

"Anyone have plans for spring break?" Alex asked, not wanting to talk about magic or give too much attention to the sympathetic looks she was receiving.

"No." Bran gave her an odd look. "Didn't seem wise to leave Ravenslake given the circumstances."

"Jenny? Lance?" Alex looked at them hopefully.

Jenny was frowning slightly and watching her with a thoughtful expression. Alex really didn't feel comfortable with the way her gaze was settled on her. Jenny shrugged and tugged up the blade of grass between her fingers. Shifting on the grass, Alex rolled her shoulders as she began to feel restless herself.

"I'm staying," Jenny replied. "Just wasn't sure what would happen, and in a weird way this feels like the safest place to be."

"That's understandable." Nicki gave a small reassuring smile to Jenny. "You haven't distanced yourself from us and Arthur's probably more than a little angry at the moment."

You had to love Nicki's willingness to say what they were all thinking. Or not, based on the grimace Jenny made. Lance shifted a bit closer to her and put a hand over hers for a moment. There was an almost audible sigh of relief from the whole group and Alex smiled a little at the reminder she hadn't been the only one hoping they'd work it out.

"So, anyone have ideas on what to do with Timothy?" Aiden lay back in the grass. "He doesn't seem to be going anywhere."

"Weren't you the one who wanted a Brownie?" Alex teased, feeling her lips curve up in a real smile. "I seem to recall a conversation along that train of thought."

"Well, I wouldn't recommend bringing him to a dorm," Aiden answered with a chuckle. "And while my mother may be Irish, I don't think she'd really take well to having a Brownie in the house."

"And Gran would never go for it," Nicki offered with a grin. "But we do need to talk about what to do next year," Nicki reminded them all with a more serious expression. "Summer will be here any day now and we need to have housing figured out."

"We were talking about getting a house together," Bran informed Lance and Jenny helpfully. "Just to keep us away from the other students."

"Given that I was attacked in my dorm that's a good idea," Alex muttered. "Timothy didn't seem bothered by the iron around the window or the iron at Merlin's house."

"After three thousand years it makes sense that some of them would be resistant," Aiden pointed out. He didn't look happy about the idea. "At least until you draw blood."

"Balls of sunshine," Jenny murmured. "Are all your conversations like this?"

"No," Nicki assured her with a smile. "On our good days, there are a lot of Monty Python references."

"A house might be a good idea," Alex said, getting the conversation back on track. "And Timothy could come and stay there with us if he wants to."

"You'd trust him that close?" Lance gave her a slightly worried inquisitive look. "After what happened?"

"If Merlin and Morgana are right, then on the Spring Equinox, I'll be able to break the power of the Iron Chain, at least for a time. Timothy didn't want to do any of that. It was the Queen and the Iron Chain. It's power..." Alex trailed off as she began to feel chilled and the memory of those blank eyes settled on her shoulders again. A wave of guilt that was her own for actions that were not rushed over her and she had no idea how to process it. "Anyway, we should take a look at what's available when spring break is over."

"Ideally we're looking at six rooms," Bran reminded her. "Might not be easy to find."

"We'll have the help of Morgana and Merlin," Aiden said. "Honestly it wouldn't surprise me if they outright bought a house near one of theirs."

"That would be rational," Nicki agreed. "But like Alex said, we'll have that conversation after break is over and Merlin returns." Nicki turned her attention back to Alex. "So, if we're all staying together for break, is there anything special you want to do?"

"Not really," Alex answered with a shrug. "Not in town anyway."

"Okay then, let's say we don't have to worry about staying in Ravenslake? What would you like to do then?" Nicki pressed, leaning towards her.

Alex paused at the direct question and even more so when she realized that everyone was watching her and waiting for an answer. "I guess... well, I want to try and do the blood spell in Spokane," Alex replied slowly before her mood began to brighten. "If you went with me and used your magic then I could make it my own and hopefully cover the whole area with one spell!"

Judging from the looks she was receiving no one was surprised by the answer. Alex had to admit to herself that given the attack it made sense that she'd be worried about her family. Arthur was twisted. While she felt a flicker of pity for him, for the forced reincarnation that had then been altered and raised by a monster, she couldn't ignore what he'd done. Morgana had been fused to a Changeling and raised by the Sídhe, but she had sided with her own realm in the end. Arthur- Medraut, whatever and whoever he was, didn't seem conflicted at all, and Alex couldn't shake a sense of dread.

"Alright then!" Nicki grinned with a look of slight relief. "Road trip to Alex's hometown to protect it!"

"And we'll stop in Lance and Bran's towns too," Alex added quickly. She pulled herself from her thoughts. "See if we can't get some other areas protected."

"Thank you," Lance told her with a slight slump of relief. "It'll be easier knowing that they're safe."

"Remind me to get you all tickets to California sometime soon," Jenny added with a small tight smile. Alex could see the tension in her shoulders and felt a surge of sympathy for Jenny whom Arthur knew far too much about. "Lest Arthur decide that he likes the idea of returning there."

"Okay." Alex made a reminder to herself that they'd also need to protect her brother Matt's home too. "We have a plan. My last test is in an hour. I've got all my papers in otherwise. What are your schedules?"

"I'll be done tomorrow afternoon," Bran answered.

After a quick go around the circle, Alex confirmed their schedules. Excitement was building in her chest along with a drive to be useful until Merlin returned.

"We can leave Thursday morning then," Aiden remarked with a smile. "Be in Spokane that afternoon, do the spell and come back via Eugene and Portland. Hopefully, by the time we're back, Merlin will have Thor's Hammer, giving Alex a few days to practice with it and then we can break the power of the Iron Chain."

It was a plan, a solid plan. Alex felt the knot in her chest easing a little bit. They could be useful and protect most of their families before Merlin returned. With a little luck and a favor from Morgana, she might even let them go down to California upon their return. After all, they could be done with the northern cities by the end of the weekend.

Nodding in pleasure, Alex brought her sandwich up again and took another bite. It tasted no better and when she closed her eyes for a moment there was another flash of the ship hold and someone screaming.

Holding in her shiver, Alex forced a smile even as worries of just what was ahead now crept over her. It would be alright she promised herself. She and her friends would see that where their families lived was safe, and Merlin would bring her the Iron Hammer. She was the Iron Soul, and she had all of them. As long as she had them, then she could deal with this and they would find a way to stop Arthur and Scáthbás. She had to keep believing that. No matter what Arthur tried next.